The Silent S

Unveiling the Secrets of a Deadly Conspiracy

Jane Doe

Table of Contents

Chapter 1
The Arrival in Elmsbrook

Samantha Cross stepped off the bus and into the warm, late afternoon sun. Main Street in Elmsbrook looked like a picture-perfect postcard—quaint storefronts, freshly painted facades, and a cobblestone path lined with blossoming flowerbeds. Children's laughter floated through the air, blending with the soft chirping of birds. For anyone else, the scene would have felt idyllic, comforting even. But Samantha wasn't anyone else. She wasn't here to enjoy a quiet, charming town. She was here to unravel the truth.

As she adjusted her shoulder bag, her sharp, investigative eyes scanned the streets. Something was off. The calmness of the town seemed too perfect, like a layer of gloss covering cracks beneath the surface. Elmsbrook felt rehearsed, as if everyone were playing a part in a carefully choreographed play. The tension was palpable, though invisible to most. But not to Samantha.

"Afternoon, miss! Welcome to Elmsbrook!" A middle-aged man with a wide-brimmed hat tipped it toward her as he walked past. His smile was wide, too wide. Samantha offered a polite nod in return, but her instincts were already tingling. There was a certain practiced ease in his greeting, too friendly for a stranger passing by. She watched him as he continued down the street, a little too relaxed for her liking.

Keeping her movements casual, Samantha crossed the street toward the Elmsbrook Inn, the place she would call home for the next few days. A woman sweeping her front porch caught her eye, offering her a bright smile. "Need any help finding your way?" the woman called out, her tone sweet, but Samantha noticed the way her eyes darted back to the road after the offer. Wary, as if checking for someone else's reaction.

Samantha shook her head with a friendly wave. "Thank you, but I think I've got it." She continued down the sidewalk, feeling the woman's eyes lingering on her long after she'd passed. Each step down the street felt like moving through an overly constructed scene. The buildings, though charming, seemed oddly uniform, their pristine appearance too perfectly maintained for a rural town.

Something's wrong here, she thought. But what?

Ahead, the Elmsbrook Inn stood proudly at the end of the street, its floral-patterned sign swaying gently in the breeze. It looked welcoming enough, with its wooden shutters and cozy porch, but Samantha knew better than to take appearances at face value. She pushed open the door, the soft chime of a bell signaling her arrival. Inside, the lobby was as inviting as she'd expected—plush armchairs arranged neatly around a crackling fireplace, a vase of fresh flowers on the front desk. The smell of lavender and vanilla filled the air, offering a sense of warmth that felt... staged.

"Good afternoon!" A woman behind the desk looked up with a cheerful smile. "You must be Samantha Cross. Welcome to the Elmsbrook Inn. How can I help you?"

Samantha approached, her eyes discreetly scanning the room. The receptionist's appearance was immaculate—hair pulled back into a neat bun, makeup applied just right, and her uniform crisp and wrinkle-free. But there was a slight tremor in her hands as she reached for the guest book. A sign of nerves.

"Yes, I have a reservation," Samantha said, resting her bag on the desk. "Room twelve, I believe?"

The receptionist quickly flipped through her records and handed over an old-fashioned brass key. "That's right. Room twelve, second floor." Her smile remained, but her eyes flickered toward the window, just for a split second, as though checking something outside. The gesture wasn't lost on Samantha.

"Thank you," Samantha said, taking the key. She hesitated for a moment before asking, "Is everything alright? You seem… a bit on edge."

The receptionist blinked, clearly not expecting the question. Her smile faltered for just a second before it widened again, almost unnaturally. "Oh, everything's fine! It's just been a busy day, you know?" Her fingers drummed nervously on the desk as she spoke.

Samantha nodded slowly, sensing there was more behind the surface. "Of course," she replied, keeping her tone light. "I imagine it's a quiet town most days. Anything unusual happen recently?"

The receptionist's hands stilled. For a moment, Samantha thought she might not answer. "Unusual?" The woman's voice had tightened slightly. "No… nothing at all. Just the usual small-town life."

Samantha offered a polite smile, though her mind was already spinning. She could read the discomfort in the receptionist's body language. The way her eyes avoided Samantha's gaze now, the subtle shift in her posture. Something was definitely off.

"Well, thank you," Samantha said, turning toward the stairs. "I'll let you get back to your day."

"Of course! If you need anything, don't hesitate to ask," the receptionist called after her, her voice bright again. But Samantha could feel the tension underneath.

Climbing the wooden stairs, which creaked beneath her steps, Samantha's thoughts raced. The receptionist was nervous. Why? Was it just the usual paranoia that small towns fostered around outsiders, or was there something deeper here? She would need to tread carefully, but she was used to that.

As she reached her room, she paused for a moment, turning back to glance at the lobby below. The receptionist was already busy with something on her desk, her back turned. For now, the surface of Elmsbrook remained undisturbed. But Samantha knew how to dig beneath the surface.

She unlocked her door and stepped into the room, the familiar weight of the investigation settling over her shoulders. The town might try to hide its secrets behind charm and smiles, but Samantha was here for one reason: to uncover the truth.

Whatever it took.

Samantha stood at the window of her room in the Elmsbrook Inn, watching the late afternoon sun cast long shadows over the town. She had unpacked the essentials—her notebook, a few files, and her laptop—but her mind wasn't on her gear. The serene stillness of Elmsbrook was unsettling. The town's charm was too deliberate, its peacefulness too perfect. She knew this type of place. It reminded her of cases she'd worked in the past—places where darkness lurked beneath calm waters.

She made a mental list of what she had noticed so far: the overly friendly but nervous locals, the receptionist's subtle glance out the window, and the watchful eyes on the street. People here weren't just cautious around strangers—they were scared. Of what, she wasn't sure yet, but her instincts told her it was something big.

Deciding to take a walk before the evening settled in, Samantha grabbed her jacket and headed out. The air was cool, carrying with it the faint smell of pine and distant wood smoke. As she strolled down the cobblestone path, her eyes took in every detail—quiet porches, abandoned bicycles leaning against picket fences, and curtains drawn in many of the houses she passed. It wasn't the vibrant, lively town it pretended to be. Something was keeping these people indoors, out of sight.

She rounded a corner and found herself near the town square. A small park lay in the center, flanked by benches and a modest fountain that burbled quietly in the fading light. Only one figure sat on a bench near the edge of the park, his shoulders hunched, hat pulled low over his face. Samantha's pace slowed as she sized him up—he looked like any other local, but something about him felt off. He wasn't relaxed like the others who forced their smiles. He looked worried, as if he had been waiting for someone.

As if sensing her approach, the man glanced up. His eyes narrowed slightly before he stood and tipped his hat. "Evenin', miss," he said, his voice gravelly, as if it had been ground down by years of hard living.

Samantha offered a polite nod. "Good evening," she replied, keeping her tone casual, though her mind was already in overdrive. The man didn't seem surprised to see her, almost as if he had expected her to walk by.

"Stranger in town, I see," the man said, gesturing toward her with a knowing look. "Not many visitors come around Elmsbrook unless they're lookin' for somethin'."

Samantha raised an eyebrow. "And what do most visitors come looking for?" she asked, her curiosity piqued.

The man shrugged, but there was something calculated about the gesture. "Depends. Some folks look for peace and quiet. Others... well, they find more than they bargain for."

His words hung in the air, heavy with implication. Samantha's investigative instincts flared. This man knew something, and he was offering her just enough bait to pull her in. But she wasn't going to bite too quickly. She had to keep control of the conversation, steer it in a way that would get him to reveal more.

"Is that so?" she asked, her tone light. "And what do people tend to find when they're not careful?"

The man chuckled, though there was no humor in it. "Secrets, mostly. This town's full of 'em, but it don't take much diggin' to find what you're lookin' for. You just gotta know where to look... and who to talk to."

Samantha studied him carefully. He was offering her information, but she couldn't afford to trust it. In her line of work, people like him—locals who knew more than they should—often had their own agendas. Still, information was information, and she needed to gather as much as she could. But she wouldn't take his word as truth, not without verifying it first.

"And you?" she asked, tilting her head. "You seem like someone who knows a lot about this town. What should I be looking for?"

The man hesitated, glancing around as if checking to make sure they were alone. "Name's Henry Johnson," he said quietly. "Lived here my whole life. Seen things happen here... things that ain't right. People disappear, rumors spread, but nobody says a damn word. They're too scared. Too scared of what might happen if they do."

Samantha's gaze sharpened. She made a mental note of his name, filing it away for later. "Disappearances?" she echoed, keeping her voice neutral. "That sounds serious. Why wouldn't anyone say anything?"

Henry shifted uncomfortably. "Because they know better. Some people here—good people—tried to stand up, tried to do somethin'. Now they're gone. And no one knows where. It's like they vanished overnight. But there's always whispers. Whispers about the people who really run this town."

The wind rustled the trees overhead, and for a moment, silence settled between them. Samantha could feel the weight of what he wasn't saying. Whoever or whatever controlled Elmsbrook had a strong grip on its people. And if Henry's story was true, they were dangerous enough to make people disappear without a trace. But how much of this could she believe? Was Henry telling her the truth, or was he exaggerating for his own reasons?

She had to be careful. "That's quite the story, Henry," she said, her voice measured. "But you understand if I don't just take your word for it. These kinds of things need to be looked into."

Henry gave her a long, measured look. "I figured you'd say that. Don't blame you. But just know this—if you start pokin' around too much, you might not like what you find. There's a reason people keep their heads down around here."

Samantha nodded, already forming her plan. She would dig into this town's past, starting with the records of any disappearances and tracking down those whispers Henry mentioned. But she wouldn't let on to him just how seriously she was taking his words. Not yet.

"Thanks for the advice," she said with a slight smile. "I'll keep it in mind."

Henry tipped his hat again, giving her a final, wary glance before walking off into the evening shadows. Samantha watched him go, already considering her next steps. Elmsbrook's secrets were starting to reveal themselves, but she would proceed with caution. As always, the truth would come, but only after she had peeled back each layer carefully.

For now, she had enough to start. And Henry Johnson would be the first name she investigated.

Samantha walked through the quiet streets of Elmsbrook, the evening light fading into a soft amber glow. The picturesque town was winding down for the night, with only a few people left milling about. But despite the calm exterior, Samantha's instincts were buzzing. There was an eerie stillness in the air, like the town was holding its breath, waiting for something to happen.

As she made her way past a row of closed shops, she felt it—the unmistakable prickle on the back of her neck. She was being watched. Samantha slowed her pace, careful not to make any sudden movements that would give away her awareness. Instead, she casually glanced at the reflection in a nearby window, scanning the street behind her.

Nothing. The street seemed empty, but the feeling didn't fade.

She reached into her jacket pocket, fingers brushing against her phone. Her senses heightened. The town was too quiet, too still. If there was someone following her, they were good at staying out of sight. Samantha kept walking, her footsteps steady, her mind calculating her next move. She needed to confirm her suspicions.

The reflection in the window caught something—a shadow moving near a lamppost, just out of her peripheral vision. She glanced up, her heart rate increasing slightly, though she maintained her calm exterior. She needed to get a better look.

As she approached the corner of a narrow alley, her phone buzzed in her pocket. It was Turner. She hesitated for a split second before pulling it out and reading the message.

Turner: *Stay sharp. Could be more eyes on you than just the townspeople.*

Samantha pocketed the phone, her jaw tightening. Turner always had impeccable timing. She stopped in front of a closed bakery, pretending to inspect the "Closed" sign in the window, her eyes discreetly scanning the glass for any movement behind her.

Footsteps. Soft, deliberate.

There was definitely someone there.

Samantha straightened, pulling her jacket tighter around her as she turned and began walking again. This time, she let her steps take her toward a busier part of town—the diner near the square that she had passed earlier. The faint sound of voices inside offered some semblance of normalcy, and the glow of the neon sign made her feel slightly more anchored.

As she reached the entrance, she heard the sound of footsteps pause behind her, then fade. The hairs on the back of her neck still prickled, but she didn't turn around. Instead, she stepped into the diner, the bell over the door jingling softly as she entered.

The waitress behind the counter looked up from wiping down the counter and gave her a friendly nod. "Evening. Just yourself tonight?"

Samantha offered a polite smile, though her mind was still racing. "Yes, just me," she said, her voice even.

"Take a seat anywhere you like."

Samantha nodded and chose a booth by the window, positioning herself where she could see the door and anyone who might walk past outside. She reached for her phone again, her fingers tapping out a quick response to Turner.

Samantha: *Definitely being watched. Just saw a shadow near the alley. How's everything on your end?*

A minute passed before the screen lit up with his reply.

Turner: *Not surprised. Small towns like this, they always have their way of keeping tabs on newcomers. Be careful—don't let them know you're onto them just yet.*

Samantha exhaled slowly, her eyes flicking to the window. "Just another small town with big secrets," she muttered under her breath. But Turner was right. She couldn't afford to tip her hand too soon. The last thing she needed was to let them know she had spotted the surveillance, not until she had more information.

The waitress approached with a notepad in hand. "What can I get you, hon?"

Samantha smiled briefly. "Just a coffee, please. Black."

The waitress nodded and walked away, leaving Samantha to her thoughts. She casually scanned the street outside, her eyes narrowing as a figure moved at the far end of the block, just barely visible under the dim streetlight. They didn't come any closer, but the message was clear: they were watching, and they weren't trying too hard to hide it.

Her phone buzzed again.

Turner: *Need backup?*

Samantha smirked, typing out a quick reply.

Samantha: *Not yet. I'll play this one slow. See what they do next.*

Turner responded almost immediately.

Turner: *Keep me posted. Don't take any chances.*

Samantha slid her phone back into her pocket, her eyes still scanning the street. Whoever was watching her was being cautious but not invisible. That meant they wanted her to feel the pressure, wanted her to know they were there. It was a game of control, and Samantha wasn't about to give them the upper hand.

The waitress returned with her coffee, setting the steaming cup down in front of her. "You alright, hon? You seem a little on edge."

Samantha blinked, pulling herself back to the present. "I'm fine," she said, her tone neutral. "Just a long day of travel."

The waitress gave her a sympathetic smile. "Yeah, this town can feel a little... odd to newcomers. You here for business?"

"Something like that," Samantha replied, taking a sip of the coffee. It was bitter, but she barely noticed.

"Well, let me know if you need anything," the waitress said before moving on to another table.

Samantha watched her go, her mind already shifting back to the shadowy figure outside. Whoever they were, they wouldn't stay hidden for long. People who watched too closely often ended up revealing themselves sooner or later.

She would be ready when they did.

Samantha sat in the diner, her cup of black coffee now lukewarm as her eyes flicked between the window and her journal. She had only written a few notes so far, all of them fragments of thoughts, scattered pieces of a puzzle she hadn't fully formed yet. But the feeling was undeniable—there was something here, beneath the idyllic surface of Elmsbrook, waiting to be uncovered.

She tapped her pen on the edge of the notebook, the soft rhythm almost soothing. The street outside had grown quieter, with only the occasional passerby. But that same feeling from earlier, the sense of being watched, still lingered. Someone had been following her, of that she was certain. Yet, they had remained elusive, just out of reach.

"Maybe it's time to push back," she muttered to herself, though she knew she needed to move carefully. Whoever was behind the surveillance wanted her to feel unsettled, but they weren't ready to confront her directly—at least not yet. That gave her some room to work.

Her phone buzzed in her pocket again. It was Turner.

Turner: *How's it looking? Any new signs?*

Samantha glanced outside before replying.

Samantha: *Not much movement. Just a hunch at this point, but they're definitely watching.*

She set the phone aside, her gaze returning to the street. A flicker of motion caught her eye. She leaned forward slightly, watching as an older man exited a small shop across the street, his posture rigid. He wore a long, faded trench coat and a hat that cast a shadow over his face, obscuring his features. But that wasn't what made Samantha pause.

It was the way he moved—quick, deliberate, like he didn't want to be seen. He glanced over his shoulder twice, and as he crossed the street, his hand darted out to the side of the building, brushing against something on the wall. It was subtle, so subtle that anyone not paying close attention would've missed it.

Samantha narrowed her eyes. There was something there, something hidden in plain sight.

"Interesting," she murmured under her breath. She picked up her notebook and pen, scribbling a quick note:

Old man, trench coat. Shop across from the diner. Marked something on the wall—north side.

She stood up, leaving a few bills on the table for her coffee, and slid her phone and notebook into her jacket pocket. Her movements were unhurried, casual, but her mind was already racing. She needed to see what the man had touched. Whatever it was, it could be a clue, some small piece of information that might confirm her suspicions.

The door chimed as she stepped out into the cool evening air. The street was nearly empty now, with the man already several blocks ahead, disappearing into the distance. Samantha didn't follow him. Instead, she crossed the street, heading toward the shop where he had made his subtle mark.

As she approached the side of the building, her eyes scanned the brick wall, searching for anything that seemed out of place. And there it was, barely noticeable at first—a small, crude symbol scratched into the brick near the corner of the shop. It looked like a spiral, or maybe a snake coiled tightly.

Samantha crouched down to get a better look. The symbol was rough, hastily carved, but it hadn't been done carelessly. It was deliberate, like a signal or a warning. She glanced around, ensuring no one was watching, and quickly jotted another note in her journal:

Coiled symbol, scratched into brick near shop. Likely a marker. Investigate further.

Her pen paused on the page as she considered the implications. Was this some kind of code? A way for locals to communicate covertly? Or was it meant to deter outsiders, a warning to those who didn't belong? Either way, it was clear that Elmsbrook wasn't as innocent as it appeared.

Her phone buzzed again, breaking her thoughts.

Turner: *Still good?*

She typed a quick response.

Samantha: *Found something. Symbol scratched into a building. Looks like a marker. Could be important.*

Turner's reply came almost immediately.

Turner: *Don't push too hard yet. Keep gathering, stay under the radar.*

Samantha tucked her phone away, her eyes still locked on the symbol. Turner's advice was sound. She couldn't afford to push too hard, not this early. Whoever was keeping an eye on her would be watching for any signs that she had noticed their activities. She needed to play it cool, stay under the radar, just like Turner had said.

She stood up and casually made her way back toward the inn, her pace unhurried. As she walked, her mind worked through the possibilities. The symbol was too deliberate to be random graffiti, and the man's behavior had been suspicious. There was definitely something more to this town, and this clue—however small—was the first crack in the facade.

Back in her room, Samantha pulled out her journal again, flipping through her earlier notes. She added a final thought to the page:

Surveillance is active. Locals nervous. Symbol = first tangible clue. Watch for more markers.

Closing the journal, she leaned back in her chair, staring at the ceiling. It wasn't much yet, but it was enough to confirm what she had felt from the moment she arrived. Elmsbrook was hiding something, and it was only a matter of time before the truth started to unravel.

But she would have to tread carefully. This town wasn't going to give up its secrets easily.

Chapter 2
Unveiling Secrets

Samantha sat across from Dr. Margaret Caldwell in the small, dimly lit office of the local clinic. The room smelled faintly of antiseptic and old books, the walls lined with medical certificates and thick, leather-bound volumes on various health topics. Dr. Caldwell, a thin woman in her mid-fifties with wire-rimmed glasses perched low on her nose, fidgeted with a stack of papers on her desk. She had agreed to meet with Samantha after some hesitation, but her body language told the real story: she was nervous.

"Thank you for agreeing to speak with me, Dr. Caldwell," Samantha began, her voice steady and professional. "I know this must be difficult, given the circumstances."

Dr. Caldwell glanced up, her eyes shifting toward the closed door before she finally nodded. "Yes, well… Elias was a friend. A colleague, too. It's hard to make sense of it all. His… disappearance was sudden." Her voice wavered, but she quickly composed herself, clearing her throat.

Samantha leaned in slightly, her expression calm but focused. "I understand. I just want to ask a few questions about Elias's work. Anything that might help me understand what he was working on before he… vanished."

Dr. Caldwell hesitated, her fingers tapping lightly on the desk before folding in her lap. "Elias… he was a brilliant man, but sometimes, I think, his ambition got the better of him. He was working on something—something big—but he didn't talk much about it in detail. Only snippets."

"What kind of snippets?" Samantha pressed, her tone still neutral, but her mind was already on alert. She had learned from experience that even the smallest detail could unravel a case.

"Something about genetic manipulation," Dr. Caldwell said softly, her gaze dropping to the papers in front of her. "He believed he was on the verge of a breakthrough, something that would change the way we treat genetic disorders. But Elias... he was secretive. Almost paranoid in the last few months."

Samantha's eyebrows lifted slightly. "Paranoid? In what way?"

Dr. Caldwell shifted in her seat, clearly uncomfortable. "He kept talking about someone watching him. He thought his work was attracting the wrong kind of attention. I told him he was being ridiculous, that no one in a town like Elmsbrook would care about cutting-edge genetic research. But..." Her voice trailed off, and she looked down again, as if regretting the conversation.

Samantha remained still, keeping her expression neutral. "And you never saw anything unusual yourself? No one asking questions, no one following him?"

Dr. Caldwell bit her lip. "Not that I noticed. Elias was always a little dramatic, but toward the end, it was worse. He started locking his notes away, taking precautions like he was preparing for something. He even stopped discussing his research with me—his closest friend."

Samantha nodded slowly, making mental notes of everything. She could sense Dr. Caldwell wasn't telling her everything. There was more, but she was reluctant to share it. "Did he ever mention Pharmatech?" she asked directly, watching for the reaction.

Dr. Caldwell's fingers twitched at the name, and her eyes flickered with something—fear, maybe. "Pharmatech? No... not to me, anyway. Why do you ask?"

Samantha leaned back, crossing her arms. "It's just something I came across during my research. A corporation with deep interests in medical advancements. They've been linked to controversial practices before. It wouldn't be a stretch to think they might take an interest in what Elias was working on."

Dr. Caldwell's face paled, and she glanced at the door again before speaking. "If Pharmatech was involved... Elias never said anything. But I've heard rumors. Just rumors, you understand." Her voice dropped to a near whisper. "That they have... methods. Ways of controlling information. But nothing concrete. I can't say for certain."

Samantha leaned forward again, her voice calm but insistent. "Rumors often start with a kernel of truth, Dr. Caldwell. If there's anything else you know, anything that might help me, now's the time to tell me. Elias's life—his disappearance—could depend on it."

Dr. Caldwell sighed, rubbing her temples. "He was meeting someone. That much I know. He wouldn't tell me who, but he said this person had access to... things. Information, resources.

I tried to warn him, but Elias wouldn't listen. He thought he was too close to stop."

"Do you have any idea who this person was?" Samantha asked, her voice soft but firm, wanting to keep Dr. Caldwell from retreating back into silence.

"No," Dr. Caldwell shook her head. "He was vague. But after one of those meetings, he came back more frantic than ever. That was when the paranoia really set in. He started acting like... like he knew his time was running out."

Samantha felt a knot tighten in her chest. "Do you think he was afraid for his life?"

Dr. Caldwell hesitated, her voice dropping even lower. "I don't know. But I think he believed... someone was after him. I didn't take him seriously at first, but now..."

Samantha nodded slowly, her mind working through the implications. "Thank you, Dr. Caldwell. This helps a lot."

Dr. Caldwell looked at her with wide eyes, her expression strained. "Please, Miss Cross. If you're getting involved in this, be careful. Elias may have gotten too close to something dangerous. And whoever is behind it... they won't stop just because he's gone."

Samantha stood, offering a reassuring smile, but the weight of Dr. Caldwell's warning lingered. "I appreciate your concern. I'll be careful."

As she left the office, the crisp evening air hit her, but it did little to dispel the tension curling in her stomach. Dr. Caldwell had been holding back, but what she did share was enough to confirm Samantha's suspicions. Elias's research had drawn attention from dangerous places, and Pharmatech was right in the middle of it.

She made a mental note to dig deeper into Pharmatech's involvement. If Elias had met someone with resources, someone who made him paranoid, then Samantha needed to find out who that person was—and fast.

Samantha sat in her room at the Elmsbrook Inn, her laptop open in front of her, the soft glow of the screen casting faint shadows on her face. She had spent the last hour sifting through data, financial records, and news reports, cross-referencing everything she could find on Elias's research and its potential links to outside entities. And now, a name kept surfacing—**Pharmatech**.

She leaned back in her chair, tapping her fingers lightly on the table. Pharmatech wasn't just any corporation. They had their hands in numerous high-stakes medical research projects, some of which were considered cutting edge—and controversial. Their presence wasn't blatant, but there were too many connections to ignore. Shell companies, investments funneled through obscure third parties, and a string of low-profile acquisitions in the genetic research field. This was no coincidence.

Her phone buzzed beside her, a text from Turner flashing across the screen.

Turner: *Anything new?*

Samantha's eyes lingered on the phone before she picked it up and typed a quick response.

Samantha: *Found something. Pharmatech keeps coming up. Seems they've had their claws in a lot of genetic research lately, including some in Elmsbrook.*

Barely a minute passed before Turner replied.

Turner: *Pharmatech? That's heavy. You sure?*

Samantha stared at the screen, knowing exactly what Turner meant. Pharmatech wasn't just a company—it was a powerhouse. They were known for cutting-edge research but also for silencing anyone who got too close to exposing their more questionable practices. She typed back quickly.

Samantha: *Not certain yet, but I'm getting there. Too many links for it to be nothing.*

A few moments later, Turner called. His voice came through the phone, steady but with a clear undercurrent of concern.

"You need to be careful, Sam," he said, skipping any greeting. "Pharmatech's not just some small-time player. They've got the resources to make things very difficult for you."

"I know," Samantha replied, leaning forward, her eyes still fixed on the names scrolling across her screen. "But if they're involved, it could explain a lot. Elias was working on something that caught their attention. Genetic manipulation, remember? Pharmatech's been linked to projects like that before, and now they're showing up in Elmsbrook of all places?"

"Do you have any solid proof?" Turner's tone was measured, cautious.

"Not yet," Samantha admitted. "But I've found records of shell companies tied to Pharmatech funneling money into local research projects here. It's too much of a coincidence."

Turner paused for a moment before speaking again, his voice lower. "And you think Elias got in too deep with them? That he was targeted because of it?"

"I do." Samantha clicked through another file, the Pharmatech name popping up again, this time attached to a research grant given to a small lab in the region. "Dr. Caldwell said he started acting paranoid before he disappeared. She mentioned he was meeting with someone—someone who had access to resources. If that person was linked to Pharmatech..."

Turner let out a breath on the other end of the line. "That changes everything. If Pharmatech's involved, we're talking about more than just a missing researcher. They play dirty, Sam, and they've got the money and power to cover their tracks."

Samantha nodded, though Turner couldn't see her. "That's exactly what I'm thinking. I'm going to dig deeper, see how far their reach goes in Elmsbrook. They've been too quiet here, but there's something lurking under the surface."

"You're not going to let this go, are you?" Turner's tone wasn't accusatory, but it carried the weight of someone who knew exactly how determined Samantha could be once she latched onto something.

"No, I'm not," she replied, her voice firm. "If Pharmatech had a hand in what happened to Elias, I need to know. And if they're involved in anything else in this town, I need to find out how deep that involvement goes."

Turner was silent for a moment, and Samantha could almost picture him on the other end of the line, weighing the risks. "Okay," he said finally. "But tread lightly. Pharmatech isn't just going to sit back if you get too close. These guys don't play fair. If they think you're onto something, they'll make sure you disappear, just like Elias."

"I know the risks," Samantha said, her tone softening slightly. "But I'm not turning back now. I've already seen enough to know something's wrong here."

"I trust your instincts," Turner replied. "But just... don't push too hard too fast. I'll start pulling some strings on my end, see if I can dig up anything on Pharmatech's recent movements. If they've got a presence in Elmsbrook, they'll have left some kind of trail."

Samantha felt a small surge of relief. Having Turner's backup always gave her an extra edge. "Thanks, Turner. I'll keep you updated."

"You better. And Sam?" His voice took on a more serious tone. "Watch your back. Pharmatech doesn't just intimidate—they eliminate threats."

Samantha exhaled, feeling the weight of his words. "I will. Thanks."

The call ended, and Samantha set the phone down beside her, staring at the screen. Pharmatech's shadow loomed over everything now, and she knew it was only a matter of time before they realized she was digging into their business. But this wasn't new territory for her. She had faced powerful corporations before, but none quite like Pharmatech.

Taking a deep breath, she opened a new document on her laptop, quickly typing out a list of leads to follow. There were a few names associated with the shell companies she needed to investigate further, but she couldn't be hasty. Turner was right—pushing too fast could draw unwanted attention. She needed to be smart, cautious.

But most of all, she needed to get to the truth before it was too late.

Samantha sat hunched over her laptop at the small desk in her room at the Elmsbrook Inn. The late afternoon sun had dipped behind the trees, casting long shadows through the curtains, but she barely noticed. Her fingers flew across the keyboard as she navigated through the various files she had collected, organizing everything she could find on Pharmatech. Each document, each scrap of information felt like another piece of a puzzle coming together.

But then, something caught her attention. A file she had flagged earlier—a list of names connected to Pharmatech's shell companies—was missing.

Her brow furrowed, and she quickly clicked back through her folders. Nothing. The file was gone.

"What the hell?" she muttered under her breath, her heartbeat quickening. She knew she had saved it. She always backed up important files, especially ones connected to high-risk investigations like this. But now it was gone, and not just the document itself—there was no record of it ever being there.

Samantha opened her external drive, hoping to find a backup. She scanned through the contents, but again, the file was nowhere to be found.

Her frustration grew as she checked her notes. The contact information she had written down earlier—the name of a local researcher who had once worked with Elias—was missing, too. She had written it down clearly, yet the page was blank. Her journal was meticulous; there was no way she would have forgotten to write it down. She double-checked, flipping back and forth through the pages, but it was as if the name had never existed.

Her mind raced, piecing together what was happening. This wasn't an accident. The missing file, the absent name—

someone was interfering. Pharmatech. It had to be. They were covering their tracks, just like Turner had warned.

Samantha sat back in her chair, eyes narrowing as a wave of realization hit her. Pharmatech's influence had already started to reach her, creeping in like a shadow she hadn't noticed until it was too late. They were watching her movements, monitoring her progress, and now, they were erasing her leads.

Her phone buzzed on the desk, pulling her attention away from the screen. A text from Turner.

Turner: *Anything new?*

For a moment, she stared at the message, contemplating how much she should tell him. He was already concerned about Pharmatech's involvement, and now they had started to act, removing pieces of evidence right under her nose. But if she told Turner too soon, he might tell her to pull back, and Samantha wasn't ready for that. Not yet.

She typed a quick response.

Samantha: *Weird glitch. Lost some files. Could be nothing, but I'm going to check around.*

It wasn't the whole truth, but it would keep Turner from worrying—at least for now. She set the phone aside and returned to the screen, trying to retrace her steps, but the longer she searched, the clearer it became that someone had deliberately deleted the information.

Her mind worked quickly, assessing the situation. Pharmatech was more dangerous than she'd initially realized. They weren't just trying to intimidate her—they were actively removing evidence, erasing any trace of their involvement. She had to be even more careful now, more methodical.

Leaning forward, she pulled up the encryption program Turner had insisted she use on her laptop. She should have activated it earlier, but she hadn't expected them to move so fast. As the program launched, encrypting her files and securing her connections, Samantha felt a knot of frustration tighten in her chest. She wasn't just fighting against time anymore—she was up against an invisible adversary who was always one step ahead.

With her files now secure, she needed to find a way to regain the lost information. The researcher's name, the one tied to Elias—whoever they were, they could still be out there. If Pharmatech hadn't already gotten to them, they might hold the key to uncovering what Elias had been working on. But without that name, Samantha had no idea where to start looking.

Her eyes fell on her phone again. She could reach out to Turner, tell him about the missing contact, but she hesitated. If Pharmatech was willing to erase files and contacts, they were likely monitoring her communication, too. If she alerted Turner, she might risk leading Pharmatech right to him—and she couldn't afford to put him in danger.

Instead, she opted for a safer route. She opened an encrypted messaging app and sent a quick message to a contact outside Elmsbrook—someone she trusted, who had experience with corporate espionage and had helped her with similar cases in the past.

Samantha: *Lost a lead. Possible interference. Need a dig into Pharmatech's regional connections, specifically anyone tied to genetic research.*

She hit send and closed the app, feeling a small sense of relief. It wasn't much, but it was a start. If her contact could recover anything about the researcher or Pharmatech's regional operations, she might still have a chance to regain some ground.

Samantha leaned back in her chair, her gaze drifting toward the window. The sun had set, leaving the town bathed in twilight. The shadows outside seemed to deepen, growing longer and more menacing, as though reflecting the mounting tension she felt.

She knew Pharmatech was onto her now. The missing information wasn't just a fluke—it was a warning. They wanted her to know they were in control, that they could take away anything she uncovered, and if she wasn't careful, they might erase more than just documents.

But Samantha wasn't one to back down from a fight. This was just the beginning, and if Pharmatech thought they could scare her off, they didn't know her well enough yet.

With renewed determination, she closed her laptop and grabbed her jacket. If she couldn't find the information online, she'd have to do it the old-fashioned way—by hitting the ground and talking to people. She still had leads, and she wasn't about to let Pharmatech get away with whatever they were hiding.

As she stepped out into the cool night air, Samantha knew one thing for sure: the deeper she dug, the more dangerous this was going to get. But she wasn't stopping now.

The streets of Elmsbrook were quiet as Samantha made her way back from the diner, the cool evening air nipping at her skin. The town seemed to retreat into itself as night fell, the quaint charm of the day giving way to an eerie silence. The windows of the nearby shops were dark, their displays barely visible in the dim streetlights. Only a few cars dotted the road, their drivers long gone into the safety of their homes. It was the kind of quiet that made every footstep sound too loud, every breath feel too sharp.

Samantha's mind was still racing from the realization that Pharmatech was already moving against her. The missing files, the erased contact—it had shaken her more than she wanted to admit. They were watching her, or at least they were aware of her presence. She had encountered threats before, but this felt different, more calculated. The deeper she dug, the more dangerous this investigation was becoming. But that was nothing new.

As she walked, she kept her movements casual, but her senses were on high alert. Something felt off. The kind of instinct she had honed over years of investigating cases like this was buzzing in the back of her mind, warning her that she wasn't alone. She slowed her pace slightly, letting her eyes scan the area without drawing attention.

And then she saw him.

Across the street, standing in the shadows between two parked cars, was a tall, thin man. He wore a long coat, the collar turned up against the chill, and a wide-brimmed hat that obscured most of his face. Even from where she stood, she could see the glint of sunglasses reflecting the streetlights. His posture was stiff, too still for someone casually standing on a sidewalk. He was watching her.

Samantha's heart rate quickened, but her face remained neutral. She continued walking as if she hadn't noticed him, her pace unchanged. Confronting him now would be a mistake—she needed information, not a confrontation. Whoever he was, he had made himself known, and that meant he either wanted her to see him or had gotten sloppy.

As she approached the corner of the street, she slipped her phone from her jacket pocket, angling the screen so that she could discreetly capture a photo of the man without drawing attention. The camera clicked softly, the image snapping just as she turned slightly to look at a nearby storefront. The man hadn't moved. He was still there, watching.

Samantha's pulse raced, but she forced herself to stay calm. She quickly opened her encrypted messaging app and sent the photo to Turner, typing a short message to accompany it.

Samantha: *Picked up a tail. This guy's been watching me. Could be Pharmatech.*

The message sent, and she slipped the phone back into her pocket. She needed to get off the street, fast. The last thing she wanted was to make it easy for him to follow her. She knew Elmsbrook was small, but there were still enough alleyways and side streets to lose someone if she was careful.

Without altering her pace, she took a left at the next corner, moving away from the main road and into a narrower street lined with darkened shops. She cast a quick glance over her shoulder. The man had moved, now walking slowly along the opposite side of the street, still maintaining distance but making no attempt to hide his interest. He was following her.

Her mind worked quickly. If he was sent by Pharmatech, then things were worse than she thought. They weren't just erasing her files—they were actively monitoring her, and likely planning their next move. She couldn't let this escalate before she had more information.

Turning another corner, Samantha quickened her pace slightly, her eyes scanning for a place to break the line of sight. Ahead, an alleyway between two old brick buildings offered just the opportunity she needed. Without hesitating, she darted into the narrow passage, her boots hitting the pavement softly as she moved into the shadows. She pressed her back against the cold brick wall, taking a moment to listen.

Silence.

Then, after a few tense seconds, the sound of footsteps. Slow, deliberate. They were getting closer.

Samantha didn't panic. She pulled her phone out again, ready to send another message to Turner if things went south. The figure stepped into view at the end of the alley, his silhouette outlined by the faint glow of a streetlamp. He stopped, standing at the mouth of the alley, his gaze sweeping the darkened space, searching.

Her phone buzzed in her hand—Turner had responded.

Turner: *Got the photo. Be careful. He could be a scout, or worse. Stay out of sight.*

Samantha's grip tightened on her phone as the man continued to stand there, unmoving. She needed to make a decision. If she stayed hidden long enough, he might lose interest, or he could decide to come in after her. Either way, she couldn't stay here forever.

The man shifted slightly, taking a step toward the alley. Samantha held her breath, her body tensing. But just as he seemed to be making a decision, he stopped, glancing over his shoulder. Another figure appeared at the far end of the street, and with a final glance toward the alley, the man turned and walked away, disappearing into the night.

Samantha waited a full minute before stepping out from her hiding spot, her pulse still racing. She couldn't shake the feeling of being hunted, like prey caught in a game she hadn't yet figured out. But one thing was clear—Pharmatech wasn't playing around anymore. They had sent someone to watch her, to follow her, and that meant she was getting too close to something they didn't want exposed.

She took a deep breath and quickly texted Turner again.

Samantha: *Lost him for now, but he's not working alone. This is getting serious.*

As she walked back toward the inn, her mind raced with possibilities. The sense of danger was more palpable now than ever. She needed to move fast, gather as much information as she could, and stay one step ahead of whoever was watching.

The game had changed. And so had the stakes.

Chapter 3
Hidden Tensions

Samantha walked briskly through the narrow streets of Elmsbrook, her hands tucked into the pockets of her jacket. The evening was cooler than usual, the wind carrying with it a slight chill. Her mind was still buzzing from the events of the previous night. Whoever the man was that had followed her, he had disappeared, but the tension in her chest hadn't eased. She needed answers—and fast.

As she approached the park where she had first met Henry Johnson, she couldn't help but feel a wave of skepticism wash over her. Her initial conversation with him had been too easy. He had offered information, but it felt rehearsed, like he was giving her just enough to keep her interested but not enough to risk his own position. This time, she was ready to dig deeper.

Henry was sitting on the same bench, hunched over slightly, his hat pulled low. He didn't seem surprised to see her approaching. His eyes flicked up as she stopped in front of him, offering a thin smile that didn't quite reach his eyes.

"Well, well, if it isn't the curious outsider again," he muttered, straightening his posture a bit but keeping his voice low.

Samantha stayed standing, her arms crossed in front of her. "You seemed eager to talk last time. Thought I'd see if you had any more to say."

Henry shrugged, pulling his jacket tighter around himself. "Depends on what you want to hear, Miss Cross. Not much changes around here, you know."

Samantha raised an eyebrow, her gaze steady. "Not even when people start following strangers around town?"

Henry's face stiffened for a moment before he masked it with a smirk. "Sounds like you're starting to see the underbelly of this place. Told you before, didn't I? Elmsbrook has its secrets."

"Yeah, you did. And I'm starting to think you know more about those secrets than you're letting on." Samantha sat down on the bench next to him, pulling out her phone and casually placing it in her lap, its recording app already running. "Last time we talked, you mentioned people disappearing. Said it was because they got too close. Too close to what, exactly?"

Henry shifted uncomfortably, glancing around as if checking for anyone within earshot. "I already told you. People in this town know when to keep their mouths shut. Those who don't..." He trailed off, his fingers tapping anxiously on his knee.

"You told me a lot of things, but none of it adds up," Samantha pressed, her tone firmer. "People don't just vanish into thin air without someone knowing why. And if you know something about that, now's the time to come clean."

Henry's smirk faltered, replaced by a grimace. He scratched the back of his neck, his eyes avoiding hers. "Look, I don't want trouble. I'm just a man trying to get by."

"And I'm just a woman trying to find the truth," Samantha replied coolly. "So stop dancing around it, Henry. You said there are people who run this town. You weren't just talking about local politicians. You were talking about something bigger. I want to know who they are."

Henry glanced at her, his jaw tightening. "You don't want to get involved in this. Trust me, you don't."

Samantha leaned in slightly, lowering her voice. "It's too late for that. I've already got someone tailing me, my files are disappearing, and I've barely scratched the surface. So stop stalling and tell me what you know."

Henry's hands twitched, his gaze shifting nervously again. "Pharmatech. They've got their claws deep in this town. Deeper than you can imagine. But that's all I can say. They control things here, and if they find out I've been talking…" His voice trailed off, leaving the implication hanging heavily in the air.

"Pharmatech," Samantha repeated, though she wasn't surprised. The name had come up too many times to ignore. "And you're scared of them. That's why you're holding back."

"I ain't holding back!" Henry snapped, then lowered his voice quickly. "I'm just trying to stay alive. This ain't the kind of game you play around with."

Samantha's eyes narrowed. His defensiveness told her everything she needed to know. Henry knew more than he was saying, and fear was keeping him from talking. But fear wasn't going to stop her. "You told me people disappeared, Henry. If Pharmatech's involved, they didn't just disappear—they were made to disappear. You've seen it happen, haven't you?"

Henry clenched his jaw, his shoulders slumping. "Yeah. I've seen things. People getting too curious, asking the wrong questions. Next thing you know, they're gone. Like they never existed. Pharmatech don't leave loose ends."

Samantha's stomach tightened. She had suspected as much, but hearing it confirmed sent a chill down her spine. "Why haven't you disappeared yet?" she asked, watching his reaction carefully.

"I know how to keep my head down," Henry muttered. "I don't get involved. I don't ask questions."

"But you're talking to me," Samantha pointed out.

Henry chuckled darkly. "And I'm already regretting it."

Samantha stood up, slipping her phone back into her pocket. "Maybe. But you've already said enough to make yourself a target. So here's what's going to happen—I'm going to keep digging. You're going to stay alive by being smart. And if you remember anything else that might be useful, you'll let me know. Got it?"

Henry's eyes darted to hers, a mixture of fear and reluctant agreement in his gaze. "You're gonna get yourself killed, you know that?"

Samantha shrugged, her face unreadable. "Wouldn't be the first time someone's tried."

As she walked away from the park, her mind raced. Henry was holding back, but his fear told her more than he realized. Pharmatech was controlling more than just the town's economy—they were controlling the people, silencing anyone who got too close to the truth. And now, Samantha was in their crosshairs.

She would need to tread carefully, but one thing was clear: she wasn't stopping now. Henry had given her just enough to confirm what she already suspected—and enough to make her even more determined to bring Pharmatech down.

Samantha sat at her desk in the Elmsbrook Inn, the low hum of her laptop filling the silence of the room. The dim light from her desk lamp cast long shadows across the walls, but she was too focused to notice. She had been digging into Pharmatech for days, sifting through mountains of documents, financial reports, and digital breadcrumbs, trying to piece together the web of influence the corporation had spun around the town.

Her fingers moved steadily across the keyboard as she accessed yet another encrypted file, this one linked to a local government contract. Pharmatech wasn't just involved in genetic research.

The company's reach extended into Elmsbrook's infrastructure, healthcare, and even education. They had ties to nearly every public service, a fact that sent a shiver down her spine. The more she uncovered, the clearer it became that Pharmatech wasn't just a player in the background—they controlled the stage.

As the document loaded, Samantha's eyes narrowed. The title read: **Confidential Report—Elmsbrook Infrastructure Grant**. She scrolled through the pages, her heartbeat quickening as she read. Pharmatech had funneled millions into the town's public projects, but the money hadn't gone where it was supposed to. Instead, it had been used to buy influence, to secure contracts with local politicians and authorities who were now deeply in their pocket.

"Unbelievable," she muttered, shaking her head.

Her phone buzzed on the desk, and she glanced at the screen. It was Turner.

"You sound tense," Turner said after she picked up the call.

"I've just found something," Samantha replied, her voice low but urgent. "Pharmatech's influence here is worse than we thought. They've bought off local officials, used their money to secure control over everything—hospitals, schools, city projects. They've got their hands in everything."

Turner let out a slow breath. "How deep does it go?"

Samantha clicked on another file, her eyes scanning the list of names. "It goes all the way to the top. I've got documents here showing that the mayor, several council members, and even the head of the local police are tied to Pharmatech. They've been on the payroll for years."

"Jesus," Turner muttered. "No wonder you've been having trouble. If Pharmatech's controlling the town, it explains why information's been disappearing. They've got the power to bury anything they want."

Samantha felt a tightness in her chest as she read through more of the files. Pharmatech's reach wasn't just financial—it was personal. She came across emails between the mayor and a Pharmatech executive, discussing ways to silence local journalists who had started asking too many questions. Another document detailed a payment made to a local judge, ensuring a favorable ruling in a land dispute that Pharmatech had an interest in.

"They've bought everyone," Samantha said quietly, disbelief lacing her words. "This isn't just about money or influence. They're controlling the town. They're erasing people, making them disappear if they don't play along."

Turner's voice was grim. "You need to be careful, Sam. If they've got this much power, they won't hesitate to come after you if they think you're getting too close."

"I know," she replied, trying to suppress the growing unease. "But I can't stop now. This town is suffocating under Pharmatech's control. People are too scared to speak up. If we don't expose this, they'll keep getting away with it."

Turner was silent for a moment. "What's the plan?"

"I need more evidence," Samantha said, clicking through more files. "Right now, I've got enough to tie them to local corruption, but that won't be enough to take them down. I need something bigger, something that shows how far they're willing to go."

Turner hesitated. "And if you don't find it?"

Samantha's jaw tightened. "I will."

She ended the call and turned back to her laptop, the screen flickering as she opened another set of documents. This one was marked **Highly Confidential—Pharmatech Internal Use Only**. Her heart raced as she decrypted the file, waiting for what new horrors it might reveal.

When it finally opened, she was met with a list of names— names of individuals who had been flagged by Pharmatech as "potential risks." Her stomach churned as she recognized some of the names from her earlier investigations—activists, journalists, even a local doctor who had spoken out against Pharmatech's practices.

"Targets," she whispered to herself, the weight of the realization hitting her hard. Pharmatech wasn't just bribing officials—they were eliminating anyone who posed a threat.

She quickly scrolled through the file, her eyes widening as she came across a section labeled **Erasure Protocols**. It outlined detailed procedures for neutralizing "high-risk individuals," including methods of blackmail, threats, and in some cases, disappearances. The people in Elmsbrook who had vanished—they hadn't just left town. Pharmatech had made them disappear.

Samantha's hands trembled slightly as she took a screenshot of the document and saved it to a secure folder. This was it. This was the proof she needed to show just how dangerous Pharmatech truly was. But with this knowledge came a new level of danger. Pharmatech would stop at nothing to protect its secrets, and now, she was standing directly in their crosshairs.

She quickly sent the encrypted files to Turner, adding a short message.

Samantha: *I've found what we need. But it's bigger than I thought. Pharmatech's not just corrupt—they're eliminating people. I've got names, targets, and a protocol. We need to move fast before they realize what I've found.*

A moment later, Turner replied.

Turner: *Stay safe. This just became a fight for survival.*

Samantha closed her laptop and leaned back in her chair, her mind racing. The pieces were falling into place, but they were darker and more twisted than she had imagined. Pharmatech wasn't just manipulating the town—they were suffocating it, controlling everyone from the shadows.

But now she had the truth. And no matter how dangerous it became, she wasn't going to stop until everyone else knew it too.

Alex sat hunched over his laptop, the glow from multiple screens illuminating his face as his fingers moved rapidly over the keyboard. The soft clack of keys was the only sound in his small, cramped apartment. His workspace was a tangle of wires, routers, and hard drives, each serving a specific purpose in his never-ending battle to stay one step ahead of whatever he was digging into. This time, though, things were different. This time, he was up against something much larger than any of the freelance hacking jobs he'd taken before.

Pharmatech.

Samantha had been clear when she asked him to help dig into the corporation's digital footprint. At first, Alex had thought it would be routine—track their financials, pull some documents, and find out who they were connected to in Elmsbrook. But as soon as he breached their systems, he knew something was wrong. The security was too tight, too well-constructed. Every firewall he breached was followed by another, stronger one. Every backdoor he found was quickly patched. It was like they were expecting him.

"Come on, you bastards," Alex muttered under his breath as he tried another bypass. His eyes flicked to the coding screen, watching a series of numbers and symbols dance across it, trying to force their way into Pharmatech's mainframe. But no matter what he tried, every step forward was followed by two steps back.

45

The system flashed red. A security breach alert. Pharmatech's countermeasures had detected his intrusion again, and this time they were coming for him.

Alex cursed softly, immediately moving to shut down his connection. He'd been in situations like this before, but something about this attack felt different. It wasn't just a corporate firewall—this was active defense. Pharmatech wasn't just passively protecting their system; they were hunting him down the moment he poked his head inside.

He barely severed the connection in time before the trace hit his IP address.

Sweat beaded on his forehead as he leaned back in his chair, rubbing his hands over his face. "Shit," he muttered. "They're not playing around."

His phone buzzed on the desk. He glanced at the screen—it was Samantha.

"How's it going?" she asked, her voice calm but carrying the weight of expectation.

Alex let out a breath. "Not good. This is next-level stuff, Sam. I've breached corporate systems before, but Pharmatech is a whole different beast. Every time I make progress, they slam the door shut. I've never seen a system adapt this fast."

Samantha's voice remained even. "Do you think they know we're looking?"

"I wouldn't be surprised if they've got teams of people monitoring this system around the clock," Alex replied, shaking his head. "Whoever built their defenses knew exactly what they were doing. They've got everything—encrypted firewalls, dynamic security measures, and now they're trying to trace me. I barely cut the connection in time."

"Damn," Samantha muttered on the other end of the line. "So, what's our next move?"

Alex stared at his screens, his mind racing. Pharmatech was powerful—he had known that going in—but the sophistication of their defenses was beyond anything he had anticipated. If they were this determined to protect their systems, then whatever secrets they were hiding were much more dangerous than he'd originally thought.

"I can keep trying," Alex said after a moment, though there was doubt in his voice. "But I need to change tactics. Direct attacks aren't going to work; they're too well-prepared. I might need more time—weeks, maybe."

Samantha paused. "We don't have weeks, Alex. If they know we're digging into them, they'll move fast. We need something now."

Alex felt the pressure mounting. He could hear the tension in her voice, but he knew that rushing would only increase the chances of getting caught—and if they got caught, Pharmatech wouldn't hesitate to retaliate. "I'll see what I can do, but I'm telling you, this is no ordinary corporate system. We're talking military-grade protection. If we push too hard, we might trip something we can't take back."

"I trust your judgment," Samantha said, though her tone was clipped. "Just keep me updated."

The call ended, leaving Alex staring at the series of error messages blinking on his screen. Pharmatech wasn't just defending its assets—it was actively monitoring, reacting, and retaliating. They had the resources to track him down if he made one wrong move, and they wouldn't hesitate to bury him, just like they'd done to others who had gotten too close.

He ran his hand through his hair, his mind working furiously to find a way around the obstacles. Maybe brute force wasn't the answer. If he couldn't go in through the front, he'd have to find a more subtle way to infiltrate the system.

Alex pulled up a different set of tools on his laptop. Pharmatech's main servers might be untouchable, but every system had its vulnerabilities. Sometimes, the easiest way to break into a fortress wasn't through the heavily guarded gates—it was through the cracks in the wall. He'd have to find those cracks, whether they were in a secondary server, an unguarded employee's email, or a forgotten database. It would take finesse, but if anyone could do it, it was him.

He cracked his knuckles, the tension in his shoulders easing slightly. He wasn't giving up yet. Pharmatech might be powerful, but they weren't invincible. He would find a way in. He just had to be patient.

As he started running a series of tests to identify weak points in the system, he reminded himself of why he was doing this. Elias had been onto something, something big enough to get him killed—or worse. And now, it was up to Alex and Samantha to figure out what that was before Pharmatech buried the truth for good.

"Alright, Pharmatech," Alex muttered, a determined edge in his voice. "Let's see how good you really are."

Samantha sat in the corner booth of the small, dimly lit coffee shop near the town square. The place was quiet, the kind of establishment where people came to mind their own business, and tonight, that's exactly what she needed. Her fingers drummed lightly on the table as she waited, her eyes flicking toward the entrance every few seconds. She had arranged this meeting cautiously, avoiding any mention of it in her usual channels. If Pharmatech was watching, they couldn't know about this.

The door opened with a soft chime, and Samantha's gaze locked on the man who entered. He was in his early forties, a little scruffy around the edges, with a weathered jacket and a worn notebook tucked under his arm. His eyes scanned the room nervously before landing on her.

"Samantha Cross?" he asked as he approached her table, keeping his voice low.

"That's me," she replied, gesturing for him to sit. "You must be Daniel."

Daniel Hartley nodded and slid into the booth, glancing around the shop one more time before leaning in closer. "I've heard about you. You've been asking the right questions—dangerous questions."

Samantha gave him a tight smile. "That seems to be a pattern for me. But from what I hear, you've been asking those same questions for years."

Daniel's expression darkened, and he shook his head. "Yeah, I've been digging into Pharmatech for a long time. Problem is, every time I get close to something solid, they shut it down. Stories vanish, sources disappear. People don't want to talk about it, not when they know what Pharmatech can do."

"That's exactly why I reached out," Samantha said, lowering her voice. "I'm not just looking to expose them. I need to bring them down, and I can't do that alone. I need someone who knows this town, someone who has access to information that I don't."

Daniel looked at her skeptically. "And what makes you think I can help? Every lead I've had has dried up or been silenced."

Samantha leaned forward, locking eyes with him. "Because I have proof. Real proof. I've found documents that tie Pharmatech directly to local officials, payments, bribes, erasure protocols. They're not just running this town—they're controlling it. And I have names."

Daniel's eyes widened slightly, but he kept his voice calm. "Names? You're telling me you have a list of people they've... what? Paid off? Silenced?"

"Both," Samantha replied, her tone serious. "I've seen the files. They've flagged people as 'high risk' and made them disappear. Journalists, doctors, activists—anyone who posed a threat to their operations."

He let out a low whistle. "That's big. Bigger than I thought. And you're sure it's real?"

Samantha nodded. "I've cross-referenced everything. It's airtight. But the problem is, they're watching. They know I'm getting close. I need to move fast before they realize what I have."

Daniel leaned back, running a hand through his hair. "Damn. You really came prepared."

"I don't have a choice," she said, her voice firm. "Pharmatech's dangerous, but I'm not backing down. That's why I need you. You've been digging into them for years, so you must have contacts. People who've seen things. People who can speak up now that I've got proof."

Daniel hesitated, clearly weighing the risks. "I've got a few sources. Most of them are scared, though. People don't want to cross Pharmatech—they know what happens to those who do. But if you really have proof..."

"I do," Samantha said, her tone unwavering. "But we need to be smart about this. If we release everything too soon, they'll bury it before it ever reaches the public. We need to build momentum, get the right people involved."

"And who's that?" Daniel asked, his skepticism still lingering. "Who can we trust?"

Samantha tapped her fingers on the table, thinking for a moment. "We start small. Local media first, people who aren't afraid to go against the grain. Then we move up—regional outlets, maybe a few investigative journalists with bigger platforms. If we can get enough attention, Pharmatech won't be able to squash it all at once."

Daniel nodded slowly, his expression thoughtful. "I might know a few people who'd be willing to take that risk. There's a guy I used to work with—retired now, but he's still got some pull in the local press. And there's a blogger I know who's been itching to take down a big corporation. She might be reckless, but she's not afraid to get her hands dirty."

"Good," Samantha said, a sense of relief washing over her. "The more voices we have, the harder it'll be for Pharmatech to silence us."

Daniel leaned in closer, his voice dropping to a whisper. "But you realize what you're getting into, right? This isn't just some corporate scandal. If we start pulling these threads, they're going to come after us. And they don't play fair."

Samantha met his gaze, her expression hardening. "I know. But I'm not backing down. Not after what I've seen."

Daniel studied her for a moment before nodding. "Alright. I'm in. But we need to be careful. We take it slow, build our case, and then we hit them hard."

"Agreed," Samantha said, her voice steady. "We'll start with the local press, gather as much support as we can. Then, when the time's right, we release everything. It's the only way to make sure Pharmatech doesn't see it coming."

Daniel smirked, though there was a flicker of nervousness in his eyes. "You've got guts, I'll give you that."

"I'm going to need them," Samantha replied, a slight smile tugging at her lips.

As they stood up to leave, Samantha felt a sense of determination settle over her. She had an ally now, someone who knew the town and its secrets. Together, they would expose Pharmatech for what they truly were—and bring them down, no matter the cost.

Chapter 4
The Watchful Eyes

Samantha pulled her jacket tighter around her shoulders as she stepped out of the Elmsbrook Inn, her mind still buzzing with the conversation she'd had with Daniel the previous night. The air was crisp, and the quiet streets of the town seemed peaceful—too peaceful. The more she uncovered about Pharmatech, the more the town's serene facade felt like a stage set, hiding something dark and dangerous beneath.

She had spent the morning tracing another lead, following up on one of the names that had appeared in Pharmatech's confidential files. A local contractor, supposedly involved in one of the town's infrastructure projects, had suddenly gone off the grid a few months back. No one seemed to know where he'd gone, and the police reports mentioned nothing suspicious. But Samantha knew better. People didn't just disappear like that, not in a town controlled by a corporation like Pharmatech.

As she walked down the main road, her phone buzzed in her pocket. She glanced at the screen—it was Turner.

"How's it going?" his voice came through, steady but concerned.

"I've got a lead," Samantha said, her voice low as she kept her pace steady. "But something feels off. I'm heading over to one of the sites tied to the missing contractor. I want to see if there's anything they've left behind."

Turner's sigh was audible. "Just be careful. You've already had people watching you. They're not going to let you dig around without trying to make you stop."

Samantha's lips tightened into a thin line. "I know. But I need to see this through."

As she spoke, she heard the low rumble of an engine behind her. It wasn't unusual—cars passed through the town regularly—but something about the sound made her stomach tighten. She kept walking, glancing over her shoulder as casually as she could.

A dark SUV was approaching, moving slowly. Too slowly.

Her instincts flared, and Samantha's pace quickened. "I think I'm being followed," she whispered into the phone.

Turner's voice immediately sharpened. "Can you lose them?"

"I don't know yet," Samantha replied, her heartbeat speeding up. "It's just one car, but something feels wrong."

The SUV was getting closer, still creeping along the road, its tinted windows giving no hint of who was inside. Samantha made a quick decision and turned onto a side street, hoping the narrow alleyways would offer some cover. The SUV turned as well, its engine revving slightly as it picked up speed.

"Damn it," Samantha muttered, her eyes scanning the street for an escape. There was a narrow alleyway up ahead, just wide enough for her to slip through but too tight for the vehicle.

"Samantha?" Turner's voice came through the phone, tense now.

"I'm fine," she said quickly, darting toward the alley. "I've got a plan."

She ducked into the alley, her heart pounding in her chest. The SUV couldn't follow her here, but that didn't mean she was safe. She kept moving, weaving between buildings, her steps quick but quiet. When she reached the other side of the alley, she peered around the corner, checking for the SUV.

It was gone.

Her phone buzzed in her hand again—Turner.

"What the hell just happened?" he asked, his voice a mix of concern and frustration.

Samantha took a deep breath, trying to calm her racing pulse. "Someone just tried to run me down. They were following me, waiting for the right moment."

"Are you sure?" Turner pressed, his tone serious.

"Yes," she said, her voice firmer now. "They weren't just following me. They were trying to scare me—or worse."

There was a long pause on the other end of the line before Turner spoke again. "This means they're getting desperate. If they're escalating to this, they're feeling threatened by how close you're getting."

"That's what I'm thinking," Samantha agreed, her mind already racing through her next steps. "I need to be more careful. They're not going to stop at intimidation."

"They won't," Turner confirmed. "You need to take this seriously, Sam. Pharmatech doesn't play around. If they've made an attempt on you, they'll try again."

Samantha nodded to herself, though her gaze was still scanning the street, making sure the SUV wasn't lurking nearby. "I will. I'll keep a low profile from here on out."

"Good. Keep me updated, and don't take unnecessary risks," Turner warned. "You've already got enough on them to make them nervous. That's a dangerous place to be."

Samantha's lips tightened. "I'm not backing down."

"I didn't think you would," Turner said with a dry chuckle, but his tone was still tense. "Just make sure you're alive to see this through."

She ended the call and leaned against the brick wall for a moment, letting out a slow breath. The adrenaline was still pulsing through her veins, but now there was a sharper edge to her focus. The close call had been a wake-up call, a reminder that Pharmatech wasn't going to let her continue digging without consequences.

Pushing off the wall, she started walking again, this time more cautiously. Pharmatech was escalating their efforts to silence her, but if they thought a staged accident would scare her off, they didn't know her well enough. This was only going to make her dig deeper.

She pulled her jacket tighter and kept moving, her mind already working through the next steps. She needed to reach out to her contacts, keep Turner in the loop, and—most importantly—stay one step ahead of Pharmatech. If they were desperate enough to try scaring her, it meant she was getting close. And that only fueled her determination to expose them.

Samantha glanced over her shoulder one last time, ensuring the street was empty before disappearing into the shadows. The game had changed, and now it was a fight for survival.

Samantha stood outside the Elmsbrook Inn, leaning against a lamppost as she waited for Turner to arrive. The evening air was crisp, and the sun was beginning to set, casting long shadows across the sleepy town. Her close call earlier had rattled her more than she'd admit, but she was still determined to push forward. If anything, the attack had only strengthened her resolve. But she knew she couldn't keep going alone—not anymore.

The familiar sound of a motorcycle engine cut through the quiet of the street. She looked up just as Turner pulled up, parking his bike a few feet away. He swung his leg over the seat and removed his helmet, revealing his sharp features and calm, focused expression. His presence was a welcome sight—a reminder that she wasn't entirely on her own in this.

"Sam," Turner greeted her with a nod, his voice steady but tinged with concern. "You alright?"

"I'm fine," she replied, though the tension in her shoulders told a different story. "But things are heating up faster than I expected. I've already had one close call, and it won't be the last."

Turner frowned, his eyes narrowing slightly. "Yeah, I got that from your call. Pharmatech's not playing around anymore. I figured they'd ramp up the intimidation, but trying to run you down? That's a new level."

Samantha sighed and gestured toward the inn. "Come inside. We need to talk strategy."

Once inside her small room, Turner wasted no time. He scanned the space quickly, checking the windows and doors, his tactical instincts kicking in immediately. "First thing's first—we need to get serious about security. If Pharmatech is making moves, they've likely got eyes on you."

Samantha sat down at the small desk, watching Turner as he methodically assessed their surroundings. "I've been careful, but clearly not careful enough. I didn't think they'd escalate this fast."

"They're scared, Sam," Turner said, pulling a chair up across from her. "You've hit a nerve, and now they're trying to knock you off balance. They want you to feel vulnerable."

"Well, they're doing a damn good job of that," she admitted, running a hand through her hair. "But I'm not backing down."

"I know you're not," Turner said, leaning forward. "But we need to be smart about this. It's not just about surviving their attacks—we need to outmaneuver them, stay two steps ahead. If they know where you are or what you're doing, they'll always be in control."

Samantha nodded, understanding the gravity of his words. "So, what's the plan?"

Turner crossed his arms, his expression serious. "First, we set up secure communication channels. No more using your regular phone for sensitive conversations. I'll give you an encrypted device that can't be traced. We'll also need to change up your routine—make sure you're not easy to track. If they've got someone tailing you, we need to lose them."

Samantha raised an eyebrow. "You think I've got a tail?"

"I'd bet on it," Turner said flatly. "They've already tried to hit you once. They'll be watching to see what you do next."

"Great," she muttered, shaking her head. "Just what I need."

Turner leaned in, his voice low but firm. "We're not just reacting to them, Sam. We're going to turn this around. We hit them where they're not expecting it. While we keep them busy looking for you, we dig deeper—find out who's pulling the strings behind the scenes."

Samantha nodded, her mind already working through the next steps. "I've got leads, Turner. But we need time. Pharmatech's reach is everywhere. They've bought off officials, buried evidence. It's like trying to fight a shadow."

"That's exactly why we need to be smarter," Turner said. "We can't fight them head-on, not yet. We gather intel, use the information to create pressure. They've got skeletons in their closet—we find them, and we expose them."

Samantha sat back, her hands tapping lightly on the desk. "You make it sound simple."

"It's not simple," Turner said, his tone sharp. "It's going to be messy and dangerous. But if we don't do this right, they'll bury us before we can even make a move. And you know they're capable of that."

She met his gaze, and for the first time since the attack, she felt a flicker of hope. Turner's calm confidence, his ability to see through the chaos and find a clear path, was exactly what she needed. "Alright," she said, her voice steady. "What do we need to do first?"

Turner pulled a small device from his pocket—a slim, black phone, completely untraceable. "This is your new line of communication. Keep it with you at all times, and don't use anything else for sensitive calls."

Samantha took the phone, feeling its weight in her hand. "And what about tracking?"

"I've got a few tricks up my sleeve," Turner said with a small smirk. "We'll use misdirection. Make them think you're somewhere else while we move in the shadows. I've got contacts who can help us with that, but you'll need to trust me on this."

"I do," Samantha said, her eyes locking with his. "I trust you."

"Good," Turner replied, standing up. "Because we're going to need every advantage we can get. Pharmatech's powerful, but they're not invincible. We just have to play the game smarter than they do."

Samantha stood as well, slipping the encrypted phone into her pocket. "Then let's start playing."

Turner nodded, his expression unreadable but focused. "Let's take them down, one move at a time."

The attic of Elias Harding's old office was exactly as Samantha had imagined: dusty, cluttered, and filled with decades of forgotten files and boxes. The dim light from a single bulb hanging from the ceiling cast long shadows over the shelves, illuminating stacks of papers and abandoned equipment. She had been searching for hours, combing through old documents and notes, trying to piece together the final days of Elias's life.

Her fingers grazed the spine of a weathered book wedged between stacks of papers. It was small, leather-bound, and out of place amidst the chaos of loose files. Samantha tugged it free, dusting off the cover. The initials **E.H.** were embossed on the front.

"This has to be it," she muttered under her breath, flipping it open.

The handwriting inside was hurried, messy, the kind of scrawl produced by someone in a state of constant anxiety. It was Elias's journal. And it wasn't just notes on his research—this was personal.

She flipped to the first page, her eyes scanning the text quickly.

June   12th,   20XX.

I think they're onto me. I don't know how much longer I can keep this up before they come for me. I can't tell Margaret—she wouldn't understand the danger.

Samantha's breath caught. She knew Margaret had been close to Elias, but this was different. He had been hiding things from her, from everyone. The next entry was even more cryptic.

June 20th, 20XX.

Pharmatech is involved, I'm sure of it. Their interest in my research came out of nowhere. They want to control the results, twist them for their own purposes. I've seen how they operate—people disappear when they get too close. I won't let that happen to me.

Samantha's fingers tightened on the edges of the pages. Elias had known about Pharmatech's reach long before anyone else had. He had seen through their facade, but the fear in his writing was palpable. She continued reading, flipping through page after page of frantic, paranoid notes.

A door creaked behind her, and she instinctively grabbed her phone, already expecting Turner's voice on the other end.

"Samantha? What did you find?" Turner's voice crackled through the speaker.

"I found Elias's journal," Samantha said, her voice filled with urgency. "It's... It's worse than we thought, Turner. He knew Pharmatech was coming for him. There are pages of cryptic notes, but it's clear he was scared—paranoid even."

"Paranoid how?" Turner asked, the sound of movement in the background telling her he was on the move as well.

"He was convinced they were watching him," she explained, reading another entry aloud. *'I've changed my routine. I leave through the back door now. Too many strange cars parked near the house. One of them followed me yesterday.'* Her voice softened. "He knew they were watching him, but no one believed him."

Turner was quiet for a moment before responding. "Makes sense. Pharmatech has always been good at that—isolating their targets, making them look unstable. They break people down, make them question what's real."

Samantha flipped to a section of the journal filled with scientific equations and data, but it was accompanied by a deeply personal note.

August   3rd,   20XX.
I thought this research would help people. I thought it could be a breakthrough. Now I realize I'm a pawn in their game. They don't care about the science, only the control. The more I uncover, the more dangerous this becomes. I'm not safe. I don't think I've been safe for a long time.

"He wasn't just scared of Pharmatech taking his research," Samantha said, her voice heavy with realization. "He was afraid of what they would do with it. He saw his work twisted into something it wasn't meant to be."

Turner let out a slow breath. "And that's exactly what they do, Sam. They take something good, something that could change the world, and they turn it into a weapon for control."

Samantha ran a hand over her face, the weight of the journal's contents sinking in. "It wasn't just research to him. This... this was his life. And they ruined it."

"What else does it say?" Turner asked, his voice calm but urgent.

She scanned the pages, her heart sinking as she read the final entries.

August   18th,   20XX.

I'm running out of time. I've made arrangements for the data—hid it where they won't find it. If anything happens to me, someone will know the truth. They can't erase all of it, not if it's out there. But I'm scared. Scared that it won't be enough. They're closing in. I can feel it.

Samantha's throat tightened as she read the last lines of the journal. Elias had been ready for the worst, knowing that his time was running out. He had hidden the data—his research, his life's work—somewhere they couldn't reach it, but it hadn't been enough. Pharmatech had gotten to him first.

"He was prepared to disappear," Samantha said softly. "He knew they were coming for him, but he didn't stop. He kept working, kept hiding the data."

Turner's voice was grim. "And now it's on us to finish what he started."

Samantha closed the journal and stood, determination settling over her like a heavy cloak. "He hid the data, Turner. It's out there somewhere. We need to find it before Pharmatech does."

"Then we move fast," Turner said, his voice hardening. "Because if they know you have that journal, they'll come for you next."

Samantha nodded, her grip on the journal tightening. Elias's fear, his sacrifice, wasn't going to be in vain. She would find the data, and she would bring Pharmatech down.

But the clock was ticking.

Samantha sat in the dimly lit room of the Elmsbrook Inn, her laptop open on the small desk in front of her, Elias's journal beside it. The weight of what she had found was still sinking in, but there was no time to dwell. She needed to act. Turner paced the room, his arms crossed, his expression serious as they discussed their next move.

"We can't sit on this any longer, Turner," Samantha said, breaking the silence. "We have to release something. If we wait too long, Pharmatech will find out what we've uncovered, and they'll shut us down before we get a chance to expose them."

Turner stopped pacing and looked at her, his eyes narrowing in thought. "I agree. But we have to be careful about what we release. If we drop everything at once, they'll come at us hard. We need to play this strategically."

Samantha nodded, her mind racing through the possibilities. "What if we release just a portion? Something that grabs attention but doesn't expose all our cards. Just enough to get the media on our side and put pressure on Pharmatech."

Turner leaned against the wall, his arms still crossed. "That could work. We release something damning, but not enough for them to figure out the full extent of what we have. It buys us time, and it forces them to scramble. But you realize, the moment we do this, they're going to escalate. They'll come after us harder than before."

"I know," Samantha said, her voice steady. "But we can't afford to wait. We need to control the narrative before they have a chance to bury it."

Turner walked over to the desk and sat down across from her, the intensity of the situation settling between them. "Alright. What part do we release?"

Samantha pulled up the encrypted files she had gathered over the last few days. "We start with the payments. The bribes to local officials, the shell companies Pharmatech used to funnel money into Elmsbrook's infrastructure. It's concrete evidence of their corruption, but it doesn't reveal everything about the research Elias was working on."

Turner studied the files on the screen. "It's enough to get the media's attention. Once they see a corporation like Pharmatech buying off local governments, they'll start digging. It'll open the floodgates."

Samantha clicked through the documents, preparing to send them to a few trusted journalists she had been in contact with. "We need to time this perfectly. Once this goes public, they'll be looking for us. We need to be ready."

Turner stood and grabbed his phone. "I'll handle the logistics. Make sure we're not traceable. You focus on getting this to the right people."

Samantha hesitated for a moment, her finger hovering over the send button. "Are we ready for this?"

Turner's eyes softened for a moment. "We have to be. It's not just about us anymore. If we don't act, Pharmatech will keep doing what they've been doing—erasing people, controlling governments, and twisting science for their own gain."

She nodded and hit send, watching as the files were encrypted and sent to her contacts in the media. There was no turning back now.

Moments later, her phone buzzed. One of the journalists, a seasoned reporter named Leah, had already responded.

Leah: *This is explosive. I'll run with it. We'll need a statement from you to confirm. Can we talk?*

Samantha smiled grimly. "It's out."

Turner nodded, his expression unreadable. "Now we wait."

It didn't take long. Within hours, the story was breaking across several smaller outlets. Headlines began popping up on her phone: **Pharmatech Bribery Scandal Exposed in Small Town** and **Corporate Corruption in Elmsbrook: The Dark Side of Big Pharma.**

Turner's phone buzzed. He glanced at the screen. "It's happening faster than I thought. Pharmatech's already pushing back."

Samantha's phone rang, and it was Leah on the other end. "Samantha, we've published the first piece. It's gaining traction, but Pharmatech's PR team is already on damage control. They're calling the accusations baseless, saying it's the work of conspiracy theorists."

Samantha clenched her jaw. "That's expected. But this is just the beginning."

"I know," Leah replied, her voice steady but tense. "Be careful. They're going to come after you hard now that this is out there."

"We're ready," Samantha said, her voice calm but her pulse quickening. "Just keep the pressure on them. We've got more, and if they push too hard, we'll release it all."

Leah paused. "Alright. Stay safe, Samantha."

As she hung up the phone, Turner looked at her with a mixture of concern and determination. "We're in it now."

Samantha nodded, her mind already spinning with the next steps. "We need to stay one step ahead of them. If they're already pushing back, that means they're scared. But they'll retaliate."

"They will," Turner said, his voice low. "And when they do, it won't just be through the media. They'll come after us directly."

Samantha met his gaze, her voice unwavering. "Then we hit back harder."

Turner smiled grimly. "I'll start setting up the next layer of security. We need to be ready to move if they make this physical."

"They will," Samantha said, standing up from the desk. "They've already tried once. They'll try again."

Turner placed a hand on her shoulder. "Then let's make sure we're ready for them."

As the headlines continued to spread, Samantha knew the battle with Pharmatech had officially begun. They had made their move, and Pharmatech would respond, but this time, Samantha was ready. With Turner by her side and the public watching, the fight had just escalated—and she was prepared to do whatever it took to bring them down.

Chapter 5
A Mysterious Lead

Rachel sat in front of her laptop, her fingers flying over the keyboard as she typed out the next wave of media leaks. The room was dimly lit, the glow of the screen casting her face in sharp relief. Around her, printouts, notes, and files were scattered across the table—a chaotic map of the media strategy she was orchestrating. Her phone buzzed with messages from reporters, bloggers, and editors, all hungry for more details about the Pharmatech scandal.

"This has to be perfect," she muttered under her breath, eyes focused on the screen. She glanced at the clock—she had just hours to push the next leak before the news cycle shifted again. Time was of the essence, and the stakes were growing higher by the minute.

Samantha stood by the window, watching the empty street below, her arms crossed tightly. "How's it going, Rachel? You've already gotten more traction than we thought. But we need to keep the momentum."

Rachel didn't look up. "I've got it under control, Sam. The first wave worked—the bribery scandal grabbed everyone's attention. But now we need to hit them harder. Something about the research Elias was working on, something that shows how dangerous Pharmatech really is."

Samantha nodded, though her mind was still racing. "I trust you. But remember, their PR team is going to push back harder this time. We can't afford any mistakes."

Rachel sighed, leaning back in her chair. "I know. They're already starting. Just look at this."

She turned her laptop to show Samantha a news article from a major outlet with the headline: **Pharmatech Refutes Claims of Corruption, Calls Allegations 'Baseless.'**

"They're hitting back with the usual denials," Rachel explained, her voice tight with frustration. "Saying the documents were forged, that we're pushing a conspiracy. And they've got a lot of outlets on their payroll to amplify that message."

Samantha frowned. "That's what we expected, right? They'd discredit us, try to make us look like conspiracy theorists."

"Yeah, but they're going harder than I thought," Rachel said, pulling up another page. "They're flooding the media with counter-narratives, questioning our credibility, and painting us as rogue investigators with an agenda. They're muddying the waters."

Samantha walked over, studying the headlines. "They're trying to confuse the public. If they can make it seem like there's no solid proof, people will stop paying attention."

"Exactly," Rachel said, spinning the laptop back toward her. "But I've got a plan. We need to leak some of Elias's research. Just a taste of what he was working on before he disappeared. Something that shows the public what's really at stake."

Samantha raised an eyebrow. "That's risky. If we release too much, they'll know exactly what we have."

Rachel smiled grimly. "That's the point. We give them just enough to make them sweat. Let them know we're not bluffing. If we do this right, it'll shift the narrative in our favor. People won't care about Pharmatech's denials once they see the actual science."

"Do it," Samantha said after a moment of thought. "We need to keep the pressure on."

Rachel nodded, her fingers already flying across the keyboard again. "I'll prep the leak and make sure it goes to the right outlets. But we need to be prepared. Pharmatech's going to hit back hard after this."

Turner, who had been listening from the doorway, stepped into the room. "She's right. The more we reveal, the more aggressive they'll get. You're ready for that, right?"

Rachel didn't stop typing. "I've been ready since the day I joined this team, Turner. We always knew Pharmatech wasn't going to sit back and watch."

Turner chuckled dryly. "Good. Because once this hits the media, it's going to be a war out there. Their PR team won't just discredit us—they'll try to bury the story entirely. And if they can't do that, they'll come after us."

Rachel shrugged. "Let them try. We're ready."

Samantha walked over to the window again, her mind racing. "How long before the leak goes live?"

Rachel glanced at the clock. "Give me an hour. I've got the files queued up, just need to coordinate with the journalists. We release it in waves—first the small outlets, then we move to the bigger ones. Once it's out there, it'll be impossible for Pharmatech to ignore."

Turner crossed his arms. "We'll need to stay mobile. If they can't win the media battle, they'll escalate. You know that, right?"

Samantha nodded, her jaw tightening. "I know. But we can't stop now. This leak could be the tipping point. If the public sees what Elias was working on, they'll start asking the right questions. We'll have more eyes on Pharmatech than they can handle."

Rachel hit a final key, sending a series of encrypted messages to her media contacts. "It's done. The first wave will hit in an hour. Then we watch the fallout."

Samantha exhaled slowly, turning to face Rachel. "You've done good work. This is what we needed."

Rachel smiled faintly, though there was tension behind it. "Thanks. But let's not celebrate yet. We're about to kick a hornet's nest."

Turner checked his watch. "Alright, we've got some time before things start heating up. I'll get our contingency plans ready in case we need to move. Pharmatech's not going to sit around and watch themselves get dismantled in the press."

Samantha nodded, glancing back at Rachel. "We'll keep an eye on their counter-narratives. If they try to flood the media again, we'll need to adjust fast."

"Don't worry," Rachel said, her eyes focused on the screen. "We're playing chess, not checkers. Let's see how Pharmatech handles the next move."

As the team settled into their tasks, the tension in the room was palpable. They had taken the first step in exposing the truth, but the battle was just beginning. Samantha knew they were up against a powerful and ruthless enemy, but with Rachel's media strategy, they had a chance to turn the tide. The next few hours would be crucial, and Samantha could feel the weight of what was to come pressing down on her.

But there was no turning back now.

Alex sat in the dimly lit corner of the room, surrounded by multiple screens, his fingers flying across the keyboard. The glow of his monitors was the only light in the room, casting shadows over his tense face. His focus was razor-sharp, but the anxiety was creeping in. Pharmatech had been relentless, sending wave after wave of cyberattacks since they had leaked the first batch of evidence. Alex had held them off so far, but now... now things were different.

"They're coming harder than before," he muttered, not taking his eyes off the code scrolling in front of him. "I've never seen anything like this."

Samantha stood behind him, her arms crossed, watching the screens with a furrowed brow. "What's different this time?"

Alex let out a sharp breath, shaking his head as his fingers continued to work. "It's not just a basic DDoS attack or phishing attempts anymore. They're actively trying to breach our firewalls, corrupt the data. They're inside some of the smaller systems. I'm holding them off, but they're... damn it, they're smarter than I expected."

Turner, standing in the doorway, took a step forward. "How close are they to breaking through?"

Alex hesitated, his jaw tightening as he typed furiously. "Too close. I'm rerouting traffic through different servers to buy us time, but they're learning. Whoever's running this attack—this is more than just a corporation's IT team. This is military-grade."

Samantha exchanged a glance with Turner, the tension in the room thickening. "What do you need, Alex? What can we do to help?"

"Right now? Nothing," Alex said, his voice clipped with frustration. "I just need time. But they're not giving me any. I'm barely holding them at bay, and if they breach the main system, they could wipe everything. All the evidence, Elias's research... gone."

A warning alert flashed on one of the screens, and Alex's fingers froze for a split second before he jumped back into action. "No, no, no... not now."

"What is it?" Turner asked, stepping closer to the desk.

"They've breached one of our backups," Alex said, his voice rising in panic. "They're corrupting the files. I can stop them, but I need to lock down everything. If I don't, we'll lose the whole system."

Samantha leaned forward, her voice calm but urgent. "Do whatever you have to, Alex. We can't afford to lose any of this."

"I know!" Alex snapped, immediately regretting the tone. He paused for a second, rubbing his face with one hand while the other continued to type. "I'm sorry, I'm just… this is too much. I'm trying to hold everything together, but they're coming at us from all angles."

"We get it," Samantha said, her voice softening. "But you've got this. You're the best at what you do."

Alex clenched his jaw, focusing back on the screen. "I hope you're right."

Another alarm went off, this time louder, and Alex's face paled. "Damn it! They're in the main system. They're trying to corrupt the core data!"

Turner moved beside Samantha, his voice steady but intense. "What does that mean? Can you shut them out?"

"I'm trying," Alex growled, his fingers moving frantically across the keys. "I'm closing access ports, rerouting the firewalls… they're fast, too fast…"

For a few agonizing moments, the only sound in the room was the rapid tapping of Alex's fingers against the keyboard. Sweat beaded on his forehead, and his breathing quickened as he fought to keep the system from collapsing. Then, suddenly, he stopped, his hands hovering over the keyboard.

"They're out," he whispered, his voice barely audible.

Samantha let out a breath she hadn't realized she was holding. "You did it."

Alex shook his head, his eyes still glued to the screen. "They're out for now. But they'll be back. And next time, I don't know if I'll be able to stop them. They're getting better with every attack. I'm barely keeping up."

Turner took a step closer, his voice calm but firm. "Alex, you've been handling this alone for too long. What do you need? How can we reinforce the system?"

Alex leaned back in his chair, his hands trembling slightly as he stared at the screens. "I don't know. We're up against more than just Pharmatech's IT team. This is next-level. I don't have the resources to keep up with them. If they hit us again, I'm not sure we'll survive it."

Samantha placed a hand on his shoulder. "You've done more than we could've asked for. You've kept us in the fight."

Alex exhaled shakily, his eyes closing for a brief moment. "I'm just trying not to lose everything. If we lose this data, it's over. All of it... gone."

Turner nodded, glancing at Samantha. "We need to get him more support. If Pharmatech is playing this aggressively, we're going to need backup."

Samantha nodded. "Agreed. I'll reach out to some of our contacts, see if we can get extra cyber defense."

Alex opened his eyes, staring blankly at the screen. "If they get through again, I don't know if we'll have anything left to protect."

"We're not letting that happen," Samantha said firmly. "You've held them off so far. We'll make sure you have what you need to keep doing that."

Alex swallowed hard, his voice a whisper. "I just don't know how long I can keep this up."

Turner gave him a reassuring look. "You're not doing this alone. We'll find a way to get ahead of them."

Alex nodded, though the weight of the pressure was clear on his face. The battle with Pharmatech wasn't just a war of information anymore—it was becoming a personal struggle, a test of endurance that was pushing him to his limits.

Samantha straightened, her voice resolute. "We're in this together, Alex. And we're not losing."

Samantha could feel the tension crackling in the room before anyone said a word. Turner was standing near the door, his

79

arms crossed tightly over his chest, his face set in a grim expression. Across from him, Rachel sat at the small table, her laptop in front of her, tapping her fingers impatiently. The silence was thick, and Samantha knew that something was about to boil over.

Finally, Turner spoke, his voice low but sharp. "We can't keep doing this, Rachel. We're escalating too fast, and we're not prepared for the backlash. Every time we leak something, Pharmatech comes at us harder. We're one step away from them finding us."

Rachel didn't look up from her screen. "You think I don't know that? We're making progress, Turner. We have the public's attention. We can't just stop now because you're nervous."

"Nervous?" Turner scoffed, his arms dropping to his sides. "This isn't about nerves. It's about strategy. We're playing with fire, and you want to pour gasoline on it. We're not ready for what happens if Pharmatech decides to take this offline."

Rachel finally looked up, her eyes flashing with frustration. "Offline? What do you suggest we do then? Sit back and wait for them to bury us? The media is already moving on. If we don't keep pushing, we'll lose our momentum, and then we'll have nothing."

Samantha stepped forward, trying to defuse the growing argument. "Both of you, calm down. We need to think this through."

Turner turned to her, his voice hard. "I am thinking this through, Sam. And what I see is us walking straight into a trap. Rachel keeps pushing these leaks out without considering the consequences. We're not just fighting a PR war anymore. Pharmatech's already come after you, after Alex, and it's only going to get worse."

Rachel threw her hands up. "So what do you want to do, Turner? Run? Hide? We're already in this fight. If we back off now, they'll crush us anyway."

"That's not what I'm saying," Turner shot back. "But we need to be smart. This isn't just about dropping stories and hoping for the best. We need to plan each move, anticipate their response. You're throwing punches without thinking about the counterattack."

Rachel stood, her voice rising. "What's the alternative? Do nothing? Let them control the narrative? If we give them space, they'll drown us out with their PR machine, and everything we've worked for will be gone."

Samantha stepped between them, raising her hands. "Enough! Both of you." She looked at Turner first. "Turner, I get it. You're worried, and we should be. But Rachel's right—we can't just back down now. We've come too far."

She turned to Rachel. "But you have to understand Turner's point too. We're dealing with a corporation that has unlimited resources. We can't keep escalating without thinking about the long-term consequences. We're not invincible."

Rachel's frustration simmered just below the surface, but she nodded. "I know that, Sam. But we can't lose the momentum we've built. People are finally paying attention. If we hesitate, Pharmatech will bury the story, and they'll come for us harder."

Turner crossed his arms again, his expression still tense. "And what happens when they stop playing by the rules? When they stop worrying about PR and start coming after us directly? You saw what happened with Alex—Pharmatech nearly wiped everything. We were lucky. That won't happen twice."

Samantha exhaled, feeling the weight of the decision pressing down on her. She was caught between two valid points—Turner's need for caution and Rachel's drive to keep the pressure on. Both of them were right, in their own ways. The media leaks had given them leverage, but Pharmatech was a cornered beast, and they couldn't afford to underestimate how far the corporation would go to protect itself.

"We need a middle ground," Samantha said finally, her voice calm but firm. "Rachel, keep the media engaged, but we're going to scale back the frequency of the leaks. We need to be more calculated. Release only what we know will have maximum impact. And Turner…" She turned to him, her expression softening. "We're not backing down. But we'll be smarter. We'll start planning for Pharmatech's next move before they make it."

Turner's jaw tightened, but he nodded slowly. "Fine. But we need to increase security, too. If we're going to keep leaking this stuff, we can't afford to get blindsided again."

Rachel threw her hands up in exasperation. "Fine. More security, more planning. But we're still moving forward. We can't slow down too much, Sam. I'm telling you, we've got the public's attention now. This is our window."

"I understand," Samantha said, her voice steady. "But we're playing a long game now. We need to outlast Pharmatech, not burn out before we get the chance to finish this."

Rachel slumped back into her chair, still frustrated but resigned. "I just don't want to lose the momentum. You know how the media works—if we don't keep feeding them, they'll move on to the next scandal."

Samantha placed a hand on Rachel's shoulder. "We won't lose it. We just have to play this smart. Trust me."

Turner exhaled, glancing at the clock on the wall. "I'll go check on Alex, make sure everything's secure. But Sam, don't wait too long to move. We can't afford to hesitate."

"I won't," Samantha assured him.

As Turner left the room, the tension lingered, but the immediate heat of the argument had passed. Rachel stared at her screen, muttering, "We can't wait forever, Sam."

Samantha sighed and looked out the window, the quiet street of Elmsbrook still and deceptively peaceful. "We won't wait forever. Just long enough to make sure we survive this."

Samantha stood frozen in the doorway, her hand trembling as she read the report on her phone for the third time. The words blurred together, but one line remained crystal clear: **Daniel Hartley, local journalist, found dead.** The article stated that he had been found in his car, the engine still running, an apparent accident. But Samantha knew better. This wasn't an accident. This was Pharmatech.

The weight of it hit her like a wave, knocking the breath from her lungs. Daniel had been one of her most valuable informants, someone who had been feeding her information about Pharmatech's local influence, connecting the dots between the corporation and the corrupt officials they had bought off. And now he was gone.

"They killed him," she whispered to herself, her voice cracking. Her eyes flicked across the rest of the article, but the details were vague—too vague. Just like all the others. Pharmatech had erased him, just as they had done to anyone who got too close. But this time, it wasn't just some faceless figure in the files. This time, it was someone she had worked with, someone she had trusted.

Turner's voice cut through her haze. "Sam, what's going on?" He stepped into the room, concern etched on his face. "You're pale. What happened?"

Samantha couldn't bring herself to speak at first. She swallowed hard, thrusting the phone toward him, her hand shaking. Turner took it from her, his eyes scanning the screen. His face hardened as he read.

"Damn it," he muttered under his breath. "Daniel? I thought he was careful."

"So did I," Samantha said, her voice barely audible. "But it doesn't matter. I told him too much, Turner. I gave him the leaks. They found him because of me."

"No, Sam. This isn't on you," Turner said, stepping closer, but his words barely registered.

She sank into the nearest chair, her hands gripping the arms tightly. "Yes, it is. He trusted me, and I put him in the line of fire. And now he's dead because of it."

Turner crouched down in front of her, his voice firm but gentle. "Pharmatech killed him. Not you. They're the ones pulling the strings. You can't take this on yourself."

Samantha shook her head, tears welling in her eyes. "I'm responsible for this. I didn't think it through, I didn't... I pushed too hard, too fast, and now Daniel's dead. What if it happens again? What if we keep pushing and more people die?"

Turner sighed, his hand resting on her knee in a comforting gesture. "We knew this was dangerous, Sam. Daniel knew it too. Everyone who's been helping us knew what was at stake."

"But I didn't expect this," she said, her voice breaking. "I didn't expect them to go this far."

"They'll go as far as they need to protect themselves," Turner said, his tone grim. "That's what makes Pharmatech so dangerous. But if we stop now, if we let this break us, then Daniel's death is for nothing. You know that."

Samantha closed her eyes, tears slipping down her cheeks. "I don't know if I can keep going, Turner. What if this keeps happening? What if every person who helps us becomes a target?"

For a long moment, the only sound in the room was the ticking of the clock on the wall. Turner stayed quiet, watching her, knowing that no amount of words could take away the guilt she felt. But after a while, he spoke again, his voice softer this time.

"Sam, you're doing what no one else would. You're fighting something bigger than all of us. And yes, it's dangerous. Yes, people are getting hurt. But that's not on you. That's on them. You didn't choose this fight—they did. And if you stop now, you're giving them exactly what they want."

Samantha stared at him through teary eyes. "But how do I keep going, knowing that people might die because of me?"

"You don't do it because it's easy," Turner said quietly. "You do it because it's right. Because if we don't keep fighting, who will?"

Samantha wiped her eyes, her heart still aching with the weight of Daniel's death. She had never wanted this—never wanted to be responsible for anyone's life, let alone their death. But Turner was right. If they stopped now, Pharmatech would win, and Daniel's death would be just another casualty swept under the rug.

"I don't know if I can live with this," she whispered.

Turner stood and placed a hand on her shoulder. "You're not in this alone, Sam. We'll get through this. We'll finish what Daniel started. But you have to decide if you're still in this fight."

For a long moment, Samantha didn't move. She sat there, staring at the floor, feeling the crushing weight of her responsibility pressing down on her. But somewhere, deep inside, a fire still burned. She couldn't let Pharmatech win. Not after everything. Not after Daniel.

She stood slowly, her resolve hardening despite the pain in her chest. "I'm still in."

Turner gave her a small nod of approval. "Good. Because we've got work to do."

As he left the room, Samantha stood alone for a moment, staring at the phone in her hand. Daniel's death was a brutal reminder of the cost of this fight. But it was also a reminder of why they couldn't stop now.

Pharmatech had made a fatal mistake by killing Daniel—they had pushed her too far. And now, there was no turning back.

Chapter 6
Beneath the Surface

The morning light filtered through the curtains of Samantha's makeshift office at the Elmsbrook Inn, but the atmosphere inside was far from calm. Samantha sat at her desk, her laptop open in front of her, several notifications flashing urgently on the screen. She had barely slept since Daniel's death, and now, as the reality of Pharmatech's latest move came crashing down on her, it felt like everything was slipping through her fingers.

"We've been hit," Rachel said from across the room, her voice tight with frustration as she scrolled through her phone. "Pharmatech's PR machine is in full swing. They're flooding the media with counter-narratives, calling us frauds, accusing us of fabricating evidence. It's everywhere."

"They're not just going after our reputation," Alex added, his voice tense as he leaned over his laptop. "They've frozen our accounts. Every donation, every financial channel we had—blocked. We can't access a single dollar."

Samantha's heart sank. "They've taken out everything?"

"Yeah," Alex said, his face pale. "I'm trying to find a way around it, but they've tied up every asset we have. They're using shell companies and financial hold orders. It's a mess."

Turner, who had been standing by the window with his arms crossed, turned to face them, his expression hard. "They've got the resources to keep this going for as long as they want.

They're not just trying to shut us down—they're trying to destroy us."

Samantha rubbed her temples, trying to think. The past few weeks had been a blur of small victories and sudden losses, but this—this was different. Pharmatech had clearly decided that they weren't going to play defense anymore. They were launching an all-out assault on her team, and it was working.

"They're hitting us on every front," Samantha said, her voice steady despite the panic rising in her chest. "If we don't push back, we're finished."

"We can't push back if we don't have any resources," Rachel said bitterly. "We've got no money, no legal standing, and they've got the media wrapped around their finger. What are we supposed to do?"

Samantha stood, walking toward the window, her hands trembling slightly. She stared out at the quiet street, a stark contrast to the chaos she felt inside. She could see how Pharmatech was dismantling everything they had built, one move at a time. "We need to regroup. We can't let them control the narrative."

Turner's voice was cold but steady. "Regrouping won't stop them from bleeding us dry. They'll keep pushing until we're completely discredited, and by the time we can respond, no one will believe a word we say."

Samantha turned to face him, determination flickering in her eyes. "We've come too far to let them bury us now. They've escalated this into a full-on war, so we need to fight back with everything we have."

Alex looked up from his laptop, his fingers still tapping away. "I might be able to break through their financial blocks, but it's going to take time. They've got some of the best cyber defenses money can buy, and they're using every trick in the book to lock us out."

"How much time?" Turner asked, his eyes narrowing.

Alex shook his head. "I don't know. Days, maybe longer. They're throwing everything at us."

Rachel sighed, standing and pacing the room. "Even if you get us access to the money, it won't stop them from discrediting us. They're calling us conspiracy theorists, saying we fabricated Elias's research. It's all over the major news outlets."

Samantha clenched her jaw, thinking through their options. Pharmatech had money, power, and influence. They had control over the media, legal systems, and financial institutions. And yet, despite all of that, Samantha knew they still had something Pharmatech feared: the truth.

"We need to shift our focus," Samantha said, her voice sharpening with resolve. "If we can't fight them on their level, we need to fight them on ours. We release more of the research. Not just leaks—everything. Elias's work, the financial records, the corruption we've uncovered. We make it public. And we do it now."

Rachel stopped pacing, her eyes widening. "Everything? Sam, that could be dangerous. If we release it all, Pharmatech will know exactly what we have, and they'll come after us even harder."

"They're already coming after us," Samantha shot back. "But if we release everything, we force them into the light. They won't be able to control the narrative anymore. The media can't ignore hard evidence, not if it's out there for everyone to see."

Turner stepped forward, his voice low but intense. "If we do this, we need to be prepared for what comes next. Pharmatech won't just attack us in the press—they'll come after us personally. And they won't hold back."

"I know," Samantha said, her eyes meeting his. "But we're out of options. If we don't do this, we lose. We lose everything."

Alex nodded slowly, his fingers moving faster on the keyboard. "I can set up a secure data drop. We'll upload the files to multiple platforms at once—news sites, independent outlets, even social media. If we hit them all at the same time, Pharmatech won't be able to stop it."

Rachel frowned, biting her lip. "It's risky. But it might be our only shot."

Samantha glanced around the room, meeting each of their eyes in turn. "This is it. If we're going to take Pharmatech down, this is how we do it. We release the truth, all of it, and let the world see who they really are."

Turner nodded, his expression grim but determined. "Then let's do it. But we need to be ready for whatever comes next."

As Alex began preparing the data drop, the room fell into a tense silence. Samantha could feel the weight of their decision bearing down on her, but she knew it was the right one. They were out of time, out of money, and out of options. The only thing left to do was fight.

And this time, they were going all in.

Turner sat at the small, worn table in the Elmsbrook Inn, his eyes fixed on the map in front of him. The room was dimly lit, the soft glow of a lamp casting long shadows across his focused face. A series of marked locations dotted the map—points of escape, places to hide, and routes they could take to evade Pharmatech's tightening grip on their every move. Turner's mind worked like clockwork, his tactical background honed through years of planning high-stakes operations, but this time the stakes felt even higher.

"We can't stay here much longer," Turner said, not looking up from the map. "Pharmatech's got eyes everywhere. They're going to start sending people to track us, maybe even worse. We need to stay ahead of them."

Samantha sat across from him, watching him work. She could see the intensity in his eyes, the way he was already anticipating Pharmatech's next move. "What do you have in mind?"

"We're going dark," Turner said simply, his voice steady. "We need to disappear, at least for a while. No phones, no online communication unless it's secure. I've already set up alternate channels for us to stay in touch—encrypted, untraceable."

Rachel leaned against the wall, arms crossed, a look of concern on her face. "And what about the safe houses? You mentioned something earlier."

Turner nodded. "I've arranged for a few places we can lay low. They're outside Pharmatech's immediate reach—old contacts I trust. They don't know much about our situation, just that we need to disappear for a bit."

Samantha raised an eyebrow. "You think they'll keep us off the grid? Pharmatech's got deep pockets and a lot of resources. If they really want to find us…"

"They won't," Turner cut in, his voice calm but firm. "I've made sure these locations are off the radar. Remote places, no digital footprint. Pharmatech might have resources, but they're not going to waste time chasing shadows if they think we've gone dark."

Alex glanced up from his laptop, where he'd been working to secure their data files. "What about their surveillance systems? Pharmatech's got access to satellites, drones, God knows what else. If they really want to track us, they'll find a way."

"I've already thought of that," Turner replied. "We'll use routes that avoid major highways, back roads, and places where they're less likely to expect us. And when we do have to communicate, it'll be through encrypted channels I've set up. They won't be able to trace anything back to us."

Rachel frowned. "This all sounds great, but what about supplies? We can't just disappear without any resources. We need money, gear, food, everything."

Turner gave her a small, knowing smile. "Already taken care of. I've got caches set up at each safe house—supplies we'll need for at least a few weeks. It's not luxurious, but it'll keep us going."

Samantha leaned in, her eyes narrowing. "And how long do you think we'll need to stay off the grid?"

Turner paused for a moment, considering his answer. "Long enough for us to regroup. Pharmatech's coming after us hard, but we can use this time to plan our next move. They'll be looking for us, but we'll be the ones watching them."

Alex sighed, rubbing his temples. "So, we just disappear and hope they lose interest?"

"Not exactly," Turner said, shaking his head. "We'll still be active, just not where they expect. We'll keep releasing information, strategically. Pharmatech will scramble, but they won't be able to pin us down."

Samantha sat back, her mind racing. "You really think we can stay ahead of them? They've already frozen our assets, and they've got the media running their disinformation campaigns."

"That's why we need to move now," Turner replied, standing up from the table and pointing at the map. "Pharmatech thinks they've cornered us, but we still have options. If we stay here, we're sitting ducks. But if we disappear, we can control the narrative from a distance. We're not backing down, just repositioning."

Rachel crossed her arms. "And what about the people we leave behind? The contacts, the allies—won't they be vulnerable if we go dark?"

Turner's eyes met hers, his expression serious. "They knew the risks. We'll do what we can to protect them, but we can't save everyone. The more we stay in one place, the more vulnerable we become. This is the only way to stay ahead."

Samantha nodded, understanding the grim reality of the situation. "When do we leave?"

"Tonight," Turner said without hesitation. "I've got the routes mapped out. We'll break up into smaller groups, head to different safe houses. Once we're settled, we'll reconnect through the secure channels."

Alex stood, looking over at the map. "And after that?"

"After that," Turner said, his voice calm but full of determination, "we regroup, we strategize, and we hit Pharmatech harder than ever."

Samantha met Turner's gaze, feeling a renewed sense of purpose. "Let's do it. We can't let Pharmatech win."

Rachel uncrossed her arms, finally nodding in agreement. "Fine. I'm in. But this better work, Turner. I'm not getting off the grid just to sit around and wait."

"It'll work," Turner assured her, rolling up the map. "Trust me, they won't see us coming."

As they gathered their things, the weight of what lay ahead settled over the team. They were about to go dark, stepping into the shadows where Pharmatech's reach couldn't easily find them. But as long as they stayed one step ahead, they had a fighting chance.

And Turner was going to make sure they stayed ahead.

The tension in the small, dimly lit room was palpable. Samantha stood near the window, staring out into the darkness, lost in thought. The safe house Turner had set up felt more like a trap than a refuge. Something wasn't right, and she couldn't shake the feeling that they were being watched—no matter how carefully Turner had covered their tracks.

Behind her, the team was gathered around the table, quietly discussing their next steps. Turner's voice was calm, methodical, while Alex and Rachel spoke in hushed tones, still rattled by Pharmatech's relentless attacks.

Then, out of nowhere, the door burst open, and Turner stormed in, his face dark with fury. He held a laptop in one hand, his knuckles white from the grip.

"Everyone, shut up and listen," Turner said, slamming the laptop down on the table. The room went silent as all eyes turned to him.

"What the hell is going on, Turner?" Rachel asked, looking between him and Samantha, her confusion mirrored by Alex.

Turner's jaw clenched, and he turned the laptop toward them, tapping a few keys before a series of encrypted messages appeared on the screen. "This," he growled, "is what's been going on."

Samantha walked over, glancing at the screen, her heart sinking as she read the messages. The encryption was Pharmatech's signature—she recognized it instantly. Someone had been feeding them information. Someone close.

"No…" Alex whispered, taking a step back. "That can't be right. We've been careful."

"Careful?" Turner scoffed, his voice filled with anger. "We've been compromised. Every step, every plan we've made—they've known about it before we even moved. That's why Pharmatech's been ahead of us at every turn."

Rachel crossed her arms, her eyes narrowing. "You're saying someone in this room is working for Pharmatech?"

Turner nodded grimly. "Yes."

Samantha's blood ran cold. "Who?"

Turner's eyes moved to Alex, his expression hardening. "Alex."

"What?" Alex's face went pale. "No, I've been with you from the beginning. I've put everything into this—why would I betray you?"

"Because you've been in the system," Turner said, his voice low and dangerous. "You've had access to all of our data, all of our communications. And now, these encrypted messages, leading directly to Pharmatech—there's no other explanation."

Alex shook his head furiously. "No. No way. This has to be a mistake. Turner, you know me. Sam, you know me!"

Samantha stood frozen, her mind reeling. She had known Alex for years. He had been with her from the start, helping her dig through Pharmatech's digital walls. But now... she couldn't deny what was in front of her.

"I didn't do this," Alex pleaded, his voice cracking. "I swear."

Samantha stepped forward, her voice shaking with controlled anger. "Then explain how Pharmatech has been ahead of us every step of the way. Every time we've made a move, they've been waiting. How do you explain that?"

"I—I don't know!" Alex stammered. "I'm telling you, I didn't leak anything! Someone else must have gotten into the system. It wasn't me."

"Someone else?" Turner snapped. "You're the one in charge of our security, Alex. You said everything was locked down, that Pharmatech couldn't breach us."

Alex looked desperate now, his eyes wide as he tried to defend himself. "I swear to you, I didn't do this. I don't know how they're getting this information, but I didn't—"

Rachel cut him off, her voice icy. "You expect us to believe that after everything? You've had full access to all of our communications, our finances, our safe houses. And now you're telling us this is just a coincidence?"

Samantha's heart pounded in her chest, and she could feel the weight of the betrayal crushing down on her. She wanted to believe Alex, wanted to trust him. But the evidence was undeniable.

"Turner," she said, her voice barely a whisper. "Are you sure?"

Turner nodded, his expression firm. "I've been tracking the leaks for days. Every trace leads back to Alex's IP address. There's no other way."

Alex's eyes filled with tears. "Please, you have to believe me. I wouldn't do this to you, to any of you. They must've hacked into my system. I don't know how, but I—"

Samantha raised her hand, cutting him off. "Enough, Alex."

The room fell silent as she stared at him, her heart breaking. She had trusted him, relied on him, and now everything was falling apart. She couldn't afford to be emotional, not now. Not when Pharmatech was so close to taking them down.

"We can't take any chances," she said quietly, her voice filled with resolve. "Turner, secure the system. Isolate Alex's access. He's done."

Alex's face fell, his voice trembling. "Sam, please…"

But Samantha had already turned away. Her trust had been shattered, and there was no time to dwell on the betrayal. If Pharmatech had gotten this close, then they were running out of time.

Turner moved quickly, locking Alex out of the system as Rachel stood by, her arms still crossed and her expression unreadable.

"I'm sorry," Samantha whispered, though she wasn't sure if it was to Alex, to herself, or to the team as a whole. "But we have to keep moving."

With Alex now sidelined, Samantha realized something painful and undeniable—she could no longer afford to rely solely on her team. The stakes were too high, and the dangers too real. If she wanted to finish this fight, she would have to take matters into her own hands.

Pharmatech was closing in, and now, more than ever, Samantha knew she was on her own.

Samantha stood outside the unassuming clinic, the wind biting at her face as she stared at the faded sign that read **Elmsbrook Medical Center**. Inside, she knew Dr. Caldwell was waiting, though whether she was expecting this confrontation or not,

Samantha couldn't be sure. After everything that had happened—the betrayal, the relentless attacks from Pharmatech—this felt like the final piece. Dr. Caldwell had been evasive for too long, hiding behind a veneer of nervousness and silence, but that was no longer an option.

Taking a deep breath, Samantha pushed open the door and stepped inside. The small waiting room was dimly lit, its sterile scent a sharp contrast to the growing tension in Samantha's chest. She spotted Dr. Caldwell at the far end of the hall, talking quietly with a nurse, her shoulders hunched and weary.

Samantha walked toward her, her footsteps deliberate, the sound echoing through the narrow space. Dr. Caldwell turned at the noise, her eyes widening as she saw Samantha approaching.

"Miss Cross," Dr. Caldwell greeted her, though there was a tremor in her voice. "I wasn't expecting you today."

"I wasn't planning on coming," Samantha said evenly, "but we need to talk."

Dr. Caldwell hesitated, glancing nervously toward the nurse, who quickly excused herself and disappeared into a side room. Left alone with Samantha, the doctor's posture stiffened, her hands fidgeting with the edges of her white coat.

"I don't know what you're hoping to find," Dr. Caldwell said, her voice tight, "but I've already told you everything I can."

Samantha shook her head, stepping closer, her voice calm but firm. "No, you haven't. And you know it."

101

Dr. Caldwell blinked rapidly, her discomfort obvious. "I—what are you talking about?"

"You've been holding back, Doctor," Samantha said, her eyes locking onto Caldwell's. "You've known more about Elias's research, about Pharmatech, this entire time. You've been hiding it, and I need to know why."

For a moment, Dr. Caldwell said nothing. Her eyes dropped to the floor, her fingers twisting nervously in her lap. Samantha could see the internal battle playing out, the fear that had been haunting the doctor for months, maybe even years. But there was no time left for hesitation. Samantha stepped closer, her voice softening, but her resolve unyielding.

"I know you're scared, but if you don't help me now, more people are going to get hurt. Elias trusted you, didn't he? He shared his research with you, or at least parts of it. And you know where it is."

Dr. Caldwell's breath hitched, and her hand fluttered to her throat. Her voice wavered when she finally spoke. "I... I didn't want to be involved. Elias was my friend. I didn't know how deep this went until it was too late."

"You knew what Pharmatech was capable of," Samantha pressed. "You've seen what they've done—what they're doing. And you've kept quiet because you're afraid they'll come after you. But staying silent won't save you. If we don't stop them, they'll keep going."

Dr. Caldwell's eyes filled with tears as she finally looked up, the weight of her fear etched into every line on her face. "I… I didn't know it would come to this. I thought I could protect myself, keep my head down, but you're right. Elias… he gave me something before he disappeared. I didn't understand all of it, but he told me to hide it, to keep it safe."

Samantha felt her heart skip. "What did he give you?"

"Data," Dr. Caldwell whispered. "Research, files, recordings. I didn't know what to do with it. He said it was everything—his work, his discoveries, everything Pharmatech wanted to control. But he told me that if I was ever found with it, it would mean… the end."

Samantha nodded slowly, her pulse quickening. "Where is it?"

Dr. Caldwell hesitated again, her eyes darting toward the door, as if expecting someone to burst in at any moment. "I hid it in a place where no one would think to look—an old property Elias used to own, outside of town. It's in a safe, buried under the floorboards."

Samantha's mind raced as she processed this. Finally, the location of Elias's hidden research was within reach. This was the break they needed.

"Give me the address," Samantha said quietly, though her heart pounded in her chest. "I'll get the files, but I need to know everything—every detail."

Dr. Caldwell's hands shook as she reached into her pocket and pulled out a small piece of paper. She handed it to Samantha, her eyes filled with fear and resignation. "If you go there, you'll be putting yourself in danger. Pharmatech is watching everything. If they find out you're going after this... they'll stop at nothing."

Samantha took the paper, her fingers gripping it tightly. "I know."

Dr. Caldwell wiped at her eyes, her voice barely above a whisper. "Elias thought he could protect me by giving me this. He believed that if I stayed quiet, I'd be safe. But it's too late now, isn't it?"

Samantha's gaze softened, though she couldn't offer comfort. "They're not going to stop, Doctor. Not unless we finish what Elias started."

Dr. Caldwell nodded slowly, the fight leaving her shoulders. "Please... be careful."

Samantha turned and walked toward the door, the weight of the mission ahead pressing down on her. She had the location, the key to everything Elias had tried to protect. But as she left the clinic, her thoughts turned dark—retrieving the data would put her squarely in Pharmatech's crosshairs.

And this time, there would be no turning back.

Chapter 7
Echoes of the Past

The sound of their footsteps echoed in the quiet, dimly lit hallway of the storage facility. Samantha led the way, her heart racing as she scanned the darkened corridors. The air was thick with tension, and every shadow felt like a threat. Behind her, Turner and Rachel moved silently, their faces set with determination. They were close—so close to retrieving Elias's data. But they all knew they weren't the only ones closing in.

"This is it," Turner whispered, gesturing toward a heavy steel door at the end of the hall. "That's where the safe is. We need to move fast."

Samantha nodded, her eyes flicking to Rachel. "Do you have the codes?"

Rachel pulled out a small device from her backpack, her fingers moving quickly over the touch screen. "Give me a minute. I've been working on decrypting the facility's security codes for days. Should be able to bypass the lock."

Samantha glanced back down the hallway. They had been lucky so far. The place was eerily quiet, but she knew that Pharmatech wasn't far behind. She could feel it—a sense of impending danger looming over them. She clenched her fists, willing Rachel to hurry.

Turner moved closer to her, his voice low. "We need to be in and out before anyone knows we're here. You know they've got people on this."

"I know," Samantha replied, her voice tense. "But we can't leave without the data. If we lose this, we lose everything."

Rachel let out a frustrated sigh. "Almost got it… just one more—there!" The door clicked, and a soft green light flashed on the lock. "We're in."

Without another word, Turner pushed the door open, and they stepped inside. The room was small, dimly lit, and filled with old storage crates and metal shelves. In the far corner was the safe—exactly where Dr. Caldwell had said it would be.

"There it is," Samantha breathed, her heart pounding in her chest. "Let's get this done."

Turner approached the safe, pulling out a set of tools. "This is old-school. No digital locks, just a manual combination. It'll take a bit, but I can crack it."

Rachel moved to the doorway, keeping watch. "We don't have much time. Pharmatech's got operatives all over this place. They'll be here soon."

Samantha felt the pressure mounting, her nerves on edge. "Just keep watch. Turner, how long do you need?"

"Five minutes, tops," Turner said, already working on the lock.

Samantha turned to Rachel. "Any sign of movement?"

Rachel shook her head, but her expression was tight with anxiety. "Not yet. But I'm picking up encrypted communications—someone's nearby. We need to move faster."

Turner's hands worked quickly, his face a mask of concentration as he twisted the dial on the safe. Samantha stood beside him, her eyes darting between the safe and the door. The seconds dragged on, each one feeling like an eternity.

"There's chatter on their channels," Rachel said, her voice urgent now. "They know we're here. We've got less than two minutes before they reach this part of the building."

Turner grunted, adjusting his grip on the safe's handle. "Almost there…"

Samantha's heart pounded in her ears, her hands shaking as the reality of the situation settled in. This was it—their final chance to retrieve Elias's data, the last piece of the puzzle that could bring Pharmatech down. But they were running out of time.

"Come on, Turner," she muttered, her voice filled with desperation.

Turner's hand moved one final time, and there was a soft click as the lock disengaged. "Got it," he said, pulling the door open.

Samantha's breath caught as she looked inside. There, in a small metal box, were several USB drives and a thick stack of papers—Elias's research. The data they had been searching for all this time.

"Grab everything," she ordered, her hands trembling as she scooped up the USB drives and stuffed them into her bag. Turner grabbed the papers, shoving them into his jacket.

Rachel stepped away from the door, her face pale. "We've got company. They're coming. We need to go—now."

Samantha didn't need to be told twice. "Let's move."

They bolted from the room, Turner slamming the door shut behind them. Samantha's pulse raced as they sprinted down the hallway, her bag heavy with the precious data. The sound of footsteps echoed behind them, growing louder. Pharmatech's operatives were close—too close.

"This way!" Turner shouted, leading them down a side corridor. "We've got to lose them before we reach the exit."

Rachel glanced behind them, her face tense with fear. "They're catching up!"

Samantha's lungs burned as she ran, the adrenaline coursing through her veins. She knew they couldn't afford to get caught. If Pharmatech got their hands on them—or the data—it would all be over.

Turner led them through a series of narrow hallways, ducking and weaving through the facility's labyrinthine layout. But the sound of their pursuers was growing louder, closing in with every step.

"We're almost there," Turner said breathlessly, pointing toward a door at the far end of the corridor. "That's the exit."

Samantha could see the door, but she also knew they were running out of time. "Go, go, go!"

They burst through the door, spilling out into the cold night air. The sound of shouting echoed behind them, and Samantha knew they had only moments to escape.

Turner pointed toward a nearby alley. "There's a car waiting around the corner. Let's move!"

They sprinted for the alley, Samantha clutching the bag tightly against her chest. The data was safe—for now. But as they reached the car and sped away into the night, she knew one thing for certain: this was far from over.

Pharmatech would be coming for them. And next time, they wouldn't stop until everything—everyone—was destroyed.

The air inside the safe house felt thick with tension. Samantha sat at the table, the USB drives in front of her, the weight of Elias's data pressing down on her shoulders. Around her, the team moved with quiet urgency. Rachel was at her laptop, furiously typing as she set up the next series of secure uploads. Turner was by the window, peering out into the night, his hand resting near the holster on his hip. Every second felt heavier than the last, and Samantha could feel the storm that was about to break over them.

"They're throwing everything at us," Rachel muttered under her breath, her eyes glued to the screen. "I'm getting pings from

Pharmatech's legal team—cease and desist orders, threats of lawsuits. They're trying to shut us down through the courts."

Samantha rubbed her temples, exhaustion tugging at her. "How bad is it?"

"Bad," Rachel replied. "They've filed injunctions in five different states, trying to block any news outlet that publishes the data. If we go public with this, they'll bury us under legal fees before we even get a chance to fight back."

Turner, still standing by the window, turned to face them. "Legal threats are the least of our worries. I've been watching the street. We've got a black SUV parked two blocks away, same one I saw tailing us yesterday. They're watching the house."

Samantha looked up, alarm flashing in her eyes. "You're sure it's them?"

Turner's expression was grim. "Pharmatech's not being subtle anymore. They want us to know they're watching. It's intimidation."

Rachel slammed her laptop shut, frustration bubbling over. "Intimidation, legal threats... what's next? Blackmail?"

As if on cue, Samantha's phone buzzed on the table. The screen flashed with an unknown number, and her stomach tightened. She exchanged a look with Turner, then picked up the phone and pressed it to her ear.

"Hello?"

A cold, clipped voice answered. "Miss Cross. I assume you're aware that you're in over your head."

Samantha's grip tightened on the phone. "Who is this?"

The voice chuckled softly. "You know exactly who this is. And you know exactly what we're capable of."

"Pharmatech," she spat, her blood boiling. "What do you want?"

"We want you to stop," the voice said coolly. "You've meddled enough. This ends now, or there will be consequences."

Samantha glanced at Turner, who was watching her intently, his expression hard. "Consequences?" she said, her voice steady despite the fear crawling up her spine. "Is that a threat?"

"It's a promise," the voice replied, the tone darkening. "You and your team are standing in the way of something much larger than you understand. We suggest you walk away while you still can."

Samantha's jaw clenched, anger rising in her chest. "You think you can scare us off with a phone call? We have the truth, and we're going to expose everything."

The voice remained calm, unbothered. "Miss Cross, we've been very patient. But that patience is running out. Your little team is hanging by a thread. How much longer do you think you can hold out before we destroy everything you've built?"

Samantha's heart raced, but she refused to show weakness. "You're already losing. Why else would you be calling me?"

The voice paused, then spoke again, this time with an edge of menace. "You have no idea what's coming. Walk away, or we'll make sure you regret it."

Before she could respond, the line went dead. Samantha lowered the phone, her hand trembling slightly. She looked up at Turner and Rachel, their faces tense with anticipation.

"That was Pharmatech," Samantha said, her voice low. "They want us to stop."

"They're scared," Turner replied, stepping closer. "They wouldn't be making threats like that if they weren't."

Rachel stood up, pacing the room. "Scared or not, they're not playing around. We can't ignore this. They'll come at us from every angle—legally, physically. It's only going to get worse."

"I know," Samantha said quietly. "But we can't back down now. We're too close."

Turner's gaze hardened. "They're watching us, Sam. That SUV isn't here to keep an eye on things—they're planning something. We need to move, and soon."

Samantha took a deep breath, her mind racing. "We're out of time, then. We need to get the data out now. No more waiting."

Rachel nodded, her fingers flying over her keyboard again. "I'm setting up the uploads to multiple outlets—encrypted, but we'll need to move fast. Once it's out there, they can't stop it."

Turner checked the clip on his sidearm, his voice calm but resolute. "We need to split up after the upload. We can't all be in the same place when they make their move."

Samantha felt the weight of the decision bearing down on her, but she knew Turner was right. Pharmatech had resources they couldn't match, and the team was now in direct danger. They had to finish this before it was too late.

"We'll finish the upload and scatter," Samantha said, her voice filled with determination. "Pharmatech won't be able to stop us once it's out."

Turner stepped toward the door, peering out once again. "We need to stay on the move. Once they realize we're not backing down, they'll come after us with everything they have."

Samantha's phone buzzed again—this time, a text from a blocked number:
Last chance, Miss Cross. Walk away, or we'll make you.

She stared at the message, her stomach knotting with fear, but her resolve never wavered. "Let them try," she muttered, putting the phone down.

Rachel hit a final key on her laptop. "Uploads are set. It's all going live in five minutes."

Turner met her gaze, his expression serious. "This is it, Sam. There's no turning back now."

Samantha nodded, feeling the weight of their situation sink in. They were up against a corporation that had everything to lose—and everything to gain by silencing them. But they weren't going to be silenced. Not anymore.

"Let's go," Samantha said, her voice steady. "We finish this now."

With that, the team moved swiftly, packing up their gear and preparing to scatter into the night. As they stepped outside, the black SUV remained parked down the street, its presence a menacing reminder of what was at stake.

Pharmatech had made their last stand. But so had they.

Alex sat hunched over his laptop in the dimly lit room, his fingers flying over the keyboard, beads of sweat dotting his forehead. The faint hum of the computer and the rapid clicking of keys were the only sounds in the room as he faced the final cyber showdown with Pharmatech's security team. He'd been here before, countless times, but this time felt different. The stakes were higher, the opposition sharper, and the pressure nearly unbearable. He had to secure the data and ensure it reached the public, or everything they'd fought for would be lost.

"Pharmatech's experts are good," Alex muttered, his voice barely above a whisper. His eyes never left the screen, the lines of code flashing by in an endless stream. "They've set up countermeasures I've never seen before. But we're still in this."

Samantha, standing by the door, crossed her arms tightly, her expression tense. "Can you break through? We don't have time, Alex. We need that data out now."

"I know!" Alex snapped, though the frustration wasn't directed at her. "I'm working on it, but they've locked down every backdoor I've ever used. It's like they knew I was coming."

"They probably did," Turner said from across the room, pacing as he kept an eye on the windows. "They've been ahead of us the whole time. They've probably got their best team on you right now."

Alex gritted his teeth, focusing on the screen. Pharmatech's digital defenses were unlike anything he had faced before— layer after layer of firewalls, encryption, and adaptive countermeasures that seemed to shift and evolve with every move he made. Every time he breached one defense, another would rise in its place, more formidable than the last.

"They're playing chess, not checkers," Alex muttered. "But so am I."

Another warning flashed across the screen: **Intrusion detected. Countermeasures activated.**

"Damn it!" Alex slammed his hand on the desk, his frustration boiling over. "They're onto me again. They've triggered a full lockdown."

Samantha stepped forward, her voice calm but urgent. "Can you bypass it?"

Alex stared at the screen, his mind racing. "I'm trying, but they've set up a dead man's switch. If I trip it, they'll wipe the data clean before I can even get to it."

Turner stopped pacing and crossed his arms, his face grim. "So what's the play?"

Alex's fingers moved rapidly over the keys again. "I'm going to have to trick them—make them think I'm taking one path while I sneak in through another. It's risky, but it's our only shot."

Samantha exchanged a worried glance with Turner. "And if it doesn't work?"

Alex's eyes flickered toward her, a determined gleam in them. "If it doesn't work, we lose everything."

Without waiting for a response, Alex dove back into the battle. Pharmatech's security system was relentless, throwing new obstacles at him with every passing second. He dodged digital traps, navigated around honeypots designed to trace his location, and launched decoys to distract the security team. His heart raced as he pushed the limits of his skills, knowing that one wrong move could cost them everything.

"They're adapting," Alex muttered through clenched teeth. "They're learning my moves."

"They're playing defense," Turner said. "So hit them where they're not looking."

Alex smirked slightly, despite the tension. "Already ahead of you."

With a few keystrokes, Alex activated a false lead, sending Pharmatech's security team chasing after a phantom intrusion in a completely different sector of their system. It was a gamble, but it bought him precious seconds to work. His hands moved even faster now, exploiting the temporary hole in their defenses.

"I'm in," he breathed, his voice filled with a mix of relief and disbelief. "I've got access to the data vault."

"Good," Samantha said, her voice filled with hope. "Now secure it."

Alex's fingers danced across the keyboard, pulling up file after file—everything Elias had hidden from Pharmatech. Research logs, recordings, financial records—all of it was there, buried deep within the system.

But just as he began transferring the data, another warning flashed on the screen: **Counterattack detected. Trace initiated.**

"They're tracing me!" Alex shouted, his eyes wide with panic. "They've figured out what I'm doing."

"Can you finish the transfer?" Samantha asked, her voice sharp.

"I can try," Alex said, his hands moving frantically as he fought off Pharmatech's countermeasures. The screen flickered, the data transfer crawling at a painfully slow pace. Every second felt like a lifetime.

"They're coming for us," Turner warned, his eyes flicking to the windows. "We need to get out of here, Alex."

"I'm almost there!" Alex shouted, his pulse racing. "Just a few more seconds…"

The screen flashed red as Pharmatech's security team launched a final assault, flooding Alex's system with attempts to lock him out. His fingers flew over the keyboard, blocking and dodging every attack they threw at him. His breath came in short gasps, the pressure mounting with every passing moment.

Then, just as the system threatened to crash, the transfer completed.

"I've got it!" Alex cried, his face breaking into a triumphant grin. "The data's secure!"

Samantha let out a breath she didn't realize she was holding. "You did it."

But before they could celebrate, Alex's screen flashed one final warning: **Immediate evacuation recommended. System breach imminent.**

"We need to move—now!" Turner barked, already grabbing his bag.

Alex didn't hesitate. He yanked out the USB drive containing the precious data and shoved it into his pocket, his heart still racing. "Let's get the hell out of here."

As they rushed toward the exit, Alex couldn't help but glance over his shoulder at the screen, where Pharmatech's system was scrambling to recover from his assault. He had won this round, but he knew they weren't finished. Pharmatech was coming, and they wouldn't stop until they had them cornered.

But for now, they had the data. And that was enough.

As they burst into the cold night air, the weight of the final cyberbattle still fresh in his mind, Alex knew the fight wasn't over. But they were one step closer to bringing Pharmatech down.

And this time, they had the upper hand.

Samantha sat at the long wooden table in the safe house, her laptop open in front of her. The dim glow from the screen illuminated her face, her eyes focused on the files Alex had just decrypted. She had waited for this moment—Elias's hidden research, the full extent of Pharmatech's corruption—all of it was here. It was bigger than she had imagined. Darker. The truth was more terrifying than any of them had anticipated.

Turner stood behind her, his arms crossed, watching the screen intently. Rachel was next to him, her face pale as she read over Samantha's shoulder. The room was silent except for the soft hum of the laptop's fan, the weight of what they were about to uncover settling over them like a heavy fog.

"This is it," Samantha said quietly, scrolling through the files. "This is everything Elias was working on."

Turner leaned forward, his eyes narrowing. "What are we looking at here?"

Samantha took a deep breath, clicking on one of the documents labeled **Human Trials**. "Pharmatech wasn't just funding Elias's research for medical advancements. They were using his breakthroughs to develop something else. Something far more dangerous."

Rachel's brow furrowed as she scanned the document. "What is this? These are... people. Names, dates... and experiments."

Samantha nodded grimly. "Elias stumbled onto a way to manipulate human DNA—targeted gene therapy that could alter genetic traits. But Pharmatech twisted it. They started using it to experiment on people, trying to create 'perfect' human subjects. They used prisoners, refugees, people with no legal standing—no one would notice if they disappeared."

Turner's jaw clenched. "You're telling me they were experimenting on humans? That's insane."

"It's worse than that," Samantha replied, her voice tight with anger. She clicked on another file, this one filled with financial records. "Pharmatech covered it up. They funneled billions into black-budget projects, bribed government officials, silenced whistleblowers. Anyone who got too close either disappeared or was paid off."

Rachel shook her head, disbelief in her eyes. "How did they hide this for so long? This is… this is monstrous."

"They own everyone who could have stopped them," Turner said, his voice cold. "Politicians, law enforcement, media outlets. This isn't just about profits—it's about control. They're rewriting the rules."

Samantha's hands trembled as she opened the last file, a personal journal entry from Elias. His handwriting was messy, the letters frantic and rushed. She read aloud, her voice heavy with emotion.

"I didn't mean for it to go this far. The research was supposed to save lives, to cure diseases. But now, I see what they've done. They've turned my work into something evil. If you're reading this, it means I didn't make it. It means they found me. Please, whoever you are, you have to stop them. You have to make this public before more people suffer. The truth is out there, hidden in the data. It's up to you now."

Samantha's voice broke as she finished reading, the weight of Elias's final plea settling on her shoulders. She closed the journal and looked up at Turner and Rachel, her face filled with determination.

"We have to release this," Samantha said, her voice steady. "The world needs to know what Pharmatech is doing. This can't stay hidden any longer."

Turner nodded, his expression grim. "Once we release this, they'll come after us with everything they have. They won't let this go without a fight."

"I know," Samantha replied, standing up from the table. "But if we don't do this, more people will die. More people will suffer because of what Pharmatech is doing in the shadows. We can't let them win."

Rachel swallowed hard, her fingers trembling as she reached for her laptop. "I'll start preparing the upload. Multiple platforms, independent news outlets. We need to make sure this can't be taken down."

Samantha moved to the window, staring out into the darkness. She could feel the danger closing in around them, the looming presence of Pharmatech's reach. But she couldn't let fear stop her. Not now. Not when they were so close to bringing the truth to light.

"They'll hit back hard," Turner warned, coming to stand beside her. "You know what's coming. They've already killed for this."

"I know," Samantha said softly. "But we can't stop now. Elias gave his life to hide this, to protect this information. We owe it to him—and to everyone who's been hurt by Pharmatech—to make sure the truth is exposed."

Turner nodded, placing a hand on her shoulder. "You're right. But you need to be ready. Once this goes live, there's no going back."

Samantha took a deep breath, steeling herself. "I'm ready."

Rachel worked quickly, her fingers moving over the keyboard with precision. "The files are uploading now. It'll take a few minutes, but once they're live, Pharmatech won't be able to shut it down fast enough."

Samantha's phone buzzed on the table. She picked it up, seeing another unknown number flash across the screen. She hesitated for a moment, then answered.

"Miss Cross," the familiar, cold voice from Pharmatech greeted her. "You still have a chance to walk away from this. Don't make the mistake of going public with that data."

Samantha's heart pounded, but her voice was steady as she responded. "It's too late. The truth is already out there."

A pause. Then the voice lowered to a menacing whisper. "You're making a mistake. You won't survive this."

Samantha hung up, her hand trembling slightly. She turned to Rachel. "How long?"

Rachel glanced at her screen. "Thirty seconds. Then the world will know."

Samantha exhaled slowly, watching as the final countdown began. This was it. They had done everything they could. In just a few moments, Elias's research, Pharmatech's darkest secrets, and their web of corruption would be exposed to the world.

"Here we go," Rachel whispered as the final file uploaded.

Samantha felt a mix of fear and relief as the data went live. The world would finally see the truth. But now, they had to survive the consequences.

Pharmatech wasn't going to let this go without a fight.

Chapter 8
Pharmatech's Reach

Samantha sat in the darkened room, the only light coming from the flickering television in front of her. News anchors from around the world filled the screen, their voices blending together in a chaotic, frenzied chorus of breaking news reports. Every major network had picked up the story. Pharmatech, once untouchable, was now at the center of a global scandal that was unraveling faster than anyone could have anticipated.

Rachel sat beside her, her laptop open, her eyes glued to the live feeds pouring in from every corner of the internet. "It's everywhere," she whispered, half in disbelief. "We actually did it."

Turner stood by the window, his arms crossed, watching the street below for any sign of trouble. His expression was hard, unreadable, though Samantha knew he was thinking the same thing they all were: This was far from over.

The television crackled, the voice of a seasoned news anchor filling the room.

"Breaking news tonight: Pharmatech, one of the world's largest biotechnology companies, is facing allegations of human experimentation, corruption, and a vast cover-up spanning decades. Leaked documents reveal that Pharmatech has been conducting illegal gene therapy trials on human subjects, using prisoners and vulnerable populations without their consent. The fallout has been immediate, with Pharmatech's stock plummeting and several key executives reportedly going into hiding…"

Samantha leaned forward, her heart pounding. "They're finally being exposed."

"They are," Rachel said, still typing furiously on her keyboard. "But look at this." She turned her laptop toward Samantha, revealing social media feeds flooded with Pharmatech's PR responses. Carefully crafted statements were being released, attempting to downplay the severity of the leaks, casting doubt on the legitimacy of the data.

"'Baseless accusations… fabricated evidence… misinformation,'" Rachel read aloud, rolling her eyes. "They're pulling out all the stops."

"They'll spin it as long as they can," Turner said from across the room. "But that doesn't change the fact that their empire is crumbling. We've done real damage."

Samantha nodded, but she couldn't shake the feeling of unease settling in her chest. "Yeah, but they won't go down quietly. They're already trying to control the narrative."

"They can try," Rachel said, her tone fierce. "But this is too big. It's out there now. Every major outlet is picking up the story, and people are talking about it. They can't just sweep this under the rug."

The television flashed again, cutting to an interview with a legal expert.

"Pharmatech could be facing a series of criminal investigations and class-action lawsuits in the coming weeks," the expert said, his tone grave. "But what's most concerning is the involvement of high-level government officials who may have been complicit in covering up these illegal experiments…"

Samantha exchanged a glance with Turner. "This goes deeper than we thought."

Turner nodded. "It always does."

Rachel let out a deep breath. "We've shaken the foundation, but Pharmatech's still got resources. They'll start leaning on their allies in government, in the media. They'll fight this tooth and nail."

"They're already hiding," Samantha said, her eyes narrowing. "The executives—they've gone underground. But they can't stay hidden forever."

Turner moved away from the window, walking over to the table. "They're scared. That's a good thing. But don't forget, they've got connections. They'll be pulling strings behind the scenes to cover their tracks."

"We need to keep the pressure on," Rachel said, determination in her voice. "If we let up now, they'll recover."

Samantha nodded. "We won't. But we need to be careful. Pharmatech isn't just going to let this go. They'll come after us with everything they have."

As if on cue, Samantha's phone buzzed. She glanced at the screen—an unknown number, again. Her stomach tightened as she picked it up, answering with a cautious, "Hello?"

The voice on the other end was cold, calculated. "You think this is over, Miss Cross? You've made a lot of enemies tonight."

Samantha's heart skipped a beat, but she kept her voice steady. "It's over for Pharmatech. The world knows what you've done."

The voice chuckled softly, a sound that sent chills down her spine. "You've started something you can't control. Pharmatech isn't just a company—it's a system. And systems don't fall because of a few leaks."

"Systems fall when people stop trusting them," Samantha countered. "And right now, the world is watching your empire burn."

There was a pause on the other end, and then the voice spoke again, more menacing this time. "You're in over your head. If you think we're going to let you walk away from this, you're mistaken. Watch your back, Miss Cross. We'll be watching."

The line went dead, leaving a cold silence in its wake.

Samantha slowly lowered the phone, her hand trembling slightly. She looked at Turner and Rachel, her voice steady but laced with fear. "They're coming after us. They won't stop."

Turner's expression darkened. "Let them come. We're ready."

Rachel's eyes flickered with worry, but she straightened in her seat. "We've exposed them. They're just desperate now. We need to keep moving—keep digging, keep getting the truth out."

Samantha nodded, her mind racing. "We will. But we need to be smart. They'll use everything they have left to bury us."

The television flashed again, showing footage of protests outside Pharmatech's headquarters. Crowds were gathering, demanding justice, calling for the company to be dismantled. The media coverage was relentless, and it was clear that Pharmatech was on the ropes.

But Samantha knew better than to believe the fight was over. Pharmatech wasn't going down without a brutal, dangerous struggle.

As she stared at the screen, watching the chaos unfold, she felt the weight of what they had done settle over her. They had pulled back the curtain on one of the most powerful corporations in the world. But now, they were in the crosshairs of a beast that had been wounded but not yet killed.

"Keep monitoring the feeds," Samantha said quietly to Rachel. "We need to stay ahead of their moves."

Rachel nodded, her fingers already flying over the keyboard. "I'm on it."

Turner stepped closer to Samantha, his voice low. "We need to lay low for a while, Sam. They'll send people after us."

"I know," Samantha replied, her eyes fixed on the screen. "But we can't hide forever. This isn't just about survival anymore. We have to finish what we started."

Turner nodded, his expression grim. "Then we need to be ready. Because this is far from over."

Samantha took a deep breath, her gaze hardening as the weight of the coming battle settled on her shoulders. Pharmatech's empire was crumbling, but the fight for justice had only just begun.

The weight of the media fallout hung heavy in the air as Samantha sat alone in the small, sparsely furnished room of the safe house. The past few days had been a blur of breaking news stories, threats, and growing pressure from Pharmatech's relentless counterattacks. She rubbed her tired eyes, exhaustion settling into her bones. The rest of the team had scattered, each member dealing with the personal consequences of what they had unleashed.

Her phone buzzed on the table beside her. She glanced at the screen: it was Rachel.

"They're coming after me, Sam," Rachel's voice was strained, the tension evident even through the phone. "I just got served. Pharmatech's legal team has filed defamation suits against me, and it's not just one. They've got lawyers lined up, throwing everything they can at me."

Samantha swallowed hard. "Rachel, I'm so sorry. We knew this could happen, but… we didn't think they'd move this fast."

"They're trying to bankrupt me," Rachel continued, a slight tremor in her voice. "I'm already getting emails from clients saying they can't work with me anymore. Pharmatech's doing everything they can to isolate me."

Samantha leaned back in her chair, staring up at the ceiling. "They're trying to scare us, make us second-guess everything. But Rachel, we knew this fight wasn't going to be easy."

"I know," Rachel said softly. "But it's one thing to say that, and another to live it. It's real now. And it's only going to get worse."

Samantha closed her eyes, the guilt heavy on her chest. "You're not alone in this. We'll get through it."

Rachel let out a bitter laugh. "I hope so. But you should know… I'm going into hiding for a while. Turner's helping me get off the grid. I can't risk being tracked."

Samantha's eyes flew open. "Wait, you're leaving?"

"For now, yes," Rachel replied. "Pharmatech's not going to stop. I need to disappear until things settle down."

Samantha gripped the phone tightly, her heart sinking. "Be safe, Rachel. And stay in touch when you can."

"I will," Rachel promised. "Take care of yourself, Sam."

As the call ended, Samantha stared at the phone, feeling the isolation creeping in. One by one, her team was being pushed to the edge, forced into hiding or legal battles that threatened to destroy everything they had built together. She knew it was the price of exposing a company as powerful as Pharmatech, but the personal toll was heavier than she had imagined.

Turner's voice cut through her thoughts. "Rachel's going dark, isn't she?"

Samantha nodded without turning around. "She has to. Pharmatech's all over her—lawsuits, threats. They're doing everything they can to ruin her."

Turner crossed the room and sat across from her, his face lined with the same exhaustion she felt. "It was always going to come to this. We shook the hornet's nest, and now we're paying for it."

Samantha sighed, leaning forward and resting her head in her hands. "I knew the risks. But seeing it unfold like this... I didn't think it would happen so fast."

"They're trying to isolate you," Turner said quietly. "Make you feel like you're alone in this."

"I am alone," Samantha whispered, her voice barely audible. "Rachel's gone, Alex is in the middle of a legal battle with Pharmatech's lawyers, and the media is already starting to turn. They're planting doubts, trying to make me look like the one who's unstable."

Turner reached across the table, his hand resting on hers. "You're not alone, Sam. I'm still here. And I'm not going anywhere."

Samantha's eyes met his, and for a moment, the weight on her chest felt a little lighter. "I don't know how much more of this I can take, Turner. They're coming at us from every angle, and I'm... I'm tired."

"I know," Turner said softly. "But we've come too far to stop now. You didn't expose them just to watch everything fall apart."

She took a deep breath, trying to steady herself. "I know. But I wasn't prepared for this. For how personal it would get."

Turner leaned back, his expression dark. "That's exactly what they're counting on. They're trying to break you. But you're stronger than that."

Samantha stood up, walking over to the window. The street outside was quiet, but she knew that danger lurked in every shadow now. She felt it constantly—Pharmatech's reach extending into every part of her life, her team's lives. Nothing felt safe anymore.

"They've already threatened me," Samantha said, her voice flat. "Calls, emails. They're coming after me personally. If they can't stop the media, they'll try to ruin my reputation, my credibility."

"They'll try to make you look like a liar, like you made it all up," Turner said, standing and moving beside her. "But we have the truth on our side."

Samantha shook her head, her mind racing. "The truth isn't always enough. People believe what they want to believe, especially when Pharmatech has the power to rewrite the narrative."

Turner placed a hand on her shoulder. "Then we make sure they can't rewrite it. We keep pushing, keep the pressure on. We have to be smarter, faster than they are."

She turned to face him, her eyes filled with a mixture of fear and determination. "What if it's not enough, Turner? What if we've lost before we've even had a chance to win?"

Turner's gaze was steady. "It's enough. You've already done what no one else could. Now we just have to survive the fallout."

Samantha's chest tightened, but she nodded, knowing he was right. The fight wasn't over—not by a long shot. But the sacrifices they were making now, the personal toll it was taking on all of them, felt like too high a price.

"I don't want anyone else to get hurt," Samantha whispered, her voice cracking slightly.

Turner's grip on her shoulder tightened. "No one else will. You've done everything you can. Now it's time to finish what we started."

Samantha looked out the window again, the weight of the battle ahead settling over her. She had come too far to back down now. Even as her team scattered and the pressure mounted, she knew there was no turning back. The fight for the truth had already claimed too much.

And the only way to win was to see it through to the end.

The safe house had never felt more suffocating. Samantha sat at the small kitchen table, her laptop open in front of her, emails, court documents, and news alerts filling the screen. Pharmatech's counterattack was swift and brutal. Despite the damning revelations and the ongoing media frenzy, the corporation had begun to regroup, and their retaliation was as cold and calculated as expected.

Rachel's voice crackled over the phone's speaker, frustration bleeding into every word. "They've filed another lawsuit, Sam. This one's for defamation and breach of contract, claiming we stole proprietary information. Their legal team is everywhere. If they can't kill the story, they'll bury us in paperwork."

Samantha rubbed her temples, feeling the weight of it all pressing down on her. "How many suits is that now?"

"Five," Rachel replied grimly. "And those are just the big ones. There's a dozen smaller cases popping up too—cease and desist orders, demands for retractions. They're throwing everything at us."

Turner, who had been pacing the room, stopped and leaned against the wall, arms crossed. "They're trying to drown us. They know they can't undo the damage from the leaks, so they'll make us pay another way."

Samantha nodded, her gaze still fixed on the screen. "They've already started. Every outlet that published the story is getting hit with lawsuits. They're calling the documents forgeries, claiming we doctored everything."

Rachel sighed, her voice full of weariness. "They're losing control, but they're trying to make the public doubt us—make us look like frauds. And with enough noise, some people will believe it."

Samantha gripped the edge of the table, her knuckles turning white. "We knew this was coming, but it doesn't make it any easier. If they can convince enough people that this is all fake, they might survive this."

"Barely," Turner interjected. "Pharmatech's stock is still plummeting, and investors are starting to panic. Their executives are in hiding, but they're not dead yet. They're wounded, but that's when they're most dangerous."

The TV in the corner flickered to life, and a news report blared through the room. "Pharmatech's latest statement denies all allegations, insisting that the documents leaked by the whistleblower, Samantha Cross, were heavily manipulated. They've hired top-tier legal teams to combat the growing number of lawsuits, but questions remain about the company's long-term viability."

Samantha turned to the screen, her chest tightening. "They're pushing back hard. The media's starting to split—some outlets are digging deeper, but others are parroting Pharmatech's talking points. If they can control enough of the narrative, we'll lose ground."

Rachel's voice came through the phone again. "They've already gotten a few influential journalists on their side. One of the major networks just ran a segment questioning the validity of the research documents. They're sowing doubt."

Turner pushed off the wall, his expression hard. "We need to get ahead of this. What's our next move?"

Samantha leaned back in her chair, her mind racing. "We can't just react. That's what they want—they're trying to throw us off balance, make us second-guess everything."

"They want to exhaust us," Rachel added. "They know most whistleblowers burn out when the legal pressure starts."

Samantha stood up and paced the room, her frustration growing. "We can't let them do that. We need to stay proactive, keep the focus on their crimes. If we let them drag us into a legal quagmire, we'll be stuck fighting court battles while they quietly rebuild."

Turner nodded. "So we go on the offensive. Hit them again."

"How?" Rachel asked, skepticism creeping into her tone. "They're locking everything down. Most of the media is too scared to publish anything new, and their legal threats are working. Even some of our smaller allies are starting to pull back."

Samantha paused, staring at the ceiling as she thought. "We need to find a way to keep the pressure on without getting bogged down in their games. Something they can't control."

Turner raised an eyebrow. "Like what?"

Samantha's eyes lit up with an idea. "Grassroots. We take this to the public, bypass the media. Social media, independent platforms, even rallies if we need to. Pharmatech can control the press, but they can't silence millions of people at once."

"That's risky," Turner said, though his expression softened as he considered it. "But it could work. If we can get enough people talking, they'll be forced to respond."

Rachel chimed in, excitement returning to her voice. "We've already got a huge social media following from the leak. We could amplify that, start a campaign to expose their smear tactics. If we can show people how they're trying to manipulate the story, it'll turn more of the public against them."

Samantha nodded, feeling a renewed sense of determination. "Exactly. We show the world how they're trying to spin this, how desperate they are to cover their tracks. We can't just sit here and wait for them to grind us down."

Rachel was already typing on her laptop, her fingers flying over the keys. "I'll start drafting something now—maybe a hashtag campaign, something that calls attention to their tactics."

Turner crossed his arms, a faint smile on his lips. "Pharmatech thinks they can outlast us, but they've underestimated how much we're willing to fight."

Samantha turned to him, her expression fierce. "They think we'll break, that we'll give up once they make it personal. But they're wrong."

The phone buzzed again, and this time, it was Alex's voice on the line. "Sam, it's me. Just a heads-up, but Pharmatech's lawyers are coming after me hard. They've frozen some of my accounts, trying to cripple me financially."

Samantha's heart sank, but her resolve hardened. "I'm sorry, Alex. I knew they'd target you. Stay strong—we're going to push back."

"I'm with you," Alex said, his voice steady despite the pressure. "Just wanted you to know they're not letting up. But neither am I."

Samantha hung up and turned back to the room. The battle wasn't just in the courts or on TV—it was everywhere. And they had to be ready for whatever came next.

"We need to keep fighting," Samantha said, her voice firm. "Pharmatech's wounded, but they're not dead. If we stay on the offensive, we can finish this."

Turner gave her a nod of approval. "Let's make sure they never recover."

Samantha looked back at the television, where the news continued to report Pharmatech's denials and legal moves. This was their retaliation—Pharmatech was striking back with everything they had. But Samantha knew that as long as they stayed united, as long as they kept pushing, they had a chance to win.

And they weren't backing down.

Samantha stood on the rooftop of the safe house, the city skyline stretched out before her, glowing softly in the late evening light. The wind was cool against her skin, a stark contrast to the whirlwind of events that had unfolded over the past few weeks. She watched as the city buzzed below, people going about their lives, unaware of the battle that had been fought—at least, not in the same way she was. The world knew now, thanks to her and her team, but the weight of that knowledge sat heavy on her shoulders.

Turner's footsteps echoed softly as he approached from behind. He stood beside her, his presence a grounding force amid the chaos. "You've been up here a while."

Samantha didn't turn to face him. She kept her eyes on the city, her thoughts racing. "I needed some air. To think."

"About what?" Turner asked, his voice quiet.

"About all of it," she replied, exhaling slowly. "Everything we've done, everything we've uncovered. We exposed Pharmatech. The world knows what they are now. There's going to be justice, but…"

Turner looked at her, waiting. "But what?"

Samantha finally turned to him, her expression weary. "But it doesn't feel like enough. We've only just scratched the surface. Pharmatech is still fighting, and they've got enough power and money to drag this out for years. People are already starting to doubt, to question if we were right."

"They're doing that because Pharmatech's PR machine is still working," Turner said, his tone firm but calm. "But the truth is out there. That can't be undone."

Samantha nodded, but there was a hollowness to her gesture. "I know. And I'm proud of what we did. We put everything on the line—our careers, our safety. But... I just didn't expect it to feel so unfinished."

Turner was silent for a moment before speaking again. "It's because it's not over yet. This fight isn't something you can wrap up neatly. Corporations like Pharmatech don't just collapse overnight."

Samantha sighed, her hands gripping the edge of the rooftop railing. "You're right. It's just... I didn't realize how much this would cost. Rachel's gone underground, Alex is facing legal hell, and I've lost count of the threats I've gotten. It's like we're just waiting for the next attack."

"You've held up this long," Turner said, his voice low and steady. "You're stronger than you think."

Samantha turned to face him fully now, her gaze soft but tired. "Am I? I'm not so sure anymore. The investigation took everything out of me, Turner. I lost parts of myself along the way that I'm not sure I'll ever get back."

Turner's expression softened. "You didn't lose yourself, Sam. You found what you're capable of. You found out what it takes to stand up to a company like Pharmatech. And yeah, there's a cost to that. But it's worth it."

Samantha's eyes flickered with a mix of emotions—doubt, exhaustion, but also something deeper. "Was it? I look at what we've accomplished, and I'm proud of it. I am. But when I think about what's ahead, I don't know if I can keep doing this. The fight doesn't end just because we won this battle."

Turner nodded, understanding in his eyes. "That's how it works when you take on something this big. It's not just about winning one fight—it's about keeping up the pressure, making sure they don't recover. You've come this far, and yeah, it's been brutal. But you're not alone in this."

Samantha smiled faintly, appreciating his support. "I know. I just... I didn't expect the personal toll to hit this hard."

Turner stepped closer, his voice softening. "It's not just about the fight anymore, is it?"

Samantha shook her head, a lump forming in her throat. "No. It's about what I've given up. The things I've sacrificed to get here. I've lost people along the way—friends, allies, and maybe even parts of myself. And I don't know if I'm ready to keep losing more."

Turner placed a hand on her shoulder, a reassuring weight. "You didn't do this because it was easy. You did it because it was right. That's what makes you different from them, Sam. You didn't back down."

"I know," she said softly. "And I won't back down. But I need to be ready for the cost next time. I can't lose sight of who I am just because I'm fighting them."

Turner nodded. "You won't. Because you've already proven you can stand up to them. And whatever comes next, you'll handle it. You're stronger than you were at the start of this."

Samantha looked back out at the city, her heart heavy but her resolve stronger. "I didn't expect to come out of this feeling so... unfinished. Like there's still more to do, more to uncover. Pharmatech isn't the only one out there, and if we don't keep going, there'll be others like them."

"There always will be," Turner said quietly. "But you've made a difference, Sam. You've shown that even the most powerful can be taken down."

Samantha smiled, but there was a sadness behind it. "I just wish it didn't feel so lonely."

"You're not alone," Turner reminded her. "Not as long as you've got people like me, Rachel, Alex. We're still here. And we're not going anywhere."

Samantha nodded, letting the moment sink in. The battle against Pharmatech wasn't over, and she knew that there would be more sacrifices ahead. But for now, there was a sense of closure—an understanding that she had changed, and that this fight had become a part of her.

"I'll keep going," Samantha said, her voice filled with quiet determination. "I have to. For Elias, for Rachel, for everyone who's been hurt by Pharmatech."

Turner smiled. "Then let's get ready for whatever comes next."

Samantha exhaled slowly, her heart feeling a little lighter as she looked out at the horizon. The fight was far from over, but now she knew she had the strength to face whatever was coming next.

And for the first time in a long time, she felt ready.

Chapter 9
The Web Tightens

Samantha sat in front of her laptop, staring at the headlines scrolling across the screen, each one more infuriating than the last.

"Leaked Pharmatech Documents: Truth or Elaborate Hoax?"
"Whistleblower Samantha Cross Accused of Manipulating Evidence"
"Conspiracy or Corruption? The Battle Over Pharmatech's Future"

She exhaled sharply, running a hand through her hair as her eyes flicked to the next headline. The media storm that had initially exposed Pharmatech was now being redirected, twisted into something far more dangerous. Pharmatech wasn't just defending itself anymore—they were manipulating public opinion, sowing doubt where there had once been outrage. It was a strategy Samantha had feared, but seeing it unfold in real-time made her blood boil.

"They're turning everything around," Rachel said from across the room, her voice tight with frustration. She sat at the small table, scrolling through social media feeds. "Look at this: people are already starting to question whether the leaks were real. Pharmatech's PR team is putting out statements faster than we can respond."

Turner leaned against the wall, arms crossed, his expression unreadable. "They're using the same tactics they always do—

confusion, misinformation. They don't need to disprove the leaks. They just need to make people doubt."

Samantha clenched her fists, her anger rising. "And it's working. Look at this." She gestured toward the screen, showing the latest poll results. A significant portion of the public was now undecided about the legitimacy of the data, with a growing number believing Pharmatech's narrative that the documents had been manipulated.

"They've got powerful people backing them too," Rachel said, shaking her head. "Corporate allies, political figures—everyone's chiming in, saying Pharmatech's being unfairly targeted."

"They've spent years building relationships," Turner added. "They're calling in every favor, pulling every string."

Samantha could hear the exhaustion in his voice. "And now the media is playing right into their hands," she said bitterly. "Half the outlets that were covering the story are either walking it back or questioning us."

Turner stepped forward, his voice calm but determined. "They're trying to paint us as conspiracy theorists. That's always been their fallback—discredit the messenger, confuse the message."

Rachel snorted, her frustration spilling over. "And people are buying it! Look at this." She pulled up a thread from a popular social media platform. Comments were flooding in, some defending Samantha's team but many more accusing them of being part of a larger hoax.

"Pharmatech's too big to take down. This is probably a smear campaign."
"I wouldn't be surprised if these so-called whistleblowers were paid off by Pharmatech's competitors."
"It's all fake. These conspiracy nuts will believe anything."

Rachel shook her head, her voice filled with disbelief. "How did we go from being the heroes to this?"

Samantha slammed her laptop shut, standing abruptly. "Because Pharmatech knows how to manipulate people. They've done it for years. All they need is to plant a seed of doubt, and it grows into a full-blown narrative that they're the victims."

"They're smart," Turner said. "They've managed to turn the tide before, but this is different. They're up against the truth, and no matter how much they spin it, that truth is still out there."

Samantha paced the room, her frustration bubbling over. "But how do we fight back? Every time we make a move, they counter it with more noise. They've got more resources, more connections. We can't respond to every lie they throw out."

"We don't have to," Turner said, his voice steady. "We just need to stay focused on the truth. Keep pushing it out there. People will see through the lies eventually."

Rachel glanced at Turner, doubt in her eyes. "Eventually? Turner, they're controlling the narrative right now. People aren't waiting for the truth—they're making up their minds based on the loudest voices. And Pharmatech is louder."

Samantha stopped pacing and turned to face them both, her jaw tight with frustration. "We need to change tactics. We can't just keep playing defense, responding to every attack. If we do that, they'll wear us down."

"So what's the move?" Turner asked, watching her carefully.

Samantha took a deep breath, her mind racing. "We need to find a way to cut through the noise, to remind people why this matters. We have the truth on our side, but right now, Pharmatech is flooding the conversation with distractions. We need to remind people what's really at stake."

Rachel's eyebrows lifted. "How? They've already buried the human trials in legalese, and the media's too scared to dig deeper without hard proof."

"We focus on the human cost," Samantha said firmly. "We need to tell the stories of the people Pharmatech hurt. Real people, real names. We've been caught up in the data, the documents—but this is about more than just files on a screen. It's about the lives they destroyed."

Turner nodded slowly, seeing where she was going. "If we put a face to the story, it becomes harder to dismiss. People might doubt documents, but they can't ignore someone standing in front of them, telling their story."

Rachel seemed hesitant. "That's risky, Sam. If we bring people forward, Pharmatech will go after them, just like they've gone after us."

"I know," Samantha said quietly. "But that's the only way we fight back. We can't hide anymore. If we don't bring these stories to light, Pharmatech wins. And more people will get hurt."

Turner studied her for a moment before nodding. "It's a bold move. But it's the right one."

Samantha met his gaze, her resolve hardening. "I'm done letting Pharmatech dictate the terms. We fight back on our own terms now."

Rachel sighed, closing her laptop. "Alright. I'll start reaching out to some of the victims' families, see who's willing to go public. But Sam… this is going to get ugly."

"It's already ugly," Samantha said. "We've been fighting them in the shadows, trying to expose the truth. But now it's time to bring it into the light."

Turner placed a hand on her shoulder. "We're with you."

Samantha nodded, a renewed sense of purpose settling over her. The backlash was fierce, but she knew they couldn't let it break them. Pharmatech was wounded, but they were far from defeated. And if they were going to finish this fight, they needed to change the narrative—and they needed to do it now.

"We'll take them down," Samantha said, her voice steady. "But we have to show the world the real story."

And this time, there would be no more hiding.

Turner sat in the corner of the safe house, the glow of his laptop screen illuminating his tense features. His fingers moved quickly over the keyboard as he juggled between secure communication channels and encrypted emails. It had been days since Pharmatech's smear campaign had begun, and the pressure was mounting. But Turner was focused, working silently behind the scenes, ensuring that they stayed one step ahead of the corporation's relentless assault.

"Turner, do you think this will hold?" Samantha's voice broke through the quiet, her eyes filled with concern as she sat across from him.

Turner didn't look up from his laptop. "It has to," he said, his tone even. "I'm coordinating with a few other whistleblowers from similar cases. They've faced companies like Pharmatech before, and they're giving us advice on how to stay ahead legally."

Rachel, seated on the couch, shook her head. "That's great and all, but I'm more worried about what happens when Pharmatech stops playing in the courts. You know they've got more than just lawyers on their payroll."

Turner paused, his jaw tightening as he glanced over at her. "I'm already working on that, too. I've got a few safe locations lined up if we need to move again. But for now, we stay here. It's quiet, and we're not showing up on any of their trackers."

Samantha leaned forward, her voice dropping to a whisper. "How can you be so sure? They've found us before. What makes this place different?"

"I've taken extra precautions," Turner said, finally lifting his gaze to meet hers. "New communication protocols, no digital footprint from this location. And I'm coordinating with some legal experts who've helped whistleblowers disappear before. It's not foolproof, but it's better than what we had last time."

Rachel folded her arms, a skeptical look crossing her face. "So what, we just keep running forever? What's the endgame here, Turner?"

"The endgame is survival," Turner replied bluntly. "We can't fight Pharmatech if we're not alive to do it."

Samantha sighed, rubbing her temples. "And the legal side? How are we handling that?"

Turner switched screens on his laptop, pulling up a series of documents. "I've been in touch with a legal team specializing in corporate whistleblower cases. They've agreed to represent us pro bono—for now, at least. They're prepping for what's coming, and we need to be ready."

Rachel raised an eyebrow. "Pro bono? What's the catch?"

"No catch," Turner said. "They've been fighting cases like this for years. They believe in what we're doing. And more importantly, they know how to handle companies like Pharmatech."

"Great," Rachel said, her voice laced with sarcasm. "So we have lawyers who believe in us. But belief doesn't pay the bills, Turner. What happens when Pharmatech drags this out in court for years? They'll bankrupt us before we even get a chance to prove anything."

Turner narrowed his eyes, his voice dropping to a low growl. "That's why I'm coordinating with other whistleblowers. Pharmatech has enemies, and not just us. We're not the only ones who've been hurt by them. There are people out there who want to see them fall, and they're willing to help."

Samantha frowned. "Help? What kind of help?"

"Financial, legal, and… let's just say, logistical support," Turner replied, his expression unreadable. "We're not fighting this war alone. We have allies, even if we haven't met them all yet."

Rachel leaned back, crossing her arms. "And these allies… can we trust them? Or are we just trading one problem for another?"

Turner's lips tightened into a thin line. "We don't have a lot of options, Rachel. Pharmatech's gunning for us, and we're out of time. If these people are willing to stand with us, we take their help."

Samantha nodded slowly, absorbing the weight of Turner's words. "What about the other whistleblowers? Have they dealt with anything like this before?"

Turner's eyes darkened. "Some of them have. And some didn't make it out alive."

Rachel's face paled, but she didn't say anything.

"Look," Turner continued, his voice softer now, "we're in deep, and we're not going to come out of this unscathed. Pharmatech has the resources to fight this for as long as they need to. Our job is to stay out of their crosshairs and keep the truth alive. That means moving when we need to, staying hidden, and making sure they can't bury us."

Samantha stared at him, her expression a mix of exhaustion and determination. "And what happens if they find us again? What then?"

Turner didn't flinch. "Then we keep moving. We'll have to stay flexible. But we won't go down without a fight. I've been in contact with a network of whistleblower protection groups— they know how to get people out of situations like this."

Rachel snorted. "Situations like this? I doubt they've seen anything like Pharmatech. These people play dirty."

Turner shot her a hard look. "That's why we're going to be smarter."

Silence fell over the room for a moment, the weight of their situation pressing down on them all.

Samantha broke the silence, her voice low. "So what's next?"

Turner glanced at the clock on the wall, then back at his laptop. "We stay here for another 48 hours. I've got a few more safe houses lined up if we need them. I'll be coordinating with the legal team and our new allies in the meantime."

Rachel shook her head, muttering to herself. "Running. Always running."

Turner ignored the comment, his voice steady and calm as he addressed Samantha. "We stay sharp. Pharmatech's regrouping, but so are we. And this time, we're not going to be caught off guard."

Samantha nodded, though her heart still pounded with doubt. "We'll be ready."

Turner met her gaze, his expression unwavering. "We have to be."

The air in the safe house was thick with tension. Samantha could feel it pressing down on her as she sat at the small, cluttered table in the kitchen, staring blankly at the map Turner had spread out earlier. The room was dimly lit, and the hum of the generator outside was the only noise breaking the suffocating silence. Rachel sat across from her, arms crossed, her face pale with exhaustion and frustration.

"This wasn't the plan," Rachel muttered, shaking her head. "We didn't sign up for this."

Samantha looked up slowly, her eyes meeting Rachel's. "What do you mean? We knew what we were getting into."

"No, we didn't," Rachel shot back, her voice rising slightly. "We knew Pharmatech was dangerous, but I didn't think it would come to this. Legal threats, being hunted, constantly looking over our shoulders—this isn't what I expected."

Turner, who had been standing by the window, keeping watch as always, glanced over his shoulder. "You knew they wouldn't just roll over, Rachel. We're threatening their entire operation. What did you expect?"

"I expected some pushback, sure," Rachel said, her frustration spilling over. "But not this level of retribution. I mean, look at what's happening. They're dragging us through the mud, attacking us in the media, hitting us with lawsuits. And now we're hiding in some cabin in the middle of nowhere, hoping they don't find us. How long do you think we can keep this up?"

Samantha stood, the weight of Rachel's words hitting her hard. "We can't back down now, Rachel. We've come too far."

Rachel's gaze hardened. "Too far for what, Sam? What exactly have we accomplished? Pharmatech is still standing, stronger than ever, and we're the ones who are being torn apart."

"We've exposed them," Turner interjected, his voice calm but firm. "The world knows what they've done."

"Do they?" Rachel shot back. "Because right now, it feels like Pharmatech is the one controlling the narrative. People are starting to doubt us. The media's questioning everything. They're painting us as frauds and conspiracy theorists. What's the point of exposing them if no one believes us?"

Samantha ran a hand through her hair, frustration gnawing at her. "That's why we need to keep fighting. If we give up now, then everything we've done—everything Elias gave his life for—will be for nothing."

Rachel sighed, her arms dropping to her sides. "I'm just not sure if I can keep going. The pressure is… it's too much, Sam. I didn't think it would get this personal."

Samantha felt her stomach twist. She had seen this coming for days—the exhaustion in Rachel's eyes, the way she avoided conversations about their next steps. The tension was palpable, and now it was all coming to a head.

"We're all feeling the pressure," Samantha said softly, stepping closer to Rachel. "But we're in this together. We can't stop now."

Rachel's eyes flashed with something like guilt. "I know you're trying to hold everything together, Sam, but I don't know if I'm built for this. I didn't sign up to be hunted. I didn't think it would get this far."

Turner crossed the room, his voice more intense now. "If we quit, Rachel, Pharmatech wins. They'll keep experimenting on people, keep ruining lives. They'll erase everything we've done like it never happened."

Rachel threw up her hands. "I get it, Turner! I know what's at stake. But I also have a life outside of this. A family. What happens if they come after them? I can't risk that."

Samantha's chest tightened. "Rachel, we can protect you. Turner's set up safe houses, and we have allies—"

"Allies?" Rachel cut her off. "You mean the whistleblowers we've never met? The lawyers working for us pro bono? Sam, we're just pawns in this game, and Pharmatech is playing a whole different level."

Samantha swallowed hard, feeling the sting of Rachel's words. She had tried to keep the team united, to stay strong for everyone, but the cracks were showing. "I'm not asking you to stay if you don't want to, Rachel. But you need to understand that if we stop now, they win. Everything we've worked for falls apart."

Rachel's shoulders slumped, her anger giving way to something closer to despair. "I just don't know if I can do it anymore. I'm scared, Sam. I didn't realize how scared I was until now."

Turner moved beside Samantha, his voice softening slightly. "We're all scared, Rachel. But that's why we're doing this— because if we don't stand up to them, no one will. And they'll keep getting away with it."

Samantha stepped closer to Rachel, her voice gentle. "You don't have to make a decision right now. But please, don't give up on this yet. We need you. I need you."

Rachel's eyes glistened with unshed tears, and for a long moment, she was silent, staring at the floor. Finally, she took a shaky breath and nodded. "I'll try, Sam. I just... I need time."

Samantha exhaled, relief washing over her, but the uncertainty lingered in the air. The team was fracturing, and she could feel the weight of every decision pressing down on her. She turned to Turner, who met her gaze with a quiet understanding. He didn't say anything, but the look in his eyes told her everything she needed to know: they couldn't afford to lose anyone else.

As the tension in the room slowly eased, Samantha realized that the fight ahead wasn't just against Pharmatech—it was against the growing doubt within her own team. And that battle was far from over.

The tires screeched, and Samantha's world spun violently as the car lurched sideways, the force slamming her into the driver's door. Her hands gripped the steering wheel, white-knuckled, as she fought to control the vehicle. The headlights of the truck that had swerved into her lane loomed in her rearview mirror before it sped away into the night, its engine roaring like a beast in the darkness.

Heart pounding, Samantha pulled the car to a stop on the shoulder, her breath coming in ragged gasps. The road around her was silent now, but the near-miss played on a loop in her mind, the unmistakable, deliberate move of the truck cutting across the highway at just the right moment. It wasn't an accident. It couldn't have been.

Her phone buzzed, its sudden ring jolting her. She fumbled for it with trembling hands, recognizing Turner's number.

"Sam? Are you okay?" Turner's voice was sharp, edged with concern. "You didn't answer my last message."

Samantha tried to steady her breathing, glancing in the rearview mirror again as if expecting the truck to return. "I—I'm fine, Turner. Just... something happened. There was a truck. It came out of nowhere and almost... it almost ran me off the road."

There was a pause on the other end, then Turner's voice, low and tense. "Are you sure it was an accident?"

Samantha closed her eyes, gripping the phone tighter. "No. No, I'm not sure at all. I think... I think it was them."

Turner cursed under his breath. "That's Pharmatech. They're trying to rattle us, or worse. Sam, you need to get out of there. Where are you?"

Samantha took a deep breath, fighting to calm the storm inside her. "I'm not far from the safe house. I can make it back, but... Turner, this is getting worse. We knew they'd push back, but this? They're trying to kill me."

"You need to lay low for a while," Turner said, his voice firm. "We'll regroup, but you can't stay out there by yourself. They're escalating."

Samantha's hands trembled as she rested them on the steering wheel, the weight of his words sinking in. She had seen the lengths Pharmatech would go to protect their secrets, but

159

this—this was different. They weren't just attacking her reputation anymore. They wanted her gone.

"I don't know if I can keep doing this, Turner," she admitted, her voice barely above a whisper. "What if next time, they actually succeed? What if they find the rest of us?"

Turner's voice softened, but there was still steel behind it. "Sam, we can't stop now. That's what they want. If we go underground and disappear, they'll take the win and bury the truth. We need to go on the offensive."

Samantha blinked, surprised. "Offensive? How? They've got more resources, more people, and now they're trying to kill us."

"We don't have to fight them alone," Turner said. "I've been talking to some investigative bodies—journalists, government watchdogs. They can help us. If we get the right people involved, we can expose Pharmatech on a bigger scale than we've already managed. But we have to act fast, before they can silence us."

Samantha shook her head, leaning her forehead against the steering wheel. "You don't understand. They're everywhere. They'll find us. And I can't risk more lives, Turner. This isn't just about the data anymore—it's about survival."

Turner's voice remained calm, but it was laced with urgency. "Sam, listen to me. If we go into hiding now, if we disappear and play defense, Pharmatech wins. They'll clean up their mess, spin the narrative, and erase everything we've done. But if we go public, if we bring in external bodies, we can make this too big for them to contain. They won't be able to kill us all."

Samantha let out a shaky breath, staring out into the dark expanse of the highway. "You're asking me to take a huge risk. They're not just after me—they'll come for all of us."

"I know," Turner said softly. "But we're already at risk. The difference is, if we go on the offensive, we might actually have a chance to end this."

Samantha was quiet for a long moment, the weight of the decision pressing down on her. She had spent so much time running, trying to stay ahead of Pharmatech's attacks, but the danger was closing in. They were playing a game she couldn't win on their terms.

"What if I'm not ready to go on the offensive?" she asked, her voice trembling. "What if we make this worse?"

Turner's reply was gentle but firm. "Sam, this is the only way to make sure they don't destroy everything we've worked for. You've come too far to back down now. You have to trust that we can take them down."

Samantha swallowed hard, feeling the fear tighten in her chest. But beneath the fear, there was a flicker of something else—resolve. Turner was right. Hiding wouldn't stop Pharmatech. They needed to bring their fight into the light, where Pharmatech couldn't cover their tracks.

She sat up, her grip on the steering wheel tightening. "Okay," she said, her voice stronger now. "I'll come back to the safe house, and then we go on the offensive. But we need to be smart about this."

Turner's voice held a note of relief. "We will be. I'll make the calls. You just get back here safely."

Samantha nodded, though he couldn't see her. "I will."

As she started the car again and pulled back onto the road, her heart still raced with the remnants of fear. But this time, there was something else driving her—a renewed sense of purpose. Pharmatech might have tried to silence her, but she wasn't backing down.

They had taken their shot.

Now, it was her turn.

Chapter 10
Into the Shadows

The safe house felt smaller every day. Samantha sat by the window, staring out at the forest that surrounded the isolated cabin. The silence outside was deceptive, hiding the relentless storm brewing inside her mind. Inside, the tension was palpable, thick enough to feel in the air. It had been days since the close call on the highway, and since then, the team had gone into hiding. But instead of finding safety in their seclusion, they were slowly coming undone.

Rachel paced the small room, her steps echoing off the wooden floor. "This is impossible," she muttered, her voice sharp. "We're sitting ducks here. We've been locked up in this cabin for days, and what have we accomplished? Nothing."

Samantha glanced over at her, but she didn't respond. She knew Rachel was right—on some level, they were all thinking the same thing. The safe house was supposed to be a place where they could regroup, but instead, it felt like a prison. And with each passing day, the weight of their situation grew heavier.

Turner, sitting at the table with a map spread out in front of him, didn't look up as he replied. "We're here because it's the only option right now. Pharmatech's hunting us, Rachel. We can't afford to move until we know what their next move is."

"And what if their next move is finding us here?" Rachel shot back, her voice rising. "What if they're just waiting for us to get comfortable, waiting for the right moment to strike?"

Turner's jaw tightened, but he kept his tone calm. "We've taken precautions. This place is off the grid, and I've made sure we're not traceable. They won't find us."

Rachel scoffed, throwing her hands up in frustration. "You can't know that for sure. They've already proven they can track us down when they want to."

Samantha closed her eyes, trying to tune out the rising tension. It was always the same argument—Rachel's fear clashing with Turner's logic. But she couldn't blame either of them. The truth was, she wasn't sure how much longer they could last like this. Every day in hiding felt like borrowed time, and Samantha couldn't shake the feeling that Pharmatech was regrouping, preparing for a final strike.

"We can't keep going like this," Rachel said, turning to Samantha now. "Sam, you know it. We're not outmaneuvering them—we're just hiding. And hiding isn't going to be enough."

Samantha exhaled slowly, standing from her spot by the window. "I know, Rachel. But right now, we don't have another option."

Rachel's frustration boiled over. "What do you mean we don't have another option? We've exposed Pharmatech, but it doesn't even feel like it matters anymore. They're still out there, and we're the ones trapped."

Turner finally looked up from the map, his voice calm but firm. "Rachel, the alternative is walking right into their hands. We need to stay here until we've figured out our next move. Going out there without a plan is suicide."

"And sitting here doing nothing isn't?" Rachel shot back. "What happens if they find us here? We're cornered, Turner. We have no way out."

Samantha rubbed her temples, trying to stay focused. "We need to stop fighting each other. Pharmatech's the enemy, not us."

Rachel shook her head, her voice softer now, but still full of doubt. "I'm not fighting you, Sam. I just… I'm scared. We're all scared. And I don't know if we've really won anything."

Samantha felt her chest tighten at Rachel's words. She knew Rachel wasn't alone in feeling that way—she herself had been plagued by the same doubts. Yes, they had exposed Pharmatech, but what had it really accomplished? The corporation was still standing, and for all they knew, they were just waiting for the perfect moment to retaliate.

"What if they're just regrouping?" Samantha said quietly, almost to herself. "What if we haven't outmaneuvered them at all, and they're just waiting for us to make a mistake?"

Turner looked at her, his expression unreadable. "We've hurt them, Sam. They're not invincible. But they're also not stupid. They'll come for us if they get the chance."

Samantha felt a wave of exhaustion wash over her. The constant running, the pressure, the fear—it was wearing her down. She wanted to believe they had a chance, but the longer they stayed in hiding, the more the doubts crept in.

"I'm starting to wonder if we're fighting a losing battle," Samantha admitted, her voice barely above a whisper.

Turner stood up, his gaze intense as he walked over to her. "We're not losing, Sam. Not yet. But we need to keep moving forward. If we stop now, they win."

Samantha met his eyes, searching for the certainty she so desperately needed. "I'm just tired, Turner. I don't know how much longer we can keep this up."

He placed a hand on her shoulder, his voice steady. "I know. But we have to hold it together. We've come too far to fall apart now."

Rachel, standing by the door, sighed heavily. "I don't want to give up, Sam. But I'm scared. Every time we move, every time we try to push forward, they're right there. And I don't know if I'm ready for what happens next."

Samantha nodded, understanding the weight of Rachel's words. She felt it too—the uncertainty, the fear of the unknown. But there was something else, buried deep beneath the exhaustion: a flicker of hope. They had exposed Pharmatech, and even though the road ahead was dangerous, they couldn't afford to stop.

"We'll find a way," Samantha said softly, more to herself than anyone else. "We have to."

The silence in the room returned, but it wasn't as suffocating as before. The tension still lingered, but now, there was a shared understanding. They were scared, they were tired, but they weren't broken. Not yet.

Turner looked at both of them, his voice firm and resolute. "We'll make it through this. But we need to stay strong, together. We can't let them tear us apart."

Samantha nodded, feeling a flicker of resolve return. "You're right. We can't let them win."

Outside, the forest remained silent, but inside, Samantha felt a renewed sense of purpose. They were still fighting, and as long as they were together, they hadn't lost yet.

The room felt like a pressure cooker, the air thick with tension. Alex sat hunched over his laptop at the table, his fingers moving frantically over the keys, trying to hold the digital line against Pharmatech's relentless cyberattacks. The screen flickered as wave after wave of attempted breaches hit their encrypted network. Beads of sweat formed on his forehead, and his eyes were bloodshot from days of little sleep.

"They're getting smarter," Alex muttered through gritted teeth, his voice barely above a whisper. "They're adapting to everything I throw at them."

Samantha stood behind him, watching the screen, her arms crossed. "Can you hold them off?"

"For now," Alex replied, his voice tense. "But I don't know how much longer. Every time I patch a hole, they find another way in. It's only a matter of time before they break through."

Turner, pacing the room like a caged animal, shot a glance at Alex. "Then we need to go on the offensive. We can't just sit here and wait for them to crush us. We need to take the fight to them."

Rachel, leaning against the far wall, folded her arms tightly across her chest. "What do you mean, 'take the fight to them'? We're barely holding on as it is, Turner. If Pharmatech breaks through, we're finished."

Turner stopped pacing and faced her, his expression hard. "I mean we need to stop playing defense. We've been reacting to everything they do, and it's wearing us down. We should be reaching out to international media outlets, pushing the story harder. Make it impossible for Pharmatech to silence us."

Rachel scoffed, her frustration boiling over. "International media? And how exactly do you think that's going to help? Pharmatech owns half the media already, and the other half is too scared to touch this. The more we expose, the more they bury us in legal threats and disinformation."

Turner stepped closer, his eyes narrowing. "So what, Rachel? You want to just sit here and wait for them to break us? You think hiding is the answer?"

"I'm saying we need to be realistic!" Rachel's voice cracked, her emotions spilling out. "You keep pushing for more, for us to do more, and every time we take a step forward, they hit back twice as hard. Look at us! We're falling apart."

Samantha, sensing the tension spiraling out of control, interjected. "Turner, we've already taken huge risks. Going international could make things worse. We're stretched thin as it is, and Alex is barely keeping us afloat."

Alex didn't look up from the screen but nodded. "Yeah, I'm doing everything I can, but I can't guarantee this will hold much longer. They're relentless, Sam. It's like they're testing us, looking for a weak spot."

Turner ran a hand through his hair, his frustration mounting. "And they'll find it if we keep sitting here waiting for them to. We need to stay ahead of them, push the narrative harder. If we go international, we'll reach people who aren't under Pharmatech's thumb."

Rachel threw her hands up, her voice shaking. "And what if we do that and they come after us harder? What if they come after my family? Turner, you keep talking about fighting back, but you don't seem to care about the personal cost. This isn't just a game of chess for me—this is my life!"

Turner's expression softened for a moment, but his voice remained firm. "I do care, Rachel. But if we back down now, they'll come after all of us. They won't stop just because we lay low. They'll find us, one by one, and it'll be over. The only way we survive this is by staying on the offensive."

Rachel's eyes filled with tears, her voice breaking. "I'm not like you, Turner. I can't keep pretending like I'm okay with all of this. I can't keep waking up every day wondering if today's the day they find us. I'm scared, okay? I'm scared, and I don't know if I can do this anymore."

The room fell into a heavy silence. Samantha glanced between them, the weight of Rachel's words hanging in the air. She had seen this coming—the cracks in the team, the fear and exhaustion creeping in. But hearing it out loud made it real in a way she hadn't fully acknowledged before.

"Rachel," Samantha said softly, stepping toward her. "I get it. We're all scared. But we've come this far. If we stop now, everything we've done, everything Elias did, will be for nothing."

Rachel wiped at her eyes, shaking her head. "I just don't know if I'm strong enough for this, Sam. Every day, it feels like we're losing more ground, and I don't know if I can handle what's coming next."

Turner, his voice gentler now, spoke up. "We're all in this together. None of us are handling this perfectly. But I need you to trust me on this—we can't let up. We can't hide forever. The only way to end this is to keep pushing until Pharmatech has no choice but to back down."

Alex suddenly cursed under his breath, his fingers flying over the keys. "They're hitting us again. Stronger this time. I'm blocking them, but they're persistent."

Samantha moved beside Alex, her heart pounding. "Can you hold them off?"

"I'll try," Alex replied, his voice strained. "But they're getting closer."

Turner turned back to Rachel, his voice urgent. "We need to keep fighting. This is how they wear us down, by making us doubt ourselves, by pushing us to the edge. But we've got something they don't—the truth. And we need to use that."

Rachel let out a shaky breath, her hands trembling. "I just don't know if it's enough, Turner."

Samantha placed a hand on Rachel's arm. "It is. We're stronger than they think we are. We've already exposed them, and we've survived everything they've thrown at us so far."

Rachel looked at Samantha, her eyes filled with fear and doubt, but there was a flicker of hope there too. "Okay," she whispered. "I'll stay. But if this gets any worse…"

"It won't," Turner said, his voice resolute. "We'll make sure of it."

As Alex continued to fend off Pharmatech's latest attack, the room fell back into a tense silence. The pressure was mounting, and Samantha knew that the internal fractures were widening. But for now, they were still holding on. Barely.

Samantha sat at the small kitchen table, the dim light from a single lamp casting long shadows across the room. The tension from earlier still lingered in the air, thick and oppressive. Alex had managed to block Pharmatech's latest cyberattack, but only just. Rachel had retreated to her room, emotionally drained, while Turner sat across from Samantha, silently studying the map in front of him.

Her phone buzzed on the table, breaking the heavy silence. Samantha glanced at the screen, her heart skipping a beat. It was Dr. Caldwell. She hesitated for a moment before answering.

"Dr. Caldwell?" Samantha's voice was cautious.

"Samantha," the older woman's voice was low, almost a whisper. "I don't have much time. I've found something— something Elias never intended for anyone to see."

Samantha's grip tightened on the phone. Turner looked up from the map, his eyes narrowing as he picked up on the urgency in her tone. "What is it? What did you find?"

"I was going through some of Elias's old files," Dr. Caldwell continued, her voice shaky. "Buried deep in his research was a series of encrypted documents. I thought they were just technical notes, more data on the gene therapy, but when I decoded them... it was something else. It goes deeper, Samantha. Much deeper."

Samantha stood, pacing the small room, her pulse quickening. "How much deeper, Dr. Caldwell?"

There was a pause on the other end of the line, and Samantha could almost hear the hesitation in Dr. Caldwell's breathing. "It's not just about the gene therapy," she said quietly. "Elias was working on something far more dangerous. Pharmatech didn't just want to control his research for profit. They were using it as a cover for something else—a partnership with government officials, high-level corruption that ties directly into public health policies."

Turner leaned forward, his expression darkening as he caught Samantha's side of the conversation. "What are you talking about, Dr. Caldwell? Government corruption?"

"Yes," Dr. Caldwell replied, her voice growing more urgent. "It wasn't just about creating 'perfect' human subjects, as we initially thought. Elias discovered that Pharmatech had been secretly collaborating with certain government agencies. They've been using his research to justify new policies under the guise of public health initiatives. But these initiatives... they're not what they seem."

Samantha stopped pacing, the weight of Dr. Caldwell's words hitting her like a tidal wave. "You're saying they're using Elias's research to influence government policy?"

"Exactly," Dr. Caldwell confirmed. "They're using his findings as a way to push through experimental medical treatments on a national level, but the real purpose is control. Pharmatech has been lobbying for years, shaping policy, and they've been covering it up by claiming it's in the name of 'medical advancement.' But what they're really doing is consolidating power."

Samantha sank into a chair, her mind racing. "Why didn't Elias tell me this? Why didn't he reveal it before?"

Dr. Caldwell's voice wavered. "I don't think he fully understood the scope until it was too late. He believed in his work, in what he was trying to achieve, but when he realized what Pharmatech was really after… it broke him, Samantha. He didn't know who to trust anymore."

Turner stood up, his face hard with anger. "This changes everything," he muttered, pacing in frustration. "We're not just dealing with a corrupt corporation. We're dealing with something much bigger—government officials, lawmakers. Pharmatech isn't just influencing policy, they're writing it."

Samantha rubbed her temples, trying to process the enormity of what Dr. Caldwell was saying. "How far does this go, Dr. Caldwell? How many people are involved?"

"I don't know exactly," Dr. Caldwell admitted, her voice trembling slightly. "But it's widespread. I've found evidence that ties key officials to Pharmatech's board of directors. They've been passing laws that benefit Pharmatech's agenda for years. And the medical community… some of the most respected institutions are involved. They've been manipulated into endorsing treatments, all under the guise of 'advancing science.'"

Samantha's heart raced as she exchanged a glance with Turner. "This is bigger than we thought," she whispered.

Turner nodded grimly. "It always is."

Dr. Caldwell continued, her tone urgent. "Samantha, this isn't just about taking down Pharmatech anymore. This could bring down entire governments if the truth gets out. But you need to be careful. If they know you've uncovered this… they'll stop at nothing to silence you."

Samantha swallowed hard, the gravity of the situation settling in. "We'll be careful, Dr. Caldwell. But we need that information. Can you get it to us?"

"I'm sending it now," Dr. Caldwell replied. "But you have to act fast. I don't know how long I can stay hidden. They're already watching me, and if they find out what I've uncovered…"

"We'll protect you," Turner said, his voice steady. "Just get us the files, and we'll make sure the world knows the truth."

There was a brief pause before Dr. Caldwell spoke again, her voice softer now. "Be careful, Samantha. This isn't just about justice anymore. It's about survival."

Samantha closed her eyes, her chest tightening. "I understand."

As the call ended, Samantha looked at Turner, her mind still reeling from the revelation. "They're not just influencing the medical world—they're controlling it. Pharmatech has their hands in everything."

Turner nodded, his expression grim. "And now we know why they've been fighting so hard to shut us down. If this gets out, it'll expose corruption on a global scale."

Samantha felt a surge of fear, but also a renewed sense of determination. The stakes were higher than she had ever imagined, but now, more than ever, they couldn't afford to back down.

"We have to move fast," she said, her voice steady despite the fear bubbling inside her. "Before they make their next move."

Turner placed a hand on her shoulder. "We will. But we need to be ready. This is just the beginning."

As Samantha nodded, she knew one thing for sure—this fight was no longer just about exposing a corrupt corporation. It was about dismantling an entire system of power, one that would stop at nothing to protect itself. And they were now on the front lines of that battle.

Samantha's fingers drummed anxiously on the table as she stared at her laptop screen. The data from Dr. Caldwell had arrived, a treasure trove of damning evidence that could not only take down Pharmatech, but expose the network of corruption that stretched far beyond the corporation. But they were running out of time. Pharmatech's counterattacks had been relentless, both in the digital realm and in the shadows. Every passing hour increased the chance that the truth would be buried or erased forever.

"They're ramping up the attacks," Alex muttered, eyes fixed on his screen, his voice tense. "They're trying to breach every security measure I've got. It's like they know we've got something huge."

Samantha nodded, her pulse quickening. "They do. And if we don't move fast, they'll bury us before we can release anything."

Turner, pacing near the window, glanced over at her. "We've been playing defense for too long. Pharmatech's been dictating the pace of this fight, but we need to change that."

Rachel, sitting at the table with her arms crossed, shot Turner a skeptical look. "And how do we do that? They've got more resources, more power, and more reach. We've barely been keeping up."

Turner stopped pacing and looked directly at Samantha. "We force their hand."

Samantha raised an eyebrow. "How?"

"A live broadcast," Turner said, his voice steady but filled with urgency. "We go public, right now. No more encrypted files, no more leaks to journalists who take weeks to vet the information. We release the biggest piece of data in real time. They won't have time to react or cover it up. We drop it all, right where the world can see it."

Rachel shook her head in disbelief. "Are you crazy? A live broadcast? They'll track us down the minute we go live."

Turner's jaw tightened. "They're already tracking us. We've been running, hiding, and fighting back in bits and pieces, and all it's done is buy us time. This isn't about hiding anymore—

it's about forcing Pharmatech into a corner, making them deal with the fallout publicly."

Samantha glanced at the laptop, her heart racing. "Turner's right. If we broadcast this, there's no going back for Pharmatech. The minute the data's out, it becomes too big to suppress. Even if they try to erase it, people will have seen it."

Rachel frowned, her voice filled with doubt. "And what happens to us? If we go live, they'll find us in minutes."

"We won't need more than a few minutes," Turner replied firmly. "We release the data, all of it, and let the world handle the rest. Pharmatech won't be able to scramble fast enough to shut it down. And once it's out there, they'll be in full damage control mode."

Samantha leaned forward, her mind spinning. "We'd need a secure connection, a platform that's hard to take down. We can't risk Pharmatech sabotaging the feed before we finish."

Alex, still typing furiously at his laptop, glanced up. "I can set that up. I'll bypass the usual networks and route it through a series of encrypted servers. They might find us eventually, but it'll buy us enough time."

Rachel let out a frustrated sigh. "And what about the legal side of this? Once we do this, it's not just Pharmatech coming after us—it's everyone. The government, other corporations tied to this… we'll be enemies of the state."

Samantha locked eyes with Rachel. "We already are. Look at everything we've uncovered. This is about more than just us now. If we don't release this, if we don't get it out there, then everything we've fought for means nothing."

Rachel's expression softened, though fear still clouded her eyes. "I'm not ready to be a martyr, Sam. I don't know if I can do this."

Turner stepped forward, his voice firm but compassionate. "We're not asking you to be a martyr. We're asking you to help finish what we started. You don't have to stay for the whole thing, Rachel. But we need you to see this through, just long enough to make sure the truth comes out."

Rachel swallowed hard, glancing between them. After a long moment, she exhaled slowly and nodded. "Okay. But if this goes south, I'm gone."

Samantha gave her a reassuring nod. "That's fair."

Alex cleared his throat. "I've got everything set. We can stream through a secure platform. They'll try to take it down, but with the connections I've set up, we'll have at least ten minutes before they can shut it off. That's all we need."

Samantha stood, her heart pounding in her chest. "Then let's do it."

Turner moved quickly, pulling up the data files on the screen. "We start with the most explosive part—Pharmatech's link to government corruption, the bribery, the illegal testing. Once that's out, the rest will fall into place."

Rachel bit her lip, anxiety clear on her face. "This could ruin lives."

Turner glanced at her. "Pharmatech's already ruined lives, Rachel. We're just making sure people know about it."

Samantha took a deep breath, her hands shaking slightly as she moved to the center of the room. She looked at Turner, Alex, and Rachel, the weight of their journey pressing down on her. "We've come this far. Let's finish it."

Alex nodded, his fingers hovering over the keyboard. "We're live in three... two... one..."

The screen flickered, and suddenly, Samantha found herself staring into the camera. Her voice was steady as she spoke, the enormity of what they were about to reveal giving her strength.

"My name is Samantha Cross," she began, her voice clear and unwavering. "And what you're about to see will change everything you think you know about Pharmatech, government health policies, and the true cost of unchecked corporate power."

Turner stood beside her, silent but strong, as the data began to flash across the screen—documents, names, numbers. The truth laid bare for the world to see.

There was no turning back now.

Chapter 11
A Dangerous Ally

The small room felt like it was vibrating with tension. The air was thick, charged with a sense of urgency that weighed down on everyone. Alex sat at the table, hunched over his laptop, his fingers moving at lightning speed across the keyboard. He was setting up the broadcast, every keystroke a lifeline in their last-ditch effort to release the damning evidence against Pharmatech. Across from him, Rachel was typing furiously, her face pale with concentration. Turner stood near the window, scanning the perimeter, his body coiled with the same tension that gripped the entire team.

"We're running out of time," Alex muttered, his voice strained. "Pharmatech's already got eyes on us. I can feel them trying to push through the firewalls. I don't know how much longer I can hold them off."

"Just focus," Turner said, his tone clipped. "We need to make sure everything is in place. We only get one shot at this."

Rachel's fingers paused over her keyboard, and she glanced at Alex. "What's our backup if they break through before we're ready?"

"There isn't one," Alex replied, not looking up from his screen. "I've already rerouted everything through secure channels, but if they breach the encryption, it's over. They'll shut us down in minutes."

Samantha hovered nearby, watching her team as they worked frantically. The pressure was suffocating, and she could feel it pressing down on her like a weight she could barely hold up. This was it—the final move. If they failed here, everything they had fought for, everything Elias had sacrificed, would be for nothing.

"How much time do we have before they hit us?" Samantha asked, her voice tight with anxiety.

Alex shook his head. "Could be five minutes, could be twenty. I'm doing everything I can to slow them down, but they're not messing around anymore."

"We need at least ten minutes to get the full broadcast out," Rachel said, her voice betraying a tremor of fear. "If we cut it short, the most important parts won't even make it through."

Samantha moved closer to Turner, lowering her voice. "Do you think they know where we are?"

"They'll know soon," Turner replied, glancing at her with a grim expression. "Pharmatech's not stupid. They've probably been tracking us through digital breadcrumbs, trying to triangulate our location. That's why we need to move fast."

Samantha felt her stomach knot with tension. "So, we're working against two ticking clocks—the cyberattacks and the physical threat. Great."

Turner nodded. "That's about the size of it."

Rachel let out a shaky breath, her hands hovering over the keyboard. "I'm not going to lie—I'm terrified."

Samantha turned to her, her voice softening. "You're doing great, Rachel. We all are. We just have to get through this. We've come too far to turn back now."

Rachel looked up, meeting Samantha's eyes. "I know. I just… I can't stop thinking about what happens if we don't get this out in time. If Pharmatech buries us before anyone even knows the truth."

"We're not going to let that happen," Turner said, his voice firm. "We've got a plan, and we stick to it. Alex has set up the broadcast. Rachel, you're handling the release of the files. We do this step by step, and we don't panic."

"I'm almost ready," Alex said, typing faster now. "Just a few more connections to make and we'll be live."

Samantha could feel her pulse quicken as she watched him work. Every second felt like a lifetime. She glanced at the clock—five minutes had passed since they'd started preparing. Pharmatech was out there, pushing against their defenses, closing in with every keystroke.

"We need to hit them where it hurts," Turner said, his gaze fixed on Alex. "The more damaging the information we release, the harder it'll be for them to recover. If we can get the government ties and the bribery schemes out there first, Pharmatech will have to go into full crisis mode."

Alex nodded, his face tense with concentration. "I'm prioritizing the most explosive files. Once we're live, the system will automatically push the biggest pieces first. That way, even if they shut us down halfway through, the core information will still get out."

Rachel leaned back in her chair, staring at the screen. "And what if they manage to spin it, even after we release everything? What if they're ready with a counter-narrative?"

"They'll try," Turner replied, his voice steady. "But we've got the truth. Once this hits, it's going to be too big for even Pharmatech to control. People will start asking questions, and those questions will lead to investigations. They can't silence everyone."

Samantha placed a hand on the back of Rachel's chair, squeezing gently. "This is our moment. We've been fighting for this since the beginning. We've faced every obstacle they've thrown at us, and we're still standing. We can do this."

Rachel took a deep breath, nodding slowly. "You're right. I just… I wish I didn't feel like the walls are closing in."

"They are," Alex muttered, still typing furiously. "But we're going to knock them down."

Samantha glanced at Alex. "How much longer?"

"Almost there," Alex said, his fingers flying across the keyboard. "Once I hit this last sequence, we'll be live. You ready for the show?"

Samantha swallowed hard, the gravity of the situation pressing down on her. "Ready as I'll ever be."

Turner checked his watch, his movements deliberate and calm despite the tension radiating through the room. "We're out of time for second guesses. When we go live, they'll know exactly where we are. We have to be prepared to move fast."

Alex hit a final key, the screen flashing brightly. "We're live in three... two... one..."

The tension in the room reached a fever pitch as Samantha stepped in front of the camera. This was it. The moment that would decide everything.

She took a deep breath, her heart racing, and began. "My name is Samantha Cross, and the information you're about to see will reveal the truth about Pharmatech—about their corruption, their control over our government, and the lives they've destroyed in their pursuit of power."

The truth was out, and there was no going back now.

The room hummed with tension as the team prepared for the broadcast, but there was a sense of quiet determination in the air. They were minutes away from releasing the truth, from exposing everything Pharmatech had worked so hard to bury. Alex was focused on his screen, ensuring the feed was stable. Rachel was finalizing the documents, her face pale but resolute. Turner was keeping a watchful eye on the clock, his usual calm veneer masking the high stakes of the moment.

Suddenly, Alex's fingers froze on the keyboard. His brow furrowed, and he glanced sideways at Rachel. "Something's off."

Samantha, standing by the window, turned sharply. "What do you mean?"

Alex's face paled as he scanned the screen. "There's a security breach in the system. Someone's been tampering with the feed."

Turner moved closer, his expression hardening. "What kind of tampering?"

"I'm not sure yet," Alex muttered, his fingers flying over the keys again. "But it looks like someone's rerouted some of the broadcast data. They're trying to divert it somewhere else— possibly to Pharmatech."

Samantha's blood ran cold. "Who? How could they even get access?"

Alex was silent for a moment, his eyes narrowing as he pulled up the internal logs. His face went pale. "It's coming from within our network. Someone on our team is behind this."

The room went deathly quiet.

Rachel stood up from her seat, looking horrified. "That's impossible. We're all in this together. No one here would—"

"Someone would," Turner interrupted, his voice low and dangerous. His eyes scanned the room, landing on each team member with a piercing gaze. "Pharmatech's reach goes deeper than we thought. If someone here's been compromised, we're in more danger than we realized."

Samantha stepped forward, her heart pounding. "Who? Alex, can you trace it?"

Alex typed furiously, his jaw clenched. "Give me a second… It's coming from… Rachel's terminal."

Rachel's eyes widened in shock. "What? No, that's not possible. I haven't touched anything! I've been working on the files this whole time, you've seen me!"

Turner moved toward her, his expression dark and unreadable. "Rachel, if you're lying—"

"I'm not lying!" Rachel snapped, panic rising in her voice. "I swear, I haven't done anything! It wasn't me!"

Samantha stepped between them, her mind racing. She knew Rachel had been struggling, but could she have really been working with Pharmatech this whole time? The thought sent a chill through her, but there was no time to second-guess. They were minutes away from going live, and if there was a traitor in their midst, everything could fall apart.

Alex's voice cut through the tension. "Wait… It's not Rachel. It's being routed *through* her terminal, but the real source is… Turner's."

Samantha's heart stopped. She turned slowly, her eyes locking onto Turner, who stood still, his face blank and unreadable.

"You've got to be kidding me," Rachel muttered, her voice trembling.

Turner met Samantha's gaze, his expression steely. "I didn't betray anyone. This has to be a mistake."

Alex stood up, his voice shaking. "It's no mistake. The data reroute is coming directly from your system. You've been leaking information to Pharmatech."

Samantha's mind reeled. Could it be true? Turner, the one who had kept them together, the one who had pushed them to take risks, to fight back harder—had he been playing them all along?

"You were the one pushing for us to go live," Samantha said, her voice cracking as she stepped closer. "Was that part of the plan? To sabotage everything at the last minute?"

Turner's face hardened. "I've been with you since the beginning, Sam. I didn't do this. You know that."

"Do I?" Samantha shot back, anger flaring in her chest. "Because right now, it looks like you're the one who's been feeding Pharmatech information from the start."

Turner shook his head. "I wouldn't do that. Everything we've done, everything we've fought for—it's real. I've been risking my life just like the rest of you."

Samantha looked into his eyes, searching for something—anything—that would make her believe him. But there was no time for hesitation. The breach was real, and if Turner had been compromised, everything they'd worked for was in jeopardy.

"We don't have time to debate this," Alex said urgently. "If we don't stop the leak now, it's over."

Samantha's heart raced. She had to make a decision.

"Cut him off," she said, her voice steady despite the storm inside her.

Turner's eyes flashed with anger. "You can't be serious."

Samantha met his gaze. "I don't know if you're lying or not, Turner, but I can't take that chance. We need to secure the broadcast, and if that means cutting you off, I'll do it."

For a moment, Turner said nothing. Then, slowly, he nodded. "Do what you have to do."

Alex moved swiftly, his fingers flying over the keyboard. In seconds, Turner's system was isolated from the rest of the network.

"We're secure," Alex said, his voice tight. "But we need to move now. Pharmatech will be on us in minutes."

Samantha turned back to the camera, her heart pounding. She didn't know if she had made the right call, if Turner had been lying or if she had just cut off their strongest ally. But there was no time to dwell on it. They had to go live.

"We go now," she said, her voice firm.

Rachel, still shaken, nodded and hit the final key.

The broadcast was live.

Samantha took a deep breath and faced the camera, her voice steady. "This is the truth about Pharmatech. And nothing is going to stop it from coming out."

As she spoke, she could feel the weight of Turner's betrayal—or maybe his innocence—hanging over her. But for now, they had to keep moving.

The truth was out there, and no one could take it back.

The room was silent but for the hum of the equipment, the tension so thick it was almost palpable. Alex, sitting at his laptop, was the first to break the silence. "We're live," he whispered, though his voice was strained with the intensity of the moment.

Samantha stood in front of the camera, her heart pounding in her chest. Rachel sat just out of frame, scrolling through the documents they were about to unleash on the world. This was it—the moment they had been working toward for so long, the moment Pharmatech had been trying to stop with every trick in the book.

Samantha took a deep breath, steadying herself. "This is Samantha Cross," she began, her voice clear but heavy with the gravity of what she was about to reveal. "What you are about to see will expose one of the most powerful corporations in the world—Pharmatech—and their corrupt dealings with both governments and public institutions. The evidence we are about to present will reveal a network of bribery, illegal experimentation, and a cover-up that has cost lives."

Rachel looked up from her screen, her voice just above a whisper as she spoke to Samantha, though the camera couldn't pick it up. "We're good on the files. Ready when you are."

Samantha gave her a slight nod before turning her attention back to the camera. "Over the past year, my team and I have gathered irrefutable evidence that connects Pharmatech to illegal human trials and government officials who have knowingly allowed this to happen. These are not just rumors— these are facts backed by official documents, emails, and financial records."

Rachel tapped a key on her laptop, and the first document appeared on the broadcast—a leaked email exchange between top Pharmatech executives and a government official approving an illegal trial under the guise of medical research.

Samantha continued, "This email, from a senior Pharmatech executive to a member of the regulatory body overseeing public health policy, discusses the approval of an experimental gene therapy trial. These trials were not approved by any ethics committee. Instead, they were carried out in secret, using vulnerable populations as test subjects."

The camera zoomed in on the email, and the screen lit up with names, dates, and chilling details of human experimentation. Rachel's fingers hovered over her keyboard, ready to bring up the next wave of evidence.

But then Alex's voice cut through the moment, sharp with tension. "Pharmatech's trying to shut us down. They've launched another attack—stronger this time."

Samantha's pulse quickened, but she kept her eyes on the camera. "How long do we have?"

Alex's fingers flew over the keyboard, his face tight with concentration. "They're coming at us hard. I can hold them off for a few minutes, but we don't have much time. Keep going."

Samantha's heart raced, but she pressed on, knowing the window to reveal the truth was rapidly closing. "Next, we'll show you the financial records that tie Pharmatech directly to top political figures. These payments were disguised as charitable donations, but in reality, they were bribes—money exchanged for silence and support."

Rachel hit a key, and a new screen filled with spreadsheets and transaction records appeared. Names of high-ranking officials alongside staggering sums of money. The implications were explosive.

Samantha's voice grew stronger, fueled by the urgency of the moment. "These records prove that Pharmatech's influence extends far beyond the medical industry. They have corrupted politicians, bought their way into policy decisions, and ensured that their illegal activities remain hidden from the public."

Alex's voice came again, a low warning. "They're breaking through. We've got maybe two more minutes before the stream gets cut."

Rachel's eyes flickered with panic. "We haven't even gotten to the worst part yet."

Samantha nodded, turning back to the camera, her voice firm. "We don't have much time, so here is what you need to know. Pharmatech has been conducting experiments on human subjects—innocent people who were never given the chance to consent. These experiments were conducted in secret, and the consequences have been devastating."

Rachel pulled up the final set of documents—internal Pharmatech memos detailing the results of these illegal trials. The memos outlined failures, deaths, and attempts to cover up the true extent of the damage. Names were redacted, but the horror of what had happened to the test subjects was undeniable.

Samantha took a deep breath. "Pharmatech has been responsible for deaths. And not just one or two—dozens. Maybe hundreds. These are human lives lost to corporate greed. And the officials we trust to protect us have been complicit in this."

Alex swore under his breath. "They're almost through."

Samantha's eyes locked on the camera, her heart pounding in her chest. "We're running out of time. This information cannot be erased. Share this broadcast. Spread it across every platform you can. Pharmatech will try to silence us, but they can't silence the truth if enough of you hear it."

She looked at Rachel, who hit the key to send out the final wave of files across multiple servers. The data surged out into the world, too fast for Pharmatech to stop it now.

Alex's fingers flew over his keyboard. "They've breached the outer firewall. We're seconds away from losing the feed."

Samantha took a final breath, her voice resolute. "To the people watching—Pharmatech will come for us. But they can't come for all of you. Spread the truth. Expose them. Don't let this disappear."

The screen flickered, the connection slowing as Pharmatech's assault on their system hit full force.

"Three… two…" Alex muttered, sweat dripping down his forehead. "And we're—"

The screen went black.

The room fell into silence. Samantha's heart pounded in her chest as she turned to Alex. "Did we get it out?"

Alex nodded slowly, exhaustion etched across his face. "We did. The files are out there. Pharmatech's too late."

Rachel slumped back in her chair, her hands trembling. "Then it's done."

Samantha exhaled, her body finally releasing the tension that had built up over the past hour. "Now we wait."

Outside, the world would soon know the truth. There was no going back now.

The silence that followed the broadcast's abrupt end was suffocating. Samantha sat in the chair, her heart still racing, the adrenaline slowly draining from her system. The room was thick with the weight of what had just happened—what they had just done. It felt as though the entire world had shifted in the moments since they'd gone live.

Rachel was the first to break the silence. "Do you think it worked?" Her voice was small, unsure. She looked pale, still shaken from the betrayal and the broadcast's chaotic finish.

Samantha glanced at Alex, who was staring intently at his screen, monitoring the web traffic. "Alex?"

Alex nodded slowly, his eyes scanning the data as it streamed in. "It worked. It's everywhere. News outlets are already picking it up, even some international ones. Twitter, Reddit, Instagram—it's all blowing up."

Turner, who had been standing near the window, finally turned around. His expression was calm, but there was a quiet intensity in his eyes. "Pharmatech won't be able to recover from this."

Rachel let out a breath she hadn't realized she was holding. "God, I hope so."

Samantha leaned forward, rubbing her temples. The tension that had been building for days, maybe even weeks, was beginning to crack, but the relief was tempered by a gnawing sense of uncertainty. "What happens now?"

Alex spun his laptop around to show them the news feed, already filling with headlines.

"BREAKING: Major Corruption Scandal Exposed— Pharmatech Linked to Illegal Human Trials"
"Explosive Documents Reveal Government Ties to Pharmatech's Illegal Testing"
"Pharmatech Faces Financial Collapse After Leaked Data Rocks Corporate World"

Samantha's eyes skimmed over the articles, her pulse quickening. Every major news outlet had picked up the story within minutes of their broadcast ending. It was everywhere— on television, in newspapers, online. Pharmatech's name was now synonymous with corruption, greed, and suffering.

"This is just the beginning," Alex muttered, scrolling through the updates. "The stock market's reacting already. Pharmatech shares are plummeting. Investors are pulling out. Board members are resigning left and right."

Turner folded his arms across his chest, nodding grimly. "It's going to be a feeding frenzy. Once this news gets out, everyone's going to want a piece of Pharmatech's carcass."

Samantha felt the enormity of it all weighing down on her. She had known this would happen—she'd planned for it—but seeing the fallout unfold in real-time was something else entirely. "What about the government ties?" she asked, her voice low. "Are they reporting on that yet?"

Alex nodded. "Yep. Multiple outlets are picking it up. People are already calling for investigations into the officials named in the documents. This is going to go all the way to the top."

Rachel sat down hard in the nearest chair, burying her face in her hands. "I can't believe we actually did it."

Samantha gave her a small, tired smile. "We did. But it's not over."

Turner's eyes flicked toward her. "She's right. This is just the beginning of the fallout. Pharmatech might be going down, but they're not going to let it happen without a fight."

Rachel frowned. "What do you mean? Their board is falling apart, and the media's already calling for heads. What more can they do?"

"They'll fight this in court," Turner said, his voice steady. "They'll tie it up in legal battles for as long as they can. And don't forget, they've got allies in high places. Government officials, powerful friends. We may have started the fire, but they're going to try and put it out."

Samantha nodded, her expression somber. "Turner's right. The legal battle is going to be long, messy, and brutal. Pharmatech will pull every string, call in every favor. They're not dead yet."

Rachel looked at them both, fear creeping back into her eyes. "So, what are we supposed to do? We're not exactly legal experts."

Samantha sighed, leaning back in her chair. "We've done our part. We got the truth out there. Now we let the legal system—and public opinion—do the rest. But we're going to need to stay vigilant. Pharmatech will come after us, and they'll come hard."

Turner gave a grim nod. "They'll try to discredit us, spin the narrative, paint us as rogue whistleblowers with an agenda. But the evidence is too strong this time. They can't bury it."

Alex's phone buzzed, and he glanced at the screen before looking back at them. "The government's already launching investigations into the officials named in the documents. This is about to get ugly."

Samantha stood, crossing her arms as she gazed out the window. She felt a strange mix of relief and dread—relief that the truth was finally out, but dread at what lay ahead. "Pharmatech's fall might take years. We've shaken the tree, but now we have to wait for the fruit to drop."

Rachel looked up at her, eyes wide with exhaustion. "Do you think we'll be safe?"

Samantha hesitated for a moment, then shook her head. "No. They'll come for us. They'll try to discredit us, sue us, maybe even worse. But we have to be ready for that. We've come too far to let fear stop us now."

Turner stepped forward, his voice steady. "We'll be ready. And we won't stop until Pharmatech and everyone involved pays for what they've done."

Samantha turned to face her team, her eyes filled with resolve. "This is just the beginning. We've won this battle, but the war isn't over."

The news on the screen continued to update, flashing images of Pharmatech's CEO giving a hurried statement outside corporate headquarters, journalists shouting questions, and financial analysts predicting the company's collapse. But even as the world reacted, Samantha knew the real fight was only just beginning.

Pharmatech had been exposed, but now came the hard part— surviving the fallout.

Chapter 12
Crossing Lines

The safe house was eerily quiet, a far cry from the storm they had just unleashed on the world. The dim glow of the laptop screens cast long shadows across the room as Samantha and her team sat in silence, each lost in their own thoughts. The thrill of the broadcast's success had already begun to fade, replaced by the heavy weight of the consequences they now faced.

Samantha broke the silence, her voice soft but tinged with exhaustion. "It's done. Pharmatech is falling apart, but... it feels like we've only just started."

Rachel, seated at the far end of the room, looked up, her face pale and drawn. "We should be celebrating, right? I mean, we did it. We brought them down."

Samantha met her gaze, her expression weary. "Yeah, but it doesn't feel like a victory, does it?"

Rachel shook her head, her hands trembling slightly as she spoke. "No. It doesn't. It feels like... like we're the ones who are about to be destroyed."

Turner, who had been leaning against the wall, crossed his arms and sighed heavily. "Pharmatech's going down, but they're not dead yet. And the people backing them? They've got deep pockets and powerful friends. We're not exactly out of the woods."

Rachel let out a shaky laugh, the sound bitter. "So what was the point of all this? We risked everything, and now we're sitting here in hiding, waiting for the next hit. They'll come for us. You know that, right?"

Alex, sitting at his laptop, chimed in, though his voice was flat. "They've already started. I've been monitoring chatter online. Pharmatech's PR team is trying to paint us as rogue activists, conspiracy theorists. They're throwing everything they've got at us."

Samantha sighed and rubbed her temples, feeling the weight of the last few days pressing down on her. "We knew this was coming. They were never going to let us get away with this without a fight. But we have the truth on our side. That has to count for something."

Turner shook his head, his expression grim. "The truth is only as strong as the people who believe it, Sam. And Pharmatech still controls a lot of the narrative, even in their weakest moment."

Rachel sat forward, her voice growing sharper. "So what now? We keep running? Hiding? Waiting for someone to find us?"

Samantha's eyes flickered with guilt as she glanced around the room, taking in the exhaustion etched on each of their faces. Rachel's fear, Alex's weariness, Turner's frustration—it was all there, unspoken but heavy in the air.

"We regroup," Samantha said quietly. "We need to stay hidden for now, let the dust settle. But we don't stop. The legal battle will take years, and Pharmatech's going to throw everything they have at us, but we can't let up."

Rachel groaned, running a hand through her hair. "I'm so tired, Sam. I don't know how much more of this I can take. Every time I close my eyes, I think about what they could do to us—what they'll do to me."

Samantha stepped closer, her voice soft but filled with empathy. "I know. I'm tired too. We've been running for so long, and it feels like it'll never stop. But we've come too far to quit now. The world knows the truth because of us."

Alex leaned back in his chair, rubbing his eyes. "I don't think any of us were ready for this. I thought once we exposed them, it'd be over. But it's not. It's just the beginning of a different kind of fight."

Turner's voice was low but steady as he spoke. "You're right, Alex. But that's why we need to be smart. We've got to be prepared for whatever they throw at us next. We can't afford to make any mistakes."

Rachel let out a frustrated sigh. "It just feels like we're alone in this. Even though the whole world saw what we did, it feels like we're the ones who'll pay the price."

Samantha nodded slowly, understanding the weight of Rachel's words. "It feels that way because we're the ones on the front lines. But we're not alone. People are waking up. The investigations are starting, the media is all over Pharmatech, and public pressure is building."

Rachel's eyes darkened with doubt. "But what about us? What happens to us? We can't hide forever."

Samantha's heart sank as she thought about the uncertain future ahead. "I don't know, Rachel. I really don't. But I do know that if we hadn't done what we did, they'd still be out there, hurting people, destroying lives. And now, at least, we've made it harder for them to keep doing that."

Turner stepped forward, his voice more gentle now. "Look, this is the hardest part—the aftermath. But we're not powerless. We've exposed Pharmatech, and the world's watching now. The spotlight's on them, not us. If they come after us, it'll be in full view of the public. That's not a fight they want to have."

Alex glanced at Turner, his expression still grim. "Maybe. But we can't rely on public opinion to keep us safe. We need to be ready for whatever comes next."

Samantha nodded, a quiet determination settling over her. "We will be. But right now, we rest. We take a breath. Then we get ready to keep fighting."

Rachel looked at her, her eyes softening. "I hope you're right, Sam. I really do. Because I don't know how much more of this I can take."

Samantha gave her a tired smile. "None of us do, Rachel. But we've survived this far. We'll make it through the rest."

The room fell quiet again, but this time it wasn't the silence of fear or tension—it was the silence of people who had survived the worst and were bracing themselves for the next storm. Samantha knew the road ahead would be long and full of challenges, but for now, they had each other. And for the moment, that was enough.

Days had passed since the broadcast, but the frenzy outside their secluded safe house hadn't diminished. The world had latched onto the Pharmatech scandal like a ravenous animal, dissecting every piece of evidence Samantha and her team had exposed. News outlets from every corner of the globe were running stories on Pharmatech's collapse, its corrupt ties to governments, and the devastating human trials that had come to light. Headlines screamed of betrayal, greed, and death, while images of Pharmatech's headquarters, now surrounded by protestors, dominated the airwaves.

Samantha sat at the edge of the dining table, watching a news segment on her laptop. The anchor's voice was smooth, almost too rehearsed. "With investigations now underway, former Pharmatech executives are under intense scrutiny. Government officials implicated in the scandal are beginning to step down as pressure mounts. The public outrage is palpable, but questions remain: How deep does this go? And will justice be served?"

She closed the laptop with a sigh, rubbing her temples. The world might be screaming for justice, but she knew better. This was only the beginning of a very long fight. The noise from the media storm would die down soon enough, and what remained would be the ugly legal battles, the underhanded deals, and the attempts to silence or bury the truth.

Her phone buzzed on the table, startling her. Another message from an unknown number. Another journalist. They had been reaching out non-stop, each trying to secure an exclusive interview, to be the one to get the next big story.

"Samantha, this is Diane Matthews from The Globe. I've been following the Pharmatech story closely and would love to speak with you about your next steps. We can offer you a platform to tell the full story—one that won't be influenced by corporate interests. Please consider meeting with me."

Samantha didn't respond. She had received at least a dozen similar messages in the past 48 hours, some from reputable sources, others from smaller, lesser-known publications. But how could she know which were genuine? Which reporters truly wanted to uncover the truth, and which ones were quietly working for corporate interests, trying to manipulate the narrative?

She stood, walking over to the window and pulling the curtains aside. The view of the surrounding forest was peaceful, a stark contrast to the chaos she knew was brewing beyond. For now, they were safe, hidden. But they couldn't stay here forever, and the offers from journalists and investigators were growing harder to ignore.

"What's going on in that head of yours?" Turner's voice cut through the quiet as he entered the room.

Samantha turned, her expression tired. "More messages. Journalists, investigators, all wanting to talk. It's overwhelming."

Turner leaned against the doorframe, arms crossed. "You can't trust them, Sam. Not yet. Not with everything still so raw. Most of them are probably just looking for a scoop, and the ones who seem legit… they could be working for someone else. Pharmatech still has people out there, even if they're not as bold as they used to be."

"I know." Samantha nodded, sinking back into her chair. "But we can't stay silent forever, either. If we don't get ahead of this, someone else will control the narrative, and I can't let that happen."

Turner's face darkened. "Whoever we talk to has to be clean. No ties to corporate money, no hidden agendas. That kind of journalist is rare."

Samantha's phone buzzed again, pulling her attention. Another name flashed on the screen—someone she recognized from a well-known independent news outlet, one with a reputation for hard-hitting investigative journalism. Her fingers hovered over the screen. Could this one be different? Could they trust anyone at this point?

Turner watched her carefully. "You thinking of responding?"

She hesitated, then shook her head. "Not yet. Not until we're sure."

"You're right to be cautious," Turner said, moving closer. "They're all circling like vultures. Pharmatech's empire is crumbling, but there's still plenty of money in keeping some parts of the story buried. If we're not careful, we'll be used as pawns."

Samantha felt the weight of his words pressing down on her. Every choice they made now would have far-reaching consequences, and the wrong move could unravel everything. They had won the battle with the broadcast, but this—the media storm, the public scrutiny—was a different kind of war.

"The problem is, we need allies," Samantha said softly, more to herself than to Turner. "If we keep hiding, we're going to lose momentum. People will start asking questions about why we aren't speaking out, and Pharmatech will take advantage of that."

Turner nodded, his gaze steady. "I get it. But we need to play it smart. We've got one shot to tell this story our way. Once we pick a platform, we can't go back."

Samantha looked out the window again, her thoughts racing. She knew Turner was right. They needed to choose carefully. They had fought too hard to expose the truth to let it slip away now. But every day they waited, the media narrative spun further out of their control.

"We'll need to vet whoever we decide to work with," Turner added, his tone more serious now. "Make sure they're in it for the right reasons. Not just for the story, but for the truth."

Samantha nodded slowly, her mind made up. "I'll start reaching out, but carefully. No commitments until we're sure."

Turner gave her a small nod of approval. "Good. We need to stay sharp. This isn't over yet."

Samantha took a deep breath, her fingers tightening around her phone. The media storm was only growing stronger, and the world was watching. But for now, they would bide their time. Trust was a precious commodity, and she wasn't about to give it away so easily.

As she stared down at the screen, she knew that the next step they took would be just as critical as the last. The truth was out there, but now they had to protect it—and themselves—before the vultures closed in.

The café was quiet, tucked away in a part of the city where no one would expect to find Samantha Cross or Dr. Caldwell. It was the kind of place where people came and went without giving each other a second glance—perfect for a meeting that needed to be off the radar. Samantha sat at the far corner table, her back to the wall, watching the door. Her fingers traced the rim of her coffee cup absently, though she hadn't taken a sip. Her mind was elsewhere, lost in the aftermath of the storm they had unleashed.

The door opened with a soft chime, and Samantha looked up, spotting Dr. Caldwell as she stepped inside. The older woman moved with a kind of cautious grace, her eyes scanning the room until she found Samantha. She gave a small nod before making her way over, her face etched with the weariness of a battle that had lasted far longer than any of them had anticipated.

"Thank you for meeting me," Dr. Caldwell said as she sat down, her voice soft but sincere.

Samantha smiled faintly, though her own exhaustion mirrored Caldwell's. "Of course. I wasn't sure if I'd ever see you again."

Dr. Caldwell gave a small, tired laugh. "I wasn't sure either. But I needed to speak with you, one last time. To thank you, and to... well, to make sure you understand what comes next."

Samantha leaned forward slightly, her expression serious. "What do you mean?"

Caldwell sighed, her hands resting on the table. "You've done something incredible, Samantha. You and your team exposed Pharmatech. You brought the truth to light, and for that, you should be proud. But you need to know, this battle—this fight—is far from over."

Samantha's brow furrowed. "I know Pharmatech isn't dead yet. They still have resources, and they'll drag this through the courts for years. But we've dealt them a massive blow."

Dr. Caldwell shook her head gently. "It's not just about Pharmatech. Yes, you've crippled them, and the world is watching them burn, but there are still forces at play—forces that operated in the shadows long before Pharmatech. These are the people, the networks, that benefited from Pharmatech's influence. They're the ones who will try to rebuild, who will step into the vacuum that's been created."

Samantha felt a cold knot form in her stomach. "You're saying that even after everything, we've only scratched the surface?"

Caldwell met her eyes, a sadness there that spoke of too many years of watching the wrong people win. "Exactly. Pharmatech was a piece of the puzzle, but the system that enabled them, the people behind the scenes who profited from their actions—that's still intact. Pharmatech's fall is a victory, yes, but those hidden forces… they're already working to adapt, to shift their influence elsewhere."

Samantha exhaled slowly, her gaze dropping to the table. "So, what do we do? If we've only taken down one piece, how do we stop the rest?"

Dr. Caldwell reached out, placing a hand over Samantha's. "You can't do it alone, Samantha. No one can. But what you've done is start a movement. People are watching now, people who were blind to it before. You've shaken the foundations of their power, and that's something they can't ignore."

Samantha nodded, though her mind was already racing with the implications. She had known this fight would take everything she had, but she hadn't realized just how deep it went—how many layers of corruption had yet to be exposed.

Caldwell leaned back, her voice softening. "I wanted to warn you because I know how exhausting this can be. You've made enemies, powerful ones, and they won't stop just because

Pharmatech is falling. They'll regroup. They'll come after you in ways you won't see coming. You need to be prepared for that."

Samantha looked up, meeting Caldwell's gaze. "I won't stop. I can't stop."

Caldwell smiled, though it was tinged with sadness. "I know you won't. But don't lose yourself in this fight. It's easy to become consumed by it. I've seen it happen to others, to people who believed they could take down the whole system. It wears on you, changes you."

Samantha clenched her jaw, determination hardening her expression. "I know what's at stake. And I'm ready for whatever comes next."

Dr. Caldwell's smile faded, her eyes filled with understanding. "You've done more than most people would ever dare to, Samantha. Just remember, the road ahead is long. And the people you're fighting—some of them won't show themselves until it's too late."

There was a heavy silence between them, one filled with unspoken fears and shared understanding. Samantha knew Caldwell was right. They had exposed Pharmatech, but the true power behind the corporation—the people who had remained hidden in the shadows—were still out there.

After a moment, Caldwell stood, her hand resting briefly on Samantha's shoulder. "Take care of yourself, Samantha. And take care of your team. You'll need each other for what comes next."

Samantha nodded, watching as Caldwell turned and walked toward the door, her figure disappearing into the afternoon crowd.

Samantha remained at the table for a long time, the weight of Caldwell's warning settling over her. She had known from the beginning that this fight would be difficult, but now, sitting there alone, she realized just how far-reaching the battle truly was. The war against Pharmatech might have been their most public victory, but the war against the hidden forces behind it was only just beginning.

And this time, she would be ready.

The dim light of the safe house flickered softly in the early evening. Samantha sat by the window, her gaze drifting over the empty horizon. The room was quiet, almost too quiet, as the reality of what had transpired began to settle in. She had done it—exposed Pharmatech, avenged Elias, and uncovered one of the biggest corporate scandals the world had ever seen. And yet, the victory felt hollow, the price they had paid looming larger with each passing moment.

She leaned her forehead against the cool glass, the weight of exhaustion pressing down on her. The fight had taken everything from her—her sense of security, her peace of mind, and most painfully, her relationships. Every step forward in the investigation had come at a cost, and now that the storm had passed, she was left with the quiet aftermath. It was in this silence that the personal toll began to truly sink in.

Turner's voice broke the stillness as he entered the room, his footsteps barely audible on the worn floorboards. "You're quiet," he said, leaning against the doorframe.

Samantha didn't look up. "Just… thinking," she murmured.

He stepped closer, crossing his arms as he stood next to her. "About what?"

She sighed, her breath fogging up the window for a moment before it cleared. "About everything. About how we got here, about Elias… about what we've lost."

Turner nodded, though he didn't press her for more. He could sense the weight she was carrying. "You're thinking about Elias, aren't you?"

She closed her eyes, the memory of Elias's face flashing through her mind—the way his eyes had sparkled with hope when he first talked about his research, the passion he'd had for changing the world. "I promised him I'd finish what he started," she whispered. "I didn't think it would cost so much."

Turner leaned against the wall, his voice quiet. "It always costs more than we think."

Samantha turned to him, her eyes searching his face. "Do you ever wonder if it was worth it? If what we've done… if it's enough?"

Turner met her gaze, his expression serious. "It was worth it, Sam. Exposing Pharmatech, making them pay for what they did—that's not something a lot of people could have pulled off. And you didn't just do it for Elias. You did it for everyone they hurt, for everyone who never got a chance to fight back."

"But what about the ones we couldn't save?" Samantha's voice trembled, the guilt surfacing. "All those people Pharmatech experimented on, the lives they destroyed. We didn't get to them in time."

Turner's jaw tightened, his voice softening. "We can't save everyone. You know that. But you made sure that what happened to them won't happen to anyone else. That's something."

Samantha nodded, though the ache in her chest didn't ease. She had always known the risks, always understood the sacrifices, but now that it was over—now that the truth was out—she was left with the stark reality of what it had cost. Her life had been consumed by this fight, and in the process, she had lost parts of herself she wasn't sure she'd ever get back.

"I just… I wonder if this is it for me," she said, her voice barely a whisper. "If my life is always going to be this—running, fighting, losing people I care about."

Turner's eyes softened as he looked at her, his usual hardened exterior giving way to something more vulnerable. "You're not alone, Sam. I know it feels like it sometimes, but you've got people around you who believe in what you're doing. You've got us."

She smiled faintly, the gesture tinged with sadness. "I know. But it's different now. I've made enemies, Turner. Powerful enemies. This isn't just about exposing one corporation anymore. It's about fighting a system that's been built on greed and corruption, and I'm not sure if I'll survive that."

"You will," he said firmly, his voice filled with certainty. "Because you're stronger than you think. You've survived this far, and you'll survive what comes next."

Samantha looked back out the window, the sky fading into shades of gray as the sun dipped below the horizon. She knew he was right, but that didn't make the path ahead any less daunting. She had thrown herself into this fight to bring justice for Elias, to tear down the corrupt systems that had taken so much from them, but now that the battle was over, she was left with the question of what came next.

"I don't know if I can stop," she admitted quietly. "Even if I wanted to. There's still so much more out there. So many more people like Elias. And as long as they're out there, I don't think I can walk away."

Turner gave her a small, understanding nod. "Then don't walk away. Keep fighting. But don't forget to live, too. This fight is important, but so is what comes after."

Samantha's chest tightened as she thought about what "after" even looked like. She had been fighting for so long, she wasn't sure she knew how to be anything else. But maybe Turner was right. Maybe there was still something to live for beyond the fight.

She turned to him, her resolve hardening. "I won't stop. I can't. But I'll try to find some balance. I'll try to remember that there's more to life than this."

Turner gave her a rare smile, the kind that only appeared when he knew something had shifted in her. "That's all anyone can ask for."

As he turned to leave, Samantha sat back down, the weight of everything settling around her like a cloak. The world outside was still spinning, still full of danger, but she was ready to face it. The fight wasn't over, not by a long shot. She had made powerful enemies, enemies who would come for her in ways she couldn't yet imagine. But she had also exposed the truth. She had brought justice for Elias, for the victims Pharmatech had left behind.

And now, as the night settled in, Samantha Cross made her choice. She would keep fighting. She would face whatever came next, knowing full well the risks ahead. Because some truths were worth fighting for, no matter the cost.

With a deep breath, she stood, her resolve unshakable. The road ahead was long, but Samantha was ready.

Chapter 13
The Price of Truth

The courtroom was sterile, almost suffocating in its stillness. Samantha sat at the witness stand, her palms pressed tightly together, a bead of sweat forming at the base of her neck. The atmosphere was tense, a far cry from the raw danger of the field but just as heavy with threat. Pharmatech's legal team, a small army of high-priced lawyers in tailored suits, sat at the opposing table, watching her with calculated indifference. They were waiting for her to slip up. One misstep, and they would tear her apart.

Her heart raced as she glanced at Turner, sitting just behind the defense table, his expression unreadable but reassuring. He gave her a small, almost imperceptible nod. He was there, just like he always was, ready to step in if things got out of hand. But for now, it was her fight. She was the key witness in a legal battle that had quickly turned into the trial of the century.

"Miss Cross," the prosecutor's voice rang out, pulling her back to the present. The lawyer, a sharp-eyed woman with a no-nonsense demeanor, paced in front of the jury box, every word measured and deliberate. "You were the one who spearheaded the investigation into Pharmatech's illegal activities, correct?"

Samantha cleared her throat, keeping her voice steady. "Yes. My team and I uncovered evidence that exposed Pharmatech's use of illegal human trials, bribery, and corruption on a global scale."

The prosecutor nodded. "And this investigation, it cost you a great deal, didn't it?"

Samantha hesitated for a moment, thinking of Elias, of the lives ruined by Pharmatech. "Yes," she replied, her voice quieter now. "It cost a lot of people everything."

There was a moment of silence before the prosecutor continued. "But despite the risks, despite the threats, you chose to move forward with the truth."

"I did," Samantha said, her eyes hardening. "Because it was the right thing to do."

Before the prosecutor could continue, one of Pharmatech's lawyers stood. "Objection, your honor. We're not here to discuss morality, but facts. Miss Cross's personal motivations are irrelevant to these proceedings."

The judge, a stern-faced man with graying hair, looked at the lawyer with mild annoyance. "Overruled. Continue, Counselor."

The prosecutor didn't miss a beat. "Miss Cross, in the course of your investigation, you came across documents, emails, and financial records linking Pharmatech to various government officials. These records showed not only illegal human trials but also deep corruption within the company and external entities. Is that correct?"

"Yes," Samantha replied, nodding. "Pharmatech used its wealth and influence to bribe officials, cover up deaths, and manipulate public health policies. We found evidence of direct involvement from members of their board and political figures around the world."

Another murmur spread through the courtroom, and Samantha felt the weight of their eyes on her. She knew what this was—a chess game. Pharmatech was going to throw everything they had at her, not just to save themselves but to discredit her, to make her look like a rogue conspirator instead of a truth-seeker.

Turner had warned her. He'd sat her down the night before and gone over every possible line of attack Pharmatech's lawyers would use, every tactic they'd employ to twist her words.

"They'll try to make you out to be irrational," Turner had said, his voice calm but serious. "They'll go after your credibility, your motivations. They'll say you had an agenda."

Samantha had nodded, knowing full well what was coming. "And what if they do?"

"We counter with facts," Turner had replied. "That's what they're scared of. The facts are on your side. But you need to stay calm. Don't let them provoke you."

Now, sitting under the courtroom's glaring lights, she could feel the truth of Turner's words. The facts were on her side, but the lawyers would twist everything if she gave them an inch.

Sure enough, the next lawyer from Pharmatech's team stood, straightening his suit jacket as he approached the witness stand. His eyes were cold, calculating, the kind of lawyer who lived for moments like these.

"Miss Cross," he began, his voice smooth, almost patronizing, "while we certainly respect your dedication, there's something we need to clarify for the court. Your investigation into Pharmatech—it was personal, wasn't it?"

Samantha's jaw tightened. "It was about finding the truth."

The lawyer smirked, as if she had just proven his point. "Yes, but it was personal, too, wasn't it? After all, Elias Harding, the scientist whose work you claim to have been protecting—he was close to you, wasn't he?"

Samantha's throat tightened. She had known this was coming, but it didn't make it any easier to face. "Elias was a friend," she said, her voice steady.

"More than a friend, though, wasn't he?" the lawyer pressed, his tone suggestive. "You've admitted in previous interviews that his death affected you deeply. So, isn't it possible that your motivation to expose Pharmatech was driven by personal grief, rather than a quest for justice?"

Samantha's pulse quickened, but she forced herself to remain calm. Turner's voice echoed in her mind. *Don't let them provoke you.*

"My motivation was to stop Pharmatech from hurting more people," she said, her voice firm. "Elias's death was tragic, but it's not the reason I did this. I did it because Pharmatech was breaking the law, and people were dying."

The lawyer arched an eyebrow, clearly trying to bait her. "But you can't deny that your personal connection to Elias played a role in your decisions, can you?"

Samantha didn't hesitate. "My connection to Elias made me understand just how dangerous Pharmatech's experiments were. But this was never about revenge. It was about justice—for Elias, and for everyone else Pharmatech exploited."

The lawyer's smirk faded slightly, and he stepped back, adjusting his tie. "No further questions, your honor."

Samantha exhaled slowly as the judge called for a brief recess. The pressure inside the courtroom, the constant attempts to discredit her, to twist her motives—it was exhausting. But as she stepped down from the stand and walked toward Turner, who stood waiting by the door, she knew she couldn't stop. This was only the beginning of a long battle, one she had no choice but to see through.

"You held your ground," Turner said quietly, his voice calm as always.

"They're trying to break me," she replied, her voice heavy with fatigue.

"They won't," Turner said, meeting her gaze. "You're stronger than they are. And they know it."

Samantha gave him a tired smile. "Let's hope you're right."

Turner nodded, his eyes filled with certainty. "I am. But you need to be ready, Sam. This is going to get worse before it gets better."

She knew he was right. The legal battle was just beginning, and Pharmatech's remaining power brokers would stop at nothing to tear her down. But she had come this far. And no matter what they threw at her, she wouldn't back down now.

Samantha sat in the corner of the law office, the air humming with tension. Turner had left to meet with a legal consultant, and she was alone with her thoughts for the first time in days. The legal proceedings against Pharmatech were well underway, but the pressure on her was growing unbearable. She was constantly in the public eye, her name dragged through the mud by Pharmatech's high-powered legal teams, who had begun their relentless campaign of character assassination.

Every day, new headlines appeared, each more damning than the last. They accused her of being a rogue whistleblower, an attention-seeker driven by personal vendettas. They dredged up her past, twisting every personal detail they could find into something malicious. Pharmatech was fighting dirty, and Samantha knew it was only going to get worse.

She was lost in thought when Turner walked back into the room, his expression serious but with an underlying energy that caught her attention. "We've got something," he said, sitting across from her.

Samantha raised an eyebrow, not daring to hope for good news. "What do you mean?"

"People are stepping forward," Turner said, a slight smile creeping onto his face. "Former employees. People who worked for Pharmatech—who saw things. And they're willing to testify."

Samantha blinked in surprise, trying to process what he was saying. "Testify? You're serious?"

Turner nodded. "A few of them have already come forward. They've been watching from the sidelines, waiting to see if someone would take down Pharmatech. After the broadcast and the media frenzy, they've decided it's time to speak up."

Samantha felt a strange mix of emotions. "I didn't think anyone else would step forward... not with how dangerous this is."

Turner leaned back in his chair, his eyes sharp. "They're still scared, but they've seen what you've done. It's given them courage. They think they can help."

Samantha let out a slow breath, her mind racing. This could change everything. With former employees corroborating her claims, the case against Pharmatech would gain serious momentum. It wouldn't just be her word against theirs anymore—it would be a unified front.

"Who are these people?" she asked, leaning forward, her curiosity piqued. "What did they do at Pharmatech?"

Turner pulled out a file and handed it to her. "The first one is a woman named Lisa Grant. She worked in the research division, handling data from the human trials. She's got documents, internal memos—proof that Pharmatech knew about the deaths in those trials and covered them up."

Samantha flipped through the file, her heart pounding as she scanned the details. "This... this is incredible."

"There's more," Turner added, his voice growing more intense. "Another employee, Mark Wills, worked in their finance department. He was part of the team that managed the payments to government officials. He's willing to testify about the bribes Pharmatech paid to keep everything under wraps."

Samantha stared at Turner, almost unable to believe what she was hearing. "This could blow the whole case wide open."

Turner nodded. "It could. But you need to know that the minute these people step forward, Pharmatech's going to ramp up their attacks on you. They'll come at you harder than ever."

Samantha frowned, the weight of his words sinking in. "I know. But we can't turn back now. If these employees are willing to stand with us, we have to move forward."

Turner studied her for a moment, his expression unreadable. "You're right. But I need you to be ready, Sam. These aren't small fish we're dealing with. Pharmatech has connections, power. They'll make it personal."

"They already have," she said, her voice firm. "They've been going after me for weeks. And I'm still here."

Turner smiled, though there was a flicker of concern in his eyes. "I know. But this is going to get a lot uglier."

Samantha set the file down and looked up at Turner, her resolve hardening. "Let them try. I didn't come this far to back down because they're throwing more dirt my way."

Turner nodded, satisfied with her determination. "All right. I'll set up meetings with the former employees, and we'll coordinate their testimonies with the legal team."

As Turner left the room, Samantha's mind swirled with the possibilities. For the first time in weeks, she felt a glimmer of hope. The fight wasn't over, but for the first time, it felt like the tide might be turning in her favor. If these employees could provide the evidence they promised, Pharmatech would have no choice but to face the consequences of their actions.

But even as she felt the momentum shifting, Samantha knew Turner was right—this new support made her an even bigger target. Pharmatech wouldn't go down quietly, and they would use every resource at their disposal to discredit her and anyone associated with her.

Her phone buzzed, pulling her from her thoughts. It was a news alert, and as she opened it, her heart sank. The latest headline read: **"Samantha Cross: Hero or Rogue? Former Colleagues Speak Out About Her Obsession with Revenge."**

She scrolled through the article, her stomach twisting. Pharmatech's media machine was in full swing, and they had found people willing to speak against her—former coworkers, acquaintances, anyone who could cast doubt on her integrity. They were painting her as unstable, driven by personal grudges, twisting her motives into something sinister.

She closed the article and set the phone down, her mind racing. She had expected this, but it still stung. No matter how much truth she uncovered, Pharmatech had the power to manipulate the public narrative.

But she wouldn't let it stop her. The truth was out there, and more was coming. The former employees stepping forward could be the key to finally breaking Pharmatech's stranglehold on power. And despite the attacks on her character, despite the growing dangers, she knew one thing for certain: she wouldn't back down.

As she stared out the window, her resolve only grew stronger. Pharmatech could try to discredit her all they wanted. But she had the truth on her side, and now, she had allies willing to stand with her.

The battle was far from over, but for the first time, Samantha felt like she had the upper hand.

The news coverage had shifted dramatically. What had started as a barrage of attacks on Samantha's character, an orchestrated smear campaign by Pharmatech's PR machine, was now being overshadowed by a groundswell of support from international media outlets. Headlines from reputable publications across

Europe and Asia framed her as a courageous whistleblower, a symbol of the fight against unchecked corporate power. Samantha sat in the living room of their safe house, scrolling through the flood of articles on her laptop, the change in tone striking.

"Samantha Cross: The Woman Who Took on a Giant"
"Whistleblower Who Exposed Pharmatech Corruption Gains Global Support"
"A Lone Voice Against Corporate Greed: Cross Becomes a Symbol for Change"

The media momentum was undeniable. People around the world were starting to see the truth for what it was—an enormous, systemic abuse of power. And Samantha, once painted as a vengeful rogue, was now the face of that truth.

"Looks like you've got fans," Turner said from the doorway, breaking her concentration. He crossed the room with his usual calm demeanor, though there was a lightness in his step that hadn't been there before. "The Guardian, Le Monde, even Al Jazeera—they're all backing you now. Not bad for someone they called a conspiracy theorist a week ago."

Samantha closed the laptop and sighed. "I didn't sign up for the fame, Turner. This wasn't supposed to be about me."

Turner shrugged, dropping into the chair across from her. "You exposed the biggest corporate scandal in decades. People are going to pay attention, whether you like it or not. But this is a good thing. The more people rally behind you, the harder it gets for Pharmatech to tear you down."

"I know," Samantha said, though her voice was distant. "But it also means the stakes are even higher now."

Turner tilted his head, studying her. "What's really bothering you?"

Samantha hesitated before answering. "I'm not naive, Turner. All this attention—it's great for the case, but it also makes me a bigger target. Pharmatech has friends, powerful friends, and they're not going to let this go without a fight. If they can't discredit me publicly, they'll try to take me out another way."

Turner leaned forward, his voice serious. "You're not wrong. With the spotlight on you, you're more valuable—and more dangerous—to them than ever. But you've got people watching your back now. We've come this far, Sam. We can't start doubting ourselves."

Samantha sighed, rubbing her temples. "It's not just doubt. I'm getting threats, Turner. Every day, there's a new email, a new message telling me to back off, to drop the case. They're getting more specific."

Turner's expression darkened. "Have you told the team about this?"

"Not yet," she admitted. "I didn't want to worry anyone. But some of them… they're not from random trolls. They're from people who know where we are, who know too much about my life."

Turner stood abruptly, his eyes sharp with alarm. "Why the hell didn't you tell me sooner?"

Samantha shrugged, trying to downplay it, but her voice wavered. "Because what are we going to do? We're already in hiding. What's the next step? Go deeper underground? I can't keep running forever, Turner."

He paced the room, his fists clenched. "These aren't empty threats, Sam. If they've found a way to get to you, that means we need to tighten our security. We're not just dealing with Pharmatech anymore. These are the shadowy allies you were worried about."

Samantha bit her lip, the weight of his words sinking in. "You think it's them, don't you? The people behind Pharmatech?"

Turner stopped pacing and turned to face her. "It makes sense. Pharmatech's power is crumbling, but the people who benefited from their corruption aren't going down without a fight. They'll do whatever it takes to protect themselves."

Samantha nodded slowly, her mind racing. The threats weren't just about silencing her anymore. They were a warning. A signal that the real battle had just begun. "So what do we do?"

Turner's jaw tightened as he considered the options. "We stay ahead of them. We use the media support to our advantage. Keep shining the light on Pharmatech and their allies. The more public this gets, the harder it'll be for them to make a move in the shadows."

She sighed, leaning back in her chair. "That sounds good in theory, but what if they're not afraid of the spotlight anymore?

What if they're willing to do whatever it takes, no matter how public it is?"

Turner crouched in front of her, his voice low but resolute. "Then we fight them with everything we've got. You're not alone in this, Sam. And they know that. The media, the legal system, the people—they're all on your side now. We use that momentum to push back harder than they can."

Samantha met his gaze, the intensity of his words filling her with a renewed sense of determination. She was tired—exhausted, even—but she couldn't back down now. Not when the world was finally listening. Not when she had the power to make real change.

"I'm not afraid of them," she said, her voice firm. "I just… I didn't expect it to get this far."

Turner smiled, though there was a hint of sadness behind it. "None of us did. But you've been leading this fight from the start, and you're not about to give up now. We'll protect you, Sam. No matter what."

Samantha nodded, the knot of fear in her chest loosening just slightly. The threats were real, the danger was growing, but so was the support. International journalists were now digging deeper into Pharmatech's connections, and public pressure was mounting. The media was turning the tide in her favor, and Pharmatech's remaining power brokers were scrambling.

But she knew, deep down, that this was only the beginning of the next phase of the battle. The real threats were still out there, lurking in the shadows. And they wouldn't stop until she was silenced—or until she brought them all down.

"We push forward," Samantha said, standing up, her resolve hardening. "We expose everything. And we don't stop until Pharmatech and their allies have nowhere left to hide."

Turner nodded, his face serious but filled with quiet pride. "Then let's get to work."

The safe house was quieter than usual. The legal battle against Pharmatech had been raging for weeks, with no signs of slowing down, but for the first time in months, the team was all together. Samantha sat at the head of the table, her gaze moving across the familiar faces of those who had fought alongside her. They were tired, worn down by the endless pressure, but they were still here. At least for now.

Turner sat to her left, his posture relaxed but his eyes as sharp as ever. He'd been her constant ally, the one person who had never wavered. Across from him, Alex fiddled with a loose cable on his laptop, always connected to something, always on alert. Rachel sat near the window, her expression distant, her eyes reflecting the toll this fight had taken on her. There was a heaviness in the room that none of them could ignore.

Samantha cleared her throat, drawing everyone's attention. "I know we've been through a lot," she began, her voice quiet but steady. "And I know I've asked more of you than I ever had any right to. But I wanted to get us all together today because... well, I think we all need some closure."

Rachel's eyes flicked to hers, a mixture of relief and sadness in them. "Closure," she echoed softly, almost as if testing the word.

Samantha nodded. "This fight isn't over—far from it. The legal battles are just starting to heat up, and there are still so many people out there—powerful people—who will do anything to keep the truth buried. But we've done something important. We've exposed them. We've shown the world what they are, and because of that, we've made a difference."

There was a moment of silence before Alex spoke up, his voice tinged with exhaustion. "It doesn't feel like it sometimes. Like we're just getting dragged deeper and deeper into this mess."

Samantha gave him a soft smile. "I know it feels that way. And maybe it'll feel like that for a while. But what we've done—it's already having an impact. Pharmatech's board is crumbling, and the media is digging deeper into the corruption we uncovered. Investigations are starting all over the world. We lit the spark, Alex, and that matters."

Turner leaned forward, his eyes meeting Samantha's. "It's going to get harder before it gets easier. You know that, right? They'll keep coming for us. The people backing Pharmatech won't just let this go."

"I do know," Samantha replied, her voice firm. "But I'm ready for it. And I'm ready to keep fighting. But I also know that not everyone can keep going the way we have. This battle—it's taken a toll on all of us."

Rachel shifted in her seat, her hands clasped tightly in her lap. "You don't have to sugarcoat it, Sam. We've all paid a price. Some more than others."

Samantha turned to her, her voice softening. "I know, Rachel. I know how much this has cost you. And I don't blame you if you need to step away."

Rachel looked down, her fingers tightening around her hands. "I'm proud of what we've done. I really am. But… I can't keep living like this. The threats, the pressure—it's not just me anymore. My family's worried sick, and I don't want them to have to live in fear."

Samantha nodded, her heart heavy. "I understand. You've given so much already, and no one will think any less of you for stepping back. You deserve peace, Rachel. After everything we've been through, you deserve that."

Rachel swallowed hard, blinking back tears. "I just hope… I hope you know I'm not giving up on what we started. I just can't be in the middle of it anymore. I need to take care of myself."

Samantha reached across the table, squeezing Rachel's hand gently. "You've earned that. And you've done more than most people ever would. You helped expose one of the biggest corporate scandals in history. No one can take that from you."

Rachel gave a small, grateful smile, though the sadness in her eyes lingered. "Thanks, Sam. I just... I need to breathe again, you know?"

Samantha nodded. "I get it."

There was a long pause before Turner spoke again, his tone lighter than before. "Well, I'm not going anywhere," he said, a half-smile tugging at the corner of his mouth. "Someone's got to make sure you don't get yourself killed out there."

Samantha chuckled softly. "I'd be lost without you, Turner."

He gave her a firm nod, his eyes gleaming with determination. "You're not going to lose me. We've still got work to do. The world might know about Pharmatech now, but there's a lot more under the surface. And I'm here for the long haul."

Alex glanced up from his laptop, offering a rare smile. "Same here. I mean, who else is going to keep us from getting hacked every five minutes?"

Samantha laughed, the sound light but filled with emotion. "I'm lucky to have you guys."

Turner raised an eyebrow. "You're not lucky, Sam. You earned this. You earned every bit of it. And we're with you because we believe in what we're doing."

Rachel stood, pushing her chair back with a heavy sigh. "I might not be in the trenches with you anymore, but I'll always be on your side. You know that, right?"

Samantha stood as well, pulling Rachel into a tight hug. "I know. And we'll always be here if you need us."

When they finally pulled apart, Rachel gave a nod to the rest of the team. "Take care of yourselves. All of you."

"We will," Turner said, his voice low but filled with certainty.

As Rachel walked toward the door, a weight lifted from the room. Samantha knew it was the right decision for her, even if it hurt to see her go. She turned back to the table, her gaze moving from Turner to Alex, and she felt a surge of renewed strength.

"We keep going," Samantha said quietly. "For Elias. For everyone Pharmatech hurt. We keep going until the fight is finished."

Turner gave a nod of agreement. "We'll finish what we started. Together."

And with that, the next chapter of their battle began.

Chapter 14
The First Strike

Samantha stood at the edge of the city park, the late afternoon sun casting long shadows on the empty benches and pathways. It was eerily quiet for such a busy area, and that alone set her on edge. She had come here because the message had said it was urgent—an anonymous tip that promised to reveal the last piece of the puzzle. She wasn't naïve enough to trust it blindly, but after everything, she couldn't ignore any possible lead.

As she scanned the surroundings, her phone buzzed in her hand. It was a simple message, just two words: *Turn around.*

Her heart skipped a beat, but she didn't hesitate. Slowly, she turned, her eyes locking onto a figure standing across the park. He was tall, dressed in a dark suit that screamed power and wealth, the kind of man who wasn't used to hearing "no." His presence felt wrong here, out in the open, too exposed for someone who moved in the shadows. But then again, this wasn't a man who feared exposure.

"Samantha Cross," the man said, his voice smooth, almost too friendly for the way he watched her. "I'm glad you came."

Samantha kept her expression neutral, but her pulse quickened. "Who are you?"

He smiled, but it didn't reach his eyes. "My name's not important. But what I represent is. Let's just say I'm here on behalf of some very powerful people."

"Pharmatech," Samantha said, her voice steady, though the tension in her chest grew tighter.

"Among others," he replied, taking a step closer. "We have mutual interests, you and I. You've stirred up quite a storm with your little crusade, haven't you?"

She crossed her arms, keeping her posture defensive but calm. "I didn't start this to make friends."

The man chuckled, his tone condescending. "No, I imagine you didn't. But here's the thing, Samantha. What you've done—it's impressive. You've hurt some very powerful people. But it's also time for you to stop."

Samantha clenched her jaw, a wave of anger surging through her. "Stop?"

"You've made your point," he said, his tone like that of a teacher speaking to a wayward student. "Pharmatech is crumbling, the media's in a frenzy, and everyone's watching. But you know as well as I do that this isn't just about Pharmatech anymore. There are other forces at play. Bigger forces. And those forces aren't going to tolerate any more interference from you."

Samantha's heart raced, but she refused to let him see her fear. "You think you can intimidate me into backing down?"

He tilted his head, as if genuinely considering her question. "It's not about intimidation, Samantha. It's about understanding. You've pushed hard enough. You've won. But there's a line, and if you cross it… well, let's just say your life becomes a lot more difficult."

She took a step toward him, her eyes narrowing. "Are you threatening me?"

The man's smile widened, but his eyes remained cold. "Threats are so crass. I prefer to think of it as offering you a choice. You've made enemies, powerful ones, but you still have a way out. Walk away now, and all of this—the lawsuits, the investigations—it'll settle down. You can go back to your life, be the hero in the public eye. But keep pushing? You won't like what happens next."

Samantha felt a surge of the same fear she had felt when this all started, when the weight of what she was up against had first crashed down on her. But this time, there was something else— something stronger. She had come too far to let this man, or the shadowy figures behind him, scare her into silence.

"You don't get it, do you?" she said, her voice firm. "I'm not walking away. Not now, not ever. You can throw all the threats you want at me, but I won't stop."

The man's smile faded, his expression darkening. "I don't think you understand what's at stake here, Samantha."

"Oh, I understand perfectly," she shot back, her voice rising. "This isn't just about Pharmatech anymore, is it? This is about the entire system that let them get away with what they did. You and your 'powerful people' are scared, and you should be."

His eyes flashed with irritation, and he stepped closer, his voice dropping to a low, dangerous tone. "You think you're untouchable? You're not. I could make one call, right now, and you'd disappear. No one would ever know what happened to you."

Samantha's heart pounded in her chest, but she stood her ground. "Maybe you could. But if I disappear, if anything happens to me, the whole world will know exactly who's behind it. Do you really want that kind of attention?"

The man stared at her, his jaw clenched. For a moment, neither of them moved, the tension between them crackling like electricity. Finally, he spoke, his voice cold. "You're making a mistake."

Samantha shook her head. "The only mistake I'd make is backing down now. You can try to scare me, but it won't work. I'm not afraid of you."

He studied her for a long moment, then let out a slow breath. "You should be."

With that, he turned and walked away, his figure quickly disappearing into the shadows of the park. Samantha stood there for a moment, her heart still racing, the echoes of the confrontation lingering in her mind. The fear was still there, deep in her chest, but she wouldn't let it control her. Not anymore.

She had faced worse than this. And no matter how many threats they sent her way, she wouldn't stop. They could try to intimidate her, but she had something they didn't—truth, and the courage to keep fighting for it.

As she walked away from the park, her phone buzzed again. This time, it was Turner. "Everything okay?" he asked, his voice tense.

Samantha smiled to herself, her resolve solidifying. "Yeah, everything's fine. We've got a lot of work ahead, but I'm ready for it."

"Good," Turner replied, the relief clear in his voice. "Because it's not over yet."

Samantha slipped her phone back into her pocket, the weight of the encounter still lingering, but her determination stronger than ever. No matter what came next, she would be ready. She wasn't fighting just for herself—she was fighting for everyone who had been hurt, silenced, or exploited. And that was something no threat could ever take away from her.

The tension from her encounter with the mysterious man lingered in Samantha's mind as she left the park. Each step felt heavier, and though her defiance had been real, the weight of the threats against her gnawed at the edges of her resolve. She was no stranger to danger, but this felt different. This man wasn't just issuing empty words; he had the resources and the connections to make good on his promise.

Her phone buzzed again, pulling her from her thoughts. It was Turner, his voice steady but edged with urgency. "Where are you?"

"I'm on my way back," she replied, keeping her voice even.

"Don't. Come to the warehouse," Turner said. "Now."

Samantha's heart skipped a beat. The warehouse was one of their off-the-grid locations, rarely used unless there was a serious security threat. "What's going on?"

"I'll explain when you get here," Turner's tone left no room for argument.

Samantha hailed a cab, her mind racing as she processed the urgency in his voice. The ride felt like an eternity, but soon she found herself outside the nondescript building on the outskirts of the city. Turner was waiting for her by the entrance, his sharp gaze scanning the surroundings before he waved her inside.

As the heavy door closed behind her, Turner led her into the dimly lit interior, where Alex was already at a desk, surrounded by monitors. Rachel had left the team, but it seemed the rest of them were still deeply entrenched in the fight.

"What's going on?" Samantha asked, her eyes moving between Turner and Alex.

Turner didn't waste any time. "That man you met today—he's not just a nobody. He's part of a network of power players who've been pulling the strings behind Pharmatech for years.

They're not happy with you, Sam. They're afraid of what you might do next."

Samantha crossed her arms, her mind flashing back to the cold, calculated way the man had tried to intimidate her. "He told me to back off, that if I kept pushing, they'd make me disappear."

Turner's jaw tightened. "That's not an empty threat. I've been digging, and it turns out this guy—his name's Richard Bowen—he's part of a much larger operation. Pharmatech's fall is just a small piece of what they're trying to protect."

Samantha's stomach twisted. "So they're not just after me because of Pharmatech. They're trying to silence me before I uncover whatever comes next."

"Exactly," Turner said, his voice grim. "And they're escalating. We've intercepted communications between some of these higher-ups. They're discussing more 'permanent' ways to deal with you."

Samantha took a breath, the familiar fear tightening her chest. "So what do we do?"

Alex swiveled in his chair, typing furiously as he brought up files on the monitors. "We've been tracking Bowen's movements, trying to get ahead of whatever they're planning. He's scheduled a meeting with several key players tomorrow night—high-end restaurant, private rooms, the works."

Turner stepped forward, his voice low but firm. "We're going to use this meeting to get to him before he can act. You've rattled them, Sam. They're scared of what you know and what you could expose. If we can take Bowen out of play, we'll weaken their grip."

Samantha frowned, her thoughts racing. "But we're not just talking about Bowen, are we? There are others."

Turner nodded. "He's the face of it right now, but he's not the only one. This is a network, and we'll have to dismantle it piece by piece. Bowen's the immediate threat. We deal with him first."

"And how do you plan to do that?" Samantha asked, her eyes searching Turner's face for answers.

Turner leaned in closer, lowering his voice. "We neutralize him, quietly. No media, no public exposure yet. We gather what we need and force his hand. He has connections, but we know how to use that against him."

Samantha's heart pounded. "You want to confront him directly?"

Turner's eyes were sharp, unwavering. "Yes. But I'll handle it. You've done enough. They won't see me coming, and I know how to make sure he doesn't walk away from this without giving us what we need."

Samantha shook her head. "I'm not sitting on the sidelines for this, Turner. He came after me. He threatened me."

Turner's expression softened, but his voice remained firm. "I know. But if you're there, you'll be their primary target. I can move in and out before they know what's happening."

Alex chimed in, not looking away from his screen. "Turner's right, Sam. We've traced some chatter, and they're watching you. Bowen's people might already be keeping tabs on your movements."

Samantha clenched her fists. "So what? I hide while you put yourself in danger?"

Turner stepped closer, his tone calming but resolute. "I'm trained for this. You're the key to all of this, Sam. If something happens to you, everything falls apart. Let me handle Bowen. We'll get what we need, and you'll stay safe."

Samantha wanted to argue, to demand that she be part of the confrontation, but she knew deep down that Turner was right. He was tactical, methodical. He could get in and out without them even knowing he was there.

"Fine," she said, though her voice was tight with frustration. "But you keep me updated. I want to know everything."

Turner nodded. "I will. But trust me on this, Sam. We're not letting them win. Not after everything."

Samantha looked at him for a long moment before finally letting out a breath. "Okay. But be careful. I can't lose anyone else."

Turner gave her a reassuring smile. "You won't. This ends tomorrow."

As Turner and Alex moved into action, setting the final pieces of their plan in motion, Samantha watched them with a growing sense of unease. The final confrontation was coming, and while Turner was ready to face it, she knew that this battle, like all the others, would be dangerous.

She had faced so many threats along the way—corporate cover-ups, media smear campaigns, personal attacks—but now, she was dealing with the remnants of Pharmatech's most dangerous allies. And she was determined to see it through to the end, no matter the cost.

The courtroom was packed. Reporters filled the gallery, their pens poised, waiting to capture the verdict that would echo across industries and governments worldwide. The tension in the air was palpable as the judge entered, his robes sweeping behind him. Samantha sat at the front of the courtroom, her hands clasped together tightly in her lap. Turner was beside her, his presence grounding as always, though his expression was serious. He knew, just as she did, that this moment was critical.

"All rise," the bailiff intoned, and the courtroom shuffled to its feet. The judge nodded to the assembled crowd and took his seat, flipping through the case files on his desk. Samantha's heart raced as she stole a glance at the opposing side. The key figures of Pharmatech sat at their table, their expressions a mixture of steely resolve and thinly veiled fear. Today, the courts would decide their fate.

The judge's voice was firm, but without drama, as he began reading his judgment. "After careful consideration of the evidence presented, and in light of the overwhelming proof of corporate malfeasance, bribery, illegal human trials, and the cover-up of fatalities, this court finds the defendants guilty of all charges."

A collective breath seemed to leave the room, the weight of the moment pressing down on everyone present. Samantha closed her eyes for just a second, the rush of relief mixed with a bittersweet sense of finality washing over her. The room was silent as the judge continued, listing the specific charges and the sentences to be carried out. Each name called, each sentence handed down, felt like a small piece of justice delivered.

"Mr. Andrew Moss," the judge intoned, his voice flat, "you are sentenced to 25 years in federal prison for your role in orchestrating the illegal human trials and for the gross violations of ethics and law under your leadership at Pharmatech."

Samantha watched as Moss, once one of the most powerful men in the pharmaceutical industry, stood stone-faced, his hands clasped behind his back. He didn't flinch, but there was a slight tremor in his jaw that betrayed the truth: he knew it was over.

"Mr. Henry Driscoll," the judge continued, "you are sentenced to 18 years in prison for your part in covering up these atrocities, including falsifying reports and bribing government officials to turn a blind eye."

Turner leaned in, whispering to Samantha, "It's really happening. They're going down."

She nodded slightly, her heart still pounding. It was surreal. After all the months of investigation, the countless sleepless nights, the fear, the threats—this was it. The people responsible for so much pain and suffering were finally being held accountable.

But the feeling of victory was tempered by something darker. As the judge read the last of the sentences, Samantha couldn't help but think about all the others—the nameless, faceless victims whose lives had been destroyed by Pharmatech's greed. Some had died without ever knowing what was done to them, others had been silenced long before she'd had the chance to uncover the truth.

The judge's voice cut through her thoughts. "This ruling sets a new precedent for corporate accountability in the medical industry. It is this court's hope that it will serve as a warning to other companies, that no one is above the law, and that whistleblowers like Miss Cross deserve protection, not persecution."

Samantha felt a swell of emotion at the mention of her name. She hadn't done this for recognition—she had done it because it was the right thing to do—but hearing the court acknowledge her role was something she hadn't expected. It was a victory, no doubt, but it came with a heavy cost.

After the judge finished, the courtroom erupted into murmurs. Reporters rushed to file their stories, lawyers whispered in hushed tones, and the Pharmatech defendants were escorted out in handcuffs, their expressions grim. Samantha stayed seated, watching it all unfold around her.

Turner put a hand on her shoulder. "You did it."

She exhaled slowly, the weight of the moment settling in. "We did it. But it doesn't feel like enough."

Turner frowned. "What do you mean? These guys are going away for a long time."

Samantha shook her head, her voice low. "It's not just them. Pharmatech was a symptom, not the disease. There are still so many people out there—so many systems in place—that will let this kind of thing happen again."

Turner was quiet for a moment, then he nodded. "You're right. This fight isn't over. But you made a huge difference today, Sam. You've set the stage for change."

Samantha glanced at the media frenzy happening just outside the courtroom doors. She knew her face would be plastered across headlines again, heralded as the whistleblower who took down Pharmatech. It would send a message, no doubt. But the bitter truth was that there were still many like Pharmatech, lurking in the shadows, waiting for their moment to strike.

"Do you think it'll be enough?" she asked, her voice softer now.

Turner looked at her, his eyes serious. "It's a start. And that's more than most people ever get. You've inspired others, Sam. There will be more whistleblowers because of what you've done. People will speak out because you showed them it's possible."

Samantha nodded, her gaze distant as she thought about the road ahead. "I hope so. Because this isn't the end. Not for me, and not for the fight."

Turner stood, offering her his hand. "One battle at a time."

She took his hand, standing alongside him as the courtroom began to clear. As they walked toward the exit, the sounds of reporters and flashing cameras grew louder. The world outside was waiting for her, eager to hear her story.

Samantha paused just before the door, turning to Turner with a small smile. "Let's give them something to remember."

Turner chuckled. "You always do."

They stepped into the spotlight, the battle won, but the war far from over.

The sun was setting over Elmsbrook, casting the town in a warm, golden glow. Samantha stood outside the safe house for what she knew would be the last time. The weight of the recent legal victory still clung to her, bittersweet and heavy, but the relief was short-lived. This chapter was closing, but a new one was already beginning to take shape.

Turner walked out of the house, joining her as they stood in the cool evening air. "You sure you're ready to leave all this behind?" he asked, his tone light but carrying the underlying seriousness that marked everything between them these days.

Samantha smiled, though there was a touch of sadness in it. "It's not about leaving it behind," she said. "It's about moving forward. Elmsbrook served its purpose. I got what I came for."

Turner nodded, leaning against the doorframe. "Yeah, but what about you? You've been running on fumes for months. Maybe it's time to take a break, Sam. You earned it."

She sighed, running her fingers through her hair as she looked out at the fading horizon. "I thought about it. But I can't, Turner. There's too much left to do."

Turner raised an eyebrow, sensing there was more. "You've got something on your mind. What is it?"

Samantha hesitated for a moment, then reached into her jacket and pulled out her phone. She scrolled through the messages until she found the one she had been replaying in her mind since she'd received it.

"I got a tip," she said, handing the phone to Turner. "About another case. Different company, but the same kind of corruption. It's happening again, Turner. I can't just sit by and watch."

Turner glanced at the message, then back at her, his expression unreadable. "When did you get this?"

"Two days ago," she admitted, meeting his gaze. "I didn't want to say anything until the trial was over. But it's serious, Turner. The person who reached out... they're scared. They don't know where to turn, and I can't ignore it."

Turner sighed, rubbing the back of his neck as he handed the phone back to her. "You're really going to dive back in, aren't you?"

Samantha nodded, her resolve solidifying. "I have to. There's no one else who will."

Turner studied her for a long moment before finally shaking his head, a small smile tugging at the corner of his mouth. "You never stop, do you?"

She returned the smile, though her eyes were serious. "Not when it comes to this."

They stood in silence for a moment, the weight of the decision hanging in the air between them. Turner finally broke the quiet, his tone thoughtful. "Where's the lead taking you this time?"

"West Coast," she said. "Big tech company. They're involved in something similar to Pharmatech—illegal experimentation, covering up deaths. It's all very hush-hush right now, but the person who contacted me says they have evidence."

Turner let out a low whistle. "So, you're going to jump right back into the fire?"

Samantha shrugged. "What else is there? I can't just let it go. These people need someone who's not afraid to take them on."

Turner's expression softened. "And that someone's always going to be you, huh?"

She smiled, a quiet confidence settling over her. "Yeah, I guess it is."

The door to the safe house creaked open behind them, and Alex stepped out, his ever-present laptop bag slung over his shoulder. "I heard something about the West Coast. Are we packing up already?"

Samantha turned, her smile widening. "You didn't think we'd stop here, did you?"

Alex shrugged, his familiar deadpan tone cutting through the moment. "Figured you might want a vacation. But no, of course not. We're going straight back into the chaos, right?"

Samantha chuckled. "You're catching on."

Turner crossed his arms, looking between them. "You know what this means, right? It means more threats, more danger. Maybe worse than before."

"I know," Samantha said, her voice firm. "But this is what we do now. We're not just fighting for Elias or for Pharmatech's victims anymore. We're fighting for everyone they've hurt, and everyone they'll hurt if we don't stop them."

Alex gave a slight nod, his voice softening. "I'm with you, Sam. Whatever comes next."

Turner sighed, but the smile on his face told her he wasn't going anywhere either. "Well, looks like we're all in this together again. Just promise me one thing."

"What's that?" Samantha asked, raising an eyebrow.

"Promise me we'll stay one step ahead this time," Turner said. "I'm not looking to get ambushed by any more shadowy corporate hitmen."

Samantha laughed, the sound light but full of determination. "I'll do my best."

As the sun dipped below the horizon, casting the last of its golden light over the town, Samantha felt a sense of closure settling over her. Elmsbrook had been the beginning—a battle hard-fought and hard-won—but the war was far from over. There were new enemies to face, new truths to uncover. And she was stronger now, more determined than ever.

"We leave tomorrow," she said, her voice steady. "We'll follow the lead, get to the truth, and keep pushing forward."

Turner nodded, his eyes gleaming with the same fire she felt burning in her chest. "Then let's get to work."

As they walked back into the house to prepare for the next phase of their journey, Samantha allowed herself one last look at the place that had changed everything. Elmsbrook had been a battleground, a crucible that had tested her in ways she hadn't imagined. But now, she was leaving it behind, ready to face whatever came next.

She wasn't just a whistleblower anymore. She was a force. And nothing would stop her.

Chapter 15
The Betrayal

The wind was crisp and cool as Samantha stood on the balcony of a small hotel on the West Coast, overlooking the sprawling city below. It had been days since she and her team had arrived, the fresh case already beginning to consume her attention. But tonight, for a few quiet moments, she let herself step back and reflect, the weight of everything they had endured settling heavily on her shoulders.

In the distance, the ocean's waves crashed rhythmically against the shore, a calming contrast to the whirlwind that had been her life over the past year. She had been through battles, both in the courtroom and in the streets, against people who wielded far more power than she had ever imagined. And yet, she had survived.

But survival had come at a cost.

Turner stepped out onto the balcony, his presence familiar and grounding. "Thought I'd find you out here," he said quietly, leaning on the railing beside her. "You've been in your head a lot these past few days."

Samantha smiled faintly, not taking her eyes off the horizon. "Yeah. Just thinking."

"About what?" Turner asked, though his tone was soft enough to tell her he already had an idea.

She sighed, letting the weight of her thoughts spill out. "About everything. About what we've done, what we've lost, and what it's cost us to get here."

Turner nodded, his gaze following hers. "You've been carrying a lot on your shoulders, Sam. More than anyone should have to."

"I chose this," she said quietly, her voice steady but tired. "From the moment I decided to take on Pharmatech, I knew it wasn't going to be easy. I just… I didn't know how hard it would really be."

Turner looked at her, his expression softened with concern. "No one could've known. But we did it. You did it. And it made a difference."

Samantha turned to face him, her eyes reflecting the depth of what she'd been holding back. "But at what cost? We lost people along the way, Turner. Rachel's gone. Elias—" She paused, swallowing back the familiar sting of grief. "We've all sacrificed something. And some days I wonder if I'm losing myself in all of this."

He was silent for a moment, then he spoke, his voice firm but kind. "You're still you, Sam. But yeah, this kind of fight changes people. It has to. But that's not always a bad thing."

She looked down, the memories of everything they had been through swirling in her mind—the endless threats, the nights when fear kept her awake, the constant uncertainty of what each new day would bring. It had been a relentless journey, one that had tested her in ways she hadn't been prepared for. And yet, despite everything, she had never felt more certain of her purpose.

"I don't regret it," she said, her voice growing stronger. "None of it. The fear, the loss—it was all worth it. Because people like Pharmatech, like the ones we're going after now, they can't be allowed to win. Someone has to stand up to them."

Turner smiled, a faint but proud expression on his face. "That someone's always going to be you, isn't it?"

Samantha let out a soft laugh, shaking her head. "Maybe. I don't know if I'm capable of walking away anymore. There's always going to be another fight, another company hurting people to make a profit. How can I turn my back on that?"

Turner gave her a knowing look. "You can't. But you don't have to carry it all by yourself either. You've got people willing to stand with you. That counts for something."

She nodded, her gaze drifting back to the horizon. "I know. And I'm grateful for that. But at the end of the day, it's still a lonely path, isn't it? Fighting like this... it isolates you."

Turner didn't argue. He knew she was right. "Maybe. But the people you're fighting for—they may never know your name, but they'll feel the impact of what you've done. You've saved lives, Sam. You've changed the game. That's not a small thing."

Samantha allowed herself a moment to take that in. The victory against Pharmatech had been a turning point, not just for her but for so many others who had felt powerless against the corporate machine. It had given them hope. It had set a precedent.

"I learned a lot along the way," she said quietly, her voice carrying a weight of wisdom. "I learned that fighting for what's right doesn't mean you'll win every battle. And even when you do win, it's not always clean. It's messy. It hurts. But that's why it matters."

Turner nodded. "Yeah, it does."

She turned to face him fully now, her eyes filled with a quiet determination. "And I know it's not over. Not by a long shot. There are more like Pharmatech out there, more people willing to exploit, to hurt others for power and money. I can't walk away from that."

Turner's smile was gentle, but there was a fierceness behind it. "Good. Because the world needs more people like you."

Samantha allowed herself a small smile in return, though her mind was already on the next fight. She had sacrificed so much to get here, but the fight wasn't about her. It never had been. It was about the people who couldn't fight back, the victims who needed someone to stand up for them. That was what kept her going, what would always keep her going.

As the sun finally dipped below the horizon, leaving the sky awash in the soft glow of twilight, Samantha felt a renewed sense of purpose settle within her. The journey had changed her, but it had also made her stronger. And now, with new battles on the horizon, she was ready to move forward.

"Let's get ready," she said, her voice steady. "We've got a lot of work to do."

Turner grinned, the fire in his eyes matching hers. "Lead the way, Cross."

And with that, they turned back toward the next chapter, the next fight, and the new beginning that awaited them. The road ahead would be dangerous, but Samantha was ready. She knew what it meant to fight for what mattered, and she wasn't afraid of the cost anymore.

The familiar chime of her phone broke the stillness of the early morning. Samantha sat at a small café in the heart of the West Coast city, nursing a cup of coffee as she scanned through emails and messages. The overwhelming response to her victory against Pharmatech hadn't waned; if anything, it was growing. Each day, new messages poured in—some from media outlets requesting interviews, but more often from people she never expected to hear from.

Her phone buzzed again, and she opened the latest message. It was from a young woman in Argentina, the subject line stark and simple: **Thank you.**

The message itself was raw, personal:

"Samantha, my name is Lucia, and I've been following your story since the Pharmatech case broke. I work in a research lab here in Buenos Aires, and I've been seeing things... things that shouldn't be happening. For so long, I was afraid to say anything, afraid to lose my job or worse. But after

258

watching you take on Pharmatech, I've decided I can't stay silent anymore. You've shown me that standing up to people like them is possible. Thank you for giving me the courage to fight back. I'm not sure what happens next, but I'm not afraid anymore."

Samantha stared at the screen, the words sinking in. She could almost feel the fear and hope embedded in the message, as if the woman on the other side had poured all her anxiety and bravery into that short email. Her heart tightened. She had never expected her fight to inspire others in such a direct, personal way.

Before she could process it, another message came through, this one from a man in India.

"Miss Cross, my name is Rohit. I work in a factory that manufactures pharmaceuticals, and for years, I've watched them cut corners—using unsafe materials, lying about quality controls. I've tried to raise concerns, but I've been shut down at every turn. I thought no one cared. But after seeing what you did to Pharmatech, I realized it's not about waiting for someone else to fix things. It's about us, the people, taking a stand. I've begun organizing my coworkers. We're going to speak out. Thank you for leading the way."

Samantha shook her head in disbelief. She had known, of course, that the Pharmatech case would send ripples across industries, that it would force corporations to rethink how they operated. But this? These personal stories, these brave souls reaching out from every corner of the world—it was more than she had ever imagined.

Turner walked into the café, his jacket slung over his shoulder. He spotted her at the corner table and made his way over, his usual calm demeanor in place. "You're up early," he said as he slid into the chair opposite her.

Samantha smiled slightly, still absorbing the impact of the messages. "Yeah, couldn't sleep much. The usual."

Turner raised an eyebrow, glancing at her phone. "What's got you so focused?"

She handed him her phone, letting him read the messages for himself. As Turner scrolled through the emails, his expression shifted from curiosity to quiet understanding. "Wow. They're really reaching out to you, huh?"

"More than I expected," Samantha said, leaning back in her chair. "I've gotten messages like these from all over— Argentina, India, South Africa… People who've been afraid to speak up for years. Now they're saying they're ready to fight back."

Turner set the phone down on the table, his eyes meeting hers. "That's because of you, Sam. You showed them it can be done. That it's worth the risk."

She shook her head, a hint of disbelief still lingering in her voice. "I never thought it would turn into this. I just wanted to expose the truth about Pharmatech, to stop them from hurting more people. But this… this is something bigger."

"Because you've sparked something," Turner said, his tone thoughtful. "It's not just about one company anymore. It's about people realizing they have power. You gave them the push they needed."

Samantha stared out the window, the early morning light casting long shadows across the street. "I guess I never saw myself as part of something like that. I always thought I was just fighting my own battles, trying to fix the wrongs in front of me."

"And you did," Turner said. "But sometimes when you fight your own battles, you end up leading a lot more people than you expected."

She smiled, the weight of his words sinking in. "I've never really thought of myself as a leader."

"Well, you are now," Turner said, his voice gentle but firm. "Whether you planned for it or not, people are looking to you, Sam. You've shown them what's possible, and they're going to keep looking to you for guidance."

Samantha felt a sense of purpose deepening within her. She had always known that the fight against corruption was bigger than just one company or one case, but now it was clear that the ripple effect of her actions had turned into a wave. There were others out there—brave individuals ready to take the risk, to expose the powerful forces exploiting them. And they were looking to her for strength.

"Do you think I'm ready for that?" she asked, her voice softer now.

Turner leaned back in his chair, his expression warm. "You've been ready for a long time. You just didn't know it."

Samantha smiled, feeling a mix of pride and responsibility settle over her. "There's so much more to do, Turner. So many more people to help."

"And you'll get to them," he said. "But you don't have to do it alone. These people who are reaching out? They're part of the fight now. You've started a movement, Sam. And movements don't rely on just one person. They grow."

She nodded, letting his words sink in. The messages kept coming, and with each one, her resolve only strengthened. It was no longer just about her battle—it was about all of them, the people around the world who were ready to stand up and fight.

With a deep breath, Samantha picked up her phone and began typing a response to Lucia.

"Thank you for your courage. Know that you're not alone. Keep fighting, and remember, together, we're stronger."

She sent the message and looked up at Turner, her eyes filled with determination. "It's time to move forward."

He smiled, nodding. "Lead the way."

Samantha sat at the long oak table in the rented office space, her laptop open in front of her, files spread out on every available surface. The space was bare, utilitarian—nothing more than a temporary headquarters for the next phase of her work. She'd rented it for the month, just long enough to gather new allies and strategize their next steps. The hum of the overhead lights buzzed softly, the only sound in the otherwise empty room.

It felt strange to be starting over, but it was also energizing. The messages she'd received over the past few weeks had sparked something inside her. This was bigger than just Pharmatech. There were hundreds of other corporations, governments, and institutions abusing their power, and people around the world were finally ready to fight back.

As she stared at the map on the wall—a visual representation of the many leads and whistleblowers that had reached out from all corners of the globe—her phone buzzed. She picked it up, smiling when she saw the name on the screen.

"Rachel," Samantha said warmly as she answered the call, leaning back in her chair.

"Hey, Sam," Rachel's voice came through, filled with a familiar lightness. "I heard you're starting to build a new team. I'm guessing you're calling in all the old favors?"

Samantha chuckled. "You know me too well. But I'm not going to ask you to come back into the trenches. I know you've earned your peace."

Rachel hesitated on the other end of the line. "Yeah, I've been enjoying the quiet. But that doesn't mean I'm not here for you.

Whatever support you need—advice, connections, even just someone to rant to—you know I've got your back."

"I know," Samantha said softly, her voice filled with gratitude. "I won't drag you into another storm. But I'll take you up on that support. You have no idea how much it means to know you're still in my corner."

"I wouldn't be anywhere else," Rachel replied. "Just because I'm stepping back doesn't mean I've stopped believing in what you're doing. You're making a difference, Sam. I'm proud of you."

Samantha's chest tightened with emotion. "Thanks, Rachel. That means a lot."

They talked for a few more minutes, catching up on life outside the fight. Rachel seemed content, finally finding some peace after everything they had been through. Samantha could hear the lightness in her voice and was glad that, for at least one of them, the weight of the world had eased.

When the call ended, Samantha set the phone down and took a deep breath. Rachel wasn't the only one who had stepped back from the fight, but she wasn't alone either. Her phone buzzed again, and this time it was Turner.

"How's it going in the new place?" Turner asked, his voice as steady and reliable as always.

"Quiet so far," Samantha said, glancing around the empty office. "But I'm getting ready to bring people in."

"You've already got a list, don't you?" Turner chuckled.

"Of course I do," Samantha replied, a smile tugging at her lips. "I've been reaching out to some of the people who contacted me after the Pharmatech case. Journalists, former investigators, a few whistleblowers who are still figuring out their next steps. It's coming together."

"I figured," Turner said. "I'm not surprised. You've always been good at rallying the troops."

Samantha leaned back, her tone more serious now. "What about you, Turner? Are you in this for the long haul? Or are you thinking about stepping back too?"

There was a pause on the other end of the line, but it didn't last long. "I'm not going anywhere, Sam. I told you before—this fight isn't over. I'm with you."

Relief flooded through her. "I'm glad. I didn't think I'd lose you, but… after everything we've been through, I wouldn't blame you if you wanted to disappear for a while."

Turner chuckled. "Nah. Besides, someone's gotta make sure you don't get yourself into too much trouble."

Samantha laughed. "That's true. And believe me, there's going to be plenty of trouble ahead."

"I'm counting on it," Turner replied, his voice filled with quiet confidence. "So, what's the plan?"

"I'm meeting with a few of the new people tomorrow," she said. "Journalists who've been working on some big cases involving corporate corruption. I think they'll be valuable allies moving forward. After that, I'll be reaching out to a few more whistleblowers who've been laying low. They need someone to help them figure out how to go public safely."

"Sounds like you've already got things rolling," Turner said approvingly.

"Yeah, but it's still early days," Samantha admitted. "It feels like we're building something new, something bigger than before. But it's going to take time."

"Good things usually do," Turner said. "But if anyone can make it happen, it's you."

Samantha smiled. "I couldn't do it without you."

"Wouldn't let you," he replied, and she could hear the grin in his voice.

After they hung up, Samantha stood and walked over to the large map pinned on the wall. Red pins marked key locations—places where corporate corruption had been reported, regions where whistleblowers had contacted her, leads on new investigations waiting to be followed. She reached out and touched one of the pins, thinking of the people behind each of those dots. They were waiting, hoping, and trusting her to lead the way.

Her phone buzzed again, this time a message from someone new—a former employee of a multinational oil company with

266

evidence of environmental violations and government payoffs. Samantha read the message and smiled to herself.

The fight was far from over. But this time, she wouldn't be alone. She was building a team—a network of people willing to expose the truth, to stand up against the forces that sought to exploit the vulnerable. And with each new ally, each new voice added to the fight, she felt the momentum building.

Samantha took a deep breath, her gaze fixed on the map. There was a long road ahead, filled with new battles, new risks, and new victories. But for the first time in a long while, she felt ready. The fight wasn't just hers anymore—it belonged to everyone who had joined her cause.

With a renewed sense of purpose, she picked up her phone and began drafting her next message. It was time to bring the team together.

The train rumbled beneath Samantha's feet as she sat by the window, watching the landscape blur past in shades of green and gold. The world outside seemed peaceful—far removed from the chaotic storms she had weathered over the past year. The cities, the corruption, the battles fought in courtrooms and corporate offices—they felt distant now. But Samantha knew better. That calm, serene world was an illusion. Behind it all, corruption was lurking, always ready to exploit, to silence, to destroy.

She sipped her coffee, feeling the warm bitterness spread through her as the train raced onward. The phone in her lap buzzed softly, but she let it sit there for a moment, savoring the brief stillness. The messages hadn't stopped since the trial. New leads, new allies, and more stories of corporate greed and abuses of power. It was overwhelming at times, but this was the path she had chosen.

Her phone buzzed again, pulling her back to reality. With a sigh, Samantha picked it up and glanced at the screen.

Turner: *You sure about this next step?*

Samantha smiled to herself, tapping out a quick reply.

Samantha: *You really asking me that?*

A few seconds later, her phone buzzed again.

Turner: *Just checking. You know me, I gotta make sure you're not biting off more than you can chew.*

She shook her head, smiling as she replied.

Samantha: *I always do, Turner. That's kind of my thing.*

The next message came almost immediately.

Turner: *Fair point. But seriously, don't hesitate to call. This one sounds even nastier than Pharmatech.*

Samantha leaned back, thinking about the next case waiting for her. It was a new beast—an international corporation with tendrils in everything from oil extraction to government contracts. The people who had reached out to her, whistleblowers from within the company, were terrified. And rightfully so. This wasn't just about cutting corners or bribing officials; it was about environmental devastation and human rights abuses. The scale was staggering.

But if anyone knew how to take down a giant, it was Samantha Cross.

She typed a final message before pocketing her phone.

Samantha: *I'll be careful, Turner. I've got this.*

She stared out the window for a moment, lost in thought. The last year had shaped her in ways she hadn't expected. The battle in Elmsbrook, the fight to expose Pharmatech, had pushed her to her limits—and beyond. She had learned how deep the rot went in these systems, and how far the powerful were willing to go to protect themselves. It had been exhausting, terrifying at times, but it had also been necessary. Elmsbrook had tested her resolve, and in the end, she had come out stronger.

The train slowed as it approached a small station. Samantha glanced at her reflection in the glass. Her face was calm, her eyes steady, but she could see the subtle changes—the lines of tension, the weight of responsibility that she carried now. She wasn't the same person who had arrived in Elmsbrook all those months ago, suspicious but uncertain of the full extent of what she was getting into.

Now, she knew exactly what she was up against. And she was ready for it.

As the train pulled into the station, the sound of her phone buzzing again broke the silence. This time, it wasn't Turner.

Alex: *You're going solo on this one? Not your usual style.*

She chuckled to herself before typing back.

Samantha: *Just for now. I'm meeting the whistleblowers on my own first. Easier to keep a low profile that way.*

His response was immediate.

Alex: *Keep me posted. I've got eyes on their digital trail. If anything looks sketchy, I'll let you know.*

Samantha appreciated the quiet support. Alex wasn't the type to join her on the ground, but his work behind the scenes had saved her more times than she could count. She could rely on him to dig up the digital dirt while she handled the face-to-face work. It was a good system. A necessary one.

Samantha: *Thanks, Alex. I'll touch base after the first meeting.*

The train came to a stop, and Samantha stood, gathering her things. She slipped her phone into her jacket pocket, mentally running through the details of her upcoming meeting. The whistleblowers were scared, but they were brave. That combination had a way of creating powerful allies—if they could trust her, and if she could protect them.

As she stepped off the train and onto the platform, the crisp air hit her, refreshing and invigorating. The city she had arrived in was bustling but anonymous—perfect for staying under the radar. She glanced up at the tall buildings, the streets crowded with people going about their lives, unaware of the battles being fought behind the scenes.

A voice came from behind her, familiar and steady.

"You really think this is the last one, Sam?"

She turned, surprised to see Turner standing there, hands in his jacket pockets, a knowing smile on his face.

"I thought you weren't coming," she said, though she couldn't hide her smile.

"Changed my mind," he shrugged. "Besides, you know me. Can't let you have all the fun."

Samantha laughed softly, shaking her head. "I appreciate the company. But you know this is just the beginning, right?"

Turner's grin widened. "Oh, I know. I've accepted that you'll never stop."

She looked out at the city again, her heart steady but full of anticipation. "The fight never really ends, does it?"

"Nope," Turner said, stepping up beside her. "But that's what we're here for."

Samantha nodded, feeling the weight of her purpose settle comfortably over her shoulders. Elmsbrook had been the beginning, a trial by fire that had forged her resolve. But there were bigger battles ahead, and she was ready for them.

As they walked down the busy street, side by side, Samantha allowed herself a brief moment of reflection. The journey had been hard, and it would only get harder. But this was her mission now—to keep pushing, to keep fighting, no matter how powerful the enemies were.

The road ahead was long, but Samantha Cross was ready for whatever came next.

And this time, she knew she wasn't alone.

Chapter 16
Running Out of Time

The dimly lit office smelled of coffee and old paper, the remnants of late nights and too many meetings crammed into one small space. Samantha sat at the cluttered desk, surrounded by piles of documents, hastily scribbled notes, and her laptop glowing in front of her. The whistleblower had been right—the corruption they were up against went deeper than she had initially thought.

She had spent days poring over financial records, leaked emails, and confidential reports, trying to piece together the bigger picture. What had begun as a straightforward investigation into a tech company involved in environmental violations had quickly spiraled into something far more sinister. This was no ordinary corporation cutting corners for profit; it was part of something larger, something darker.

Samantha leaned back in her chair, running a hand through her hair as she tried to wrap her head around the scope of what she was discovering. The dots were beginning to connect, and what they were forming wasn't just another case of corporate greed. It was a network—hidden, powerful, and well-protected.

Her phone buzzed on the desk, cutting through the silence. She glanced at the screen and saw Turner's name.

"Hey," she answered, rubbing her eyes. She hadn't slept much in days, but this was no time to rest.

"Any progress?" Turner's voice came through the line, calm but focused.

Samantha sighed, swiveling in her chair to face the window. Outside, the city was waking up, the early morning light casting long shadows across the streets. "Yeah," she said, her tone serious. "But it's not what we thought."

Turner was silent for a moment, waiting for her to continue.

"This isn't just about one company," she said, her voice lowering. "What I'm finding… it's part of something bigger. A network that reaches across multiple industries—energy, pharmaceuticals, even finance. They're connected in ways that are almost impossible to trace."

"But you're starting to trace them," Turner replied, always quick to pick up on the undercurrent of her thoughts.

Samantha nodded, even though he couldn't see her. "Barely. They're good at covering their tracks. Whoever's running this, they've been doing it for a long time. They know how to stay hidden."

Turner's voice was steady, but there was a hint of concern. "How dangerous are we talking?"

Samantha took a deep breath. "Very. These people aren't like Pharmatech. They're not flashy. They don't have public faces you can take down in court. They operate quietly, in the background, pulling strings while everyone else plays their games. And I'm pretty sure they've been watching me since the Pharmatech case."

Turner cursed softly under his breath. "So, what's the next move?"

"I keep digging," she said, leaning forward, her hands resting on the edge of the desk. "But we need to be careful. This isn't something we can blow open all at once. If we do, they'll bury us before we even get close to the truth."

Turner was quiet for a beat, then his voice returned, more serious than before. "Just tell me what you need."

Samantha smiled, feeling a small spark of relief knowing she could count on him. "I need more eyes on this. Quietly. I'm going to pull in Alex and see if he can help with some of the digital trails. I've got a few leads, but I need to move slowly. These people are dangerous, Turner. More dangerous than anything we've faced before."

"I've got your back," he said, his voice firm. "Just say the word."

Samantha hung up and stared at the screen in front of her, the web of names and companies slowly coming together. Every document she uncovered, every hidden file, added a new layer to the conspiracy. But the more she uncovered, the more she realized how deep this went. Pharmatech had been a monster, but this—this was a machine. A silent, powerful force that had been quietly influencing everything from government policies to environmental disasters for decades. And now, she was in its crosshairs.

She pulled up another file on her laptop, scanning through the financial records of a small, seemingly benign energy company. At first glance, it looked clean—too clean, in fact. But as she dug deeper, she found a series of shell companies, all with ties to the same shadowy figures that had cropped up in her other research. They were operating through subsidiaries, burying their tracks in a labyrinth of offshore accounts and complex corporate structures.

The deeper she went, the more dangerous it became.

Her gut told her that this was only the beginning of a much larger battle, one that would make Pharmatech look like a small-time operation. These new enemies weren't content with one industry; they were controlling entire sectors, manipulating economies, and shaping policies in ways that most people would never even notice.

Samantha stood and walked over to the window, staring out at the city below. She felt the familiar tension building in her chest—the mix of fear and adrenaline that always came when she was on the verge of uncovering something big. The weight of what she was facing was immense, but so was the importance of what she was doing.

This was the fight. The real fight.

As she looked out at the skyline, a sense of clarity washed over her. She knew what needed to be done, and she was ready for whatever came next. There would be more danger, more threats, but she was stronger now, more resolute than ever.

The silent resistance had begun, and she was ready to meet it head-on.

Samantha sat in the corner of the bustling café, a cup of untouched coffee cooling beside her as she typed furiously on her laptop. Her mind raced with the possibilities and connections she was starting to uncover. What had started as an investigation into a tech company's environmental violations had opened up a larger web, one that stretched back to the Pharmatech case and, more disturbingly, to Elias's death.

She stopped typing, staring at her screen for a moment. The realization had been gnawing at her for days now—some of the names she had come across in this new case had a chilling familiarity. People she had thought were peripheral in the Pharmatech investigation were now emerging as key players in this shadowy network. It made her wonder if Elias had been on the verge of exposing something much larger than she ever imagined.

Her phone buzzed beside her, snapping her out of her thoughts. She glanced down at the message.

Turner: *Got your back, as always. Any progress with the old contacts?*

Samantha tapped out a quick reply:

Samantha: *Reaching out to a few of them now. I'm hoping some of the old team can help us track down more leads. Some of the names I'm seeing—Turner, they're familiar. Too familiar.*

Her phone buzzed almost immediately.
Turner: *Familiar how?*

Samantha hesitated for a moment before responding.
Samantha: *Elias. I think some of the people we're looking at now were involved in what happened to him. He was onto this long before I was.*

There was a brief pause before Turner replied.
Turner: *Then it's time we dig deeper. Meet me in an hour? I've been going through some old files, too.*

Samantha agreed and closed her laptop, her mind buzzing. This wasn't just about a new threat anymore; it was connected to everything she had been fighting for from the very beginning. Elias had always said his research had drawn attention from dangerous people, but she had never realized how deep it went. Now, she was beginning to understand.

An hour later, she met Turner at a quiet diner on the outskirts of the city. The place was nearly empty, giving them the privacy they needed. Turner was already seated, a folder of documents spread across the table in front of him.

"You've been busy," Samantha said as she slid into the seat across from him.

"Always," Turner replied with a half-smile, though his expression was serious. "You were right. Some of the names you mentioned—they were involved in Elias's work, either directly or through shell companies that funneled money into Pharmatech's research."

Samantha's heart sank. "So this network we're chasing—it's been in play for years. Elias knew about it, or at least parts of it."

Turner nodded grimly. "I think he knew more than he let on. Maybe he didn't realize the full extent of what he was uncovering, but he was close."

She stared at the documents Turner had brought. "What else did you find?"

Turner pulled out a specific report, sliding it across the table to her. "Remember when Elias mentioned those offshore accounts? He thought they were just being used to hide Pharmatech's illegal experiments, but it turns out those same accounts are tied to this new company you're investigating. They've been laundering money through these shell companies for years—through energy, tech, pharmaceuticals, even defense contracts."

Samantha's pulse quickened. "So they're using the same playbook."

"Exactly," Turner said, leaning forward. "This goes beyond anything we dealt with during the Pharmatech case. They're more sophisticated, more connected. But the patterns are there if you know where to look."

Samantha flipped through the report, her mind racing. "We need more. This is enough to get us started, but if we're going to take them down, we need hard evidence—something that directly links these people to the crimes we suspect."

Turner leaned back, his gaze steady. "That's why we're going to have to bring in some of the old team. People we can trust. This thing is too big to take on alone."

Samantha nodded. "I was thinking the same thing. I've already reached out to a few of my contacts from the Pharmatech investigation. Most of them are still working in the field, and I'm hoping they can help us dig deeper."

"Good," Turner said. "But we need to be careful. If these people realize we're onto them, they won't hesitate to cover their tracks—and take us out if they have to."

Samantha's jaw tightened. "I know. But we don't have a choice. We're already in this too deep."

Turner gave her a long look, his expression softening for a moment. "You know, you don't have to keep pushing yourself like this. No one would blame you if you took a step back."

Samantha shook her head, her voice firm. "I can't. Elias didn't back down, and neither can I. If this network is as big as we think it is, then it's not just about one company or one case anymore. It's about everything—corruption, exploitation, and the people who are suffering because of it."

Turner sighed but nodded. "I figured you'd say that. Just know I've got your back, like always."

Samantha smiled, grateful for his support. "I don't doubt it. Let's just hope some of the others are willing to help too."

As they finished going over the documents, Samantha's phone buzzed again. This time, it was a reply from one of her old contacts—Monica, a journalist who had helped expose Pharmatech's ties to government corruption.

Monica: *Samantha, I've been following your recent work. If you need help, I'm in. This new case sounds like it's even bigger than what we uncovered before. Let's talk soon.*

Samantha's heart lifted. Monica had always been a reliable ally, someone who wasn't afraid to dig deep and get her hands dirty when it came to exposing the truth.

She showed the message to Turner, who nodded approvingly. "Monica's good. She'll help us get what we need."

Samantha tucked her phone back into her pocket, feeling a renewed sense of purpose. The web they were untangling was vast, but piece by piece, they were getting closer to the truth.

"Let's do this," she said, her voice steady and determined. "It's time to bring them down."

The room buzzed with quiet conversation, the sound of pens scratching against paper and fingers tapping on keyboards filling the air. Samantha stood near the back of the room, watching as the small gathering of whistleblowers and journalists worked together, hunched over files, laptops, and coffee-stained documents. What had started as a solo effort, then a small team with Turner, had now grown into something far more significant—a loose coalition of people dedicated to uncovering corruption, not just in one company, but across industries and borders.

She had called them together, but she hadn't expected it to grow this quickly. It had been less than a month since she'd begun reaching out to her old contacts and a few new whistleblowers. Now, her fight had turned into something bigger, a movement that spanned multiple continents.

"Samantha," a voice called from the other side of the room. She looked up to see Monica, the sharp-eyed journalist who had worked with her during the Pharmatech case, waving her over.

Samantha crossed the room, dodging stacks of papers and empty coffee cups. "What's up?" she asked, sitting next to Monica at a cluttered table.

Monica tapped her screen, her voice low but excited. "I've been going through some of the financial records we uncovered last week, the ones linked to the offshore accounts. There's a clear trail here, but what's interesting is that this account isn't just tied to one corporation. It's funding multiple shell companies, all involved in different sectors—tech, pharmaceuticals, energy. They're spreading the money around, making it harder to track, but it's all connected."

Samantha leaned in, her mind racing. "They're laundering money across industries, just like we suspected."

Monica nodded. "Exactly. But here's the kicker—there's a pattern. The money flows through a series of banks in places like Switzerland, the Caymans, all the usual suspects. But it always ends up funding specific projects. I've got a list of three major companies that are currently under investigation for environmental violations, and guess who's backing them?"

Samantha's stomach churned as she stared at the screen. It was the same shadowy network she'd been tracing since the beginning of this investigation. "They're funding everything—covering their tracks by making it look like separate operations."

"Yep," Monica said, her tone grim. "They're smarter than we gave them credit for."

Samantha rubbed her temples, feeling the weight of the situation settle over her again. The network was massive, and now that she had rallied so many whistleblowers and journalists, the stakes had only gotten higher. More people were involved. More people were risking their lives to expose this. And their enemies knew it.

She glanced over at Turner, who was sitting at another table with Alex, both of them poring over encrypted documents. Turner caught her eye and gave her a small nod, but she could see the concern etched in his face.

"They're going to start pushing back harder," Samantha said softly, her voice barely above a whisper. "We're making too much progress too fast. They'll come after us."

Monica leaned back in her chair, crossing her arms. "We knew that was coming. The more we expose, the more desperate they'll get. But we've got people on our side now, Sam.

Journalists from The Guardian, investigative teams in Germany and Japan—they're all on board. They're tired of seeing this kind of corruption go unpunished."

Samantha nodded, though the weight on her chest didn't ease. "It's just… it feels different this time. Bigger. They're not just trying to cover up a scandal. They're trying to protect an entire system."

"And that's why we can't back down," Monica said, her voice steady. "We've got momentum now, and we're not in this alone anymore. Look around."

Samantha did. The room was filled with people—journalists, data analysts, whistleblowers—who had all come together because they believed in what they were doing. They believed that this fight was worth the risk. But she could also sense the tension, the unspoken fear that lurked beneath the surface of their conversations. Everyone here knew that the more they uncovered, the more dangerous their enemies became.

As if reading her thoughts, Monica leaned forward, her voice softening. "Look, I know it's a lot. You've become the face of this movement, whether you wanted to or not. But you're not responsible for everyone here. We all know the risks. We're all choosing to fight."

Samantha met her gaze, her heart heavy but resolute. "I know. But that doesn't make it any easier."

Monica smiled, a small, reassuring gesture. "No one said it would be. But you've done something incredible here, Sam.

You've built a resistance. You've given people hope. And you've shown them that the powerful can be held accountable."

Before Samantha could respond, Turner walked over, a file in his hand. "We've got a problem."

Samantha's pulse quickened. "What is it?"

Turner's face was grim. "I've been tracking some digital chatter. It looks like they've noticed us. The people behind the shell companies—they're starting to coordinate. We intercepted a few encrypted messages talking about shutting down certain 'leaks.' They're getting nervous."

Samantha felt her stomach drop. "How much do they know?"

"Not everything, but they know enough to be dangerous. We need to be careful," Turner said. "They're not just sitting back anymore. They're preparing to strike."

Monica exchanged a glance with Samantha. "So it begins."

Samantha straightened her shoulders, her mind already working through their next steps. "Then we push forward. We tighten security, limit communication to encrypted channels, and make sure we're not all in one place at the same time. We don't stop."

Turner nodded, his eyes steady. "I'll get the team on it."

As he walked away, Samantha turned back to Monica, her voice firm. "This fight isn't just about exposing them anymore. It's about survival. We need to be smarter than they are, faster. We need to stay ahead."

Monica smiled, her expression fierce. "We're ready. Let's take them down."

Samantha took a deep breath, feeling the weight of leadership settle fully on her shoulders. The resistance was growing, but so were their enemies. It was only the beginning, and she knew the battles ahead would be even harder. But with every new ally, with every piece of evidence they uncovered, they were getting closer to the truth.

And she wouldn't stop until it was exposed.

The dim glow of monitors cast long shadows across the room as Samantha and her team gathered around the central table. It was late, but no one looked tired. The adrenaline of their recent discoveries had them wide awake. Files were strewn across the table, and the air was thick with the tension of unspoken realization—they had uncovered something bigger than any of them had expected.

Turner leaned over one of the documents, his brow furrowed as he scanned the latest batch of evidence. "It's all connected," he muttered, half to himself. "These shell companies, the offshore accounts—it's not just about money laundering. It's about power. These guys are funding everything, from corrupt political campaigns to industries that are wiping out entire ecosystems."

Samantha nodded, her eyes fixed on the map they had pinned to the wall. Red strings connected countries and corporations, marking the intricate web of influence they were beginning to uncover. "It's global," she said quietly. "They've been doing this for years, maybe decades. It's not just environmental destruction—it's control. They're buying politicians, controlling resources, shaping laws."

Monica, who had been sifting through digital records, looked up. "I found something. It's a communication between two of the CEOs we've been tracking. They're discussing a meeting with a lobbyist group in Washington. Apparently, they're pushing to weaken environmental regulations. The scary part is they've already bought off a few senators to make sure it happens."

Samantha's pulse quickened. "Which group?"

Monica tapped a few keys, bringing up a series of encrypted messages on her screen. "It's a lobbying firm we've seen before—Camden Strategies. They're the same ones who were working behind the scenes during the Pharmatech trial, pulling strings to keep the case quiet."

Turner slammed the folder he was reading shut, his voice sharp with frustration. "This isn't just about one industry, Sam. They're in everything—energy, agriculture, pharmaceuticals. They're stripping resources, destroying ecosystems, and paying off whoever they need to stay untouchable."

Alex, sitting quietly in the corner with his laptop, finally spoke up. "I've been digging into the environmental violations linked to these companies. They're dumping toxic waste into rivers, clear-cutting forests, displacing entire communities. And every time someone tries to speak out, they get silenced—sometimes permanently."

Samantha's stomach turned. She knew this mission would be dangerous, but hearing the extent of the destruction laid out so plainly made her more determined than ever. "They've been able to hide because no one's looking at the bigger picture," she said, her voice steady despite the heaviness of the revelation. "But we are. And now that we see what they're doing, we have to stop it."

Turner shook his head, leaning back in his chair. "Sam, this is bigger than anything we've faced. These aren't just corporations we're going after—they're governments, too. People in positions of power. We're talking about political figures with global influence. They're not going to let us just waltz in and expose them."

Samantha met his gaze, her eyes hard with resolve. "I know. But we don't have a choice. If we don't do something, they'll keep getting away with it. They'll keep destroying everything in their path and paying off anyone who stands in the way."

Monica looked from Turner to Samantha, her voice calm but insistent. "She's right. We have enough evidence to start. We need to go public, build pressure. If we get the right media outlets on this, if we mobilize the activists, we can make this too big for them to ignore."

Turner's expression softened, but the concern was still clear in his eyes. "We need to be smart about this. They're watching us.

If we push too hard too fast, they'll bury us before we can get the story out."

Samantha nodded, understanding the gravity of what they were about to do. "We'll move carefully. We'll build alliances. There are whistleblowers we haven't reached yet, people inside these companies who've been too scared to come forward. If we can protect them, we can get even more information."

Alex looked up from his screen, his voice quiet but certain. "I can create a secure network, something encrypted that'll allow them to share documents anonymously. It'll be risky, but if we can get them to trust us, we'll have everything we need."

Samantha smiled. "Good. Do it. We're going to need as many people on the inside as possible."

Monica glanced at the map on the wall, her voice contemplative. "You realize this could go on for years, right? Taking down one company, exposing one scandal—that's one thing. But this… this is a machine. A global network of corruption. We could be fighting this for the rest of our lives."

Samantha looked at her team, the weight of their words sinking in. She knew what was at stake. This wasn't just another investigation. It was a battle for the future—of the environment, of democracy, of justice. They were up against forces that had remained hidden for far too long, and now that the light was shining on them, those forces would stop at nothing to stay in the shadows.

But Samantha felt no fear, only resolve.

"I don't care how long it takes," she said firmly. "We keep going until they have nowhere left to hide."

Turner met her gaze, his expression unreadable for a moment before he smiled, the familiar gleam of determination returning to his eyes. "Then let's get to work."

Monica leaned back in her chair, her smile mirroring Turner's. "It's going to be a hell of a ride."

Samantha stood, the energy in the room shifting as she took charge. "Start reaching out to the whistleblowers we haven't contacted yet. Alex, set up the secure network. Turner, we need to start planning how we'll release the information to the press without tipping them off too early. And Monica, you get in touch with our media contacts—make sure they're ready for what's coming."

As her team nodded and moved into action, Samantha felt a familiar sense of purpose settle over her. The mission ahead was dangerous, and the enemies they were facing were more powerful than anything they'd dealt with before. But they had something those enemies didn't—truth.

And that was a weapon more powerful than any money or influence.

The fight was far from over. In fact, it had only just begun. But Samantha knew one thing for certain: no matter how long it took, she wouldn't stop until justice was served.

Chapter 17
The Journal

The sun had long since set, casting the city in a blanket of darkness, the only light coming from the flickering streetlamps outside Samantha's small office. She was used to late nights by now, working long after everyone else had gone home, but tonight felt different. There was an unsettled energy in the air, a feeling that something big was about to happen.

Her phone buzzed on the desk, the screen lighting up with a notification. She reached for it absentmindedly, assuming it was another update from Turner or Monica. But as soon as she saw the message, her heart skipped a beat.

Anonymous: *I know what you're looking for. I can help.*

Samantha sat up straighter, narrowing her eyes at the message. It was vague, but the timing was too perfect to be coincidental. She'd received anonymous tips before, but none had come through such an untraceable channel. Her usual contact methods were heavily encrypted, but this one had bypassed everything, slipping through the cracks of her security measures like it had been deliberately placed in front of her.

Without hesitation, she typed a reply.

Samantha: *Who are you?*

There was a long pause. For a moment, she thought whoever had sent the message wasn't going to answer. Then, her phone buzzed again.

Anonymous: *Someone who can bring down your enemies. But you have to trust me.*

Samantha's jaw clenched. She had learned a long time ago that trust was dangerous, especially in situations like this. Too many times, she had seen people turn on her, their loyalties shifting as easily as the wind. Whoever this person was, they knew about her investigation, and that alone made them a threat.

She decided to push for more information.

Samantha: *I don't trust people who hide behind anonymous messages. If you want my help, you'll have to do better than that.*

This time, the reply came almost immediately.

Anonymous: *I'm inside. I work for them. If you want proof, I'll give it to you. Meet me tomorrow. 8 PM. The old factory on Ridge Street.*

Samantha stared at the message, a cold shiver running down her spine. The old factory on Ridge Street—she knew it well. It had been abandoned for years, the kind of place no one visited unless they had something to hide. This felt too much like a setup.

Before she could reply, another message came through.

Anonymous: *I know you don't trust me, and you shouldn't. But I can give you what you need to take them down. Come alone. If you bring anyone, the deal's off.*

Her instincts screamed at her to ignore the message. This had all the hallmarks of a trap—vague promises, shadowy figures, a suspicious meeting place. But something gnawed at her, a curiosity she couldn't shake. If this person really was on the inside, they could have the information she needed to bring down the entire network.

But could she afford the risk?

The door to her office creaked open, and Turner stepped inside, his expression wary as he tossed a file onto her desk. "You look like you've seen a ghost," he said, eyeing her carefully. "What's going on?"

Samantha held up the phone. "I got a message. From someone claiming to be on the inside."

Turner's brow furrowed. "Inside the network?"

She nodded. "They say they can help, but they're being cryptic. They want me to meet them tomorrow night at the old factory on Ridge Street. Alone."

Turner frowned, crossing his arms. "That sounds like a trap."

"I know," she said, her voice steady but thoughtful. "But what if it's not? What if they're telling the truth? If they really have information, we could blow this thing wide open."

Turner shook his head, his expression darkening. "Or you could walk into an ambush. These people aren't playing games, Sam. They've already tried to take us out before. If this is a setup, they'll make sure you don't walk out of there."

Samantha chewed her lip, considering her options. Turner was right—this could easily be a trap, a way to get her alone and vulnerable. But the promise of inside information was too valuable to ignore. If there was even a small chance that this source was legitimate, she had to investigate.

"I'm not going in blind," she said finally. "I'll do some digging on this 'source' before tomorrow. Maybe I can figure out who they are, or at least what their connection is to the network."

Turner's eyes softened, though the concern remained. "You don't have to go alone. We could set up a perimeter, have backup nearby in case things go south."

She shook her head. "No, if they see anyone else, they'll bolt. I'll have to handle this myself."

Turner sighed, his hand running through his hair. "I don't like it. But I know I can't stop you. Just... be careful. These people are dangerous."

Samantha smiled, though it didn't reach her eyes. "I will. But if this is what I think it is, it could be the break we've been waiting for."

Turner nodded reluctantly, stepping back toward the door. "I'll be nearby. Just in case."

After he left, Samantha sat in the quiet of her office, her mind whirling with possibilities. This could be the lead that finally cracked open the entire network—or it could be a death sentence. Either way, she had to be prepared for whatever came next.

She pulled out her laptop and began searching, tracing digital footprints and checking the encrypted routes of the message she had received. Whoever this person was, they were careful— there were no obvious markers, no signatures she could track. But there was something about the language in the messages that felt familiar, a cadence she had seen before in the way certain people within the network communicated. It was enough to make her pause.

This wasn't just a random informant. They knew her, they knew how she operated, and they knew the stakes of what they were offering.

Tomorrow, she would find out whether they were friend or foe. And she would be ready for either.

The next morning, the soft glow of early daylight filtered through the blinds in Samantha's office. She sat at her desk, her eyes focused on the file she had been reviewing since the night before. The anonymous tip had kept her mind buzzing, filled with possibilities and the risks that came with trusting an unknown contact. She barely noticed when Turner walked in, his footsteps quiet but purposeful. He had been pacing the office for a while, gathering his thoughts.

"Samantha," Turner began, his voice steady but carrying an undercurrent of tension. "We need to talk about this meeting."

Samantha looked up from her notes. "I know what you're going to say."

Turner pulled up a chair across from her, crossing his arms as he leaned back. "Do you? Because from where I'm sitting, it sounds like you're planning to walk into a potential ambush, all because some anonymous source promises you the truth."

She sighed, setting her pen down. "I'm not walking into anything blind, Turner. I'm being careful."

He shook his head, clearly unconvinced. "Careful isn't good enough. We're not dealing with low-level players anymore. These are professionals, Sam. They know how to manipulate, how to misdirect. You can't trust anyone inside that network."

"I don't trust them," Samantha said, her voice firm. "But if there's even a chance that this contact is real, we could be looking at the information we need to take this whole operation down."

"And if it's a setup?" Turner countered, leaning forward. "Then what? You'll be alone in a dark factory with no backup, facing people who have more resources and experience than we do. You need to think strategically."

Samantha leaned back in her chair, folding her arms. "That's why I'm doing my homework. I've been digging into the source all night. Whoever they are, they've covered their tracks well, but I've seen enough to know they're connected. The language in the messages, the references to key players—it's not just someone fishing for information."

Turner exhaled slowly, running a hand through his hair. "I'm not saying we ignore it. I'm saying we proceed with caution. Extreme caution."

"I'm listening," Samantha replied, her tone softening slightly.

Turner straightened in his chair, his military instincts kicking in. "First, we encrypt everything—communications, files, everything. I've already set up a more secure protocol for our internal messaging. If we're going to engage with this person, it has to be through channels that can't be easily traced."

Samantha nodded. "Agreed."

"Second," Turner continued, his voice taking on that familiar tactical edge, "we don't go in without a safety net. I know you said they don't want anyone else involved, but we need eyes on the area. Surveillance from a distance. If something goes wrong, we need to be able to extract you."

Samantha frowned. "You think they'll try something?"

Turner gave her a hard look. "I don't know. But if they're as dangerous as we think they are, we can't afford to assume anything. I'll set up a perimeter around the factory, minimal presence, but enough to get you out if things go sideways."

She studied his face, seeing the genuine concern etched in his expression. Turner was always the cautious one, always thinking three steps ahead, anticipating the worst-case scenarios. It was part of what made him such an invaluable partner. And even though Samantha was used to pushing the envelope, she knew he was right.

"Okay," she said after a moment. "We'll do it your way. But I need to meet this person face-to-face. If they're legit, we could get our hands on something big."

Turner softened slightly, relieved to see she was listening. "I get that. But you have to understand—you're not just dealing with people who want to hide the truth. These are people who will do anything to keep their secrets buried. You've already made enemies, Sam. Big ones. You walk into that factory without a plan, and you could be handing them everything they need to silence you permanently."

Samantha met his gaze, her voice quiet but resolute. "That's why we need to be smarter than them. We're not just chasing shadows anymore, Turner. We're exposing them. And if this person is telling the truth, they could help us tear the whole network down."

Turner sighed, rubbing the back of his neck. "You've always been the risk-taker."

"I'm careful when it counts," she shot back with a small smile.

"Sure you are," Turner replied, a hint of amusement in his voice. "Just make sure this doesn't turn into one of those situations where you regret that risk."

Samantha glanced back at the files on her desk, feeling the weight of the decision pressing down on her. Turner had a point—she needed to be careful. But she couldn't afford to ignore the opportunity this contact represented. If they were legitimate, this could be the breakthrough they needed.

"I'll prepare for the worst," she said after a moment, her tone serious. "But I'm going to meet them."

Turner stood, pushing the chair back. "Then we'll do it right. I'll set up the perimeter, and we'll keep communications locked down. And Sam—don't take any unnecessary chances. We've come too far to lose everything now."

Samantha watched him go, the gravity of his words sinking in. He was right—they had come too far. But as dangerous as this new mission was, it also held the potential for a major victory. She couldn't let fear stop her.

As the door closed behind Turner, Samantha picked up her phone, staring at the message from the anonymous source. She would proceed carefully. She would be ready for anything.

But she wasn't backing down.

The fight had only just begun.

The tension in the air was palpable as Samantha and her team gathered in the secure conference room. The walls were thick with soundproofing, the windows heavily tinted to ensure their privacy. Turner stood at the head of the room, his face grim as he reviewed the latest developments on the projector screen. Samantha sat beside him, her arms crossed, deep in thought. Something had been gnawing at her for days, a sense that something wasn't quite right within their coalition of whistleblowers.

"We've been compromised," Turner said, breaking the silence. His tone was calm, but there was an edge to it—one that suggested they were standing on the edge of a serious threat. "There's a mole."

A ripple of unease passed through the room. Monica, seated across from them, exchanged a concerned look with Alex, whose fingers were poised over his laptop keyboard. Samantha's eyes narrowed as she glanced at Turner. They had suspected it, but now it was confirmed.

"How sure are we?" Samantha asked, her voice steady, though her mind was racing.

Turner clicked through a series of slides, revealing encrypted communications they had intercepted in the past week. "There's been chatter. Subtle at first, but then Alex picked up on some strange patterns in our internal messaging. Someone's been pulling information out of our channels, and they're doing it without tripping any of our usual security measures."

Alex nodded, leaning forward. "Whoever this is, they're good. Really good. They've been using our own encryption to disguise their activities, piggybacking on the legitimate whistleblowers' messages. But I managed to trace some of the metadata, and it led me back to one of our newer contacts."

Samantha's stomach tightened. "Which one?"

Alex tapped a few keys, pulling up a file on the screen. "It's someone who joined the coalition about three weeks ago. Goes by the name of Jordan Everett, claims to be an environmental engineer who used to work for one of the corporations we're targeting. At first, everything seemed legit—they had documents, inside knowledge of some of the environmental violations we were already tracking."

"But?" Samantha prompted, sensing there was more.

"But," Alex continued, "as I dug deeper, I found inconsistencies in their story. The timelines didn't match up perfectly, and some of the documents they provided were just too polished—like they'd been prepared specifically to feed us false leads."

Monica crossed her arms, frowning. "So, what are we looking at? Someone feeding us misinformation to derail the investigation?"

Turner nodded. "It's worse than that. They've been gathering sensitive intel—names, locations, upcoming moves we were planning to make public. If we hadn't caught this, they could have blown our entire operation wide open."

Samantha clenched her fists, anger rising in her chest. She had been careful, so careful, but it wasn't enough. Someone had slipped past their defenses, and it could have cost them everything. "So, what's our next move?" she asked, her voice sharp.

"We're going to expose them," Turner said, his eyes hard. "But we have to do it carefully. We need to make sure they don't realize we're onto them until it's too late. If they sense anything's wrong, they could bolt—and take all the information they've gathered with them."

Samantha nodded, already calculating their next steps. "We'll need to feed them disinformation. Make them think they're still getting valuable intel, but in reality, we'll be leading them into a trap."

Turner's mouth twisted into a grim smile. "Exactly. We give them just enough to keep them interested, but nothing that can actually harm the operation."

Monica leaned forward, her voice tinged with frustration. "But how did they even get in? We vet everyone who joins. How did we miss this?"

Alex sighed, rubbing his temples. "They're good at what they do. Probably have years of experience in corporate espionage or intelligence gathering. It's not surprising they slipped through the cracks."

Samantha glanced around the room, her gaze landing on each of her team members. They were all dedicated, committed to the cause. But the reality was that they were up against a well-funded, well-organized machine. The shadowy network they were fighting wasn't going to sit back and let them dismantle it without a fight.

She exhaled slowly. "We have to tighten security. No more internal messages without encryption. Everything goes through secure channels from now on, and we double-check every new contact. No exceptions."

Turner nodded in agreement. "I'll personally handle the extraction. Once we have them isolated, we'll dig into who they're working for."

Samantha locked eyes with him, her voice quiet but firm. "I want to be there."

Turner raised an eyebrow. "Are you sure? It could get... messy."

"I need to know," Samantha insisted. "This is too big. I want to see who's behind this."

Turner didn't argue, simply nodding. "Alright. We'll do it together."

Monica leaned back in her chair, her face thoughtful. "This is just the beginning, isn't it? We expose one mole, and there's probably a dozen more waiting to take their place."

Samantha's jaw tightened. "Maybe. But we're not stopping. If they want a fight, they've got one."

Later that evening, Samantha sat in the dimly lit safe house, her phone buzzing quietly in her hand. It was a message from Turner.

Turner: *Everything's set. We'll move tomorrow. Keep things tight.*

Samantha stared at the screen, the weight of the situation pressing down on her. They had been so close to disaster. The mole had come too close to tearing down everything they had built. But they were still standing.

She sent a quick reply:

Samantha: *I'm ready. Let's end this.*

The fight was only getting harder, but Samantha knew one thing for certain: they wouldn't stop until every last piece of the shadow network was exposed.

The cold, empty warehouse echoed with the sound of footsteps. Samantha stood in the center of the large, dimly lit room, her arms crossed tightly across her chest. Turner was beside her, his posture tense as they waited for the arrival of their target. The air felt thick with anticipation. This was the moment they had been preparing for—confronting the mole who had nearly brought their entire operation crashing down.

The sound of a door creaking open broke the silence, and soon Jordan Everett—who had infiltrated their coalition—was led in by one of Turner's men. Everett's face was pale, his eyes darting around the room with barely concealed panic. He was visibly shaken, no longer the calm, collected informant they had first believed him to be.

Samantha stepped forward, her gaze icy and unrelenting. "Jordan, or whoever you are, I think it's time you told us the truth."

Everett swallowed hard, his hands trembling as they remained cuffed behind his back. "I— I don't know what you're talking about."

Turner stepped closer, his voice low and dangerous. "Cut the crap. We know you've been feeding information to the people we're trying to expose. You nearly got us killed."

Samantha studied Everett's face carefully, watching the flicker of fear in his eyes. He looked like a man on the edge, someone who had been cornered and knew there was no easy way out. For a moment, the only sound in the room was the distant hum of the warehouse's old lighting system.

"I didn't have a choice," Everett finally muttered, his voice cracking. "You don't understand—these people, they're everywhere. They've got eyes on everything."

Samantha's jaw tightened. "Then help us understand. Start talking."

Everett's eyes darted between Samantha and Turner before settling on the floor. He took a deep breath and began to speak, his voice barely above a whisper. "It's bigger than anything you've seen before. It's not just one company or one industry. They're connected—energy, pharmaceuticals, defense, tech. They've got influence in governments all over the world. They control entire economies."

Samantha's stomach turned as Everett's words sank in. She had suspected that the network was vast, but hearing it confirmed was something else entirely. "How deep does it go?" she asked, her voice firm but steady.

Everett hesitated, then continued, his voice shaking. "They've been building this system for decades. Everything is connected—corporate interests, politicians, lobbyists, even some law enforcement. They make sure that nothing stands in their way. Anyone who tries to expose them gets... removed."

Turner glanced at Samantha, his expression grim. "This is the kind of operation that takes years to build. They've got layers of protection—legal, financial, physical. They're not just covering up a few crimes. They're controlling entire systems."

Samantha felt the weight of the revelation pressing down on her. It wasn't just about uncovering corruption in a single company or even a single sector. This was an entire machine, designed to keep the powerful in power while exploiting the vulnerable.

Everett's voice broke through her thoughts. "I didn't want to betray you. But they have leverage—on me, on my family. If I didn't give them what they wanted, they would've killed us."

Samantha's anger flared. "And what about the people they're hurting? The ones suffering because of this machine you're part of?"

Everett looked up, desperation in his eyes. "I didn't know how bad it was at first. They told me it was just about protecting trade secrets, keeping competitors out of the market. But then I started seeing things—documents, meetings. People disappearing. I tried to back out, but by then it was too late. They were watching me."

Samantha stepped closer, her voice cutting through the room like ice. "What else do you know? If you want any chance of walking away from this, you'll give us everything."

Everett nodded, his breath coming in ragged gasps. "They're planning something big. I overheard a conversation last week—there's a deal going down in the next few months, something global. They're using environmental disasters as cover, pushing policies that'll give them control over key resources."

Samantha's mind raced. "Where? What are they targeting?"

"They didn't say exactly, but it's somewhere in Southeast Asia," Everett replied. "They're going after natural resources—water, minerals, land. And they're bribing officials to make it happen. If they pull it off, they'll have control over a huge portion of the global supply chain."

Turner's fists clenched at his sides. "They're destabilizing entire regions, all for profit."

Samantha could feel her pulse quickening. The stakes were even higher than they'd realized. This wasn't just corporate greed—it was a full-scale operation designed to reshape global power structures. She took a deep breath, her voice cold and sharp. "You're going to help us stop them."

Everett looked up at her, his face pale. "I'll help, but you have to protect me. They'll come after me if they find out I'm talking."

"We'll protect you," Turner said, his voice steady. "But you're going to need to give us everything you know. Names, contacts, locations. We need to know exactly who's involved and how we can get to them."

Everett nodded quickly, clearly desperate. "I'll give you everything. I just— I need to disappear after this. You don't understand what they'll do."

Samantha's eyes were hard, but she nodded. "You give us what we need, and we'll make sure you stay safe."

As the weight of the situation pressed down on her, Samantha realized just how far-reaching this fight was. The network she was up against wasn't just protecting corporate interests—they were controlling entire nations, manipulating economies, and destroying lives on a massive scale.

But now, she knew. And she wasn't going to stop until every last piece of the system was exposed.

Chapter 18
A Desperate Gamble

The city streets were louder than usual, filled with the sound of protest chants and the rumble of marching feet. Samantha stood by the window of her office, watching the unfolding scene below. A crowd had gathered, hundreds strong, holding signs and banners demanding justice, transparency, and accountability. Their voices, once quiet and scattered, had risen to a collective roar. The truth her coalition had uncovered was spreading, and the public was beginning to wake up to the reality of the corrupt system that had been operating in the shadows for years.

But with the awakening came chaos. Civil unrest was growing, not just in this city but across the country, even internationally. Protests had erupted in major urban centers, fueled by the leaks Samantha's coalition had strategically released to the press. The revelations of environmental destruction, political manipulation, and corporate greed had ignited a firestorm, one that couldn't be ignored any longer.

Samantha turned from the window and sat at her desk, scrolling through her phone. The headlines were all variations of the same theme: *"Corruption Exposed—Corporate Elites Behind Global Environmental Catastrophes," "Protests Erupt as Leaked Documents Reveal Government Collusion with Big Business," "Calls for Justice Grow Louder Amid Rising Civil Unrest."*

The truth was out, but it wasn't enough. The people behind this sprawling network of corruption weren't going down without a fight.

Turner walked into the room, his expression grim. "It's spreading fast," he said, tossing a folder onto her desk. "I just got word that protests are now happening in five major cities, and more are being planned. But it's not just the people who are reacting."

Samantha looked up at him, sensing the weight behind his words. "What do you mean?"

Turner folded his arms, his jaw tightening. "The elites are pushing back. Hard. They've ramped up their disinformation campaigns, flooding the media with counter-narratives. We're being painted as conspiracy theorists, anarchists trying to destabilize the government."

Samantha sighed, scrolling through her phone again to see the latest barrage of headlines. Sure enough, several mainstream outlets were running stories about "radical activists" and "misinformation campaigns," attempting to discredit everything her coalition had worked to expose. It was a classic move—shift the narrative, muddy the waters, make it harder for the public to know what was real.

"They're using the media to turn the story against us," Samantha said, her voice tight with frustration. "We knew they would. But it's happening faster than I expected."

Turner sat across from her, his eyes narrowing. "It's not just the media. They've got political pressure working behind the scenes. Some of the politicians we know are in their pocket are already introducing measures to clamp down on protests. Curfews, stricter surveillance laws—all under the guise of 'maintaining public order.'"

Samantha closed her eyes for a moment, the weight of the situation pressing down on her. "So now we're not just fighting a corporation. We're fighting an entire system."

Turner nodded. "That's what it was from the beginning, Sam. It's just clearer now. The deeper we go, the more tangled this gets."

Samantha opened her laptop and began typing, her mind already spinning with next steps. "We need to get ahead of this. If they control the media, they'll control the public narrative. We can't let them drown us out."

"And how do you plan on doing that?" Turner asked, leaning forward.

Samantha looked up, her eyes sharp with determination. "We use the one thing they can't control—independent media. The journalists and platforms that aren't tied to corporate interests. We've already built relationships with them during the Pharmatech case, and we've got more allies now. We need to flood the alternative channels with the truth."

Turner considered her words, then nodded slowly. "It's a good plan. But it won't be enough to sway everyone. They've got too many resources, too many people in their pocket."

Samantha's phone buzzed again, and she glanced at the screen. It was another message from one of the whistleblowers in her coalition. The cracks in the system were becoming more visible, but with those cracks came more danger. They were close to something explosive, and the pushback from the elites was only going to get more aggressive.

"Maybe," she said, her voice softer now. "But we don't need everyone. We just need enough people to see the truth for what it is. Enough to make it impossible for them to ignore."

Turner leaned back in his chair, his expression thoughtful. "You're right. But we need to be prepared for what comes next. These protests are just the beginning. The more pressure we put on them, the more desperate they'll get. They're not going to back down easily."

Samantha knew he was right. The system they were up against had been built over decades, designed to protect the powerful at the expense of ordinary people. The elites had control over governments, media, and law enforcement. They had every tool necessary to maintain their grip on power, but Samantha had something they didn't—truth. And she wasn't going to stop until it was fully exposed.

"They're trying to silence us," Samantha said quietly, her eyes fixed on the headlines flashing across her screen. "But they can't hide forever."

Turner stood, his voice steady as ever. "We'll need to keep tightening security within our ranks. If they've planted moles before, they'll try again. And they'll start targeting the whistleblowers directly. We need to protect them."

Samantha nodded. "I'll make the calls. We'll need to keep everything encrypted, and make sure our safehouses are secure."

As Turner headed for the door, he paused, glancing back at her. "You know this fight is going to get uglier, right? They're not just going to discredit us. They'll come after us in other ways."

Samantha met his gaze, her voice unwavering. "I know. But I'm ready."

Turner gave her a slight nod, then left the room, leaving Samantha alone with her thoughts. She looked back out the window at the crowds below, their voices rising in unison, demanding accountability. The people were awake now.

But the system they were up against was vast, and the battle had only just begun.

Samantha took a deep breath, steeling herself for what was coming. She had fought too hard to stop now, and no matter how powerful the elites were, she would find a way to bring them down.

The cold light of early dawn filtered through the blinds of the safehouse as Samantha paced the room, her mind racing. The tension among her team had been building for days, ever since the first personal threat had arrived. What had once felt like a distant, dangerous mission had suddenly turned intimate, invasive. They had expected retaliation, but none of them had anticipated just how far the shadow network would go.

Her phone buzzed again, the screen lighting up with another message—a photo this time. Her stomach twisted as she stared at it. It was a picture of her sister, Claire, standing outside her office, completely unaware that she was being watched. Samantha quickly swiped away the image, but the message lingered in her mind. The network had taken this fight out of the shadows and into their personal lives.

Turner entered the room, his expression dark. "We've got a problem," he said quietly, handing her a folder. "They're moving faster than we thought. These threats aren't just warnings anymore. They're targeting families—your sister, Monica's parents, Alex's wife. They're making it personal."

Samantha's hands tightened around the folder as she glanced at the images inside. Photos, addresses, details that only someone deep within the network would know. It was clear now that the game had changed. The shadow network was pulling out all the stops to make sure they were too distracted, too scared, to continue.

She set the folder down and looked up at Turner. "We knew they'd fight back," she said, her voice steady, though she felt the knot of fear twisting in her chest. "But we didn't know it would get this personal."

Turner's jaw tightened. "They're trying to break us."

"Are they?" Samantha asked, though she already knew the answer.

Turner glanced toward the door, then lowered his voice. "Alex is losing it. He hasn't said much, but I can tell. He's worried about his family. He's feeling guilty for dragging them into this."

Samantha nodded grimly. She had noticed it, too. Alex had always been steady, calm under pressure, but recently, there had been cracks in his composure. The cyberattacks had escalated, and now the threats were reaching into his home, his personal life. She knew how much Alex's family meant to him. This wasn't just a mission anymore—it was putting everything he loved at risk.

"I'll talk to him," Samantha said, her voice quiet. "We can't afford to lose him."

Turner gave a short nod and left the room. Samantha took a deep breath, gathering herself before walking down the narrow hallway toward Alex's workspace. She found him hunched over his laptop, fingers flying across the keys as he tried to patch up another breach in their security system. His face was pale, his eyes red from lack of sleep.

"Alex," Samantha said gently, stepping into the room.

He didn't look up, continuing to work as if nothing was wrong. "I'm almost done with the new encryption layer. Just a few more adjustments."

Samantha moved closer, her tone soft but firm. "That's not what I'm here to talk about."

Alex's fingers slowed, and he finally stopped typing, his shoulders slumping as he leaned back in his chair. He rubbed his hands over his face, his voice low and strained. "They sent me a picture of Zoe. She was at the park with our daughter. They were watching her, Sam. Watching my family."

Samantha's heart ached at the pain in his voice. She sat down across from him, choosing her words carefully. "I know. They're doing it to all of us. They want to scare us, make us stop."

Alex shook his head, his hands trembling slightly. "It's not just about me anymore. My family didn't sign up for this. I didn't realize how deep this would go, how dangerous it would get. If something happens to them because of me..." He trailed off, his voice breaking.

Samantha leaned forward, her eyes filled with empathy. "Alex, I get it. I really do. My sister's in their sights, too. This isn't what any of us wanted, but we're in it now. And you're one of the best we've got. We need you. But more than that, we need you to be okay."

Alex's eyes filled with guilt and frustration. "But what if I can't protect them? I know how these people operate. I've seen what they can do. I can't live with myself if something happens to Zoe and Lily because of me."

Samantha reached out, placing a hand on his arm. "We'll protect them. All of us. We're not doing this alone. We're going to tighten security, move the families somewhere safe. But Alex, we need you focused. They want to break you. They want to make you feel powerless. That's how they win."

Alex stared at the floor, his jaw clenched. "It's hard, Sam. Hard to focus when I know they're out there, watching."

"I know it's hard," she said softly. "But we can't let them win. We've come too far. If we stop now, everything we've uncovered, everything we've fought for, it all goes away. And they'll keep hurting more people."

He was silent for a long moment, then nodded slowly, though the weight of his fear was still clear in his eyes. "Okay. I'll keep going. But I'm trusting you—trusting all of us—to keep them safe."

Samantha squeezed his arm, her voice filled with quiet determination. "We will. We'll get through this, Alex. Together."

As she stood to leave, she glanced back at him, watching as he returned to his work, though the tension in his body remained. She knew this was far from over, that the cracks in her team's resolve were starting to show. The network's attacks were growing more vicious, more personal. But Samantha was more determined than ever to hold them together.

The stakes were higher now. And the price for failure was far too steep.

Samantha sat alone in her darkened office, the quiet hum of the city outside barely audible through the thick windows. Her hands rested on the desk, motionless, as her mind raced. She stared blankly at the reports, the files, the maps—they all felt distant now, like pieces of a puzzle that had grown far too big to solve. The weight of it all pressed down on her, heavier than it had ever felt before.

For the first time since they started this mission, Samantha wasn't sure if they could continue.

The threats had come too close, hit too hard. Alex's breakdown had shaken her. He wasn't the only one feeling the pressure. Turner, Monica, even the newer members of the team—they were all showing signs of strain. The once solid foundation of their coalition was starting to crack, and Samantha couldn't help but wonder if she was pushing them too far, too fast.

Her phone buzzed on the desk, but she didn't pick it up. The messages were relentless—more leaks, more demands, more questions about the next steps. It was as if the world was constantly pressing down on her, demanding that she keep moving, keep fighting, without pause. And now, she wasn't sure if she had the strength to carry that weight any longer.

A knock at the door pulled her from her thoughts. She blinked, realizing she had been sitting in the same position for far too long. "Come in," she called, her voice quieter than usual.

Turner stepped inside, his expression unreadable. He closed the door behind him and crossed the room, sitting down in the chair opposite her desk. For a moment, he said nothing, just studying her face.

"You've been quiet," he said finally, breaking the silence.

Samantha managed a weak smile, but it didn't reach her eyes. "Just thinking."

"About what?"

She hesitated, then leaned back in her chair, her voice barely above a whisper. "About whether I'm pushing everyone too hard. Alex nearly broke today. You saw him. And I know you're feeling the pressure, too. We all are."

Turner didn't respond immediately. Instead, he let the silence linger, as if giving her the space to voice the thoughts she had been holding back.

Samantha sighed, running a hand through her hair. "I don't know if we can keep doing this. Every day, it's getting harder. The threats, the fear—it's not just about us anymore. It's about everyone we care about. How much longer can I ask people to keep risking their lives for this?"

Turner's eyes softened, though his face remained serious. "Sam, you're carrying a lot. More than most people could handle. But you're not alone in this. None of us are."

"I know that," she said, her voice strained. "But what if it's too much? What if the cost is too high? I keep telling myself that we're doing this to save lives, to expose the truth. But at what point does it stop being worth it? How can I keep asking people like Alex to sacrifice everything?"

Turner leaned forward, his voice calm but firm. "You're asking because it's the right thing to do. We knew what we were getting into when we started this. You didn't drag us into this fight. We chose it. Just like you did."

Samantha looked away, her eyes heavy with doubt. "But I'm the one leading this. Every decision I make puts us deeper into danger. If something happens to any of you... I don't know if I can live with that."

Turner's voice softened. "You think I don't feel that, too? You think I don't wonder if this fight is going to get us all killed?" He paused, his eyes locking with hers. "But then I remember why we're doing this. How many lives we've already saved by exposing the truth. How many more will suffer if we stop now."

Samantha closed her eyes, the weight of his words sinking in. "It just feels like it's never going to end."

Turner's tone remained steady. "That's because the kind of fight we're in doesn't end quickly. It's messy. It's dangerous. But we're making a difference, Sam. You've made a difference. If we walk away now, everything we've fought for, everything we've uncovered—it'll all disappear."

She opened her eyes and stared at him, searching his face for some kind of reassurance. "What if it gets worse?"

"It will get worse," Turner said bluntly. "But that's why we have to keep pushing. These people we're fighting—they thrive on fear. They're counting on us to back down. But we've come too far for that. We've shaken them. They know we're not going away."

Samantha let out a long breath, feeling the tension in her shoulders ease slightly. She knew Turner was right, but it didn't make the burden any lighter.

"I just… I don't want to break anyone," she admitted, her voice quiet.

Turner gave her a small, reassuring smile. "You're not breaking anyone. We're in this together. And yeah, it's hard. But we're fighting for something bigger than us."

For a moment, the two of them sat in silence. The room felt heavy, but there was also a quiet sense of solidarity, a reminder that Samantha wasn't carrying this burden alone.

"I don't want to quit," Samantha said finally, her voice steadier now. "But sometimes, I wonder if stepping back would protect the people I care about."

Turner shook his head. "Stepping back won't protect them. It'll only give the people we're fighting more room to hurt others. You've made this fight matter, Sam. And we're not done yet."

Samantha felt a flicker of resolve reignite within her. The doubts hadn't vanished, but Turner's words had reminded her of why they had started this fight in the first place. They weren't just exposing corruption—they were saving lives, holding the powerful accountable. And that was something worth fighting for.

She straightened in her chair, meeting Turner's gaze. "You're right. We're not done."

Turner gave her a small nod, the corner of his mouth lifting in approval. "Damn right we're not."

Samantha allowed herself a brief smile before turning her attention back to the reports on her desk. The weight of the world still pressed on her shoulders, but for the first time in days, it didn't feel quite so crushing.

"Let's get back to work," she said, her voice stronger now. "We've got a lot more to expose."

The room was buzzing with quiet conversation as Samantha and her team gathered around the long, scarred table in the dimly lit safe house. The tension that had been steadily building over the last few weeks was palpable, but there was also a growing sense of determination. The setbacks they'd faced, the personal attacks, the relentless pressure—it had all led to this moment. They needed a new plan, and Samantha knew it.

She stood at the head of the table, her hands resting on the rough wood, her eyes scanning the faces of her coalition. Alex was there, looking more composed than the last time they had spoken, though the weight of the threat against his family still lingered in his expression. Monica sat next to him, flipping through notes with a focused intensity, and Turner leaned against the wall, arms crossed, his eyes sharp as ever. Others, journalists, whistleblowers, and investigators, filled the room, waiting for her to speak.

"We've been playing this the same way for a while now," Samantha began, her voice steady, though the exhaustion in her eyes was clear. "We've been relying on media leaks, on public pressure, hoping that by exposing the truth, we could force the system to change. But it's not enough."

The room fell silent. All eyes were on her.

"Every time we release something," she continued, "they counter. They discredit us in the media, spin the narrative, and keep their grip on power. We're fighting against a network that controls the narrative. And as long as they have that power, they can keep deflecting, keep silencing us."

Monica raised an eyebrow, glancing up from her notes. "So, what's the plan? You're not saying we stop leaking information, are you?"

Samantha shook her head. "No. But we need to change our approach. We need to stop playing by their rules and start building something more strategic. It's not enough to just expose them to the public. We need to get inside. We need to use the system they've built against them."

Turner, always the pragmatist, pushed off the wall and took a step closer. "You're talking about making alliances. Legal, political. People who can fight them from the inside."

"Exactly," Samantha said, meeting his gaze. "We've focused on public exposure, but we haven't done enough to form real partnerships with the people who have the power to make systemic change. There are politicians out there, activists, lawyers who are fighting the same fight as us, but we've been working in isolation."

Monica frowned slightly. "And how do we trust that these people won't just get bought off like the rest? Everyone has a price. The people we're up against know how to play that game better than anyone."

Samantha nodded, understanding the skepticism. "We're not going to trust just anyone. We'll need to vet everyone carefully. But I've been reaching out to a few people already—lawyers who have fought against corporate giants and won, politicians who have built careers fighting corruption. If we can bring them into this, we'll have more leverage than we've ever had before."

Alex, who had been quiet up to this point, finally spoke, his voice filled with cautious hope. "So, what's the first step? How do we build these alliances?"

Samantha glanced at Turner, then back to Alex. "We start small. I've already made contact with a few key figures who are willing to help, but we need more. We need to show them that we're not just another group of whistleblowers throwing accusations around. We need to offer them something tangible—evidence, testimony, something they can take into courtrooms, into legislative sessions."

"And you think they'll listen?" one of the journalists asked from the back of the room. "We've been shouting this from the rooftops for months, and half the politicians out there won't touch it."

Turner stepped forward, his voice calm but authoritative. "They'll listen if we make it impossible for them to ignore. The media leaks have made noise, but we need more than noise. We need legal victories, political momentum. The moment we start winning cases, the tide will turn."

Samantha nodded. "Exactly. We're not just trying to expose corruption anymore. We're trying to dismantle the system that allows it to thrive. And that's going to take more than headlines—it's going to take legislation, legal action, and real political will."

Monica leaned back in her chair, crossing her arms. "It's ambitious. But it's risky. We're already being targeted. If we go this route, we'll attract even bigger enemies."

Samantha met her gaze, her voice unwavering. "We're already in their crosshairs. But if we don't change tactics, we'll lose. We can't afford to play it safe anymore. We need to be bold. We need to make this fight bigger than us."

The room fell into a thoughtful silence as her words hung in the air. Everyone in the room knew the stakes had risen, but they also knew Samantha was right. The only way to win was to go deeper, to engage in the very system that had been built to protect the powerful from consequences.

Turner broke the silence. "We'll need to start identifying key players in the legal and political arenas—people who are already on our side, even if they don't know it yet. We need to build trust with them and provide them with the ammunition they need to go after these guys."

Samantha nodded. "I've already got a few names. We start with them. We bring them in, show them what we've uncovered, and make it clear that this isn't just about one corporation. It's about an entire system of corruption."

Alex looked around the room, his voice quieter but filled with determination. "If we're going to do this, we need to be airtight. No more leaks. No more risks. If they catch wind of what we're planning, they'll double down on their attacks."

Samantha met his gaze, her voice resolute. "Agreed. We're going to be smarter, faster, and more strategic than they ever expected. This is our fight now. And we're going to win it."

The room buzzed with quiet agreement. The plan was ambitious, but it was their best chance at taking down the shadowy network that had been untouchable for too long. Samantha felt a flicker of hope—something she hadn't allowed herself to feel in weeks. They were still in the fight. And now, they had a real strategy to win.

"We start now," Samantha said, her voice cutting through the room with renewed strength. "We build our alliances, we gather our evidence, and we strike from the inside."

As the team began to mobilize, Samantha felt a new sense of purpose rising within her. The stakes were higher than ever, but so was their resolve. This was no longer just about survival—it was about changing the game entirely.

Chapter 19
Breaking the Silence

The air in the underground meeting room was tense, yet filled with a quiet urgency. Samantha sat at the head of the table, Turner beside her, as a small group of political allies filtered into the room one by one. The walls were bare, the lighting dim, and the location—an old, unused library basement—was chosen for its privacy and out-of-the-way nature. Secrecy was paramount now, and every person in the room knew they were risking more than just their careers by being there.

Senator Grace Mitchell, a seasoned lawmaker with a reputation for fighting corporate corruption, sat across from Samantha. She had been one of the first to respond to Samantha's quiet outreach, a rare politician who had refused to be swayed by lobbyists and backroom deals. Beside her was Congressman David Romero, known for his work on environmental issues, and Attorney General Janice Boyd, who had spent years trying to reform the criminal justice system. Each one of them had a reason to oppose the shadow network that Samantha's team had been battling in the dark for so long.

"We don't have much time," Senator Mitchell said, her voice low but firm. "If they suspect what we're planning, they'll come after us harder than ever. Some of my colleagues are already sniffing around, wondering why I've been so 'uncooperative' with certain bills."

Samantha leaned forward, her gaze steady. "That's exactly why we need to move now. We have the evidence, and we're building more every day. But it won't matter unless we have the political leverage to make it stick. We need people inside the system to start pushing back."

Congressman Romero nodded, his face lined with concern. "We've all seen what they can do—how they silence opposition. But this isn't just about getting the word out anymore. We need legislation, laws that prevent these corporations from buying their way out of accountability."

Samantha glanced at Turner, who was watching the room with his usual calm intensity. "We've started identifying key figures within the network—lobbyists, corporate heads, even a few politicians who are directly involved in keeping this system running. If we can target them, get the right laws passed, we can start dismantling their power from within."

Attorney General Boyd, who had been quiet until now, folded her hands on the table. "We need to be smart about this. The moment we start drafting legislation, they'll know we're coming for them. They have eyes everywhere. I've already heard whispers that they're increasing surveillance on key lawmakers. Anyone associated with this could be in danger."

"That's why we're keeping this under wraps for now," Turner interjected. "We'll continue operating in the shadows while you push forward on the political front. No one can know that we're working together. As far as the public is concerned, this is your initiative. You're leading the charge."

Senator Mitchell gave a small, tight smile. "I've been fighting these people for years, but I've never had enough backing to make real progress. If we do this right, we could finally expose them for what they are. But make no mistake—they'll fight back with everything they've got."

Samantha felt the weight of the moment, knowing the risks her new allies were taking. These were people with families, with public lives that could be destroyed if the shadow network decided to turn its focus on them. But they were also some of the few with the power to help her team finish what they had started.

"We've already begun securing more evidence," Samantha said, her voice steady but full of resolve. "Alex has cracked several of their encrypted systems. We're gathering financial records, communications between key players—everything we need to build an airtight case. But we can't release any of it until we have the political support to protect it from being buried."

Congressman Romero leaned back in his chair, his brow furrowed. "And what happens when they start pushing back? These corporations have armies of lawyers, PR firms, and media outlets ready to discredit everything we say."

Turner gave a curt nod. "They'll hit hard. We expect that. But that's why we're partnering with you. They control the narrative through the media, but if we can get the legal and political machinery working against them, they'll be forced to defend themselves on multiple fronts."

Senator Mitchell exchanged a glance with Attorney General Boyd. "We'll need more allies on the inside. A handful of lawmakers won't be enough. We need to quietly gather support, get other senators and representatives on board without tipping off the wrong people."

Samantha nodded, understanding the delicate balance they needed to strike. "We'll provide you with everything we have, but you'll need to move carefully. The moment they sense a coordinated effort, they'll tighten their grip. But if we act strategically, we can chip away at their power before they realize what's happening."

Attorney General Boyd leaned forward, her voice quiet but determined. "I've spent years fighting corruption in the legal system. I've seen firsthand how deep this goes. If we're going to make this work, we need airtight cases, indisputable evidence. And we need to be prepared for them to retaliate."

"They already are," Samantha said, glancing at Turner. "We've been dealing with personal threats, surveillance, and attacks on our families. But we've held our ground. We can't back down now, not when we're this close."

Congressman Romero rubbed his temples, clearly weighing the risks. "So, what's the first step? What do you need from us?"

Samantha met his gaze, her eyes filled with determination. "We need you to start introducing legislation that targets the heart of their operations. Environmental regulations, campaign finance reform, corporate accountability. And we'll keep gathering the evidence to support it. Once we have enough, we'll expose everything."

Senator Mitchell nodded slowly. "We'll draft the bills, but we need to keep this quiet until the right moment. If they catch wind of what we're doing too early, they'll crush us before we can even get it off the ground."

Samantha stood, the weight of the next phase of their fight settling on her shoulders. "We'll keep you supplied with everything you need—evidence, testimony, documents. But you need to stay vigilant. They'll come for you, just like they came for us."

Turner stepped forward, his voice firm. "You're in danger now. All of you. But if we stick together, we can finish this."

The room fell silent, the gravity of the situation settling over the group. They were no longer just a coalition of whistleblowers and investigators—they were now working with the very people who could change the system from the inside. But with that new alliance came greater risks, and Samantha knew they were walking a razor-thin line between success and catastrophe.

Senator Mitchell stood, followed by the others. "We'll be careful. But we're not backing down. It's time someone took these people on."

Samantha nodded. "Then let's get started."

As her new allies filed out of the room, Samantha exchanged a glance with Turner. They had taken a huge step forward, but the path ahead was fraught with danger. The stakes had never been higher, but for the first time in a long time, they had real hope.

And that, Samantha thought, might just be enough to win.

The conference call connected, and the screen flickered to life with a patchwork of faces from across the globe. Samantha sat at her desk, her laptop in front of her, as she looked at the diverse group of people who had joined the call. Activists, investigators, and whistleblowers from different countries filled the screen, each of them fighting their own battles against similar networks of corruption. It was a daunting sight, but a one that filled Samantha with a renewed sense of purpose

"This is bigger than any of us," Samantha began, steady. "We've been fighting this in isolation for to all know the stakes. And we know the risks. But i our efforts, we can make it impossible for them

Her words hung in the air for a moment, and faces on the screen—an older man with silve expression—spoke up. "I've been fi corruption in Brazil for over a decade," English. "The same companies you're i tied to illegal logging and land grabs in thd time we expose them, the government p more than just evidence. We need to pressure the international community

Samantha nodded, leaning closer to the screen. "That's exactly why we're here. This isn't just about uncovering corruption in one country anymore. These networks span continents. We need to show people that this is a global problem."

From the corner of her screen, a woman with sharp eyes and a thick French accent chimed in. "In France, we've seen corporations funneling money into political campaigns, using the same tactics you've exposed in your investigations. But our legal system is... slow. They drag out cases for years, hoping the public will lose interest."

Turner, sitting beside Samantha, finally spoke, his voice calm but forceful. "That's what they count on. They use bureaucracy and legal delays to wear us down. But if we work together, we can make it harder for them to hide. If we coordinate our efforts, share evidence, and synchronize our actions, they'll have to fight us on multiple fronts."

other voice broke in, this time from a younger activist in a. "But how do we protect ourselves? My organization has argeted by government agencies that are in bed with these ations. We're constantly being watched, and some of my es have disappeared. How can we stay safe while taking "

exchanged a look with Turner before answering. ething we've been dealing with too. The threats are 're dangerous. But we've found ways to protect cure communication channels, safehouses, and visors who can help keep us out of harm's way. e resources with you."

The young activist nodded, though the fear in her eyes was clear. "We can't afford to lose more people. But we also can't stop."

Another voice, this time from a man with a German accent, broke in. "What we need is international media. We've had some success in Germany getting the word out, but the moment these stories go public, they get buried by corporate-controlled news outlets. If we could get the media in different countries to run stories at the same time, they'd have a much harder time silencing us."

Monica, who had been quietly listening from the side, leaned forward. "That's a good point. We've built relationships with independent media here in the States, and we can start connecting you with them. If we can get simultaneous coverage in the U.S., Europe, Africa, and South America, it'll create a wave that's too big for them to suppress."

The older man from Brazil nodded. "If we go public all at once, it'll force them to react on a global scale. They won't be able to contain the damage if the entire world is watching."

Samantha felt a flicker of hope as the conversation gained momentum. This was what they needed—an international effort that couldn't be silenced by any one government or corporation. "We'll need to coordinate carefully," she said, pulling up a document on her screen. "We've started compiling evidence that links these corporations to illegal activities in multiple countries. It's not just about environmental destruction. It's about human rights violations, political manipulation, and financial crimes. If we pool our information, we can build an airtight case that will force the international community to pay attention."

The French activist spoke up again. "But how do we deal with the different legal systems? What works in the U.S. or Germany won't necessarily work in Brazil or Kenya. How do we navigate that?"

Samantha took a deep breath. "That's going to be one of the biggest challenges. Every country has its own laws, and we'll need legal experts in each region to help us. But if we can build alliances with lawyers and politicians in each country, we can start to find ways around those barriers. It's going to take time, and it's going to be difficult, but we can do it."

Turner nodded in agreement. "The key is to keep moving. We can't let them bog us down in one place for too long. If we get stalled in one country, we keep pushing in another. Eventually, they won't be able to keep up."

The room fell silent for a moment, as the weight of the plan began to sink in. It was ambitious—perhaps the most ambitious thing any of them had ever attempted. But it was also their best shot at taking down a network that had, for too long, operated without consequence.

Samantha met the eyes of each person on the screen, her voice filled with quiet determination. "We're not just fighting for one country. We're fighting for all of us. If we work together, we can expose them. And we can bring them down."

The faces on the screen nodded in agreement, one by one. The plan was set in motion, and for the first time in a long time, Samantha felt a glimmer of hope. They weren't fighting alone anymore. This was a global battle, and they were ready to take it on.

"Let's get started," she said, her voice firm. "We have a world to change."

The phone call came just after midnight. Samantha had been working late, her eyes tired but her mind still racing as she sifted through documents. When the phone buzzed, she thought it was just another update from one of their contacts. But as soon as she saw the name on the screen, a cold knot formed in her stomach.

It was Monica.

Samantha answered, her voice tense. "Monica, what's going on?"

There was a long pause on the other end of the line, and in that silence, Samantha's heart sank. Monica's voice, usually so sharp and composed, was barely a whisper. "Sam... it's David."

Samantha froze. "What happened?"

"They got him."

The words hit her like a punch to the gut. Samantha gripped the edge of the desk, her knuckles turning white. "No. No, that's not—" Her voice cracked, and she had to force herself to take a breath. "How?"

"They staged a car accident," Monica said, her voice breaking as she spoke. "It looked clean, but... we know better. He'd been getting threats for weeks, Sam. We all knew this was coming. I just—I didn't think it would be this soon."

Samantha sat back, her mind spinning. David Romero, the congressman who had thrown his entire weight behind their cause, was dead. The man who had been one of the first to stand with her, to fight for the truth, had been silenced in the most brutal way possible. She could barely process it.

"Where's his family?" Samantha asked, her voice barely above a whisper.

"They're safe," Monica replied. "Turner got them out of the house as soon as we heard. They're under protection now, but Sam... this isn't going to stop here."

Samantha's heart raced, the enormity of what had just happened crashing down on her. "No, it won't," she said, her voice suddenly hollow. "They wanted to send a message. They knew he was a threat."

Monica's voice trembled, but there was a fierce edge to it. "They wanted to break us."

The silence that followed was unbearable. Samantha stared at the wall in front of her, feeling the weight of the loss like a physical blow. David wasn't just an ally; he had been a friend, someone who had believed in their cause when others had laughed it off as impossible. He had risked everything to stand with her, and now he was gone.

"They're going to pay for this," Samantha said, her voice low but filled with a cold, hard resolve.

"They will," Monica agreed. "But we need to be smart. This was a calculated move. They're trying to scare us into backing off."

Samantha closed her eyes, her thoughts swirling. "I can't believe he's gone. I should have—"

"Don't do that," Monica interrupted, her tone sharp. "You couldn't have known. None of us did."

Samantha felt the tears welling up, but she blinked them back. "He didn't deserve this."

"No," Monica said softly. "He didn't. But we have to keep going, Sam. For him. For everyone who's depending on us."

Samantha nodded, even though Monica couldn't see her. "You're right. But God, it feels like we're losing more than we're gaining."

Monica was quiet for a moment. "We are. But that's how you know we're hitting them where it hurts. They're scared of us, Sam. And that's why they're lashing out like this. David knew the risks. We all do. He died fighting for something bigger than himself."

Samantha sat in silence, the weight of Monica's words settling over her. David had known the risks. They all had. But that didn't make the loss any easier. She felt like a part of her had been ripped away, and the guilt gnawed at her. Could she have done something differently? Could she have warned him sooner, protected him better?

"Sam," Monica said, her voice softer now. "You're not alone in this. We're still with you. We're not going to let them win."

Samantha clenched her jaw, her hands shaking as she wiped at her eyes. "I know. But it's just—David was one of the good ones. He didn't deserve this."

"None of us deserve this," Monica said, her voice hardening. "But we're in this fight now, and we're not backing down. We owe it to David to finish what he started."

Samantha took a deep breath, forcing herself to think clearly. The pain was still there, raw and overwhelming, but she knew Monica was right. If they backed down now, David's death would have been in vain. And that was something she couldn't live with.

"We keep moving forward," Samantha said, her voice steadier now. "We'll regroup in the morning. I'll reach out to Turner, and we'll figure out how to tighten security. We can't afford to lose anyone else."

Monica exhaled. "We'll be ready. And Sam? Don't carry this alone."

Samantha swallowed hard, her throat tight. "I'll try. But Monica... thank you."

"You don't have to thank me. We're in this together," Monica said softly. "Get some rest. Tomorrow's going to be a long day."

As the call ended, Samantha sat in the dark, staring at the now silent phone in her hand. The weight of David's death pressed down on her like a heavy stone. She had known this fight was dangerous, that they were going up against powerful forces who wouldn't hesitate to kill to protect their secrets. But knowing it and living it were two different things.

For a long time, she sat there, her mind filled with memories of David—his laughter, his fierce commitment to the cause, the way he had always believed they could win, even when the odds seemed impossible. And now he was gone.

Samantha wiped her eyes and stood, her resolve hardening with every step. They had taken someone she cared about, but they hadn't broken her. If anything, they had made her more determined than ever.

"We're going to finish this," she whispered to herself, her voice filled with steely determination. "For David. For everyone."

And with that, she turned back to her desk, ready to plan their next move.

The morning after David's death was thick with tension. Samantha walked into the safehouse, her steps slow but deliberate, her mind still reeling from the events of the night before. Inside, her team was already gathered, the mood somber, as if a shadow had fallen over them all. Turner stood near the door, his arms crossed tightly across his chest, while Monica sat at the table, her eyes red from sleepless hours. Alex sat across from her, staring blankly at his laptop. The room, usually buzzing with energy and the clatter of investigative work, was eerily quiet.

Samantha took a deep breath, feeling the weight of their collective grief. David's death had been a gut punch to all of them, but she couldn't afford to let that stop them. She couldn't let them falter now.

"We need to talk," she said, her voice quiet but steady. The heads in the room lifted slowly, all eyes turning to her. She saw the exhaustion, the fear, the doubt in their faces, and it mirrored her own feelings. But she pushed it down. There wasn't time to let the grief paralyze them.

Monica was the first to speak. "David…" She trailed off, her voice breaking slightly. "He didn't deserve this."

Samantha nodded, the ache in her chest tightening. "No. He didn't."

"They'll come for the rest of us," Alex said suddenly, his voice low, filled with uncertainty. "If they got David, none of us are safe."

"Alex," Turner said, his tone a warning, but Samantha held up her hand, stopping him.

"No, let him speak," she said, her voice calm. She looked at Alex, meeting his eyes. "You're right. None of us are safe. But that's always been the case. From the moment we started this fight, we knew the risks. This isn't new."

Alex looked down at his hands, clearly struggling. "But David… we thought we were careful enough. We thought we had time."

Samantha crossed the room and sat down next to him, her voice softening. "I know. I thought so too. But we can't undo what happened. What we can do is decide what we do next."

Monica spoke up, her voice firmer now. "What's left to do, Sam? They killed David. They've been after us since day one. What if this is the point where they win?"

Samantha stood, looking around the room, her eyes hardening with resolve. "This isn't the point where they win," she said, her voice growing stronger. "This is the point where they're afraid. David's death wasn't an accident, it was a message. They're scared of what we're about to do. And that means we're getting closer."

Turner nodded from his place by the door, his arms uncrossing as he stepped forward. "She's right. They're lashing out because they know we're a threat now. They wouldn't waste time on us if we weren't dangerous to them."

Alex finally looked up, his face still pale, but there was a glimmer of understanding in his eyes. "But how do we keep going after this? They'll just keep killing us, one by one."

Samantha held his gaze. "We keep going by remembering why we're doing this in the first place. We've seen what they're capable of—the corruption, the destruction, the lives they've ruined. David gave everything for this cause because he believed in it, just like we do. And I'm not going to let his death be in vain. We can't let them win."

Monica took a deep breath, her face tight with emotion. "But what if we lose someone else? What if it's you next? Or Alex? How do we protect ourselves?"

Samantha glanced at Turner, who stepped in. "We tighten security. We stay out of sight. We stop taking unnecessary risks. From here on out, every move we make is calculated, coordinated, and protected. We have safehouses. We have people who can keep us off the radar. We won't let them catch us off guard again."

Samantha looked around the room, her voice firm but compassionate. "I'm not saying this is going to get easier. It's going to get harder. They'll come after us, and we'll have to fight every day just to stay ahead of them. But we're not just a group of whistleblowers anymore. We have alliances, legal support, and now we have something even more powerful— the truth. They can't kill that."

Monica's lips pressed into a thin line as she slowly nodded. "So what's the next move?"

Samantha leaned forward, her eyes blazing with determination. "We honor David by finishing what we started. We keep exposing them, but we also protect ourselves. Turner's going to implement stricter protocols for all of us—no one works alone. Every step is documented. And we push forward with the legislation we've been planning. David's name is going to be tied to the laws that bring this network down."

Alex looked over at her, some of the fear in his eyes fading. "You really think we can pull this off?"

Samantha didn't hesitate. "I know we can. David's death was meant to scare us, to break us. But I won't let it. We won't let it. This fight isn't over. It's just beginning."

There was a moment of silence as the weight of her words settled over the room. Then, one by one, they began to nod, the fire returning to their eyes. Samantha could see it—Turner, ready to move into action; Monica, pulling herself back from the edge of despair; even Alex, slowly rebuilding the resolve that had wavered in the face of David's death.

Samantha straightened, her chest tightening with grief, but also with determination. They had lost someone important. Someone they couldn't replace. But David's death wouldn't be the end of their fight. It would be the reason they saw it through to the bitter end.

"We're going to win this," Samantha said, her voice quiet but filled with steel. "For David. For everyone they've hurt. We're going to finish what we started."

And as her team rallied around her, Samantha knew they were ready for whatever came next.

Chapter 20
The Pushback

The dim glow of multiple computer screens illuminated the room as Samantha and her team worked in quiet concentration. Papers were scattered across the long table, digital files open on laptops, and the low hum of whispered conversations filled the space. They were on the verge of something monumental, something that would shake the very foundation of the shadow network they had been fighting for so long. Every document they uncovered, every piece of evidence collected, brought them one step closer to dismantling the corrupt system that had claimed so many lives.

Samantha stood at the head of the table, flipping through a series of reports, her brow furrowed in deep thought. The weight of the past months had settled heavily on her shoulders, but she pushed through the exhaustion, knowing they were close. They had uncovered the illegal activities, the human rights abuses, and the environmental destruction tied to some of the world's most powerful elites. The web of corruption was sprawling, but now, they had the evidence to expose it all.

"We're nearly there," Samantha said, her voice low but steady. "We've connected the dots between the corporations, the governments, and the criminal networks. This is enough to bring them down."

Turner, who had been monitoring the encrypted communications between various whistleblowers, nodded in agreement. "It's solid. Financial records, witness testimony, internal emails—they can't wriggle out of this one."

Monica sat beside Alex, reviewing a document on her screen. "We've got proof of environmental destruction tied to several political figures. They've been lobbying to dismantle regulations for years, all while profiting from land deals and resource exploitation."

Samantha felt a surge of hope, but it was tempered by the knowledge that they were about to enter the most dangerous phase of their fight. She placed her hands on the table, glancing around at her team. "We have the evidence, but the final step is going to be the hardest. We're going after the people who are at the very top—those who have the most to lose. They won't go down without a fight."

Turner crossed his arms, his expression grim but resolute. "They'll come after us harder than ever. But if we don't make this push now, everything we've done will be for nothing."

Alex, who had been typing furiously at his keyboard, paused to look up. "I've been digging deeper into their security protocols, and let me tell you, it's intense. These people are running international operations like it's their own private empire. But I've found a few weak points. If we move fast, we can hit them before they even know what's happening."

Samantha gave him a nod, her mind already racing through the steps they needed to take. "Good. But we can't rush this. Every move has to be calculated. If they sense we're closing in, they'll start covering their tracks, and we'll lose the chance to expose the full scope of their crimes."

Monica leaned back in her chair, glancing between the team members. "What's the plan, Sam? How do we make sure this doesn't blow up in our faces?"

Samantha straightened, her voice firm. "We go public, but strategically. We'll release everything we have to the legal teams we've partnered with, while simultaneously leaking the most explosive pieces to international media outlets. We need this to hit hard and fast—before they can spin the narrative or bury the evidence."

Turner nodded in agreement. "It'll be like ripping off a band-aid. All at once. They won't have time to regroup."

Alex looked thoughtful for a moment, then added, "I'll make sure the data is encrypted and released in waves. That way, even if they manage to block the first set of leaks, the rest will keep coming. It'll be like a flood."

Samantha couldn't help but feel a sense of pride in her team. They had come so far, endured so much, and now they were ready for the final push. But the looming danger was undeniable. The people they were targeting were ruthless, and they wouldn't hesitate to strike back.

"We're exposing some of the most dangerous figures in the world," Samantha said, her voice heavy with the weight of their task. "Politicians, CEOs, lobbyists—they've been running this network for decades, operating in the shadows, destroying lives, and getting away with it. But not anymore."

Monica exchanged a glance with Turner, her face serious. "And what if they come for us, Sam? What if they decide we're too much of a threat?"

"They will come for us," Turner replied bluntly. "We've all accepted that risk. But we're prepared for it."

Samantha met each of their gazes, her voice filled with quiet determination. "We've taken precautions, set up security measures. And more importantly, we've built alliances. If they come for us, they'll have to face a much larger resistance than they realize."

Monica nodded slowly, a flicker of hope in her eyes. "Alright. Let's do this."

Samantha took a deep breath, her resolve strengthening. They were so close. She could feel it. They had the power to bring this shadow network crashing down, and she wasn't going to let fear stop them. "We gather everything—leave no stone unturned. By the end of this week, we release it all. And when we do, we make sure they have nowhere to hide."

The team exchanged glances, the gravity of their mission settling over them. They were walking into the lion's den, but they were armed with the truth, and Samantha knew that was the most powerful weapon they had.

"Let's finish this," she said, her voice filled with steely resolve. "For David. For everyone they've hurt."

With renewed determination, the team went back to work, preparing for the final push.

The safehouse was silent except for the soft tapping of fingers on keyboards and the occasional rustling of papers. The atmosphere was heavy with the knowledge that this might be the last time they worked together like this. Samantha sat at the head of the table, her hands clasped in front of her as she looked over at Turner. He was standing by the window, peering through the blinds, his face set in a hard expression. They both knew what had to be done, but the weight of the decision pressed down on them.

"We've reached the point of no return," Samantha said quietly, breaking the silence.

Turner glanced over at her, his brow furrowed. "I know. But if we're going to do this, we need to make sure it survives no matter what happens to us."

Samantha nodded, her mind already spinning through the layers of plans they'd put into place. "We've backed up the data in four different locations, right? Secure servers in Europe and Asia, plus the two encrypted drives with our trusted allies."

"Five locations," Turner corrected, moving to sit across from her. "I sent one more to our contact in South America. Just in case. But it's not the backups I'm worried about, Sam. It's the people. The moment this goes public, they'll come for everyone connected to it. We need to make sure the right people know where the data is and how to release it if anything happens."

Samantha ran a hand through her hair, her thoughts racing. "We've trusted the right people, Turner. But we can't control everything once this starts."

"No, we can't," he said, leaning forward. "But we can control what happens next. If something happens to you—or me—the data has to reach the public. That's the only thing that matters now."

There was a long pause. Samantha knew what he was saying was true. They had put their lives on the line for this, and they had come too far to turn back now. But the thought of not being there to see it through, to ensure that their mission succeeded, sent a cold chill down her spine.

"We've prepared as much as we can," she said, her voice steady despite the fear gnawing at her. "We just have to trust that the people we've chosen will do the right thing."

Turner frowned, his eyes searching hers. "Do you trust them, Sam? Do you really trust them?"

Samantha didn't answer immediately. She glanced around the room, her mind drifting to the faces of the allies they had gathered over the past few months. Politicians, lawyers, activists, journalists—each of them had their own motivations, their own stakes in this fight. Some she trusted with her life. Others... she wasn't so sure.

"I trust some of them," she admitted finally. "But we don't have a choice. We've given them enough to move forward without us if it comes to that."

Turner leaned back in his chair, his gaze never leaving hers. "We have to assume the worst, Sam. If they take us out, we need to know that everything we've fought for won't die with us."

Samantha sighed, rubbing her temples. "You're right. We can't afford to hope for the best anymore. We need to be ready for the worst."

He nodded, his voice dropping to a whisper. "I've set up a dead man's switch. If we don't check in every 48 hours, the entire data set will be released to international media automatically."

Her head snapped up, surprise flashing across her face. "You didn't tell me about that."

"I didn't want to worry you until it was necessary," Turner replied. "But it's done. If we disappear, the world will know everything within two days."

Samantha exhaled slowly, the gravity of the situation pressing down on her. "You think it'll come to that?"

"I hope not," Turner said, his tone grim. "But we can't count on surviving this. These people are ruthless, and they're not going to let us expose them without a fight."

Samantha's heart tightened in her chest, the reality of their situation sinking in deeper. They had always known this was a dangerous game, but the finality of it all was becoming clearer by the minute. They were about to go after the most powerful people in the world—people who wouldn't hesitate to kill to protect their secrets.

"What about the others?" she asked, her voice soft. "Monica, Alex... They're just as much at risk as we are."

"They know what's at stake," Turner replied, his voice hardening. "We've all accepted the risks. But we've made sure they're protected. Alex's safehouses are secure, and Monica's already in contact with the legal teams that will push the case forward."

Samantha leaned back in her chair, staring up at the ceiling. "I hate this," she muttered. "I hate that we're talking about contingency plans like this is a suicide mission."

Turner's voice softened, and for the first time in days, there was a flicker of emotion in his eyes. "I hate it too, Sam. But we've come too far to back down now."

She closed her eyes for a moment, forcing herself to breathe. They were ready. They had done everything they could to ensure the evidence would see the light of day, no matter what. But the fear still lingered, gnawing at the edges of her resolve.

After a long pause, she opened her eyes and looked at Turner. "We're going to make it, Turner. We're going to see this through."

He gave her a tight smile, but his eyes were filled with the same uncertainty that had settled in her chest. "We're going to do everything we can."

Samantha stood up, her hands still trembling slightly, but her voice firm. "Then let's make sure we're ready. We don't get a second chance at this."

Turner stood as well, his face serious. "We'll be ready."

And with that, they returned to the task at hand—securing the last pieces of their plan, knowing that the ultimate risk was now staring them in the face. There was no turning back, only the final push toward justice.

The attack came swiftly, like a tidal wave crashing against everything Samantha and her team had worked so hard to build. It started with a subtle shift in the media—articles began to pop up, questioning the credibility of the coalition, accusing them of fabricating evidence, and painting Samantha as an opportunist willing to ruin lives for personal gain. At first, the stories seemed like isolated incidents, but it didn't take long for the pattern to emerge. The shadow network was striking back, and they were doing it with precision.

Samantha stood in front of a large screen in their secure operations room, her arms crossed tightly as she watched the cascade of headlines flood the news feeds. Each one was worse than the last: *"Coalition Scandal: Are Whistleblowers Lying?"* and *"Samantha Cole: Crusader or Manipulator?"*

"It's happening," Monica said from behind her, her voice edged with anxiety. "They're trying to destroy us in the court of public opinion."

Turner stepped up beside Samantha, his jaw clenched. "It's worse than that. I just got word from one of our legal contacts—they've filed lawsuits against the coalition in multiple countries. They're going after us with everything they have."

Samantha's eyes flickered toward Turner, her mind racing. "On what grounds?"

"Defamation, illegal wiretapping, fraud—you name it. They're throwing every accusation they can think of at us, hoping something sticks," Turner explained, his voice grim. "And that's not all. I'm hearing rumors that they're trying to bribe some of our key witnesses. If they succeed, the whole case could fall apart."

Monica's fingers were flying across her keyboard, pulling up files and emails. "I'm already seeing movement on the corporate front too. They're starting to shred documents, erase digital footprints. If we don't act fast, we're going to lose critical evidence."

Samantha ran a hand through her hair, her thoughts a whirlwind of strategies and next steps. This was it—the moment she had been preparing for, the moment she had feared. The shadow network was going all-in, and if they didn't move quickly, everything they had gathered could be destroyed.

"Alex," she called out, turning toward the far corner of the room where Alex sat hunched over his laptop. "I need you to lock down every server, every piece of data we have. Make sure the backups are secure, and start tracking any digital footprints they're trying to erase. We need a record of everything."

Alex didn't look up from his screen, his fingers flying across the keyboard. "Already on it. But they're fast. I'm seeing files disappear from public databases as we speak. We'll need to dig deeper to retrieve them."

Monica looked up from her station, her face pale. "And what about the media attacks? If public opinion turns against us, even our legal allies might back off."

Samantha exhaled slowly, trying to keep her voice steady. "We'll fight that too. We have our own contacts in the media— independent outlets that aren't tied to corporate interests. We need to get our version of the story out there before their lies take hold."

Turner glanced at her. "Do you think it'll be enough? They've got the power to control the narrative, Sam. And right now, it's not looking good."

Samantha turned to face him fully, her expression hardening. "It has to be enough. We knew they'd come after us eventually. But we didn't come this far just to let them bury us. They're scared, Turner. This attack proves it."

Turner nodded, though his face remained tight with concern. "We've never seen them this desperate before. They know we're close."

Monica, still typing furiously, looked up. "And they're hitting us on every front. Not just the media. I'm getting reports of physical break-ins at some of our off-site storage facilities. They're trying to destroy the evidence."

Samantha felt a surge of anger flare up inside her. "We need to act fast. Get our people to secure those sites immediately. And any digital evidence—back it up in real-time. If they're shredding documents, we need to be one step ahead."

Alex looked up from his screen, his face a mix of frustration and determination. "I've already encrypted everything we've got on our servers, but they're moving fast. There's a chance they could hit us harder if we're not careful."

"We'll have to risk it," Samantha said, her voice firm. "We can't afford to lose what we've collected. This is what they've been trying to prevent from coming out—their worst nightmare. We have to make sure this evidence survives, no matter what."

Turner moved closer, his eyes locked on hers. "I'll take care of securing the physical evidence. We've got a few trusted allies in place, but I'll send reinforcements."

Samantha nodded, her mind already spinning with the next steps. "Good. And I'll reach out to our legal teams. They need to be ready to counter these lawsuits before they gain any real traction."

Monica's voice cut in, her tone sharp. "I'm sending updates to our media contacts now. We need to control the narrative before they drown us in their propaganda."

Samantha's eyes flickered back to the headlines on the screen, her jaw tightening. They were under siege from every angle, but she wouldn't let them be crushed. "Let them throw everything they've got at us," she said, her voice low but fierce. "We'll hit them back harder."

The team moved into action, the room buzzing with the urgent energy of people who knew they were racing against time. Samantha watched as Turner gathered his things, ready to move out, and Monica coordinated with their media contacts. Alex was hunched over his computer, pulling files and backing up data as fast as he could.

Samantha knew they were in the fight of their lives, but they weren't backing down. The shadow network was powerful, but they were vulnerable now, and Samantha was going to use every resource at her disposal to bring them down.

She turned to the team, her voice filled with resolve. "We're not going to let them win. This is what we've been preparing for. Let's show them what happens when they underestimate us."

And with that, they fought back—against the lies, the attacks, and the destruction, determined to keep the truth alive.

The clock struck midnight in the dimly lit operations room, but no one moved. Samantha stood at the center of the room, her eyes fixed on the large screen displaying a world map. Dots blinked in various countries—each one representing a media outlet or journalist they had partnered with. Her heart pounded in her chest, but her hands were steady. This was it. The moment they had spent months—years—fighting for.

Around her, the team was silent but focused. Monica and Alex sat by their computers, their faces illuminated by the soft glow of the screens. Turner stood nearby, arms crossed, his gaze sharp as he monitored communications from their global contacts.

"We're ready," Alex said quietly, his fingers hovering over the keyboard. "The servers are secured. All the files are set to go live simultaneously."

Samantha nodded. "And the media outlets?"

Monica glanced up from her screen. "Everything's in place. We have outlets in every major region—Europe, Asia, Africa, the Americas. Once we release, they'll flood the airwaves with everything we've uncovered. There's no way the shadow network can shut this down."

The tension in the room was palpable. Samantha knew the risks. Once they hit "go," there was no going back. The shadow network would retaliate hard—possibly even violently—but they had reached the point of no return. The world needed to know the truth.

"Turner," Samantha said, glancing at him. "Are the contingency plans in place?"

He gave her a sharp nod. "Every backup is secure. If anything goes wrong, the files will still reach the public. But we need to be prepared. The moment this goes live, they'll come for us."

Samantha exhaled slowly, a sense of calm washing over her. "We knew this was coming. It's time."

She turned to face the room, her team—her friends—who had fought beside her through every battle. They had lost people along the way. David's death still weighed heavily on her, but it also fueled her determination. This was for him, for all the lives shattered by the shadow network's greed and corruption.

"We've spent years exposing the corruption and lies these people have used to control the world," she said, her voice steady but charged with emotion. "They thought they were untouchable, but tonight, we're going to prove them wrong. The truth is out there, and we're not stopping until everyone sees it."

Alex's fingers twitched on the keyboard, his voice steady but strained. "Once I hit send, every piece of evidence we've gathered will flood the global media. Are we ready?"

Samantha locked eyes with him, her heart racing but her mind clear. "We're ready."

Monica exchanged a glance with Turner, then looked back at Samantha. "Whatever happens next... we did the right thing."

Samantha gave a brief nod, her jaw set. "We did."

The room fell into a brief silence, heavy with anticipation. Alex's hand hovered over the keyboard for a moment, then—without a word—he hit send.

The screens in front of them lit up instantly, showing the broadcast beginning to roll out across the globe. In London, New York, Paris, Beijing, Nairobi—within seconds, news outlets were airing stories, publishing articles, and sharing documents that exposed the full scope of the shadow network's corruption.

Emails, financial records, secret contracts, photographs, and videos—everything Samantha's coalition had gathered over the months and years flashed across the screens. The extent of environmental destruction, human rights violations, and corporate greed was now public knowledge, accessible to millions.

"They're already picking it up," Monica said, her voice barely containing her relief. "Social media is exploding. Hashtags are trending in every major city."

Samantha watched as the news began to break internationally. The headlines came in a flood: *"Global Corruption Network Exposed: Governments and Corporations in Crisis!"* and *"Whistleblowers Unveil Decades of Corporate Crimes and Political Collusion."*

Turner leaned forward, his voice low but filled with satisfaction. "They can't stop this. Even if they take us out now, it's too late."

Samantha nodded, her eyes still fixed on the screens. "It's not just us anymore. The world knows."

But even as the evidence spread like wildfire, she couldn't ignore the tightening in her chest. This was only the beginning. The fallout from these revelations would be massive. Governments would topple, corporations would collapse, and people—innocent people—could get caught in the crossfire.

"International agencies are starting to respond," Alex said, his voice edged with excitement. "Interpol, the UN—they're all launching investigations. Some of the key figures we named are already being taken in for questioning."

Samantha felt a surge of hope. This was what they had worked for—justice. But the shadow network wasn't dead yet. The forces they were up against were powerful, and they would fight back with everything they had.

"Brace yourselves," Samantha said, her voice calm but filled with urgency. "This is where it gets dangerous. They're not going to take this lying down."

Turner's phone buzzed. He glanced at the screen and frowned. "I'm already hearing reports of retaliation. Some of our allies are being harassed. We need to stay ahead of them."

Samantha's heart pounded in her chest, but her resolve never wavered. She had expected this. They had all expected this.

"We've done what we came to do," she said quietly. "Now we need to survive the storm."

Outside the safehouse, the world was already changing. Protests were erupting in major cities as people learned the truth about the shadow network's crimes. Investigations were beginning, and the once-invisible hands that had controlled so much of the global system were now exposed to the light.

Samantha took a deep breath, watching the screens as the fallout began. "This is just the beginning," she whispered.

Turner stood beside her, his voice quiet but firm. "And we're ready for whatever comes next."

Samantha gave a final nod, her gaze steady as the world responded to the truth. They had done it. The shadow network was finally crumbling, and no matter what happened next, the truth would remain.

The fight was far from over, but for the first time, Samantha felt like they had a real chance at victory.

Chapter 21
An Unseen Enemy

The streets were alive with anger. In cities across the globe, people poured out by the thousands, their voices rising in defiance. Banners waved through the air, the messages scrawled across them furious and clear: *"Justice Now," "No More Lies,"* and *"Hold Them Accountable!"* From Paris to São Paulo, New York to Nairobi, the world had awakened, and Samantha watched it all unfold from the safety of their secure location.

Her eyes were glued to the screen, where images of protests flooded every major news outlet. It was everything they had hoped for, but even Samantha hadn't anticipated the scale of the reaction. The revelations from the global broadcast had hit like a tidal wave, exposing decades of corruption and malfeasance. Now, governments were scrambling to respond, while the public demanded answers.

"This is bigger than I ever imagined," Alex said, standing beside her as he scrolled through live feeds of protests on social media. His voice was filled with awe and something like fear. "Look at this. It's everywhere. They can't ignore us anymore."

Samantha nodded, her face a mix of determination and exhaustion. "They can't silence us now. The truth is out there."

Turner entered the room, holding a tablet with even more news updates. "Governments are already feeling the heat. A couple of high-ranking officials in the U.S. and the UK have resigned. They're trying to distance themselves from the fallout, but it's too late. They're tied to the network, and they know it."

Monica sat at the table, her laptop open in front of her, eyes darting over the torrent of information coming in. "And it's not just political. Corporate heads are getting called out too. Stock prices are plummeting for some of the biggest companies we exposed. This is hitting them where it hurts."

Samantha's phone buzzed, and she glanced down at the screen. Another whistleblower had come forward. It wasn't the first that day, and she knew it wouldn't be the last. Since the broadcast, people from all over the world—whistleblowers, insiders, even former government agents—were contacting her team, ready to share their own stories of corruption, exploitation, and injustice.

She turned to the others, holding up her phone. "We've got another one. This time, it's someone who used to work with a pharmaceutical company tied to the shadow network. They're willing to talk."

Monica looked up, her eyes bright with a new energy. "They're coming out of the woodwork. The more we expose, the more people are realizing they're not alone. We need to start documenting all of this—every testimony, every piece of evidence. This is just the beginning."

Turner leaned against the wall, arms crossed. "The world's waking up. But the elites aren't going to go down quietly. They'll fight this every step of the way."

"We knew that," Samantha replied, her voice firm. "But they've lost control of the narrative. This is bigger than them now."

Outside the safehouse, the protests raged on. Samantha turned her attention back to the news feed, where footage from around the world showed a collective surge of anger and action. Protesters were gathering outside government buildings, corporate headquarters, and media outlets, demanding that those responsible be held accountable.

In Washington D.C., thousands of people crowded the streets, waving signs and chanting in unison. "No more lies! No more lies!" In Berlin, protestors had gathered in front of the parliament building, their chants echoing through the cold evening air. London, Tokyo, Johannesburg—everywhere, the message was the same: the people had had enough.

"I've never seen anything like this," Alex murmured, shaking his head in disbelief. "We knew there'd be protests, but this is... massive."

Samantha's gaze remained fixed on the screen, watching as the faces of ordinary people, furious and determined, demanded change. "It's not just about us anymore," she said softly. "This is about everyone who's been silenced, exploited, or ignored. The world is ready for justice."

Turner's phone buzzed, and he glanced at the message before looking up. "International agencies are starting formal investigations. The UN just announced they're launching a task force to look into human rights violations tied to the network."

"That's huge," Monica said, her eyes widening. "If the UN is involved, this could lead to criminal charges on an international scale."

Samantha's heart raced as she absorbed the gravity of the situation. This was everything they had fought for, everything they had risked their lives for. The corruption they had uncovered was no longer hidden in the shadows—it was out in the open, and the world was demanding justice.

"People are scared," Monica continued, glancing at her screen. "Some of the corporate leaders we exposed are already fleeing the country, trying to escape prosecution. But the ones who remain... they're going to fight back."

Samantha clenched her jaw. "Let them. We've come too far to back down now."

Alex nodded, his voice resolute. "We've got more whistleblowers coming forward every hour. The more we expose, the harder it'll be for them to cover anything up. They can't hide anymore."

Samantha glanced at Turner. "And we're ready for what comes next? For their retaliation?"

Turner met her gaze, his expression serious but confident. "We've planned for this. Our security is solid, and our contacts are ready. We won't go down easy."

Samantha nodded, her resolve hardening. "Good. Because we're not done yet."

The roar of the protests on the screen seemed to grow louder, the chants of the people rising like a tidal wave that no one could stop. Samantha felt a surge of pride and hope, knowing that they had sparked something far greater than themselves.

The world was watching, and now, finally, it was demanding justice.

"This is it," she whispered, more to herself than anyone else. "This is the change we've been fighting for."

And as the protests raged on and more whistleblowers stepped forward, Samantha knew that they had turned the tide. The shadow network was crumbling, and the world would never be the same.

Samantha sat in the conference room, the air thick with tension and the scent of stale coffee. News screens mounted on the walls showed the latest updates on the investigations: political figures, corporate executives, and high-ranking officials being led into courtrooms in handcuffs. The first wave of legal proceedings had begun, and the world was watching. But despite the growing sense of victory, Samantha couldn't shake the knot of unease in her stomach.

"The lawsuits are piling up fast," Monica said, glancing up from her laptop. She had been tracking the rapid developments in real time. "We've got trials kicking off in the U.S., Germany, Brazil, and Japan. The charges range from fraud to human rights violations. It's... overwhelming."

Alex looked up from his phone, his expression a mix of exhaustion and triumph. "I never thought we'd actually get to this point. It's surreal seeing some of these people finally face justice."

Samantha leaned back in her chair, her mind racing. "It's a step in the right direction, but we can't let our guard down. We knew this wouldn't end cleanly. The legal battles are going to drag on for years, and the people we're up against aren't going to sit quietly."

Turner, standing by the window, gave a short, sharp nod. "They're already making moves to fight back. There are loyalists in every country trying to discredit the investigations. We've gotten more threats in the last forty-eight hours than we have in the past six months."

Monica looked up from her laptop, concern crossing her face. "How bad?"

Turner met her gaze, his voice level but tense. "Serious enough. Death threats, legal intimidation, attempts to freeze our assets. It's clear they're still trying to crush us, even with everything out in the open."

Samantha exhaled slowly, her jaw tightening. "They won't stop until they've silenced us for good."

Just then, her phone buzzed. She glanced down at the message—a news alert. *"Whistleblower Group Faces Backlash from Corporations, Political Allies"* was the headline. Beneath it were quotes from high-profile figures still loyal to the shadow network, accusing Samantha and her coalition of fabricating evidence, manipulating the media, and destabilizing global markets.

"They're calling us criminals now," Samantha muttered, tossing her phone onto the table. "Claiming we're responsible for the chaos."

Monica sighed, rubbing her temples. "Of course they are. They're losing control, and this is their way of trying to claw back power. Discredit us, make it look like we're the villains."

Turner spoke up, his voice carrying the weight of experience. "We knew this was coming. They're desperate, and desperation makes people dangerous."

Samantha nodded, her mind already shifting gears. "We need to stay ahead of them. The public's on our side, but that could change if they spin this the right way. We can't afford to let them control the narrative."

Alex leaned forward, his expression serious. "So, what's the plan? How do we counter their attacks without getting dragged into a public mudslinging match?"

Samantha was silent for a moment, thinking. The victories in the courtroom were monumental, but they weren't enough. The shadow network's reach was still vast, and the system they'd spent decades building wasn't going to crumble overnight.

"We stick to the facts," Samantha said finally, her voice firm. "We keep pushing the truth, keep the focus on the crimes they've committed. If we get pulled into a war of words, we lose. Our strength is in the evidence, in the people coming forward. The world is listening—now we just have to make sure they keep listening."

Turner turned away from the window, crossing the room to stand beside the table. "That's easier said than done. I've been hearing whispers that some of our biggest corporate backers are looking to distance themselves from the fallout. They don't want to be seen as supporting a destabilizing force."

Monica's eyes widened. "Seriously? After everything we've exposed?"

Turner nodded grimly. "They're scared. The shadow network still has influence, and some people are starting to question whether they're on the right side of history. It's up to us to make sure they understand what's really at stake."

Samantha clenched her fists, feeling the frustration rise in her chest. They had come so far, but even now, the fight was far from over. The people they were up against weren't just powerful—they were insidious, able to manipulate governments, corporations, and the media at will.

"We're not backing down," she said, her voice steely. "We've fought too hard for this. We need to keep pushing forward, no matter how ugly it gets."

Monica glanced at the news feed, where more high-profile figures were being led into courtrooms. "It's starting to feel real now, isn't it? The trials, the evidence—it's all out there. But the backlash... it's stronger than I thought it would be."

Samantha shook her head. "It's a survival instinct. They've built their lives, their empires, on lies and exploitation. They won't go down without a fight."

Turner crossed his arms, his face hard. "And that means we need to be ready. The legal battles are just beginning, and the threats are only going to get worse."

Samantha met his gaze, her resolve firm. "We will be. But we can't lose sight of what we've accomplished. People are starting to see the truth. The world is changing, even if the old guard doesn't want to admit it yet."

Alex smiled faintly. "You know, Sam, some people are calling us heroes now."

Samantha gave a half-smile, but there was a shadow behind her eyes. "Heroes in some circles. Villains in others. We're not doing this for praise. We're doing this because it's right."

Monica nodded, her voice quiet but resolute. "We're not done yet. The trials are starting, but the real battle is making sure justice is served. That's going to take time."

Samantha leaned forward, her voice soft but fierce. "Then we keep fighting. We don't stop until every last one of them is held accountable. For David. For the people they've hurt. For the truth."

And as the legal battles began to unfold across the world, Samantha and her team braced themselves for the storm that was sure to follow. The shadow network was weakened, but not yet broken. The fight was far from over—but they were ready for whatever came next.

The air in the safehouse felt heavy, weighed down by the unspoken tension that clung to every corner. Samantha sat at her desk, staring blankly at the reports in front of her, but the words blurred together. She rubbed her eyes, feeling the exhaustion deep in her bones. It had been weeks since the legal proceedings had begun, and the constant pressure was starting to take its toll.

Turner entered the room, his footsteps soft but purposeful. He placed a cup of coffee beside her, his expression unreadable. "You should rest, Sam," he said quietly. "You haven't slept in days."

Samantha sighed, leaning back in her chair. "I can't afford to rest right now. There's too much at stake."

"There's always going to be too much at stake," Turner replied, his voice gentle but firm. "But if you don't take care of yourself, you're going to burn out. And we can't afford to lose you."

Samantha knew he was right, but the guilt gnawed at her. Every time she tried to step away, even for a moment, she felt like she was letting her team down—letting the people they were fighting for down. The investigations had sparked chaos, and while the public was rallying behind them, the threats from the shadow network were growing more insidious by the day.

"I just... I feel like I can't stop," she admitted, her voice barely above a whisper. "Every time I close my eyes, all I see are the people we've lost. David, the others... How am I supposed to rest when they're gone because of this?"

Turner sat on the edge of her desk, his presence steady. "You're carrying a lot. We all are. But you're not doing this alone, Sam. You have to trust the team to handle some of the load."

Samantha shook her head, her chest tightening. "That's just it, Turner. Some of the team isn't even here anymore. Monica's gone into hiding. Alex is barely holding it together after the threats to his family. Everyone's on edge. How am I supposed to keep pushing forward when everything is falling apart around us?"

Turner's eyes softened. "It's not falling apart, Sam. It's just hard. We knew this wasn't going to be easy. We're up against powerful people, and they're scared. But we're still standing."

She took a deep breath, but the weight in her chest didn't lift. "And what about Monica? She's in hiding because of me. She had to leave her home, her life..."

"She made that choice, Sam," Turner said, his voice firm. "We all did. We knew what we were getting into. This fight—it's bigger than us."

Samantha stood abruptly, walking over to the window. Outside, the streets were quiet, but she knew the danger was never far. "I just... I didn't think it would be like this," she said softly. "I thought we could expose the truth, and things would change. But I didn't expect it to cost us so much."

Turner was silent for a moment, then he joined her by the window. "It always costs more than we expect. But that doesn't mean it isn't worth it."

Samantha looked at him, searching his face for the strength she felt slipping away from her. "Do you ever regret it, Turner? The sacrifices we've had to make?"

He met her gaze, his expression unreadable. "I regret that people like David had to die. I regret that we've lost so much along the way. But I don't regret fighting for what's right."

She nodded slowly, though the ache in her chest didn't ease. The reality of their situation was harsher than she'd ever imagined. They had uncovered a web of corruption that spanned the globe, but in doing so, they had become targets. Lives had been lost, and the constant threat of violence loomed over them every day. Some members of the team had already been forced into hiding, changing their names and cutting ties with loved ones to stay safe. Alex had sent his family out of the country after they'd received a chilling threat, and now he rarely left his workstation, consumed by paranoia.

Monica had left quietly, slipping away after the latest round of threats. Samantha hadn't heard from her in days, and though she knew it was for the best, the absence gnawed at her. Every departure felt like another piece of herself being stripped away.

Turner's voice broke through her thoughts. "You're stronger than you think, Sam. You've kept this team together through everything. Don't forget that."

She gave him a small, tired smile. "Some days, I don't feel very strong."

He placed a hand on her shoulder, his touch solid and reassuring. "You don't have to feel it. You just have to keep going."

Samantha nodded, knowing he was right, but the weariness clung to her. She turned back toward the desk, glancing at the phone that had been ringing almost nonstop for weeks—calls from journalists, lawyers, new whistleblowers eager to share their stories. The world had woken up, and Samantha's coalition was at the center of it all. But with each victory came a new threat, and the pressure was unrelenting.

"I just wonder," she said softly, "if I'll ever find peace again. If any of us will."

Turner was quiet for a moment, then he said, "Peace isn't what we're fighting for right now. But when this is all over—when they've been held accountable—you'll find it. We all will."

Samantha wished she could believe him, but in her heart, she knew that nothing would ever be the same again. The shadow network had changed the course of her life forever, and the sacrifices she had made, that they all had made, couldn't be undone. But there was no turning back now. They had come too far, and too much was at stake.

She straightened her shoulders, the weight of the world still pressing down, but her resolve hardening. "Then let's make sure it's worth it," she said, her voice filled with quiet determination.

Turner nodded. "We will."

And as Samantha turned back to her work, she knew that the fight was far from over—but she wouldn't stop until justice was served, no matter the cost.

The safehouse was eerily quiet for the first time in weeks. The constant hum of activity had slowed to a rare lull, with most of the team either resting or attending to their personal lives—those that were left. Samantha sat in the dimly lit living room, a cup of coffee cooling in her hands as she stared out the window at the soft glow of the city in the distance. It was a rare moment of stillness, and for once, she allowed herself to lean into it.

The fight wasn't over, not by a long shot. There were still trials, more threats, and the ever-present weight of the shadow network's lingering power. But tonight, in this brief pause, Samantha allowed herself to reflect on everything that had brought her to this point.

She sipped her coffee, the warmth a small comfort against the chill in the room. Her mind drifted to the beginning—the moment she had uncovered the first piece of evidence, the first crack in the facade of the network. Back then, it had been her and a small team, working in secrecy, with no idea how deep the corruption truly went. Now, years later, they had pulled the entire world into their fight.

Her phone buzzed softly on the table beside her, but for once, she ignored it. Tonight, she needed this moment of quiet. Her eyes drifted to the pile of reports on the corner of the table, evidence of the ongoing investigations and the legal battles yet to come. But beneath the exhaustion, there was a glimmer of something she hadn't felt in a long time—pride.

Turner walked into the room, his steps slow, as if he, too, was savoring the rare calm. He caught her eye and gave her a small nod, taking the seat across from her.

"Quiet night," he remarked, his voice low and reflective.

Samantha smiled faintly. "For once. I almost don't know what to do with it."

Turner chuckled softly. "You could try getting some sleep."

She shook her head, her smile widening just a little. "Maybe. But I think I needed this—a moment to just... breathe."

They sat in silence for a while, the weight of everything they had been through hanging between them. But it wasn't the suffocating pressure that had accompanied their earlier struggles. It was something different now. Lighter.

"You've done something incredible, Sam," Turner said, breaking the silence. His voice was calm, but there was a depth of sincerity in it that made her pause. "I know we've still got a long way to go, but look at where we are. You exposed them. You brought this whole thing crashing down."

Samantha looked at him, searching his face for a moment before responding. "*We* did. I couldn't have done any of this without you, without the team."

Turner leaned back, his expression softening. "You're right. But don't undersell yourself. You're the one who started this. You're the one who kept us all going, even when it seemed impossible."

She sighed, the memories of those impossible moments flooding back. The late nights, the betrayals, the deaths. "It still feels like we're not finished. Like there's always one more battle."

"There will be," Turner admitted. "But that doesn't mean you can't be proud of what we've accomplished so far."

Samantha looked out the window again, her thoughts drifting. For so long, it had been hard to see past the next crisis, the next emergency. But tonight, for the first time in what felt like forever, she allowed herself to acknowledge what they had achieved.

"I didn't think we'd ever get this far," she said quietly. "When we started, it seemed like we were taking on the world. No one believed us. No one thought we could win."

"But we did," Turner said, his voice steady. "We proved them wrong. And now the world is listening."

She felt a small flicker of hope light up inside her, a warmth she hadn't felt in a long time. It was fragile, like a candle in the wind, but it was there. She thought about the protests, the international investigations, the whistleblowers who had come forward because they believed in the truth. People who had been silenced for so long now had a voice. The network was crumbling, and while there was still much work to do, they had made the first crack.

For the first time, she allowed herself to think about the future—not just the next battle, but what might come after. The idea of a world where the shadow network no longer held sway, where the corruption they had exposed could finally be eradicated, didn't seem so far-fetched anymore.

"I guess I didn't think about what would come next," she admitted. "After all of this."

Turner's gaze softened. "You're not alone in that. But whatever comes next, we'll face it. We've made it this far."

Samantha nodded slowly, feeling the truth of his words settle over her. They weren't alone in this fight anymore. The world had joined them. And that gave her hope—real, tangible hope.

"I'm proud of us," she said softly, almost as if saying the words aloud made them more real. "I'm proud of what we've done."

"You should be," Turner replied, his tone gentle but firm. "We all are."

They sat in comfortable silence again, the weight of their accomplishments finally beginning to feel lighter. Samantha closed her eyes for a moment, breathing in the quiet, the calm. The fight wasn't over, but tonight, she would allow herself this—this brief, precious moment of peace.

And for the first time in a long while, she felt hopeful about what lay ahead.

Chapter 22
The Chase Begins

Samantha stood in front of the large board in the briefing room, staring at the photos, documents, and maps pinned in a chaotic collage. The remnants of the shadow network still loomed over them, even as she had thought they'd delivered a crushing blow. Despite all their victories, new intelligence had come in suggesting that the fight wasn't over—far from it.

Turner walked in, holding a file thick with fresh reports. His expression was grim, the lines around his eyes deepening as he handed it to her.

"I hate to say it, Sam, but we've got a problem," he said, his voice low.

Samantha opened the file, skimming through the pages. Reports of quiet meetings, shadowy transactions, and old names resurfacing with new ones. "What are we looking at?" she asked, her tone sharper than usual.

"Intel shows that the network's regrouping. Some of the key players are gone, but the infrastructure is still intact. New people are stepping in to fill the power vacuum. They're trying to reclaim what they lost." Turner pointed to one name in particular, his voice dark. "This guy, Ian Mackenzie. He's one of the new heads rising up in the ranks."

Samantha frowned, recognizing the name from previous investigations. Mackenzie had always been a minor player, skirting the edges of the shadow network without fully exposing himself. He'd avoided their earlier takedowns, but now it seemed he was stepping into the power void left by the crumbling leadership.

"Mackenzie," she muttered. "We've had him on our radar before, but he never made any bold moves."

"Until now," Turner said. "He's positioning himself to take control of what's left of the network. He's got allies—new faces, but the same playbook."

Samantha set the file down, the weight of the situation sinking in. "So, this isn't over. We cut off one head, and now another's growing in its place."

Turner nodded, his eyes hard. "Corruption's like a hydra. You strike one part down, and it regenerates. We knew this was a possibility."

She leaned back against the table, arms crossed, frustration simmering beneath her calm exterior. "It's never going to end, is it? Every time we think we've won, they find a way to claw back their power."

"It's not about winning or losing," Turner said. "It's about staying in the fight."

Samantha was silent for a moment, staring at the array of information pinned to the board. The sheer scale of what they were up against felt insurmountable, but she knew they couldn't stop. "We've come too far to back down now," she said finally. "But this... it's going to get worse before it gets better."

Turner crossed his arms, standing next to her. "You're right. They'll hit back harder now, more desperate. Mackenzie and his new allies know what's at stake. They've seen what we're capable of, so they're going to play dirtier."

"Do we have any idea how deep their regrouping goes?" Samantha asked, flipping through the pages in the file. "Who else is involved?"

Turner sighed, rubbing the back of his neck. "Not yet. We've got a few names, some loose connections, but nothing solid enough to make a move. It's early. They're trying to stay under the radar, rebuild their power slowly."

"They're going to make it look like business as usual," Samantha said, almost to herself. "Acting like nothing's changed, pulling strings from behind the scenes while the public thinks the fight is over."

"That's exactly it," Turner agreed. "They want us to think we've won. But they're playing the long game."

Samantha clenched her jaw, her frustration morphing into a quiet determination. "Well, they're not the only ones who can play the long game."

Turner gave her a sidelong glance, a hint of a smirk tugging at the corner of his mouth. "I thought you might say that."

She turned to face him, her eyes sharp. "We need to stay ahead of them. If Mackenzie's taking over, we need to cut him off before he consolidates his power. What's our next move?"

Turner pulled out another sheet from the file. "I've already got a few leads. Mackenzie's been moving money through shell companies—same tactics they've always used. We can follow the money, track down his operations before he gets too far ahead."

Samantha took the sheet from him, scanning the details. "Good. We need to hit them where it hurts, make sure they don't get the chance to rebuild."

"But it's not just Mackenzie," Turner added, his voice serious. "There are others, new faces stepping in. We'll need to dig deeper, figure out who's backing him. If we're going to take them down for good, we have to be thorough."

Samantha nodded, her mind already racing with plans. "We'll bring in the team. Start following the money trail, keep eyes on Mackenzie and anyone associated with him."

Turner gave a curt nod, already moving toward the door. "I'll get on it."

As he left, Samantha remained standing in front of the board, her thoughts swirling. They had come so far, but the shadow network was like a virus—persistent, always finding new ways to survive. And now, with new leaders rising, they were entering a new phase of the fight.

She knew the stakes were higher than ever. The victories they had achieved could easily be undone if Mackenzie and his ilk managed to regroup. But she also knew that they had the experience, the resources, and the determination to keep going.

"This isn't over," she muttered to herself, her eyes scanning the photos on the board. "But neither are we."

Samantha walked over to her desk, picking up the phone. It was time to rally the team again. The fight wasn't over, but they were far from defeated. And if Mackenzie thought he could rebuild what they had worked so hard to destroy, he was about to learn how wrong he was.

She dialed Monica's number, her voice steady as the line connected. "Monica, it's Sam. We've got new intel. It's time to regroup. Mackenzie's making his move."

There was a brief pause on the other end, and then Monica's voice, sharp with understanding: "I'll be there."

Samantha hung up, her resolve hardening. The shadow network was regrouping, but so were they. And this time, she would make sure they didn't get back up.

Samantha sat at the edge of her desk, the hum of the computer screens around her barely registering as she stared at the fresh dossier Turner had just handed her. The face staring back at her was unfamiliar, but the reputation surrounding the name sent a chill down her spine.

"Damien Locke," Turner said, his voice thick with frustration. "He's not just some replacement. He's a whole new breed."

Samantha's eyes flicked over the sparse details they had gathered on this new figure. Damien Locke was known within certain circles, not for his prominence or wealth, but for his brutality. Where the previous leaders of the shadow network had been more restrained, operating in the shadows to manipulate and control, Locke was different. He thrived on direct confrontation, and his methods were ruthless.

"He came out of nowhere," Turner continued. "There wasn't even a whisper of him before the collapse. But now, he's positioned himself as the head of what's left of the network. And from what we've gathered, he's not interested in playing by the same rules as his predecessors."

Samantha's grip tightened on the edge of the desk, her jaw clenched. "What do we know about him?"

Turner leaned against the wall, crossing his arms. "Not much. He's good at keeping his past clean, or at least hidden. We do know he's ex-military, likely mercenary work after that. He's been in and out of some of the most dangerous parts of the world—Middle East, Africa, Eastern Europe. Wherever there was a power vacuum or chaos to exploit, Locke was there."

"Sounds like he's used to cleaning up messes," Samantha muttered, flipping through the file.

"Exactly. And now, he's made the network his mess to clean up. Only this time, his goal isn't just to stabilize. It's to reassert control—and do it by any means necessary."

Monica, sitting at her workstation nearby, turned toward them, concern etched on her face. "If this guy's as ruthless as the intel suggests, what's his next move? He's not going to operate with the same careful touch the old leaders did, is he?"

Samantha shook her head, closing the file. "No, he won't. Locke doesn't care about subtlety or PR spin. He's going to come after us hard. This isn't going to be backroom deals or quiet manipulation. He's going to use fear, intimidation, and violence to crush any resistance."

Turner nodded in agreement. "We've already seen signs of it. Some of our sources in Europe have gone dark, and others are reporting that Locke's people have been asking questions—dangerous ones. He's cleaning house, and he's making it clear that anyone who doesn't fall in line will be dealt with."

Samantha stared at the dossier again, the reality of their situation sinking in. Locke wasn't like the leaders they'd taken down before. He wasn't concerned with maintaining the network's delicate web of influence—he was determined to rebuild, and he'd do it by any means necessary.

Monica glanced between them, her voice tense. "So, what's our play? Do we go after him directly? Try to expose him the way we did the others?"

Turner shook his head. "It's not going to be that simple. Locke isn't concerned about public image. Exposing him won't weaken his grip—it'll just make him more dangerous. He doesn't care about maintaining legitimacy the way the others did."

"Which means," Samantha added, "we need to approach this differently."

Turner looked at her, his expression dark. "You know what that means, Sam. Locke's going to come for you. You're the one who brought down the network in the first place. If he can't rebuild without taking us out, you're going to be his top target."

Samantha met his gaze, her mind racing. She had faced threats before, but this was different. Locke was a predator—cold, calculating, and without a shred of mercy. He wouldn't just try to discredit her; he'd aim to eliminate her entirely.

"I'm not backing down," she said firmly, her voice steady despite the knot of fear forming in her stomach. "If Locke thinks he can silence us, he's wrong. We've come too far to let him undo everything we've worked for."

Monica stood, walking over to join them. "But we need to be smart about this, Sam. Locke's not going to fight us on the same battlegrounds. He'll come at us from the shadows—hit us where we're vulnerable."

"We need to tighten our security," Turner said. "Make sure everyone on the team is protected. No more solo operations. We can't afford to take any risks with this guy in play."

Samantha nodded, her mind already spinning through the steps they needed to take. "We'll go on the defensive for now, but we need to gather more intel on Locke. There has to be something in his past, some weakness we can exploit. We need to know everything about him—his operations, his allies, his plans."

"Already on it," Monica said, returning to her computer. "I'll start digging through any military or mercenary records we can find. He's got to have left a trail somewhere."

Samantha took a deep breath, her resolve hardening. "Locke's not going to stop until he's regained control. But we're not going to give him the chance."

Turner's expression remained grim, but there was a flicker of admiration in his eyes. "You know he'll try to come after you personally."

Samantha's jaw tightened. "Let him try."

For a moment, the room was silent, the gravity of their new challenge settling over them. Locke was unlike any enemy they had faced before—more brutal, more determined. But Samantha knew one thing for certain: they had fought too hard to give up now. No matter how ruthless Locke was, no matter how many resources he had at his disposal, they would fight him with everything they had.

And this time, they wouldn't just survive. They would win.

"Let's get to work," she said, her voice filled with quiet determination. "This isn't over yet."

Samantha stood at the head of the conference room, her eyes scanning the faces of the few remaining members of her core team. The room felt emptier than it had months before, the cracks of loss and exhaustion visible in every glance exchanged. But there was no time to dwell on what they had lost. They had to rebuild. The shadow network was regrouping, and now, with Damien Locke taking the reins, the fight had grown more dangerous than ever.

"Alright," she began, her voice steady, projecting confidence even though the weight of the task ahead loomed large. "We need to rebuild, but this time, we're going to do it smarter, stronger. Locke is coming for us, and he's not playing by the same rules. We need more allies, more resources, and we need to hit them on every front—political, legal, and public."

Monica leaned forward, her fingers tracing over the edge of her notebook. "Who can we trust at this point, Sam? After everything that's happened, it feels like the network has eyes everywhere. Every time we've built something solid, they've found a way to dismantle it."

Samantha met her gaze, her voice firm. "We're going to rebuild with people who've seen the truth. We can't rely on the same power players we did before. This time, we're going to have to go deeper—activists, independent media, whistleblowers who've been working in the shadows just like us."

Turner, who was leaning against the wall with his arms crossed, spoke up. "I've already started reaching out to a few contacts in government who've been quietly supportive. They're not part of the old guard—new faces, but they've got influence.

They want change, and they're starting to see that the corruption goes far beyond what they thought."

Samantha nodded. "That's exactly what we need. People who aren't tied to the old system. Locke is going to try and buy or threaten anyone with old loyalties, but we're looking for people who've got nothing to lose by exposing him. People who are as invested in this fight as we are."

Alex, who had been silent for most of the meeting, looked up from his laptop. "What about legal support? We're going to need serious backing if we're going to take Locke down in court. He's got the resources to drag this out for years if we don't build a solid legal foundation."

Monica jumped in, her voice thoughtful. "There are a few international human rights lawyers who've been circling around this issue for a while. They've been working cases on the fringes of the shadow network—corporate exploitation, environmental damage—but they haven't been able to take on the whole machine. If we give them the evidence we've gathered, I think they'll join us."

"That's a good start," Samantha said. "Reach out to them, see who's willing to come on board. We need people who aren't afraid to stand up to this. And we need them now."

Alex frowned, his fingers hovering over the keys. "And the public? Locke's going to launch a PR war. If we're not careful, he'll turn this into a battle of narratives. We need to make sure the public doesn't lose faith in what we're doing."

Samantha's eyes narrowed as she considered the question. "We go to independent media. The major outlets are still too easily bought or intimidated. But there are journalists out there who are hungry for this story, who want to expose corruption at this scale. We'll give them what they need. Full transparency, no spin."

Turner shifted his weight, his face serious. "You realize, though, that the more people we bring in, the more vulnerable we become. Locke's got the resources to infiltrate, to plant people inside our own ranks."

"I know," Samantha said, her voice quiet but filled with resolve. "But we can't do this alone. We've always been vulnerable, Turner. This fight isn't about safety—it's about doing what needs to be done, no matter the risk."

Monica nodded in agreement. "We've been playing defense for too long. It's time to go on the offensive."

Samantha turned back to the board where she had sketched out their new plan—circles around names, branches extending to media, legal teams, and political figures. It wasn't as robust as it had been before, but it was a start. "This is going to be harder than anything we've done up to this point. Locke's different from the others. He won't just let us chip away at his power. He's going to hit back hard, and when he does, we need to be ready."

Alex's voice was steady, but there was a hint of hesitation. "What if it's not enough? What if, no matter how much we build, Locke's too strong? We've seen what he's capable of."

Samantha turned to him, her eyes blazing with determination. "Then we keep building. We keep fighting. We don't have the luxury of stopping. Locke wants to rebuild the network, but we've already proven we can tear it down. He's just a man, Alex. He's not invincible."

There was a long pause as the weight of her words settled over the room. Each of them felt the magnitude of what they were about to undertake, but there was no going back. The shadow network, once thought untouchable, had been wounded, but it was not defeated. And now, with Locke at the helm, the fight would be more dangerous than ever.

Samantha stepped closer to the table, placing both hands on the surface as she looked at her team. "This isn't just about taking Locke down. It's about dismantling the system that allows people like him to exist in the first place. We're fighting for something bigger than any of us."

Monica gave a firm nod, her voice filled with quiet conviction. "Then let's rebuild. Let's take the fight to them."

Turner straightened, his face filled with the same determination. "We've come too far to stop now."

Samantha took a deep breath, feeling the flicker of hope rise again within her. "Then let's get to work. It's time to rebuild the coalition."

And as her team moved into action, the fight felt new again, as if they were just beginning. The stakes were higher, the enemy more ruthless, but this time, they were ready. Together, they would rebuild, and they wouldn't stop until the shadow network was dismantled for good.

Samantha stood at the edge of the balcony, the night air cool against her skin as she looked out over the city. The skyline glimmered with distant lights, but her thoughts were far from the view. Behind her, the team was finishing the last of their preparations. Files were being encrypted, contacts reached, and strategies finalized. This moment of quiet felt surreal, knowing the storm that was about to come.

Turner stepped out onto the balcony, joining her in the silence for a moment before speaking. "You ready for this next phase?"

Samantha turned to him, her face calm but serious. "I have to be."

He nodded, crossing his arms as he leaned against the railing. "It's a big step. We're rebuilding, but this time... it's different."

"I know," she said softly. "It feels like we're starting all over again. Except now, the stakes are even higher, and the enemies are even more dangerous."

Turner gave her a sidelong glance. "But we've done this before. We took them down once—we'll do it again."

She offered a small smile, appreciating his confidence, but the weight of the mission still pressed heavily on her shoulders. "It's different this time, Turner. Locke is more ruthless than the others. He doesn't just want to silence us—he wants to destroy everything we've built."

"And that's why we're going to be smarter," Turner replied, his voice firm. "We've learned from the mistakes of the past. We know how they operate, and now we know how to fight them."

Samantha nodded, knowing he was right. But it wasn't just the logistics of the fight that weighed on her. It was the understanding that this battle wouldn't end anytime soon. She had committed herself to a war against an enemy that would always find new ways to survive, new leaders to rise, new methods to corrupt. It was an unending struggle. But even as that reality settled in, so did her resolve.

"We'll have to be relentless," she said, turning back toward the city. "They'll come at us harder, and they'll hit us from every angle—media, politics, even physically. Locke won't hold back."

Turner's eyes darkened at the mention of Locke, his voice low. "He's already made it clear that he'll stop at nothing. But we're not exactly defenseless."

She glanced at him, appreciating the steel in his voice. "No, we're not. We've got the truth, and we've got allies willing to fight for it. As long as we keep the truth alive, they can't win."

Inside the room, Monica and Alex were packing up the final materials. Alex's voice broke through the quiet as he checked one last file on his laptop. "Everything's encrypted and backed up. We're set for the next step whenever you're ready, Sam."

Samantha turned, her gaze moving from the skyline to her team. They had been through so much together—losses, betrayals, victories—and yet they were still here. Still fighting. The bond between them had deepened in ways she hadn't expected. They weren't just her colleagues anymore. They were her family.

Monica looked up from her notes, her eyes meeting Samantha's. "What's the next move?"

Samantha stepped back into the room, her decision already made. "We start reaching out to our new contacts, make sure our coalition is stronger than ever. We need to secure legal backing, build political alliances, and start planning our next offensive against Locke. This isn't just about survival anymore. We're going to dismantle the rest of the network, piece by piece."

Alex looked up from his screen, concern flickering in his eyes. "Locke's not going to wait for us to make the first move. He'll be gunning for us the second we step into the public eye again."

"I know," Samantha said, her voice calm but filled with determination. "That's why we have to be ready for anything. But this time, we're not going to let him dictate the terms."

Turner, who had been watching silently, spoke up. "We need to take the fight to him. Make sure he knows we're not backing down, that we're coming after everything he stands for."

Samantha nodded. "Exactly. We've been on the defensive for too long. Now, we make our move."

Monica, her expression thoughtful, chimed in. "And what about the others? The ones we've brought into the coalition? Are they prepared for this?"

Samantha met her gaze, her voice steady. "They know what's at stake. Anyone who joins us now understands the risks. This isn't just about taking down a few corrupt officials anymore. It's about dismantling the entire system that allows people like Locke to thrive."

The room fell silent again, the weight of their mission settling over them. Each of them knew the dangers they were facing, but the fear that had once paralyzed them was gone. In its place was a renewed sense of purpose—a determination to see this fight through to the end, no matter how long it took.

Samantha glanced at the map pinned on the wall, a visual representation of their global network. Dots and lines connected cities and countries, showing where their allies were gathering strength. It was just the beginning, but it was enough to give her hope.

"We've got people in place all over the world," she said, her voice filling with quiet confidence. "This isn't just our fight anymore. It's global. And Locke can't stop that."

Turner stepped forward, standing next to her, his presence solid and reassuring. "No, he can't."

Samantha turned to face her team, her family, and for the first time in a long while, she felt ready for what was coming. The fight wasn't over, but she knew they had the strength to continue. Together, they had built something powerful—something that could withstand the darkness that Locke represented.

"Let's finish this," Samantha said, her voice filled with determination. "We've got a lot of work to do."

With that, the team began to move, packing up the last of their gear, preparing for the next phase of their mission. The future was uncertain, but Samantha no longer feared the unknown. She had faced it before, and she would face it again—with her team beside her.

As they stepped into the night, ready for the battles that lay ahead, Samantha allowed herself a moment of quiet reflection. The journey was far from over, but they were stronger now. And no matter how many enemies rose to challenge them, they would continue fighting for the truth.

Because that was the one thing no one could ever take away from them.

Chapter 23
A Fatal Mistake

The successful release of their data had sent shockwaves through the pharmaceutical industry and beyond. Public outcry was at an all-time high, and regulatory bodies were scrambling to respond. Samantha Cross and her team were riding a wave of momentum, but they knew the fight was far from over. Their adversaries were wounded, but not defeated.

Samantha gathered her team at the command table. Turner, Alex, Rachel, and Dr. Greene were all present, their faces a mix of determination and exhaustion.

"We've made significant progress," Samantha began, her voice strong but measured. "But we can't afford to be complacent. Our enemies are likely planning a counterattack."

Turner nodded, his eyes sharp. "Our field teams have reported increased activity from several of the organizations we exposed. They're regrouping and could retaliate at any moment."

Alex looked up from his laptop, concern etched on his face. "I've detected attempts to breach our systems again. They're more sophisticated this time. We need to reinforce our defenses."

Rachel, flipping through a stack of messages, added, "Our allies are still with us, but they're worried. We need to show them we're prepared for whatever comes next."

Dr. Greene, his voice calm and steady, said, "We need to maintain our momentum and keep the public engaged. The more eyes we have on this, the harder it will be for our adversaries to strike back without repercussions."

Samantha nodded, absorbing their input. "Let's take proactive steps. Turner, coordinate with our field teams to ensure they're prepared for any retaliation. Alex, strengthen our digital defenses and set up additional monitoring. Rachel, communicate with our allies and reassure them of our readiness. Dr. Greene, keep engaging with the scientific community and the media. We need to stay visible and vocal."

The team dispersed, each member diving into their tasks with renewed purpose. Samantha felt a surge of pride in her team's resilience and dedication. They were facing powerful adversaries, but they were not backing down.

Later that day, as the team reconvened for an update, Alex had news to share. "I've set up additional firewalls and intrusion detection systems. We're as secure as we can be, but we need to stay alert. They're not going to stop trying."

Turner added, "Our field teams are on high alert. We've secured safe locations for our whistleblowers and increased surveillance around our key assets."

Rachel, holding a report, said, "Our allies are reassured by our actions. They're ready to support us publicly if needed. We need to keep them informed and engaged."

Dr. Greene, looking up from his laptop, added, "I've scheduled several interviews with major media outlets. We need to keep our narrative strong and ensure the public stays informed."

Samantha felt a sense of urgency. "Let's move forward with these plans. We need to stay ahead of our adversaries. Turner, coordinate any necessary relocations for our whistleblowers. Alex, keep monitoring for any signs of digital intrusion. Rachel, maintain close communication with our allies. Dr. Greene, prepare for your media engagements."

As the team moved to execute their plans, Samantha took a moment to reflect on the journey that had brought them to this point. They had faced incredible challenges and emerged stronger each time. Their fight was far from over, but they were united and determined.

That evening, Samantha received a call from Julia, who had been working closely with their partners. She put the call on speaker, the team gathering around.

"Julia, what's the latest?" Samantha asked.

Julia's voice crackled through the speaker. "We've received intel that several of the organizations we exposed are planning a coordinated counterattack. They're desperate and could try anything to silence us."

Turner's eyes narrowed. "Do we have any specifics?"

"Not yet," Julia replied. "But our sources indicate they're targeting our key assets and trying to discredit our whistleblowers."

Rachel, her expression serious, said, "We need to protect our people and counter their narrative. We can't let them undermine our work."

Dr. Greene added, "We must be prepared to respond swiftly. Any attack on our credibility could weaken our position."

Samantha felt a surge of determination. "We won't let them succeed. Julia, keep us updated with any new information. Turner, double-check our security protocols and ensure our teams are ready. Alex, set up additional monitoring for any signs of digital attacks. Rachel, prepare a communication strategy to counter any false narratives. Dr. Greene, keep the media informed and ensure our story remains strong."

As the call ended, the team sprang into action. They were facing a formidable threat, but their resolve was unshaken. They had come too far to be silenced now.

Throughout the night, the team worked tirelessly, reinforcing their defenses and preparing for the worst. The sense of urgency was palpable, but so was their unity and determination.

As dawn broke, Samantha looked around at her team, feeling a deep sense of pride. They were ready for whatever came next, united in their mission and determined to see it through. The fight for justice and ethical practices was far from over, but they were stronger and more resolved than ever.

The safe house buzzed with a palpable sense of urgency. Samantha Cross and her team had fortified their defenses, but the looming threat of a counterattack kept everyone on edge. They had made significant strides in their fight for transparency and ethics, but their adversaries were formidable and desperate.

Samantha sat at the command table, surrounded by Turner, Alex, Rachel, and Dr. Greene. The air was thick with anticipation as they reviewed the latest intelligence reports.

"Julia's intel was right," Samantha began, her voice steady but intense. "Our adversaries are planning a coordinated strike. We need to be ready for anything."

Turner leaned forward, his eyes sharp. "I've doubled the security detail around our key assets and relocated our most vulnerable whistleblowers to secure locations. But we need to be prepared for digital attacks as well."

Alex, his fingers flying over the keyboard, looked up. "I've set up advanced intrusion detection systems. We'll know the moment they try anything. But they're persistent and sophisticated. We need to stay on high alert."

Rachel, holding a stack of communications, said, "Our allies are prepared to go public with their support if needed. We need to keep them in the loop and ready to mobilize at a moment's notice."

Dr. Greene nodded, his voice calm but firm. "The media is eager for updates. We need to control the narrative and ensure our story remains strong and credible."

As the team discussed their strategies, a sudden alert flashed on Alex's screen. "We've got incoming," Alex said, his voice tense.

"Multiple attempts to breach our systems. They're hitting us hard."

Samantha's eyes narrowed. "Can you hold them off?"

Alex's fingers danced over the keyboard. "I'm blocking them as fast as they come. But this is coordinated. They're using multiple vectors. We need to brace for a full-scale digital assault."

Turner turned to Samantha. "We need to activate our contingency plans. If they breach our systems, we could lose everything."

Samantha nodded. "Do it. Alex, initiate the lockdown protocol. Turner, ensure all physical security measures are in place. Rachel, inform our allies and prepare them for immediate action. Dr. Greene, get ready to engage with the media. We need to control the narrative if this goes public."

As Alex initiated the lockdown protocol, the safe house's digital defenses went into overdrive. Screens flashed with alerts and countermeasures, a digital war playing out in real-time.

Rachel grabbed her phone and began contacting their allies. "This is Rachel. We're under attack. Be ready to go public with your support. We need to show a united front."

Dr. Greene prepared his statements for the media, his calm demeanor a stark contrast to the chaos around him. "We need to emphasize the integrity of our evidence and the lengths to which our adversaries are going to discredit us."

Samantha paced the room, her mind racing. "We've faced worse. We'll get through this."

Turner, coordinating with the security teams, spoke into his earpiece. "All teams, be on high alert. We're under coordinated attack. Protect our assets at all costs."

Suddenly, Alex's face lit up with alarm. "They've breached one of our outer firewalls. We're holding them off, but they're getting closer."

Samantha's heart pounded. "Can we isolate the breach?"

Alex's fingers flew over the keyboard. "I'm working on it. If we can isolate it, we can contain the damage."

Minutes felt like hours as the team worked in a frenzy to fend off the attack. The tension in the room was palpable, each member of the team pushing their limits to protect their mission.

Finally, Alex let out a sigh of relief. "We've isolated the breach. They're locked out of our main systems, but they got close. Too close."

Rachel, still on the phone with their allies, said, "Our partners are ready to speak out. They're waiting for our signal."

Dr. Greene, reviewing his notes, added, "We're prepared to address the media. We need to go on the offensive and expose their attempts to silence us."

Samantha took a deep breath, the adrenaline still coursing through her veins. "We've held them off for now, but we need to stay vigilant. Let's go public with this. Rachel, coordinate with our allies. Dr. Greene, get ready to engage with the media. Turner, keep our security tight. Alex, continue monitoring our systems for any further attempts."

The team moved with a renewed sense of purpose, their resilience and unity shining through. They had faced a significant threat and come out stronger, but the fight was far from over.

As the team executed their plans, Samantha felt a deep sense of pride in their collective strength. They had built something powerful, and they were ready to defend it at all costs. The battle for justice and ethical practices was intensifying, but with their determination and the support of their allies, they were prepared to face whatever came next.

The safe house was a fortress of activity. After narrowly fending off the cyberattack, Samantha Cross and her team knew they had to strike back hard and fast. Their adversaries had revealed their desperation, and now it was time to capitalize on that vulnerability. The team prepared to go live with their story, ensuring the public would be on their side.

Samantha stood at the command table, surrounded by Turner, Alex, Rachel, and Dr. Greene. The air was electric with anticipation and determination.

"We need to make sure our message is clear and powerful," Samantha began. "This broadcast is our chance to expose the truth and rally support. Let's make it count."

Turner nodded. "Security is tight. We're monitoring all entry points and communication channels. Nothing gets in or out without our say-so."

Alex, checking his laptop, added, "I've set up secure lines for the broadcast. We'll be live-streaming to multiple platforms. If they try anything, we'll know."

Rachel, holding a stack of notes, said, "I've coordinated with our allies. They're ready to amplify our message as soon as we go live. We need to keep the momentum going."

Dr. Greene, his calm voice steadying the room, added, "I'll handle the scientific and ethical aspects. We need to show that we're not just fighting for ourselves, but for everyone affected by these unethical practices."

Samantha nodded, feeling the weight of their mission. "Let's do this. Rachel, are the statements ready?"

Rachel glanced at her notes. "Yes, we've got key points and responses to potential questions. We need to stay on message and keep it concise."

Turner's phone buzzed with an update. "Our security teams are in position. We're ready whenever you are."

Samantha took a deep breath. "Alright, let's get into position."

As they moved to the designated broadcast area, the team was acutely aware of the significance of this moment. They were about to confront their adversaries on a global stage, and there was no room for error.

Minutes later, they were live. Samantha stood at the forefront, flanked by her team. The camera focused on her as she began to speak.

"Good evening. My name is Samantha Cross, and I'm here with my team to expose the truth about the unethical practices in the pharmaceutical industry. We've faced significant threats and attacks, but we are determined to ensure that justice prevails."

The screen shifted to Dr. Greene, who detailed the scientific and ethical violations they had uncovered. "The evidence we present today is irrefutable. These companies have endangered lives and violated ethical standards for profit. This cannot and will not be tolerated."

Rachel took over, emphasizing the support they had garnered. "We have the backing of the scientific community and numerous advocacy groups. Together, we are calling for immediate action and accountability."

As they spoke, Alex monitored the incoming data streams. "We're getting a lot of engagement. The message is spreading fast. They're trying to interfere, but we're holding them off."

Turner, his eyes scanning the security feeds, added, "No physical threats detected. We're secure for now, but we need to stay vigilant."

Samantha continued, addressing the viewers directly. "We stand united in our fight for transparency and ethical practices. We call on regulatory bodies, the media, and the public to join us in demanding accountability. Together, we can make a difference."

The broadcast continued with statements from key allies and whistleblowers, each adding weight to their cause. As the team spoke, the response was overwhelmingly positive. Messages of support flooded in, and the momentum continued to build.

Rachel, still coordinating with their partners, smiled. "Our allies are amplifying the message. It's trending across multiple platforms. We're reaching millions."

Dr. Greene added, "The scientific community is rallying behind us. This is exactly what we needed."

Samantha felt a surge of pride and relief. "We've done it. But we need to keep the pressure on. This is just the beginning."

As the broadcast concluded, the team gathered for a quick debrief. The atmosphere was charged with a mix of exhaustion and triumph.

"That was powerful," Turner said. "We've made a strong statement."

Alex nodded, still monitoring the data. "We're seeing a massive uptick in support. They're trying to counter it, but they're failing."

Rachel, her eyes bright with determination, added, "We need to maintain this momentum. Keep engaging with our supporters and the media."

Dr. Greene's voice was calm but resolute. "We've set the stage for real change. Now we need to follow through and ensure these practices are stopped."

Samantha looked around at her team, feeling a deep sense of unity and purpose. "We've come a long way, and we've shown we're not backing down. Let's keep pushing forward. The fight for justice is far from over, but we're stronger than ever."

The team dispersed, each member diving back into their tasks with renewed energy. They had faced a significant threat and emerged victorious, but the battle was not yet won. With their newfound momentum and the support of their allies, they were ready to face whatever challenges lay ahead.

The aftermath of the broadcast left the safe house in a state of controlled chaos. The team had achieved a significant victory, but they knew they needed to consolidate their gains and prepare for the next wave of attacks. The stakes had never been higher.

Samantha Cross sat at the command table, flanked by Turner, Alex, Rachel, and Dr. Greene. The atmosphere was charged with a mixture of relief and tension.

"We made a huge impact with that broadcast," Samantha began, her voice firm. "But our adversaries won't sit idly by. We need to be ready for their next move."

Turner nodded, his eyes scanning the latest security updates. "Our security teams report increased activity around our key assets. We're on high alert, but we need to stay vigilant."

Alex, still monitoring the digital landscape, added, "The attempts to breach our systems have intensified. They're throwing everything they have at us, but we're holding them off. For now."

Rachel, holding a stack of messages from their allies, said, "We've received overwhelming support from the public and our partners. They're ready to stand with us, but they need guidance on the next steps."

Dr. Greene's voice was calm but resolute. "We've built a strong coalition, but we need to ensure our message remains clear and unified. The media is looking to us for leadership."

Samantha felt the weight of their responsibility. "Let's outline our immediate priorities. Turner, continue to coordinate with our security teams and ensure all our assets are protected. Alex, keep fortifying our digital defenses and monitor any potential threats. Rachel, work with our allies to maintain public engagement and prepare for any coordinated responses. Dr.

Greene, stay in touch with the media and reinforce our narrative."

The team dispersed to their tasks, the air thick with determination. Samantha knew they were in a critical phase. Every move had to be precise, every decision calculated.

Later that evening, as the team gathered for an update, Alex had urgent news. "We've intercepted communications suggesting a coordinated smear campaign against us. They're planning to discredit our whistleblowers and undermine our credibility."

Samantha's eyes narrowed. "Can we counter it?"

Alex nodded. "We can preemptively release additional evidence and testimonies. If we stay ahead of their narrative, we can mitigate the damage."

Rachel added, "I've been in touch with our key allies. They're ready to support us publicly. We need to coordinate our response and make sure our message is loud and clear."

Dr. Greene chimed in, "We should organize a follow-up press conference. Reinforce our findings and show the strength of our coalition."

Turner's voice was firm. "We'll need to ensure security is airtight. They might try more than just digital attacks."

Samantha nodded, her mind racing with the details. "Alright, let's move forward with this. Alex, prepare the additional evidence and secure our channels for release. Rachel, coordinate with our allies and draft the communication plan. Dr. Greene, prepare for the press conference and ensure our key messages are solid. Turner, double-check our security measures and prepare for any contingencies."

As the team moved to execute their plans, Samantha felt a surge of pride in their collective strength. They were facing formidable adversaries, but they were united and determined.

Hours later, the team gathered in the broadcast room, ready for the follow-up press conference. The atmosphere was tense but focused. Samantha stood at the forefront, flanked by her team.

"Good evening," Samantha began, her voice steady. "We've come together tonight to address recent developments and reinforce our commitment to transparency and ethical practices. Our mission is to protect the integrity of scientific research and ensure accountability within the pharmaceutical industry."

Dr. Greene stepped forward, his calm voice resonating through the room. "The evidence we have presented is irrefutable. The attempts to discredit our whistleblowers and undermine our work are desperate and baseless. We stand by our findings and will continue to fight for justice."

Rachel added, "Our coalition is stronger than ever. We have the support of the public, the scientific community, and numerous advocacy groups. Together, we will not be silenced."

Turner's eyes scanned the room, ensuring all security measures were in place. "We are prepared for any attempts to disrupt our work. Our focus remains on protecting our whistleblowers and ensuring their safety."

Alex concluded, "We have fortified our digital defenses and are monitoring all channels for any threats. We will continue to safeguard the integrity of our data and our mission."

As the press conference continued, the team received an outpouring of support from the public and their allies. Messages flooded in, reinforcing their resolve.

Rachel, still coordinating with their partners, smiled. "The response is overwhelming. We've got the momentum, and our message is resonating."

Dr. Greene nodded, his expression thoughtful. "We need to capitalize on this. Keep the pressure on and ensure our narrative stays front and center."

Turner's phone buzzed with updates from the field teams. "Our assets are secure. We're ready for any retaliation."

Samantha felt a deep sense of unity and purpose. "We've shown our strength and resilience. Now we need to keep pushing forward. The fight for justice and ethical practices is far from over, but we're stronger and more determined than ever."

As the team dispersed to continue their work, the safe house buzzed with renewed energy and determination. They had faced significant threats and emerged stronger. With their newfound momentum and the support of their allies, they were ready to face whatever challenges lay ahead.

Chapter 24
Fighting in the Dark

The safe house had become a beacon of hope and resilience. The team's successful countermeasures had staved off their adversaries' initial attacks, but Samantha Cross knew they needed to bolster their defenses and solidify their alliances. The battle was far from over, and the stakes had never been higher.

Samantha stood at the command table, surrounded by Turner, Alex, Rachel, and Dr. Greene. The atmosphere was charged with a mix of determination and anticipation.

"We've held our ground, but we need to strengthen our position," Samantha began, her voice steady and authoritative. "We need to rally our allies and reinforce our defenses. Turner, what's our current security status?"

Turner leaned forward, his expression serious. "Our security teams are in place, and we've reinforced our perimeter. We're monitoring for any signs of physical threats, but we need to stay vigilant. They're desperate and could try anything."

Alex, his eyes glued to his laptop screen, added, "Our digital defenses are holding, but they're persistent. We've detected several new attempts to breach our systems. We've blocked them, but we can't afford to let our guard down."

Rachel, holding a stack of messages, said, "Our allies are ready to stand with us. We've got support from key figures in the scientific community, advocacy groups, and even some regulatory bodies. We need to coordinate our efforts and present a united front."

Dr. Greene nodded, his calm voice providing a steadying influence. "We've built a strong coalition, but we need to keep engaging with the media and the public. Our message is strong, but we need to ensure it stays that way."

Samantha absorbed their input, her mind racing with the details. "Alright, let's outline our immediate priorities. Turner, continue to oversee security and ensure all our assets are protected. Alex, keep monitoring our systems and strengthen our digital defenses. Rachel, work with our allies to coordinate our next steps and maintain public engagement. Dr. Greene, keep the media informed and reinforce our narrative."

The team dispersed to their tasks, the air thick with determination. Samantha knew they were in a critical phase. Every move had to be precise, every decision calculated.

Later that day, as the team reconvened for an update, Alex had urgent news. "I've intercepted communications suggesting they're planning a major disinformation campaign against us. They're trying to undermine our credibility and create confusion."

Samantha's eyes narrowed. "How do we counter it?"

Alex's fingers flew over the keyboard. "We need to stay ahead of their narrative. We can preemptively release more evidence and testimonies. If we control the flow of information, we can mitigate the damage."

Rachel added, "Our allies are ready to support us publicly. We need to coordinate our response and make sure our message is loud and clear."

Dr. Greene chimed in, "We should organize a press conference to address these issues head-on. Reinforce our findings and show the strength of our coalition."

Turner's voice was firm. "We'll need to ensure security is airtight. They might try more than just digital attacks."

Samantha nodded, her mind racing with the details. "Alright, let's move forward with this. Alex, prepare the additional evidence and secure our channels for release. Rachel, coordinate with our allies and draft the communication plan. Dr. Greene, prepare for the press conference and ensure our key messages are solid. Turner, double-check our security measures and prepare for any contingencies."

As the team moved to execute their plans, Samantha felt a surge of pride in their collective strength. They were facing formidable adversaries, but they were united and determined.

Hours later, the team gathered in the broadcast room, ready for the follow-up press conference. The atmosphere was tense but focused. Samantha stood at the forefront, flanked by her team.

"Good evening," Samantha began, her voice steady. "We've come together tonight to address recent developments and reinforce our commitment to transparency and ethical practices. Our mission is to protect the integrity of scientific research and ensure accountability within the pharmaceutical industry."

Dr. Greene stepped forward, his calm voice resonating through the room. "The evidence we have presented is irrefutable. The attempts to discredit our whistleblowers and undermine our work are desperate and baseless. We stand by our findings and will continue to fight for justice."

Rachel added, "Our coalition is stronger than ever. We have the support of the public, the scientific community, and numerous advocacy groups. Together, we will not be silenced."

Turner's eyes scanned the room, ensuring all security measures were in place. "We are prepared for any attempts to disrupt our work. Our focus remains on protecting our whistleblowers and ensuring their safety."

Alex concluded, "We have fortified our digital defenses and are monitoring all channels for any threats. We will continue to safeguard the integrity of our data and our mission."

As the press conference continued, the team received an outpouring of support from the public and their allies. Messages flooded in, reinforcing their resolve.

Rachel, still coordinating with their partners, smiled. "The response is overwhelming. We've got the momentum, and our message is resonating."

Dr. Greene nodded, his expression thoughtful. "We need to capitalize on this. Keep the pressure on and ensure our narrative stays front and center."

Turner's phone buzzed with updates from the field teams. "Our assets are secure. We're ready for any retaliation."

Samantha felt a deep sense of unity and purpose. "We've shown our strength and resilience. Now we need to keep pushing forward. The fight for justice and ethical practices is far from over, but we're stronger and more determined than ever."

As the team dispersed to continue their work, the safe house buzzed with renewed energy and determination. They had faced significant threats and emerged stronger. With their newfound momentum and the support of their allies, they were ready to face whatever challenges lay ahead.

The success of their press conference had given Samantha Cross and her team a brief respite, but they knew their adversaries were far from defeated. The momentum they had gained needed to be sustained, and their coalition had to be solidified further. As they strategized their next steps, the team remained vigilant, fully aware that the next attack could come at any moment.

Samantha sat at the command table, surrounded by Turner, Alex, Rachel, and Dr. Greene. The room was filled with the hum of computers and the quiet intensity of a team preparing for the next battle.

"We need to anticipate their next move," Samantha began, her voice steady. "They'll likely try to undermine our credibility again. Turner, what's the latest on security?"

Turner looked up from his tablet, displaying the latest security feeds. "Our perimeter is secure, and we've increased surveillance around our key assets. But we're detecting unusual activity. It's subtle, but it could be a prelude to something bigger."

Alex, his fingers flying over the keyboard, added, "I've noticed increased probing on our digital defenses. They're looking for weaknesses. We've strengthened our firewalls, but we need to stay alert."

Rachel, scanning through the latest messages, said, "Our allies are concerned about the potential for another disinformation campaign. We need to keep them reassured and coordinated."

Dr. Greene, his calm voice providing a steadying influence, added, "The media is still very much on our side, but we need to maintain our narrative. Any slip could be exploited."

Samantha absorbed their input, her mind racing with the details. "Alright, let's outline our immediate priorities. Turner, increase patrols and double-check our security measures. Alex, continue monitoring for any digital threats and enhance our defensive protocols. Rachel, maintain close communication with our allies and prepare them for any coordinated responses. Dr. Greene, keep the media engaged and ensure our message stays strong."

The team dispersed to their tasks, the air thick with determination. Samantha knew they were in a critical phase. Every move had to be precise, every decision calculated.

As the day progressed, Turner approached Samantha with an update. "We've identified some of the unusual activity. It appears to be drones, likely surveillance. They're testing our defenses."

Samantha frowned. "Can we take them down?"

Turner nodded. "We have the capability, but doing so might tip our hand. We need to be strategic."

"Monitor them closely," Samantha replied. "We need to know what they're planning without revealing our own capabilities."

Meanwhile, Alex called out from his station. "I've isolated some of the probing attempts. They're sophisticated, but we've managed to block them. However, I found something interesting—a pattern that suggests they're using a backdoor. It's faint, but it's there."

Samantha's eyes narrowed. "Can you trace it?"

Alex nodded. "I'm working on it. It's going to take some time, but if we can find the source, we might be able to turn the tables."

"Do it," Samantha said firmly. "We need every advantage we can get."

As Alex continued his work, Rachel came over with an update on their allies. "I've spoken with several key figures. They're on high alert and ready to respond to any disinformation. We need to coordinate our efforts to ensure a unified front."

Dr. Greene joined them, his expression thoughtful. "We should prepare a series of preemptive statements. If they try to discredit us, we can counter with hard evidence and testimonials from our supporters."

Samantha nodded. "Good idea. Let's draft those statements and be ready to release them at a moment's notice. We need to stay ahead of their narrative."

Hours later, as the team reconvened, Alex had significant news. "I've traced the backdoor attempts to a network of servers. They're using a complex series of relays to mask their location, but I've managed to pinpoint one of the sources. It's a known front for one of the pharmaceutical companies we've been targeting."

Turner's eyes sharpened. "This could be our chance to gather more evidence. If we can infiltrate their network, we might find incriminating data."

Rachel looked concerned. "It's risky. If they detect us, it could escalate the situation."

Samantha weighed their options. "We need to be smart about this. Alex, can you set up a secure channel to access their network without being detected?"

Alex nodded confidently. "I can. It's going to take some time, but I can do it."

"Then do it," Samantha decided. "We need that information. Turner, keep our physical defenses tight. Rachel, continue coordinating with our allies. Dr. Greene, prepare to engage with the media if we uncover anything significant."

The team moved to execute their plans, the atmosphere tense but determined. They were facing formidable adversaries, but they were united and prepared for the challenge.

As the night wore on, Samantha watched her team working tirelessly. Their dedication and resilience filled her with pride. They had come so far, and though the road ahead was fraught with danger, they were ready to face it together.

They were not just fighting for themselves, but for justice and ethical practices. With every step, they were forging a path forward, determined to expose the truth and hold those responsible accountable.

The air in the safe house was charged with anticipation. Samantha Cross and her team had managed to trace their adversaries' digital attacks to a key source. Now, they were on the brink of uncovering critical evidence that could turn the tide decisively in their favor.

Samantha gathered Turner, Alex, Rachel, and Dr. Greene at the command table. The atmosphere was tense but focused.

"Alex, where do we stand?" Samantha asked, her voice steady but urgent.

Alex looked up from his laptop, his eyes intense. "I've managed to set up a secure channel. We're ready to infiltrate their network. This could give us the evidence we need to expose their operations."

Turner nodded. "We need to be prepared for any retaliation. If they realize we're inside their network, they could launch a counterattack."

Rachel, holding a stack of documents, added, "Our allies are ready to support us publicly. We need to coordinate our efforts and be prepared to release this information strategically."

Dr. Greene, his calm voice providing a steadying influence, said, "We must ensure that whatever we find is presented clearly and credibly. The media and public trust us, and we need to maintain that trust."

Samantha absorbed their input, her mind racing with the details. "Alright, let's proceed. Alex, start the infiltration. Turner, keep our physical and digital defenses on high alert. Rachel, work with our allies to prepare for a coordinated release. Dr. Greene, get ready to engage with the media."

The team dispersed to their tasks, the air thick with determination. Samantha knew they were on the brink of a significant breakthrough.

Hours later, Alex called out, "I'm in. I've accessed their network. There's a lot of data here. It's going to take some time to sift through it all, but I've already found some incriminating documents."

Samantha moved to Alex's side, peering at the screen. "Can we get copies of everything? We need to ensure we have irrefutable evidence."

Alex nodded, his fingers flying over the keyboard. "I'm downloading everything now. This could take a while, but it's worth it."

Turner, monitoring the security feeds, added, "We need to be ready for any signs they've detected us. So far, everything looks clear, but we can't be too careful."

Rachel was on the phone with one of their key allies. "Yes, we're on the verge of something big. Be ready to mobilize your networks. We need to hit hard and fast."

Dr. Greene, reviewing the preliminary data Alex had accessed, said, "This is solid. We have emails, financial records, and internal memos. It's a clear trail of corruption and unethical practices."

Samantha felt a surge of excitement and urgency. "Let's keep moving. Alex, once we have everything, we'll need to analyze it quickly. Turner, ensure our security is airtight. Rachel, coordinate the release strategy with our allies. Dr. Greene, prepare to present our findings."

As the night wore on, the team worked tirelessly. The safe house buzzed with focused energy, each member pushing their limits to ensure the success of their mission.

Finally, Alex leaned back, a satisfied look on his face. "We've got it. All the data is downloaded and secured. This is the smoking gun we've been looking for."

Samantha's eyes sparkled with determination. "Excellent work, Alex. Turner, any signs of retaliation?"

Turner shook his head. "Not yet, but we need to stay on high alert. They won't take this lying down."

Rachel, coordinating with their allies, said, "Everyone is ready. We'll release the information simultaneously across multiple platforms. They won't be able to contain it."

Dr. Greene, reviewing the final presentation, added, "This is solid. We have everything we need to make a compelling case."

Samantha felt a deep sense of satisfaction and resolve. "Let's move forward. Release the information and be ready to respond to any fallout. We've come too far to back down now."

As the team executed their plans, the air was thick with anticipation. The release of the data was met with immediate and widespread attention. News outlets picked up the story, and social media buzzed with reactions.

Rachel monitored the responses, her face lighting up with excitement. "It's working. The public is outraged, and our allies are amplifying our message. This is exactly what we needed."

Dr. Greene, preparing for a series of media interviews, said, "We need to keep the pressure on. This is our chance to force real change."

Turner's phone buzzed with updates from their security teams. "No signs of immediate retaliation, but we need to stay vigilant. They'll respond eventually."

Samantha felt a deep sense of pride in her team. "We've done it. We've exposed them, and now we need to ensure this momentum leads to lasting change."

As the team continued to work, the safe house buzzed with a sense of accomplishment and determination. They had faced significant challenges and emerged stronger. With their newfound momentum and the support of their allies, they were ready to face whatever came next.

The release of the incriminating evidence sent shockwaves through the industry and beyond. News outlets were ablaze with the revelations, and the public outcry was immediate and intense. Samantha Cross and her team watched the events unfold from the safe house, their faces a mix of satisfaction and vigilance.

Samantha stood at the command table, surrounded by Turner, Alex, Rachel, and Dr. Greene. The air was thick with a sense of achievement, but also a readiness for the inevitable backlash.

"We've struck a significant blow," Samantha began, her voice steady. "But we need to be prepared for their countermeasures. Turner, what's our current security status?"

Turner leaned forward, his expression serious. "Our security teams are on high alert. We've detected some unusual activity around our key assets, but nothing overt yet. We need to stay vigilant."

Alex, his eyes glued to his laptop, added, "I've set up additional monitoring on all channels. They're trying to regroup, but we have the upper hand for now. We need to maintain our defenses."

Rachel, holding a tablet displaying the latest media coverage, said, "The public response is overwhelmingly positive. Our allies are speaking out, and the pressure on regulatory bodies is increasing. This is our moment."

Dr. Greene, his voice calm and reassuring, added, "We need to keep the narrative focused. The media is on our side, but we need to ensure the story remains about the corruption and unethical practices, not about us."

Samantha nodded, absorbing their input. "Alright, let's keep pushing. Turner, double-check our security measures and ensure our assets are protected. Alex, continue monitoring for any digital threats. Rachel, maintain close communication with our allies and the media. Dr. Greene, keep reinforcing our message."

The team dispersed to their tasks, the air buzzing with determination. Samantha knew they had the momentum, but they couldn't afford to let their guard down.

As the day progressed, Turner approached Samantha with an update. "We've detected increased surveillance around our key assets. It looks like they're trying to gather information on our movements."

Samantha frowned. "Can we counter it?"

Turner nodded. "We've deployed additional counter-surveillance measures. They won't get anything useful, but we need to be ready for anything."

Meanwhile, Alex called out from his station. "I've intercepted some communications. They're planning a coordinated smear campaign. They're desperate to discredit us and shift the focus away from their corruption."

Rachel, looking up from her tablet, added, "Our allies are ready to counter any disinformation. We need to coordinate our response and ensure our message is clear and consistent."

Dr. Greene joined them, his expression thoughtful. "We should prepare a series of preemptive statements. If they try to discredit us, we can counter with hard evidence and testimonials from our supporters."

Samantha felt a surge of determination. "Let's move forward with this. Turner, keep our physical defenses tight. Alex, continue monitoring and intercepting their communications. Rachel, coordinate the response with our allies. Dr. Greene, prepare the statements and ensure our key messages are solid."

As the team executed their plans, the atmosphere was tense but focused. They were facing a formidable adversary, but their unity and determination were stronger than ever.

Hours later, the team gathered in the broadcast room, ready to address the public once again. Samantha stood at the forefront, flanked by her team.

"Good evening," Samantha began, her voice clear and confident. "We've come together tonight to address recent developments and reinforce our commitment to transparency and ethical practices. Our mission is to protect the integrity of scientific research and ensure accountability within the pharmaceutical industry."

Dr. Greene stepped forward, his calm voice resonating through the room. "The evidence we have presented is irrefutable. The attempts to discredit our whistleblowers and undermine our work are desperate and baseless. We stand by our findings and will continue to fight for justice."

Rachel added, "Our coalition is stronger than ever. We have the support of the public, the scientific community, and numerous advocacy groups. Together, we will not be silenced."

Turner's eyes scanned the room, ensuring all security measures were in place. "We are prepared for any attempts to disrupt our work. Our focus remains on protecting our whistleblowers and ensuring their safety."

Alex concluded, "We have fortified our digital defenses and are monitoring all channels for any threats. We will continue to safeguard the integrity of our data and our mission."

As the press conference continued, the team received an outpouring of support from the public and their allies. Messages flooded in, reinforcing their resolve.

Rachel, still coordinating with their partners, smiled. "The response is overwhelming. We've got the momentum, and our message is resonating."

Dr. Greene nodded, his expression thoughtful. "We need to capitalize on this. Keep the pressure on and ensure our narrative stays front and center."

Turner's phone buzzed with updates from the field teams. "Our assets are secure. We're ready for any retaliation."

Samantha felt a deep sense of unity and purpose. "We've shown our strength and resilience. Now we need to keep pushing forward. The fight for justice and ethical practices is far from over, but we're stronger and more determined than ever."

As the team dispersed to continue their work, the safe house buzzed with renewed energy and determination. They had faced significant threats and emerged stronger. With their newfound momentum and the support of their allies, they were ready to face whatever challenges lay ahead.

Chapter 25
The Final Showdown

The Harding Foundation had grown exponentially in the months following their landmark victory against the pharmaceutical company. Their headquarters buzzed with activity, each department humming with purpose and dedication. Samantha, Turner, Dr. Caldwell, Margaret, and Alex had become renowned figures in the fight for corporate accountability, their names synonymous with integrity and justice.

Samantha sat in her spacious office, sunlight streaming through the large windows. Her desk was cluttered with reports, but she took a moment to look out over the cityscape, reflecting on how far they had come. The door opened, and Turner walked in, carrying a steaming cup of coffee.

"You've been at it since dawn, Sam. Thought you could use this," Turner said, placing the cup on her desk.

Samantha smiled, taking a grateful sip. "Thanks, Turner. I was just thinking about our journey. It's hard to believe how much has changed."

Turner nodded, taking a seat across from her. "We've accomplished a lot, but there's still so much to do. Our latest initiatives are making waves, though. The public support is incredible."

Samantha glanced at the reports on her desk. "I know. The new whistleblower protections and the educational outreach programs are gaining traction. And our partnerships with academic institutions are stronger than ever."

Dr. Caldwell entered the office, her expression bright. "I've just received confirmation that three more universities want to collaborate with us on research projects. This will significantly boost our capacity to analyze and expose unethical practices."

Margaret followed closely behind, holding a tablet. "And I've been in touch with several victims' advocacy groups. They're eager to join forces with us. The impact we're having is profound."

Samantha felt a swell of pride. "This is exactly what we envisioned. A network of dedicated individuals and organizations working together for a common cause."

Alex joined them, his laptop under his arm. "I've been analyzing data from our latest cybersecurity efforts. We've thwarted several attempts to breach our systems. It's clear that some corporations are not happy with our work, but we're prepared for them."

Turner looked at Samantha. "We should discuss our next steps. With the momentum we have, we need to think strategically about how to expand our reach and influence."

Samantha nodded. "Let's gather the team for a strategy session. It's time to map out our future."

In the conference room, the core team assembled, joined by new members who had become integral to the foundation's operations. Samantha stood at the head of the table, a map of their global initiatives displayed on the screen behind her.

"Thank you all for joining us," she began. "We've come a long way, but our mission is far from complete. Today, I want to discuss how we can build on our successes and address the challenges ahead."

Dr. Caldwell took the floor, outlining the new research collaborations. "These partnerships will allow us to conduct more comprehensive studies and provide irrefutable evidence against unethical practices. Our goal is to set new standards for corporate transparency and accountability."

Margaret highlighted their advocacy efforts. "By working with victims' groups and other NGOs, we can amplify our message and support those directly affected by corporate misconduct. This will not only strengthen our case but also bring much-needed attention to these issues."

Alex presented his cybersecurity report. "We've enhanced our defenses, but we need to remain vigilant. Our work threatens powerful interests, and they will continue to target us. We must stay ahead of their tactics."

Turner summarized their strategic objectives. "We need to focus on expanding our educational outreach, advocating for stronger regulations, and supporting whistleblowers. By doing this, we can create a ripple effect that will lead to systemic change."

Samantha looked around the room, seeing the determination in everyone's eyes. "We've built something extraordinary together. Let's use this momentum to drive forward. Our work is making a difference, and we owe it to those who believe in us to keep pushing."

As the meeting adjourned, the team felt a renewed sense of purpose. They were united in their mission, ready to tackle the challenges ahead. Samantha returned to her office, feeling both the weight and the promise of their work.

Turner lingered, sensing her thoughts. "We've done well, Sam. But it's the people we've helped that matter the most. Their lives are better because of what we do."

Samantha smiled. "You're right, Turner. And that's what keeps us going. Together, we can achieve so much more."

They stood together, looking out over the bustling city. The Harding Foundation was a beacon of hope and change, and its future was brighter than ever. United by their commitment to justice and integrity, they were ready to face whatever lay ahead, confident in their ability to make a lasting impact.

The Harding Foundation's success had not only brought them into the public eye but also attracted the attention of potential allies and partners from around the world. As their reputation grew, so did the opportunities to expand their reach and influence. Today, Samantha, Turner, Dr. Caldwell, Margaret, and Alex were meeting with representatives from several international organizations to discuss global collaboration.

The conference room was buzzing with excitement. Samantha welcomed the representatives as they took their seats around the large table. She felt a surge of pride and anticipation. This meeting could open doors to new initiatives and amplify their impact on a global scale.

"Thank you all for being here," Samantha began, her voice steady and welcoming. "The Harding Foundation has always believed in the power of collaboration. Together, we can achieve more than any of us could alone."

Turner nodded in agreement. "Our mission is to promote corporate accountability and protect public interests. By working with you, we hope to extend our efforts and share our resources and expertise."

Dr. Caldwell added, "Our work has shown that transparency and scientific integrity are essential in addressing corporate misconduct. We're excited about the possibility of partnering with organizations that share our values and goals."

Margaret spoke next, her enthusiasm evident. "We've seen the impact of our advocacy efforts here, and we're eager to learn from and support similar initiatives worldwide. Together, we can create a more just and equitable global community."

Alex chimed in, "With the increasing threats to digital security, it's crucial that we enhance our cybersecurity measures.

Collaborating with international experts will help us protect our data and the integrity of our work."

The representatives from the various organizations introduced themselves, expressing their admiration for the Harding Foundation's accomplishments and their eagerness to work together. The atmosphere was charged with optimism and a shared sense of purpose.

A representative from a European NGO focused on environmental issues spoke up. "We've been following your work closely. The way you've mobilized public opinion and held corporations accountable is inspiring. We're particularly interested in collaborating on projects that address environmental justice."

Samantha smiled, nodding. "Environmental justice is a critical aspect of our mission. We'd be thrilled to explore joint initiatives that tackle these issues head-on."

A delegate from a South American human rights organization added, "Your support for whistleblowers has set a new standard. We face similar challenges in our region, and we believe that by working together, we can create safer environments for those who come forward with crucial information."

Turner leaned forward. "Supporting whistleblowers is vital. We'd be happy to share our strategies and learn from your experiences to strengthen our collective efforts."

The discussions continued, each representative sharing their organization's priorities and exploring ways to collaborate. Ideas flowed freely, from joint research projects and educational programs to coordinated advocacy campaigns and shared resources for cybersecurity.

Dr. Caldwell took notes, her mind racing with possibilities. "The potential here is incredible. By combining our expertise and resources, we can address these issues more effectively and on a larger scale."

Margaret added, "And by amplifying each other's voices, we can reach a wider audience and drive meaningful change."

As the meeting progressed, the sense of camaraderie and mutual respect grew stronger. They broke into smaller groups to discuss specific projects in more detail, brainstorming and outlining initial steps.

Samantha and Turner joined the group focusing on environmental justice. "One of our goals is to expose and combat the environmental harms caused by corporations," Samantha said. "What strategies have you found most effective in your work?"

The European representative replied, "Public awareness campaigns have been key for us. When people understand the impact of corporate actions on their environment, they're more likely to demand change. We've also had success with legal challenges and working with local communities to gather evidence."

Turner nodded. "We've seen similar results. I think a combined approach, leveraging media, legal action, and community involvement, could be very powerful."

Meanwhile, Dr. Caldwell and Margaret discussed human rights initiatives with the South American delegates. "Education and awareness are crucial," Dr. Caldwell said. "How do you engage with the communities you serve?"

The delegate responded, "We focus on grassroots efforts, providing education and resources directly to communities. Empowering people with knowledge about their rights and how to protect them is fundamental."

Margaret agreed. "We've found that personal stories resonate deeply with the public. Sharing the experiences of those affected can galvanize support and drive action."

By the end of the meeting, they had laid the groundwork for several promising collaborations. Contact information was exchanged, and plans were made for follow-up discussions to turn their ideas into reality.

Samantha felt a sense of fulfillment as she addressed the group one last time. "Thank you all for your enthusiasm and commitment. Today's meeting marks the beginning of what I believe will be a series of powerful partnerships. Together, we can make a significant impact on a global scale."

As the representatives departed, the Harding Foundation team stayed behind, debriefing and reflecting on the productive day.

Turner leaned back in his chair, a satisfied smile on his face. "This is exactly what we needed. Expanding our reach globally will amplify our impact and bring new perspectives and resources to our work."

Dr. Caldwell added, "The collaboration possibilities are endless. We're building a network that can tackle these issues from multiple angles and create real, lasting change."

Margaret looked around at her colleagues, pride shining in her eyes. "We're not just a foundation anymore. We're part of a global movement."

Samantha felt a renewed sense of purpose and excitement for the future. The Harding Foundation was poised to make an even greater impact, united with partners around the world. Together, they would continue to fight for justice, transparency, and accountability, confident in their ability to effect meaningful change.

The next morning, Samantha sat at her desk, reviewing the notes from the previous day's meeting. The potential collaborations with international organizations filled her with a renewed sense of purpose. The Harding Foundation was about to embark on an even greater journey, and the possibilities were exhilarating.

Turner knocked on her door, stepping in with a determined look on his face. "Morning, Sam. We've got an invitation from the Global Justice Forum. They want us to present our work and discuss our strategies for fostering international cooperation."

Samantha looked up, excitement sparking in her eyes. "That's fantastic news, Turner. This could be our chance to showcase our efforts on a global stage and attract even more support."

Dr. Caldwell and Margaret joined them, both carrying their own stacks of papers and digital tablets. "We've also received confirmation from the universities we reached out to. They're ready to start joint research projects as soon as possible," Dr. Caldwell reported.

Margaret added, "And several victims' advocacy groups are eager to begin our collaborative efforts. They see us as a beacon of hope and change."

Alex walked in, his laptop open. "I've been analyzing data from our latest cybersecurity efforts. We're secure, but we need to stay vigilant. Expanding our network means we'll have more eyes watching us."

Samantha nodded. "We'll keep our guard up. For now, let's focus on preparing for the Global Justice Forum. Turner, can you draft an outline for our presentation?"

"Already on it," Turner replied with a smile. "I'll make sure it's comprehensive and compelling."

Dr. Caldwell leaned forward, her eyes bright with ideas. "We should highlight our academic partnerships and the impact of our research. It's a critical component of our strategy."

Margaret agreed. "And we need to emphasize the human element—the stories of the victims and the real-world impact of our work. That's what resonates with people."

Samantha nodded, feeling the momentum build. "Let's get to work. This is our moment to shine."

As they worked on their presentation, the atmosphere in the office was electric with anticipation. The team collaborated seamlessly, each bringing their expertise to the table. Turner crafted a powerful narrative, Dr. Caldwell provided data and research insights, Margaret compiled stories from the victims, and Alex ensured their digital security.

Later that day, the team gathered in the conference room to review their progress. Turner stood at the head of the table, projecting the presentation onto the screen.

"Alright, let's walk through this," he began. "We'll start with an overview of the Harding Foundation, our mission, and our key achievements."

He clicked through slides showcasing their victories against corporate corruption, their advocacy for whistleblowers, and their educational outreach programs.

Dr. Caldwell spoke next. "We'll then highlight our academic partnerships and the groundbreaking research we've conducted. This will demonstrate the scientific rigor behind our work."

Margaret added, "And we'll interweave stories from the victims, showing the real-world impact of our efforts. This will humanize our work and make it relatable."

Samantha nodded, pleased with the progress. "This is excellent. It's a powerful presentation that captures the essence of our work and our vision for the future."

As they continued refining their presentation, the sense of unity and purpose was palpable. They were not just preparing for a forum—they were gearing up to inspire and mobilize a global movement.

A few days later, they arrived at the Global Justice Forum, held in a grand convention center filled with representatives from NGOs, academic institutions, and advocacy groups from around the world. The atmosphere was charged with the collective energy of individuals dedicated to making a difference.

Samantha took a deep breath as they approached the stage. "This is it. Let's show them what we're capable of."

Turner started the presentation, his voice confident and clear. "Good morning. I'm Turner Davis, and I'm honored to present the work of the Harding Foundation. Our mission is to promote corporate accountability and protect public interests. Today, we'll share our journey, our strategies, and our vision for a collaborative future."

Dr. Caldwell followed, detailing their academic partnerships and the impact of their research. "By combining scientific rigor with advocacy, we've exposed unethical practices and pushed for systemic changes. Our work is grounded in evidence and driven by a commitment to the truth."

Margaret then shared stories from the victims, her voice filled with emotion. "These are the people we fight for—the individuals and families affected by corporate greed. Their stories are the heart of our mission, and we are dedicated to ensuring their voices are heard."

Samantha concluded the presentation, her voice filled with conviction. "We believe in the power of collaboration. By working together, we can create a more just and equitable world. We invite you to join us in this mission, to share your expertise and resources, and to build a global network of advocates for justice."

The room erupted in applause, and as Samantha looked around, she saw faces filled with inspiration and determination. The Harding Foundation had made a powerful impact, and the potential for global collaboration was limitless.

After the presentation, representatives approached them, eager to discuss potential partnerships and share their own experiences. The energy was contagious, and the team felt a renewed sense of purpose and possibility.

As they left the convention center, Samantha turned to her team, a smile on her face. "We've planted the seeds for something incredible. This is just the beginning."

Turner nodded. "We're building a global movement. The Harding Foundation is stronger than ever."

Dr. Caldwell added, "Our work is resonating with people around the world. Together, we can achieve so much more."

Margaret looked around at her colleagues, pride shining in her eyes. "We're not just a foundation. We're a force for change."

Samantha felt a surge of gratitude and excitement for the future. United by their mission and driven by their unwavering commitment to justice, they were ready to face whatever challenges lay ahead. The Harding Foundation was poised to make an even greater impact, confident in their ability to effect meaningful change on a global scale.

The momentum from the Global Justice Forum carried the Harding Foundation into a whirlwind of new partnerships and opportunities. Back at their headquarters, the team was abuzz with activity, coordinating with their new allies and planning their next steps. The Foundation's influence was expanding rapidly, and with it came new challenges and responsibilities.

Samantha sat at the head of the conference room table, reviewing the latest updates with her core team. The room was filled with a sense of purpose and excitement.

"We've received interest from several international organizations to join our network," Samantha began. "This is a chance to cement our alliances and amplify our impact."

Turner nodded, glancing at his notes. "We need to prioritize our initiatives. Our resources are still finite, and we have to ensure we're making strategic decisions. What's our primary focus?"

Dr. Caldwell leaned forward. "I suggest we start with the joint research projects. The universities we've partnered with are eager to begin, and the data we can gather will be invaluable in supporting our advocacy work."

Margaret added, "We also need to maintain our momentum with the victims' advocacy groups. Their stories have been crucial in swaying public opinion, and they're counting on us."

Alex spoke up, "And cybersecurity remains a top priority. As we expand, we'll become even more of a target. I've been working on enhancing our systems, but we need continuous vigilance."

Samantha nodded thoughtfully. "Agreed. Let's start with the research projects and advocacy efforts, but keep a strong focus on security. Turner, can you draft a strategic plan for our next steps?"

"Absolutely," Turner replied, already making notes. "I'll have something ready by tomorrow morning."

Dr. Caldwell looked at Samantha. "We also need to think about long-term sustainability. We're growing fast, but we need to ensure we have the resources and infrastructure to support this growth."

Margaret chimed in, "We've had a lot of success with crowdfunding and donations, but we should also explore grants and partnerships with philanthropic organizations."

Samantha smiled. "Great ideas. Let's set up a meeting to discuss funding strategies. We need to ensure we're not just growing, but growing sustainably."

As the team dispersed to their tasks, Samantha felt a deep sense of satisfaction. They were on the brink of something truly transformative.

Later that evening, Samantha and Turner stayed behind to finalize the strategic plan. The office was quiet, the hum of the city outside the only sound.

Turner glanced at Samantha. "It's incredible how far we've come. Do you remember when it was just the five of us, trying to take down Pharmatech?"

Samantha smiled, leaning back in her chair. "It feels like a lifetime ago. We've grown so much, both as an organization and as individuals. And now, we have the chance to make an even bigger impact."

Turner nodded. "We've built something special here. But it's the people we've helped that matter the most. Their lives are better because of what we do."

Samantha felt a swell of pride. "That's what keeps us going, Turner. And that's why we have to keep pushing forward."

The next morning, the team reconvened in the conference room to review the strategic plan Turner had drafted. Samantha looked around at her team, feeling a sense of unity and purpose.

"Turner has put together a comprehensive plan," she began. "Let's go through it and make sure we're all on the same page."

Turner walked them through the plan, outlining their immediate priorities and long-term goals. "We'll start with the joint research projects, focusing on areas where we can gather critical data to support our advocacy efforts. Simultaneously, we'll strengthen our ties with the victims' advocacy groups and enhance our cybersecurity measures."

Dr. Caldwell nodded. "This approach makes sense. We'll be able to leverage our research to drive policy changes and hold corporations accountable."

Margaret added, "And by continuing to amplify the voices of the victims, we'll keep public attention on these issues. It's a powerful combination."

Alex spoke up, "I've already started implementing new security protocols. We're building a robust system that can handle the increased activity and protect our data."

Samantha felt a surge of confidence. "This is a solid plan. Let's move forward and make it happen."

Over the next few weeks, the Foundation's initiatives gained momentum. The joint research projects yielded valuable data, providing a strong foundation for their advocacy work. The partnerships with victims' advocacy groups flourished, giving a voice to those who had been silenced for too long.

One afternoon, Samantha received a call from Rachel, their key media ally. "Samantha, I have some great news. A major news outlet wants to do an in-depth feature on the Harding Foundation and our global impact. This could bring even more attention and support to our cause."

Samantha's eyes lit up. "That's fantastic, Rachel. We'd be honored. Let's set up a time for the interview."

The feature story, when it aired, was a resounding success. It highlighted the Foundation's achievements, the personal stories of the victims they had helped, and their plans for the future. The public response was overwhelmingly positive, with donations and support pouring in from around the world.

As they watched the feature together in the conference room, Samantha turned to her team, a sense of pride and gratitude swelling in her chest.

"We've come so far, and we're making a difference," she said. "This is just the beginning. With our new alliances and the support of the global community, we can achieve so much more."

Turner nodded, a determined look in his eyes. "We're building a legacy, Sam. One that will outlast us all."

Dr. Caldwell added, "And we're proving that integrity and dedication can change the world."

Margaret smiled, tears of pride in her eyes. "For Elias, and for everyone who has suffered, we'll keep fighting."

Alex grinned. "Together, we're unstoppable."

Samantha felt a renewed sense of purpose. They had faced incredible challenges, but they had persevered. United by their mission and driven by their unwavering commitment to the truth, they were ready to face whatever challenges lay ahead. The Harding Foundation was poised to make an even greater impact, confident in their ability to effect meaningful change on a global scale.

Chapter 26
The Broadcast

The aftermath of the attack on their secure lab had left the team on edge, but it had also galvanized their resolve. Samantha Cross knew they had to capitalize on their momentum and press forward. Every moment counted, and every decision could mean the difference between success and failure.

Samantha stood at the head of the command table, her team gathered around her. The air was thick with anticipation.

"Turner, what's the latest on security?" Samantha asked, her voice steady.

Turner, his expression serious, replied, "We've fortified all our locations. The lab is secure, and our surveillance teams are monitoring for any further threats. We're ready for whatever they throw at us next."

Alex, seated at his laptop, added, "I've set up additional firewalls and enhanced our monitoring systems. We're detecting a lot of digital noise, but nothing has breached our defenses yet."

Rachel, holding a stack of reports, said, "Our allies are fully engaged. They're prepared to go public with their support at a moment's notice. We need to keep coordinating with them to maintain a unified front."

Dr. Greene, his calm voice providing a steadying influence, added, "We've received requests for interviews from several major news outlets. We need to ensure our message remains clear and focused."

Samantha absorbed their input, her mind racing with the details. "Alright, here's the plan. Turner, keep our security tight and be ready for any immediate threats. Alex, continue monitoring our digital defenses and alert us to any suspicious activity. Rachel, coordinate with our allies and prepare them for the next wave of public support. Dr. Greene, handle the media engagements and ensure our narrative stays strong."

As the team moved to their tasks, the air buzzed with determination. Samantha knew they were on the brink of a significant breakthrough.

Hours later, Turner approached Samantha with an update. "We've detected increased surveillance around our secure locations. They're trying to gather intel on our movements."

Samantha frowned. "Can we disrupt their surveillance?"

Turner nodded. "We've deployed counter-surveillance measures. They won't be able to get anything useful, but we need to stay on high alert."

Meanwhile, Alex called out from his station. "I've intercepted some communications. They're planning a coordinated digital attack to coincide with another physical strike. We need to be ready for both."

Rachel, still coordinating with their allies, said, "Everyone is on high alert. They're ready to support us publicly and help counter any disinformation."

Dr. Greene, reviewing his notes for an upcoming interview, added, "We need to prepare preemptive statements. If they try to discredit us, we can counter with hard evidence and testimonials from our supporters."

Samantha felt a surge of determination. "Let's move forward with this. Turner, keep our physical defenses tight. Alex, continue monitoring and intercepting their communications. Rachel, coordinate the response with our allies. Dr. Greene, prepare the statements and ensure our key messages are solid."

As the team executed their plans, the atmosphere was tense but focused. They were facing a formidable adversary, but their unity and determination were stronger than ever.

Later, Turner's voice came through the speakerphone. "We've got movement near one of our safe houses. It looks like they're planning another attack."

Samantha's eyes narrowed. "Can you intercept them?"

Turner's response was immediate. "We're already on it. Our teams are moving to intercept."

Minutes later, Turner's update came through again. "We've engaged them. They're trying to breach the perimeter, but we're holding them off."

Samantha felt her heart race. "Keep me updated. Alex, any signs of digital interference?"

"Nothing so far," Alex replied, his fingers flying over the keyboard. "But I'm monitoring closely."

Rachel, coordinating with their allies, said, "Our partners are ready to go public with their support. This is the moment we've been preparing for."

Dr. Greene, his voice calm but firm, added, "I'll prepare to release our statements. We need to control the narrative and ensure the public understands the full scope of these revelations."

Samantha took a deep breath. "Alright, let's do this. Turner, hold the line. Alex, keep monitoring their digital activity. Rachel, coordinate the response with our allies. Dr. Greene, prepare for the media briefing."

The team moved quickly, the atmosphere charged with anticipation. They were about to take a decisive step in their fight for justice.

The sound of gunfire crackled through the speaker, followed by Turner's voice. "We've repelled the attack. They're retreating."

Samantha felt a wave of relief. "Good work, Turner. Everyone, prepare for the next phase."

As the team gathered for a quick debrief, the room buzzed with a mix of exhaustion and triumph.

"We've made significant progress," Turner said. "But we need to stay vigilant. They won't give up easily."

Alex nodded, his face lit by the glow of his screens. "I'll keep monitoring their activity. We need to stay one step ahead."

Rachel, coordinating with their allies, added, "We need to maintain a unified front. Our strength is in our solidarity."

Dr. Greene, his voice calm but firm, said, "We've set the stage for real change. Now we need to follow through and ensure our vision becomes a reality."

Samantha looked around at her team, feeling a deep sense of pride. "We've come a long way, and we've shown we're not backing down. Let's keep pushing forward. The fight for justice and ethical practices is far from over, but we're stronger and more determined than ever."

While the team diligently worked, the safe house thrived with invigorated energy and resolve. They had faced and overcome considerable threats, emerging more robust. With their newfound drive and the support of their allies, they were equipped to handle whatever challenges the future held.

The adrenaline from repelling the attack on the safe house still coursed through Samantha Cross's veins as she and her team regrouped. They had weathered the storm, but the real battle was just beginning. With their adversaries becoming more desperate, it was crucial to rally all possible support and prepare for the inevitable escalation.

Samantha stood at the head of the command table, her team gathered around her. The air was thick with determination.

"Turner, what's the status of our security?" Samantha asked, her voice steady but urgent.

Turner, his expression resolute, replied, "We've reinforced all our locations. Surveillance is tight, and our teams are ready for any further threats. But we can't let our guard down for a second."

Alex, his eyes glued to his laptop, added, "I'm monitoring their digital activity closely. They're trying to regroup and plan their next move, but we've got their systems under surveillance. We'll know if they try anything."

Rachel, holding her tablet, said, "Our allies are ready. We've coordinated a response plan with them. They're prepared to support us publicly and help counter any disinformation."

Dr. Greene, his voice calm and reassuring, added, "The media is still on our side. We need to keep our message clear and focused. The public needs to understand the gravity of these revelations."

Samantha absorbed their input, her mind racing with the details. "Alright, here's the plan. Turner, keep our security measures tight and be ready for any immediate threats. Alex, continue monitoring their digital activity and alert us to any suspicious movements. Rachel, maintain close communication with our allies and prepare them for the next wave of public support. Dr. Greene, handle the media engagements and ensure our narrative stays strong."

As the team dispersed to their tasks, the air buzzed with a sense of purpose. Samantha knew they were on the brink of a decisive moment.

Hours later, Turner approached Samantha with an update. "We've detected increased surveillance around our secure locations. They're trying to gather intel on our movements."

Samantha frowned. "Can we disrupt their surveillance?"

Turner nodded. "We've deployed counter-surveillance measures. They won't be able to get anything useful, but we need to stay on high alert."

Meanwhile, Alex called out from his station. "I've intercepted some communications. They're planning another coordinated digital attack. We need to be ready."

Samantha's mind raced. "Rachel, are our allies prepared to respond?"

Rachel, looking up from her tablet, said, "They're ready. We've briefed them on the situation and they're on standby to go public with their support."

Dr. Greene, reviewing his notes for an upcoming interview, added, "We should prepare preemptive statements. If they try to discredit us, we can counter with hard evidence and testimonials from our supporters."

Samantha nodded. "Let's move forward with this. Turner, keep our physical defenses tight. Alex, continue monitoring and intercepting their communications. Rachel, coordinate the response with our allies. Dr. Greene, prepare the statements and ensure our key messages are solid."

As the team executed their plans, the atmosphere was tense but focused. They were facing a formidable adversary, but their unity and determination were stronger than ever.

Later, Turner's voice came through the speakerphone. "We've got movement near one of our safe houses. It looks like they're planning another attack."

Samantha's eyes narrowed. "Can you intercept them?"

Turner's response was immediate. "We're already on it. Our teams are moving to intercept."

Minutes later, Turner's update came through again. "We've engaged them. They're trying to breach the perimeter, but we're holding them off."

Samantha felt her heart race. "Keep me updated. Alex, any signs of digital interference?"

"Nothing so far," Alex replied, his fingers flying over the keyboard. "But I'm monitoring closely."

Rachel, coordinating with their allies, said, "Our partners are ready to go public with their support. This is the moment we've been preparing for."

Dr. Greene, his voice calm but firm, added, "I'll prepare to release our statements. We need to control the narrative and ensure the public understands the full scope of these revelations."

Samantha took a deep breath. "Alright, let's do this. Turner, hold the line. Alex, keep monitoring their digital activity. Rachel, coordinate the response with our allies. Dr. Greene, prepare for the media briefing."

The team moved quickly, the atmosphere charged with anticipation. They were about to take a decisive step in their fight for justice.

The sound of gunfire crackled through the speaker, followed by Turner's voice. "We've repelled the attack. They're retreating."

Samantha felt a wave of relief. "Good work, Turner. Everyone, prepare for the next phase."

As the team gathered for a quick debrief, the room buzzed with a mix of exhaustion and triumph.

"We've made significant progress," Turner said. "But we need to stay vigilant. They won't give up easily."

Alex nodded, his face lit by the glow of his screens. "I'll keep monitoring their activity. We need to stay one step ahead."

Rachel, coordinating with their allies, added, "We need to maintain a unified front. Our strength is in our solidarity."

Dr. Greene, his voice calm but firm, said, "We've set the stage for real change. Now we need to follow through and ensure our vision becomes a reality."

Samantha looked around at her team, feeling a deep sense of pride. "We've come a long way, and we've shown we're not backing down. Let's keep pushing forward. The fight for justice and ethical practices is far from over, but we're stronger and more determined than ever."

As the team pressed on with their efforts, the safe house hummed with a fresh sense of purpose and resolve. They had braved significant dangers and come out fortified. Armed with new momentum and the unwavering support of their allies, they stood ready to confront any obstacles that lay ahead.

The safe house was a hive of coordinated activity. Samantha Cross and her team had managed to fend off the latest physical and digital assaults, but they knew their adversaries were growing more desperate. With their resources and resolve being tested, the team prepared for the next wave of conflict.

Samantha stood at the command table, flanked by Turner, Alex, Rachel, and Dr. Greene. The air was thick with anticipation and the faint hum of computers.

"We've successfully repelled their latest attack," Samantha began, her voice steady but firm. "But we can't afford to let our guard down. Turner, what's the status of our security measures?"

Turner, his expression resolute, replied, "All locations are fortified. Our surveillance teams are on high alert, and we've increased patrols around the perimeter. We're ready for any further threats."

Alex, his fingers flying over his keyboard, added, "I'm monitoring their digital activity closely. They're regrouping and trying to find new ways to breach our defenses. So far, we've managed to stay one step ahead."

Rachel, holding her tablet, said, "Our allies are fully engaged. We've coordinated with them, and they're prepared to support us publicly. We need to keep up the communication to maintain a unified front."

Dr. Greene, his voice calm and steady, added, "The media is still on our side. We need to keep our message clear and focused, ensuring the public understands the significance of these revelations."

Samantha absorbed their input, her mind racing with the details. "Alright, here's the plan. Turner, keep our security measures tight and be ready for any immediate threats. Alex, continue monitoring their digital activity and alert us to any suspicious movements. Rachel, maintain close communication with our allies and prepare them for the next wave of public support. Dr. Greene, handle the media engagements and ensure our narrative stays strong."

As the team dispersed to their tasks, the air buzzed with a sense of purpose. Samantha knew they were on the brink of a decisive moment.

Hours later, Turner approached Samantha with an urgent update. "We've detected increased surveillance around our secure locations. They're trying to gather intel on our movements."

Samantha frowned. "Can we disrupt their surveillance?"

Turner nodded. "We've deployed counter-surveillance measures. They won't be able to get anything useful, but we need to stay on high alert."

Meanwhile, Alex called out from his station. "I've intercepted some communications. They're planning another coordinated digital attack. We need to be ready."

Samantha's mind raced. "Rachel, are our allies prepared to respond?"

Rachel, looking up from her tablet, said, "They're ready. We've briefed them on the situation, and they're on standby to go public with their support."

Dr. Greene, reviewing his notes for an upcoming interview, added, "We should prepare preemptive statements. If they try to discredit us, we can counter with hard evidence and testimonials from our supporters."

Samantha nodded. "Let's move forward with this. Turner, keep our physical defenses tight. Alex, continue monitoring and intercepting their communications. Rachel, coordinate the response with our allies. Dr. Greene, prepare the statements and ensure our key messages are solid."

As the team executed their plans, the atmosphere was tense but focused. They were facing a formidable adversary, but their unity and determination were stronger than ever.

Later, Turner's voice came through the speakerphone. "We've got movement near one of our secure locations. It looks like they're planning another attack."

Samantha's eyes narrowed. "Can you intercept them?"

Turner's response was immediate. "We're already on it. Our teams are moving to intercept."

Minutes later, Turner's update came through again. "We've engaged them. They're trying to breach the perimeter, but we're holding them off."

Samantha felt her heart race. "Keep me updated. Alex, any signs of digital interference?"

"Nothing so far," Alex replied, his fingers flying over the keyboard. "But I'm monitoring closely."

Rachel, coordinating with their allies, said, "Our partners are ready to go public with their support. This is the moment we've been preparing for."

Dr. Greene, his voice calm but firm, added, "I'll prepare to release our statements. We need to control the narrative and ensure the public understands the full scope of these revelations."

Samantha took a deep breath. "Alright, let's do this. Turner, hold the line. Alex, keep monitoring their digital activity. Rachel, coordinate the response with our allies. Dr. Greene, prepare for the media briefing."

The team moved quickly, the atmosphere charged with anticipation. They were about to take a decisive step in their fight for justice.

The sound of gunfire crackled through the speaker, followed by Turner's voice. "We've repelled the attack. They're retreating."

Samantha felt a wave of relief. "Good work, Turner. Everyone, prepare for the next phase."

As the team gathered for a quick debrief, the room buzzed with a mix of exhaustion and triumph.

"We've made significant progress," Turner said. "But we need to stay vigilant. They won't give up easily."

Alex nodded, his face lit by the glow of his screens. "I'll keep monitoring their activity. We need to stay one step ahead."

Rachel, coordinating with their allies, added, "We need to maintain a unified front. Our strength is in our solidarity."

Dr. Greene, his voice calm but firm, said, "We've set the stage for real change. Now we need to follow through and ensure our vision becomes a reality."

Samantha looked around at her team, feeling a deep sense of pride. "We've come a long way, and we've shown we're not backing down. Let's keep pushing forward. The fight for justice and ethical practices is far from over, but we're stronger and more determined than ever."

As the team continued their work, the safe house buzzed with renewed energy and determination. They had faced significant threats and emerged stronger. With their newfound momentum and the support of their allies, they were ready to face whatever challenges lay ahead.

The safe house was abuzz with the energy of success. Samantha Cross and her team had successfully repelled the attacks, both physical and digital, launched by their adversaries. The momentum was on their side, but they knew that their enemies were far from defeated. It was time to make their final stand and push through to victory.

Samantha stood at the command table, her team gathered around her. The air was thick with a sense of urgency and anticipation.

"Turner, give us the latest on our security," Samantha began, her voice steady.

Turner, his expression focused, replied, "Our security teams have fortified all key locations. We've intercepted several communications indicating that their forces are regrouping. We need to be prepared for another wave of attacks."

Alex, typing rapidly on his laptop, added, "I'm monitoring their digital activities. They're ramping up their efforts to breach our systems, but we've managed to stay ahead of them. I've implemented additional safeguards."

Rachel, holding her tablet, said, "Our allies are fully mobilized. They're ready to go public with their support and help counter any disinformation. We need to maintain our coordination."

Dr. Greene, his calm voice steadying the team, added, "The media is on our side, but we need to keep the narrative focused. The public must understand the gravity of these revelations and the importance of our mission."

Samantha nodded, absorbing their input. "Alright, let's finalize our plan. Turner, continue to fortify our defenses and be ready for any immediate threats. Alex, keep monitoring their digital activity and alert us to any suspicious movements. Rachel, maintain close communication with our allies and prepare them for the next wave of public support. Dr. Greene, handle the media engagements and ensure our narrative stays strong."

As the team dispersed to their tasks, the air buzzed with determination. Samantha knew they were on the brink of a decisive moment.

Hours later, Turner approached Samantha with an urgent update. "We've detected increased activity near one of our secure locations. It looks like they're planning another attack."

Samantha's eyes narrowed. "Can we intercept them?"

Turner nodded. "We're already on it. Our teams are moving to intercept."

Meanwhile, Alex called out from his station. "I've intercepted communications. They're coordinating a simultaneous digital and physical attack. We need to be ready for both."

Rachel, looking up from her tablet, said, "Our partners are prepared to respond. We've briefed them on the situation and they're ready to go public with their support."

Dr. Greene, reviewing his notes for an upcoming interview, added, "We should prepare preemptive statements. If they try to discredit us, we can counter with hard evidence and testimonials from our supporters."

Samantha felt a surge of determination. "Let's move forward with this. Turner, hold the line. Alex, continue monitoring their digital activity. Rachel, coordinate the response with our allies. Dr. Greene, prepare the statements and ensure our key messages are solid."

The team moved quickly, the atmosphere charged with anticipation. They were about to take a decisive step in their fight for justice.

Turner's voice came through the speakerphone, tense but controlled. "We've engaged the enemy. They're trying to breach the perimeter, but we're holding them off."

Samantha's heart raced. "Keep me updated. Alex, any signs of digital interference?"

"Nothing so far," Alex replied, his fingers flying over the keyboard. "But I'm monitoring closely."

Rachel, coordinating with their allies, said, "Our partners are ready to go public with their support. This is the moment we've been preparing for."

Dr. Greene, his voice calm but firm, added, "I'll prepare to release our statements. We need to control the narrative and ensure the public understands the full scope of these revelations."

Samantha took a deep breath. "Alright, let's do this. Turner, hold the line. Alex, keep monitoring their digital activity. Rachel, coordinate the response with our allies. Dr. Greene, prepare for the media briefing."

The sound of gunfire crackled through the speaker, followed by Turner's voice. "We've repelled the attack. They're retreating."

Samantha felt a wave of relief. "Good work, Turner. Everyone, prepare for the next phase."

As the team gathered for a quick debrief, the room buzzed with a mix of exhaustion and triumph.

"We've made significant progress," Turner said. "But we need to stay vigilant. They won't give up easily."

Alex nodded, his face lit by the glow of his screens. "I'll keep monitoring their activity. We need to stay one step ahead."

Rachel, coordinating with their allies, added, "We need to maintain a unified front. Our strength is in our solidarity."

Dr. Greene, his voice calm but firm, said, "We've set the stage for real change. Now we need to follow through and ensure our vision becomes a reality."

Samantha looked around at her team, feeling a deep sense of pride. "We've come a long way, and we've shown we're not backing down. Let's keep pushing forward. The fight for justice and ethical practices is far from over, but we're stronger and more determined than ever."

The team's continued efforts filled the safe house with a vibrant energy and a sense of determination. They had faced significant threats and had grown stronger as a result. With their new momentum and the support of their allies, they were ready to tackle any challenges that awaited them.

Chapter 27
The Fallout

The morning light filtered through the reinforced windows of the safe house, casting a pale glow over the command center. Samantha Cross sat at the head of the table, her eyes scanning the room. The team had barely slept, but the adrenaline kept them sharp. They were on the cusp of a monumental breakthrough, and the air was thick with anticipation.

The previous night's successful defense had fortified their resolve, but Samantha knew they had to move quickly. Their adversaries were desperate, and desperate people made dangerous decisions.

"Good morning, everyone," Samantha began, her voice steady. "We've managed to repel their attacks, but we can't rest on our laurels. Today, we take the offensive."

Turner nodded, his eyes serious. "Our security teams are still on high alert. We've detected some minor movements, but nothing significant. We're ready for anything."

"Good," Samantha replied. "Alex, what's the latest on their digital activity?"

Alex, his fingers tapping rapidly on his keyboard, looked up. "They're scrambling. We've intercepted multiple communications indicating confusion and panic. They're trying to regroup, but we've got a window of opportunity here."

Rachel, holding a tablet with the latest updates from their allies, said, "Our partners are ready. They're standing by to release supporting statements and evidence as soon as we give the signal. The public is on our side, but we need to keep the pressure on."

Dr. Greene, his calm demeanor providing a steadying influence, added, "The media is eager for more information. We need to make sure our narrative remains clear and focused. The truth is our strongest weapon."

Samantha nodded, feeling a surge of determination. "Alright, here's the plan. Turner, maintain heightened security and keep monitoring any movements. Alex, continue to intercept and analyze their communications. Rachel, coordinate with our allies and prepare them for a coordinated release. Dr. Greene, draft our next public statement. We need to make sure it hits hard."

As the team dispersed to their tasks, Samantha took a moment to reflect. They had come so far, faced so many challenges, but their resolve had never wavered. The fight for justice and transparency was nearing its climax, and she could feel the tide turning in their favor.

Later that morning, Alex called out from his station. "Samantha, you need to see this. I've decrypted another batch of communications. It's explosive."

Samantha hurried over, her pulse quickening. "What do you have?"

Alex brought up a series of emails and memos on his screen. "These documents detail a direct link between their top executives and the manipulation of trial results. It's more than enough to bring them down."

Rachel joined them, her eyes widening as she read the contents. "This is it. This is the smoking gun we've been looking for."

Dr. Greene, peering over Alex's shoulder, said, "We need to package this information carefully. It has to be irrefutable and clear to the public."

Samantha nodded. "Agreed. Alex, compile the evidence into a comprehensive report. Rachel, coordinate with our allies for the release. Dr. Greene, prepare our statement. We go public today."

The hours that followed were a blur of activity. Alex worked tirelessly to organize the evidence, while Rachel communicated with their network of allies, ensuring everyone was on the same page. Dr. Greene crafted a statement that was both powerful and succinct, ready to present to the world.

By midday, everything was in place. The team gathered in the broadcast room, the atmosphere charged with anticipation.

Samantha stood before the camera, her heart pounding. "Good afternoon. Today, we present irrefutable evidence of widespread corruption and manipulation within the pharmaceutical industry. The documents we have uncovered reveal a deliberate effort to suppress negative research findings and manipulate trial results, orchestrated by top executives."

Dr. Greene stepped forward, his calm voice resonating through the room. "This evidence is clear and comprehensive. It includes emails, financial records, and internal memos that detail these companies' unethical practices. The truth can no longer be hidden."

Rachel, holding the report, added, "We've coordinated with key figures in the scientific community and advocacy groups. Together, we demand accountability and transparency. This is about more than just one company—it's about ensuring the integrity of scientific research and protecting public health."

Turner's eyes scanned the room, ensuring all security measures were in place. "We are prepared for any attempts to disrupt our work. Our focus remains on protecting our whistleblowers and ensuring their safety."

As the press conference continued, the team received an outpouring of support from the public and their allies. Messages flooded in, reinforcing their resolve.

Samantha felt a deep sense of unity and purpose. They had taken a significant step forward, but the journey was far from over. With their newfound momentum and the support of their allies, they were ready to face whatever challenges lay ahead.

The press conference had just concluded, leaving the team in a temporary lull before the inevitable storm of responses began. Samantha Cross and her team were gathered in the command center, monitoring the immediate fallout of their explosive revelations. The room was filled with a palpable sense of accomplishment mixed with nervous anticipation.

Rachel stood in front of a large monitor displaying a live feed of various news channels. "It's everywhere," she said, her voice a mix of excitement and caution. "Every major network is covering it, and social media is blowing up with reactions."

Dr. Greene, seated nearby, nodded. "We've controlled the narrative well so far. The key is to keep the momentum and ensure that our message remains clear."

Samantha, standing at the command table, watched as her team worked. "Turner, any signs of immediate retaliation?"

Turner, his eyes fixed on the security feeds, replied, "So far, nothing unusual. But we need to stay on high alert. They won't take this lying down."

Alex, typing furiously at his laptop, added, "I'm monitoring their digital communications. They're in disarray, but that makes them dangerous. We should expect them to try something desperate."

Just then, Samantha's phone buzzed. It was a call from one of their key allies, Dr. Lisa Mitchell. Samantha answered it, putting the call on speaker for the team to hear.

"Lisa, what's the latest from your end?" Samantha asked.

Dr. Mitchell's voice was clear but urgent. "The scientific community is rallying behind you. We're seeing an outpouring of support from researchers and professionals. But there's also a lot of noise from the opposition trying to discredit the evidence."

Rachel, still watching the monitors, interjected, "We need to counter that noise with more facts and testimonials. Can we get more voices from within the industry to speak out?"

Dr. Mitchell replied, "I'm working on it. We're organizing a series of statements from respected figures in the field. They'll emphasize the validity of the evidence and the necessity for transparency."

Samantha nodded. "Good. Keep us updated. We need to maintain a united front."

As the call ended, Turner received an alert on his tablet. "We've got movement," he said, his tone urgent. "A group of unidentified vehicles approaching one of our locations. It could be another attack."

Samantha's face hardened. "Turner, get a team out there immediately. We can't afford to let them disrupt our operations."

Turner nodded and quickly dispatched a security team. The room tensed as they awaited updates.

Meanwhile, Alex's face lit up with a new discovery. "I've intercepted a series of encrypted messages. They're coordinating a smear campaign against us, trying to flood the media with disinformation."

Rachel looked up from her tablet. "We need to counter this with solid facts and public support. I'll coordinate with our allies to release more statements and evidence."

Dr. Greene, reviewing his notes for the next media engagement, added, "We also need to engage directly with the public. I suggest a live Q&A session to address their concerns and reinforce our credibility."

Samantha agreed. "Let's do it. Rachel, set up the Q&A. Dr. Greene, prepare for any tough questions. Alex, keep monitoring their communications. Turner, keep us updated on the situation with the vehicles."

As the team sprang into action, the room buzzed with renewed energy. They were in the eye of the storm, but their unity and determination were unwavering.

Minutes later, Turner's voice came through the speaker. "The team has intercepted the vehicles. It's a mix of journalists and potential agitators. We're handling it."

Samantha felt a wave of relief. "Good work, Turner. Keep them contained and ensure the journalists understand the gravity of our situation."

The live Q&A session was set up quickly. Rachel coordinated with their allies to ensure a strong turnout, and Dr. Greene prepared for a range of questions. Samantha took a deep breath as she faced the camera, ready to address the public.

"Good afternoon," she began, her voice clear and steady. "We understand that the revelations we've presented are significant and may raise many questions. We're here to address those questions and provide clarity. Our goal is to ensure transparency and accountability in the pharmaceutical industry."

The questions started coming in, ranging from supportive to skeptical. Dr. Greene handled the technical inquiries with ease, providing detailed explanations that reinforced their findings. Rachel managed the flow of questions, ensuring that key points were addressed.

One particularly pointed question came in: "How can we trust that your evidence isn't fabricated?"

Samantha leaned forward, her gaze steady. "Our evidence is backed by multiple sources within the industry and has been verified by independent experts. We've worked tirelessly to ensure its accuracy because we believe in the importance of truth and integrity."

As the session continued, the public's support grew visibly. Messages of encouragement and solidarity flooded in, bolstering the team's morale.

By the end of the Q&A, it was clear that they had managed to maintain control of the narrative. Samantha looked around at her team, feeling a deep sense of pride and unity. They had faced down another wave of challenges and emerged stronger.

The battle was far from over, but with each step, they were closer to achieving their goal. Their resolve was unshaken, and with the public and their allies behind them, they were ready for whatever came next.

The safe house thrummed with a sense of anticipation. Samantha Cross and her team had successfully navigated the press conference and the live Q&A session, but they knew their adversaries were relentless. The support from the public and their allies was heartening, yet the battle for truth was still fraught with danger.

As the team gathered in the command center, Samantha reviewed the latest updates. "Turner, status on the vehicles we intercepted?"

Turner, his gaze fixed on the security monitors, replied, "The journalists were cooperative. The potential agitators were detained for questioning. We've increased patrols around all key locations. So far, no signs of immediate threat."

Alex, typing furiously at his laptop, added, "I'm still monitoring their digital chatter. They're scrambling, but there's a lot of noise. They're trying to find another angle of attack."

Rachel, her eyes glued to her tablet, said, "Our allies are standing firm. We've got a wave of new endorsements from key figures in the scientific community. The public is starting to rally behind us."

Dr. Greene, reviewing his notes for another media engagement, added, "We need to keep the narrative strong and consistent.

The truth is our most powerful weapon, and we need to wield it effectively."

Samantha nodded, feeling a surge of determination. "Alright, let's keep the pressure on. Turner, ensure our security measures are airtight. Alex, continue monitoring their communications and alert us to any significant movements. Rachel, coordinate with our allies and prepare them for another round of public statements. Dr. Greene, let's get ready for the next media briefing."

As the team dispersed to their tasks, the air was thick with purpose. Samantha knew they were on the brink of a critical turning point.

Hours later, Turner approached Samantha with an urgent update. "We've detected a significant increase in digital activity. It looks like they're planning another coordinated attack, both physical and digital."

Samantha's eyes narrowed. "Can we intercept them before they act?"

Turner nodded. "Our teams are already moving to intercept. We need to be ready for a swift response."

Meanwhile, Alex called out from his station. "I've managed to decrypt some of their latest communications. They're desperate and planning something big. We need to be prepared for anything."

Rachel, coordinating with their allies, said, "Our partners are ready. They're prepared to go public with more evidence and support. We need to keep them informed and engaged."

Dr. Greene, his voice calm and steady, added, "I'll prepare additional statements. We need to ensure the public stays informed and on our side."

Samantha felt the tension rise. "Let's move quickly. Turner, secure all locations and be ready for immediate action. Alex, keep monitoring and provide real-time updates. Rachel, maintain communication with our allies. Dr. Greene, prepare for another media engagement."

As the team sprang into action, the atmosphere in the safe house was charged with anticipation. They were on the cusp of a decisive moment in their fight for justice.

Minutes later, Turner's voice came through the speakerphone. "We've engaged the enemy. They're trying to breach our defenses, but we're holding them off."

Samantha's heart raced. "Keep me updated. Alex, any signs of digital interference?"

"Nothing significant yet," Alex replied, his fingers flying over the keyboard. "But I'm monitoring closely. They're trying to find a way in."

Rachel, coordinating with their allies, said, "We've got strong public support. Our partners are ready to release more statements if needed."

Dr. Greene, preparing for another media briefing, added, "We need to be ready to counter any disinformation they spread. The truth must remain our guiding light."

Samantha took a deep breath, feeling the weight of their mission. "Alright, everyone, stay focused. We've come this far, and we can't afford to falter now."

The team continued their work, the room buzzing with intensity. Turner's updates came in regularly, each one affirming that their defenses were holding strong. Alex's monitoring revealed no major breaches, and Rachel's coordination ensured their allies were fully engaged.

As the hours passed, the tension in the safe house began to ease. Turner's final update came through, confirming that the immediate threat had been neutralized. The team breathed a collective sigh of relief.

Samantha gathered everyone for a quick debrief. "We've successfully repelled their latest attacks, but we need to stay vigilant. This fight is far from over."

Turner nodded. "Our teams are on high alert. We're ready for any further threats."

Alex added, "I'll keep monitoring their communications. We need to stay one step ahead."

Rachel, coordinating with their allies, said, "Our partners are more united than ever. The public is on our side, and we need to keep them engaged."

Dr. Greene, his voice calm and reassuring, said, "We've set the stage for a major shift. Now we need to follow through and ensure our vision becomes a reality."

Samantha looked around at her team, feeling a deep sense of pride and unity. "We've come a long way, and we've shown we're not backing down. Let's keep pushing forward. The fight for justice and ethical practices is far from over, but we're stronger and more determined than ever."

Engaged in their work, the team brought a buzz of renewed determination and energy to the safe house. They had encountered serious threats and emerged even stronger. With their renewed momentum and the steadfast support of their allies, they were prepared to face any forthcoming challenges.

The victory from repelling the latest attacks infused the safe house with a cautious optimism. Samantha Cross and her team knew that while they had won this battle, the war was far from over. They regrouped in the command center, the glow of their monitors casting a determined light on their faces.

Samantha stood at the head of the table, a fresh sense of urgency in her posture. "Great job, everyone. But we need to stay on our toes. Turner, any further intel on their movements?"

Turner, reviewing the latest security reports, nodded. "We've detected some chatter. It seems like they're planning a major move, but we're not sure what it is yet. Our teams are ready to respond."

Alex, seated at his station, added, "I'm still monitoring their digital activities. They're desperate, and that makes them unpredictable. We need to be prepared for anything."

Rachel, her tablet filled with updates from their allies, said, "Our partners are still with us. They're prepared to release more statements and evidence to support us."

Dr. Greene, his voice calm and reassuring, added, "We need to keep the narrative focused. The public's support is crucial, and we can't let any disinformation sway them."

Samantha nodded, absorbing their input. "Alright, let's stay focused. Turner, keep our security tight. Alex, continue monitoring their communications. Rachel, keep coordinating with our allies. Dr. Greene, prepare for our next media engagement."

The team dispersed, each member focused on their tasks. The atmosphere was charged with determination.

Hours later, Turner approached Samantha with an urgent update. "We've intercepted a high-level communication. It's encrypted, but it looks like they're planning something big."

Samantha's eyes narrowed. "Can we decrypt it?"

Alex, his fingers already flying over the keyboard, replied, "I'm working on it. Give me a few minutes."

Rachel, coordinating with their allies, added, "We need to prepare for any possible scenario. Our partners need to be ready to act quickly."

Dr. Greene, reviewing his notes, said, "We should prepare a series of statements. We need to be ready to respond to whatever they throw at us."

Samantha felt the tension rise. "Let's move quickly. Turner, increase our security measures. Alex, keep us updated on the decryption. Rachel, keep our allies informed. Dr. Greene, get the statements ready."

As the team sprang into action, the atmosphere in the safe house was electric with anticipation. They were on the brink of another critical moment in their fight for justice.

Minutes later, Alex called out, "I've got it! The communication is decrypted."

Samantha hurried over. "What does it say?"

Alex's face was pale as he read the message. "They're planning to release a fabricated video that discredits us. It's a smear campaign designed to undermine everything we've worked for."

Rachel, her eyes widening, said, "We need to counter this immediately. Our allies need to release their statements and evidence now."

Dr. Greene, his voice steady, added, "We need to get ahead of this. A preemptive media engagement can neutralize their attack before it gains traction."

Samantha felt a surge of determination. "Alright, let's move. Turner, ensure our security is airtight. Alex, monitor their digital channels for any sign of the video. Rachel, coordinate the release of our allies' statements. Dr. Greene, prepare for a live press conference."

The team moved quickly, each member executing their tasks with precision. The room buzzed with focused energy.

Turner's voice came through the speakerphone. "Our security measures are in place. We're ready for any physical threats."

Alex, his eyes glued to his screen, said, "I'm monitoring their channels. No sign of the video yet, but we need to be ready."

Rachel, coordinating with their allies, added, "Our partners are releasing their statements. The public is starting to see the truth."

Dr. Greene, preparing for the press conference, said, "We need to frame our message carefully. The truth must shine through any lies they try to spread."

Samantha took a deep breath, feeling the weight of their mission. "Alright, let's do this. We've come too far to let them undermine us now."

The live press conference was set up quickly. Samantha stood before the camera, her heart pounding. "Good evening. We've just received information that our adversaries are planning to release a fabricated video designed to discredit our efforts. We want to assure you that our evidence is irrefutable and backed by multiple sources within the industry."

Dr. Greene stepped forward, his calm voice resonating through the room. "This is a desperate attempt to undermine the truth. We stand by our findings, and we will continue to fight for transparency and justice."

Rachel, holding the latest statements from their allies, added, "We are not alone in this fight. The scientific community and public advocates stand with us, demanding accountability and transparency."

Turner's voice came through the speakerphone, updating the room. "Our security teams report no unusual activity. We're holding strong."

Alex, still monitoring the digital channels, said, "The fabricated video hasn't been released yet. We're ready to counter it as soon as it appears."

Samantha felt a wave of unity and determination. "We've faced incredible challenges and emerged stronger each time. We're not backing down. Together, we will see this through."

As the press conference continued, the team received an outpouring of support from the public and their allies. Messages flooded in, reinforcing their resolve.

Rachel, coordinating with their partners, smiled. "The response is overwhelmingly positive. We've got the momentum, and our message is resonating."

Dr. Greene nodded, his expression thoughtful. "We need to capitalize on this. Keep the pressure on and ensure our narrative stays front and center."

Turner's phone buzzed with updates from the field teams. "Our assets are secure. We're ready for any retaliation."

Samantha felt a deep sense of unity and purpose. "We've shown our strength and resilience. Now we need to keep pushing forward. The fight for justice and ethical practices is far from over, but we're stronger and more determined than ever."

With the team immersed in their tasks, the safe house was alive with a surge of renewed energy and determination. Despite having encountered substantial threats, they had grown stronger. Buoyed by their newfound momentum and the backing of their allies, they were prepared to tackle any upcoming challenges.

Epilogue
A New Beginning

Samantha stood on the balcony of a secluded safe house, the faint glow of dawn creeping over the horizon. The morning air was still, but her thoughts were anything but. Below, the city was waking up, oblivious to the weight she carried. The global broadcast exposing Pharmatech had sent shockwaves across the world. Governments were scrambling, corporations were reeling, and powerful figures were falling from their pedestals. Yet, as she stared out at the sky tinged with the soft colors of sunrise, Samantha could only think of the price that had been paid.

Pharmatech had fallen, but victory had come at a steep cost. Too many lives had been lost. Too many people had sacrificed everything for the truth to see the light of day. David's face flashed in her mind, his unwavering loyalty and commitment. He had been one of the first casualties, and his death still weighed heavily on her. Samantha closed her eyes, feeling the familiar ache in her chest.

Behind her, on the small table, her phone buzzed incessantly. The screen was flooded with notifications—messages from journalists, whistleblowers, allies, and even strangers who had been moved by the broadcast. Each one was a reminder that while they had won a battle, the war was far from over.

She sighed, running her hand through her hair before turning back toward the room. The screen illuminated the dim space, casting shadows across the walls. Another message flashed across the screen:

"Thank you for everything you've done. Your courage has inspired us all."

Samantha let out a tired laugh, shaking her head. Courage. It wasn't courage that had driven her these past months. It was necessity. It was the understanding that the truth needed to come out, no matter the cost. The world deserved to know, and now, finally, they did. But what the world didn't see was the aftermath—the lives shattered, the families torn apart, the sleepless nights spent in fear of the next move.

The door creaked open, and Turner stepped out onto the balcony, a steaming cup of coffee in hand. He gave her a knowing look, his eyes scanning her face for signs of weariness.

"You didn't sleep, did you?" he asked, his tone soft but direct.

Samantha shrugged, leaning against the railing. "Couldn't."

Turner nodded, setting the coffee down beside her. He didn't push. They had been through too much for small talk, and Turner knew better than anyone how the burden of their choices weighed on her.

"You're thinking about the cost," he said quietly, his voice barely above a whisper.

Samantha sighed, her gaze drifting back to the horizon. "Aren't you? We won, but it doesn't feel like a victory. People died for this, Turner. People who believed in what we were doing."

"They knew the risks," Turner replied, his voice steady. "We all did. And it wasn't just about winning a single fight. It was about starting something bigger."

Samantha shook her head. "It doesn't feel like the beginning. It feels like an ending. David, the others... Was it worth it?"

Turner stepped closer, leaning against the railing beside her. "You know it was. Look at the world right now. Governments are being forced to answer for their actions. Corporations are finally facing consequences. People are waking up. That wouldn't have happened if we hadn't exposed Pharmatech."

Samantha remained silent, her mind still clouded with doubt. She understood what Turner was saying, but understanding didn't make it any easier. The weight of responsibility pressed down on her, heavy and unrelenting.

"And you," Turner continued, his gaze unwavering. "You've given them hope. People are listening now because of what you did. That matters, Sam. Don't forget that."

She smiled weakly, appreciating his words even if she wasn't quite ready to accept them. "It's just... I didn't expect this," she admitted. "I didn't expect it to feel so hollow."

Turner gave a small nod, his eyes reflecting the same tiredness she felt. "That's because you're thinking about the losses. But what about the gains? You changed the world, Sam. That's something."

Samantha glanced at her phone again, the notifications still coming in. Each message, each thank you, was a reminder that the world had indeed changed. Maybe Turner was right. Maybe, in the grand scheme of things, this was only the beginning.

She turned to him, her expression softening. "I guess the fight never really ends, does it?"

"No," Turner agreed. "But that's why we're here. To keep fighting."

Samantha took a deep breath, feeling the weight of her exhaustion but also something else—a spark of determination. Turner was right. The fight wasn't over, but neither was she. And that realization, as difficult as it was to accept, brought with it a sense of clarity. The battle had been hard-fought, but the mission was far from complete.

She looked back out at the horizon, the morning light brighter now, casting long shadows across the room. "I thought I'd feel relief," she said quietly. "But instead, I just feel like there's more to do."

Turner smiled, a rare flicker of warmth in his otherwise stoic expression. "There always is."

Samantha picked up her phone, scrolling through the messages one last time. She hadn't just gained a victory over Pharmatech—she had gained a new sense of purpose. The world was watching, and there were others now—people who were ready to stand up, ready to fight.

"It's just the beginning," she said, more to herself than to Turner. "We've only just started."

Turner clapped her on the shoulder, a reassuring presence at her side. "Then let's get ready for whatever comes next."

Samantha smiled, feeling a quiet resolve settle over her. The battle had taken its toll, but she wasn't done. Not yet. And as the sun rose higher, bathing the city in light, Samantha knew one thing for certain: she was ready for the next fight.

The phone buzzed again, but this time, instead of dread, she felt hope.

The safe house had an air of quiet finality, the kind that comes after the dust of battle has settled but before the next storm arrives. Samantha sat at the large wooden table in the center of the room, surrounded by the remaining members of her team. The expressions around her were a mixture of exhaustion, relief, and something else—something that lingered just beneath the surface: uncertainty.

Rachel was the first to speak, her voice soft but steady. She leaned back in her chair, her fingers tracing the edge of a coffee cup she hadn't touched. "I think it's time for me to step back," she said, her words measured. "I've done what I came here to do, but... I need to focus on my family now."

Samantha felt a pang in her chest, though she wasn't surprised. Rachel had been the driving force behind their media campaign, crafting the narrative that had brought Pharmatech's corruption to light. But it had come at a cost. The stress, the constant pressure, and the danger had worn her down.

"I understand," Samantha said, her voice quiet but warm. "You've given so much, Rachel. No one can blame you for wanting to put your family first now."

Rachel smiled faintly, though it didn't quite reach her eyes. "It's just... my kids, you know? They've been so patient with me, but I've missed too much. Birthdays, school events... I can't keep doing that. I need to be there for them."

Samantha nodded, a sense of bittersweet acceptance washing over her. "You've earned that. And you've given more than any of us could have asked for. You changed everything."

Rachel exhaled, her shoulders visibly relaxing for the first time in what felt like months. "It's time. I know it's not easy to walk away, but it's the right decision for me."

Turner, who sat across from Samantha, leaned back in his chair, his gaze steady as he watched the conversation unfold. His jaw was set, and when he spoke, his tone was unwavering. "I'm not going anywhere," he said firmly, his eyes locking onto Samantha's. "We've made too many enemies to just walk away now. I'm staying."

Samantha met his gaze, a surge of gratitude swelling in her chest. Turner had been her rock throughout this entire ordeal—solid, dependable, and fierce in his loyalty. "I didn't think you would," she replied with a small smile.

Turner shrugged, the hint of a smirk playing at his lips. "You'd get yourself killed without me."

The tension in the room eased just a bit at that, a few quiet chuckles rippling through the team. But underneath the humor, the truth lingered. They had made powerful enemies, and even though the fight against Pharmatech had been won, it wasn't the end. Not for Turner. Not for her.

Alex, who had been unusually quiet, finally spoke up. He had been through the ringer—his cyber skills had made him invaluable, but the threats to his family had left him shaken. "I'm staying too," he said, his voice low but firm. "We've come this far... I'm not stopping now."

Samantha turned to him, her expression softening. "Are you sure, Alex? You've been through a lot. No one would blame you if you needed to step back."

He shook his head, glancing down at his hands. "I've thought about it. I've thought about leaving, taking my family somewhere safe, but... I can't just walk away. Not when there's still work to be done."

"You don't have to carry all of this, Alex," Samantha said gently. "We'll understand if—"

"I know," Alex interrupted, looking up at her, his eyes dark with resolve. "But I want to. It's not just about me anymore. If we don't finish what we started, then everything we've done, all the sacrifices we've made... they'll be for nothing."

There was a heavy silence in the room as his words hung in the air. Samantha felt the weight of them pressing against her chest. He was right, of course. They had all come too far, seen too much, to simply walk away now. But the toll it had taken on each of them was undeniable.

"I don't want anyone to feel trapped," Samantha said, her voice steady but laced with emotion. "We've all made sacrifices, and if anyone feels like they need to step away, I'll support that. I mean it."

Turner raised an eyebrow, his voice gruff but warm. "We're not trapped, Sam. We're committed. Big difference."

Samantha smiled at that, a flicker of warmth breaking through the weariness that clung to her. "I just want to make sure you all know that."

Rachel's voice, quiet but resolute, cut through the room again. "We do, Sam. We know. But for me... it's time. And I don't regret a thing. You've all been like a second family to me. But now I need to be with my first family. I hope you understand."

Samantha reached across the table, taking Rachel's hand in hers. "Of course I do. And thank you. For everything."

Rachel squeezed her hand, her eyes glistening slightly. "You're going to be okay without me. You all are."

Turner grinned. "We'll manage. Just don't go too far—we might need you to save the day again."

Rachel laughed, though it was tinged with sadness. "I'll be around. Just... in a different way."

As the team shared quiet smiles, the atmosphere in the room shifted. They had been through hell together, and even though some of their paths were diverging, the bond they had forged wouldn't break. Samantha knew that much for sure.

"We've survived the worst," Samantha said softly, glancing around the table at her team—her friends. "And whatever comes next... we'll face it. Together."

And with that, they moved forward.

Samantha sat at her desk, the soft glow of the lamp illuminating the clutter of reports, legal briefs, and newspaper clippings spread across the surface. The room was quiet, but her mind was not. The world outside had shifted, the aftermath of the Pharmatech takedown reverberating across borders. She leaned back in her chair, scrolling through the latest news updates on her laptop.

The headline on the screen read: *"The Hero Who Exposed Pharmatech: Samantha Blake's Fight for Justice."* The article beneath it painted her as a fearless whistleblower, a beacon of hope in a world riddled with corporate greed. Yet, another headline just a few clicks away told a different story: *"At What Cost? The Recklessness of Samantha Blake's Crusade."* It was a reminder that not everyone saw her actions as heroic.

As she scrolled further, an endless stream of praise and criticism flashed before her eyes—journalists calling her a champion of truth, others labeling her methods dangerous.

Governments around the world were being forced to respond to the revelations she had helped bring to light. Investigations had begun in multiple countries, and high-ranking officials were resigning in disgrace. But even with the truth exposed, new dangers loomed.

The quiet of the room was interrupted by Turner's arrival. He knocked lightly before entering, his face set in its usual calm expression. He crossed the room and sat across from her, glancing briefly at the screen before meeting her eyes.

"They're calling you a hero," Turner said with a small smirk, his tone half teasing, half serious. "How does that feel?"

Samantha sighed, running a hand through her hair. "It feels... complicated," she admitted. "For every article calling me a hero, there's another saying I went too far, that I risked too much."

Turner shrugged. "They'll say what they want to say. You know that. At the end of the day, you did what was necessary."

"Necessary, maybe," Samantha replied, her voice low. "But at what cost? Look at what we've lost—people, lives, reputations. And now that we've put Pharmatech in the ground, we're under a whole new kind of spotlight."

Turner's gaze softened, and he leaned forward, resting his elbows on the desk. "You're worried about the backlash."

"I'm worried about what comes next," she said, glancing at the pile of reports in front of her. "These investigations, the media frenzy—it's only stirred up more enemies. We've exposed a lot, but there are still people out there—powerful people—who won't let this go quietly. And with Pharmatech gone, someone else is going to fill that void."

Turner's jaw tightened, and he nodded. "You're right. There's already chatter about smaller companies regrouping, trying to salvage what they can from the fallout. And we both know that someone like Locke—someone worse—is going to rise from the ashes."

Samantha's eyes darkened at the mention of Locke, the man who had emerged in the aftermath, more ruthless than those who had come before. "It's never over, is it?" she asked, more to herself than to Turner. "We think we've won, but it's just a matter of time before another threat takes its place."

Turner's voice was steady but filled with quiet resolve. "That's why we stay vigilant. We've disrupted the system, but that system will try to rebuild itself. We need to be ready."

Samantha sighed, leaning back in her chair. "I'm just not sure if we can keep fighting like this. The spotlight—it changes things. The public sees me as some kind of hero, but that's not what I am. I'm just... someone who couldn't walk away."

Turner gave her a measured look. "You're more than that, Sam. You've done what most people wouldn't even dare to do. And yeah, the public loves a hero, but that's not what you're here for. You're here for the truth."

Samantha remained silent, her mind racing. The weight of the media attention, the constant scrutiny—it was suffocating. And yet, she knew that walking away wasn't an option. The fight wasn't over. Not by a long shot.

She glanced at her phone, where yet another notification flashed. A message from a journalist asking for a comment, a story update, another demand for her to be the face of this movement. The world was watching her, waiting for her next move, but beneath the praise and the headlines, there were still those who profited from the shadows. Those who had seen her as a threat from the beginning and now had even more reason to silence her.

"I've been getting more threats," she admitted, her voice quieter now.

Turner's expression darkened. "From who?"

"Anonymous sources, mostly," she said, scrolling through her messages. "But it's more than just a few angry emails. These people—they've lost everything because of what we did. And they're not going to let it go."

Turner leaned forward, his voice sharp. "We'll deal with them. But you need to be careful, Sam. You're more exposed now than ever."

"I know," she replied, her tone resigned. "I just didn't expect to feel this vulnerable after everything we've accomplished. I thought there'd be a sense of closure, but it feels like we've only just opened a new front."

Turner stood up, his expression hardening as he placed a hand on her shoulder. "You didn't get into this fight for praise or closure. You got into it because it needed to be done. And whether the world sees you as a hero or a villain doesn't matter. What matters is that the truth is out there."

Samantha nodded, her resolve hardening once more. "You're right. The truth is out there... but the fight isn't over. It never really is."

As she turned back to the reports scattered across her desk, the weight of the battle ahead pressed down on her. The world was watching, waiting for her next move, and the remnants of Pharmatech were regrouping in the shadows. Somewhere out there, another figure was rising, ready to fill the void she had left. But Samantha knew one thing for certain—she wasn't done fighting. Not yet.

Samantha sat alone in the quiet of the safe house, the warm glow of the setting sun filtering through the windows and casting long shadows across the room. Her laptop hummed faintly on the table before her, the latest intelligence blinking on the screen—a new case, bigger and more dangerous than anything she had tackled before. The lead had come in earlier that day: a multinational corporation, with deep ties to government officials, suspected of human rights violations and large-scale environmental destruction.

The stakes were higher now, but as she stared at the screen, reading through the report, Samantha felt something she hadn't expected—calm. She was stronger now, wiser, hardened by the battles she had fought and the enemies she had faced. There was no hesitation in her mind, no doubt about what needed to be done.

Her phone buzzed next to her, pulling her attention away from the screen. It was a message from Turner. *"I've got the initial intel on the new case. It's worse than we thought. We'll need everyone on board for this one. When are you leaving?"*

Samantha smiled, her fingers hovering over the keys as she typed a quick reply: *"Tonight. Meet me at the drop location tomorrow."*

She closed the laptop with a soft click, standing from the table and glancing around the room. The safe house, which had been her refuge for months, felt like it was already in the past. Elmsbrook had been a chapter in her life—an important one—but now, it was time to move forward. The journey ahead would be long and dangerous, but for the first time in a long while, Samantha wasn't afraid. She had seen the worst of what the world had to offer, and she had survived.

The door creaked open, and Monica stepped into the room, her expression thoughtful. "You really leaving tonight?" she asked, leaning against the doorframe.

Samantha nodded, turning to her. "Yeah. The sooner I get started, the better."

Monica crossed her arms, watching her with a mixture of concern and admiration. "You're not wasting any time, are you?"

Samantha smiled faintly. "There's no time to waste. This new lead—it's bigger than anything we've faced before. If we don't move quickly, they'll bury the evidence before we can even touch it."

Monica stepped closer, her voice softer now. "You sure you're ready for this? I mean, we've been through hell already. This... this could be even worse."

Samantha met her gaze, her expression steady. "I'm ready," she said, without hesitation. "I've learned that corruption is like a hydra. You cut off one head, and another always rises. But that doesn't mean you stop fighting."

Monica nodded slowly, her eyes reflecting the same weariness Samantha felt. "You've changed, Sam. You're... different now."

Samantha laughed softly, though there was no humor in it. "I guess I have. But so have you. So has everyone."

Monica glanced at the packed bag sitting by the door. "So what's the plan? You going solo on this one?"

Samantha shook her head. "No. Turner's meeting me at the drop tomorrow. Alex will join us when he's ready. It's going to take all of us to bring this one down."

Monica smiled, though there was a hint of sadness behind it. "I'm going to miss this. Miss working with you."

"You've still got time to change your mind," Samantha said, her tone light but hopeful.

Monica shook her head. "No. I'm done. I've done my part. But... that doesn't mean I won't be rooting for you from a distance."

Samantha gave her a grateful nod, the bond between them unspoken but strong. "Thank you, Monica. For everything."

As the last rays of sunlight disappeared behind the horizon, Samantha grabbed her bag and slung it over her shoulder. Monica watched her, her voice quiet as she spoke. "You're going to win this one too, Sam. I know you will."

Samantha paused by the door, glancing back at her friend one last time. "We don't have a choice," she said softly. "We've come too far to stop now."

With that, she stepped out into the fading light, the air cool against her skin as she walked toward the waiting car. The sun had set, but there was no time for rest. Another battle awaited her—one that would take her into the heart of corruption once again. But this time, she felt ready. The road ahead would be dangerous, but she was no longer the same woman who had stumbled into this fight. She was stronger now, more resilient. And this time, she wouldn't stop until the truth was fully uncovered.

As the car pulled away, Samantha stared out the window, watching as the darkened streets of Elmsbrook faded behind her. This chapter was over, but a new one was just beginning. And as the road stretched out before her, she knew one thing for certain: no matter how many new enemies rose from the shadows, no matter how dangerous the fight became, she wasn't backing down.

With her team by her side, Samantha was ready. Ready for whatever battles lay ahead.